Praise for *Oyster* and for Janette Turner Hospital's previous books:

"*Oyster* is a precarious, sensuous masterpiece." —*Toronto Globe & Mail*

"Turner Hospital writes with mischievous energy, an outback Angela Carter with dirt under her nails and a loaded gun hiding in a Bible."
—*London Daily Telegraph*

"A writer of high tension and terrifying allure . . . she writes with powerful beauty." —Richard Eder, *Los Angeles Times*

"She fills her novels with evocative settings, characters we care deeply about, and language that is entrancingly lyrical."
—*New York Times Book Review*

"Rich and lyrical." —Margaret Drabble

"Similar to, but more focused than the mythopoetic sagas of Thomas Pynchon, *The Last Magician* is a tour de force that finally rewards the reader's persistence with extraordinary insight and vision."
—*Philadelphia Inquirer*

"Hospital is a modern magician with a very sure hand."
—*San Francisco Chronicle*

OYSTER

By the same author

The Ivory Swing
The Tiger in the Tiger Pit
Borderline
Dislocations
Charades
Isobars
The Last Magician
Collected Stories

OYSTER

Janette Turner Hospital

W. W. Norton & Company
New York London

First American edition 1998
First published as a Norton paperback 1999

Printed in the United States of America

The text of this book is composed in Sabon.
Manufacturing by Quebecor Printing, Fairfield Inc.

Library of Congress Cataloging-in-Publication Data

Hospital, Janette Turner, 1942–
Oyster / Janette Turner Hospital. — 1st American ed.
p. cm.
ISBN 0-393-04618-4
I. Title.
PR9619.3.H674097 1998 97-34071
823—dc21 CIP

ISBN 0-393-31936-9 pbk.

W. W. Norton & Company, Inc., 500 Fifth Avenue, New York, N.Y. 10110
http://www.wwnorton.com

W. W. Norton & Company Ltd., 10 Coptic Street, London WC1A 1PU

1 2 3 4 5 6 7 8 9 0

We have just enough religion to make us hate, but not enough to make us love one another.

Jonathan Swift

Contents

PROLOGUE

here we butt against another
dimension . . .

the track we leave
declares no entry or passage
disappears despite our desire
to stake a claim

Kevin Roberts, *Red Centre Journal*

If rain had come, things might have turned out differently, that is what I think now; but there were children in Outer Maroo who had never seen rain. We prayed. We cursed. We studied the hot empty sky and imagined clouds. We waited. We waited for something to happen, for anything to happen, we were avid for some event to unfold itself out of the burning nothing to save us. We were waiting, as the desperate do, for a miracle.

Unfortunately, we got it.

Then, within the space of a few months, there were more transients than there were locals, and the imbalance seemed morally wrong. There were too many foreigners in Outer Maroo.

There was also, and still, the drought. More than that, perhaps the worst thing, was a sort of mephitic fog, moistureless and invisible, that came and went like an exhalation of the arid earth itself. We gave it a name. We thought, I suppose, in some primitive way, that if we mocked it, it might decamp and leave us alone. Old Fuckatoo, we called it.

The Old Fuckatoo is roosting again, we would say, pressing handkerchiefs against nose and mouth.

The Old Fuckatoo could brood, close and suffocating, for days, then it might lift a little, depending on the sway and twist of convection in the desert air. Mostly, when it nested and tucked us under its fetid wing, the stink of dead cattle would predominate; or else that particular rank sweetness of rotting sheep. On certain days, when hot currents shimmered off Oyster's Reef, we could detect the chalk-dust of the mullock heaps, acrid; or, from the opal mines themselves, the ghastly fug of the tunnels and shafts. Sometimes there was almost nothing, just the blankness of the outback heat, and this felt like a grace newly recognised. On other days – there was no escaping it – an altogether more disturbing trace prevailed, some terrible and indefinable emanation that suggested . . . but no one wished to think about what it suggested.

Some, in retrospect, claimed it was moral decay; though it was probably the simple stink of fear.

By cunning intention, and sometimes by discreet bribery (or other dispatch) of government surveyors, Outer Maroo has kept itself off maps, and yet people do stumble into town. A man, let us say, may find himself west of the Warrego River, then west of the McGregor Range, after which he sees nothing but acacia scrub and saltbush and the dry riverbeds that tangle and untangle themselves in pale scribbles against the red earth. The man strains his eyes and scans the horizon. Here and there, a salt-pan lake, shimmering in the heat, almost blinds him, but he knows better than to believe in water. Beyond the salt pans, beyond the butter-coloured ribbons of creek sand, somewhere far far ahead, according to his map, are the dotted lines of the South Australian and Northern Territory borders, but he can see no sign of these poignant ideas of order. They leave no trace on the land.

The official map of the state of Queensland tells him that he is surrounded by mighty rivers: the Warrego, the Barcoo, Cooper's Creek, the Diamantina. He knows that sometimes, once a decade perhaps, there is significant water in these rivers. And he knows that there are, ahead of him, vast lakes and inland seas, some of which have been full twice since the century began. The official map of the state of Queensland tells the man . . . or it could be a woman. These days, it might well be a woman, alone and determined, pushing west, her camel sore-footed and refractory, the transmission gone on her four-wheel drive, the brakes seized up with red dust. The official map tells the woman that she has entered a region without roads, a cross-hatched region whose only visible cartographical features appear to be verbal:

> *Area subject to severe drought and to sudden inundation. Numerous opal fields. Extreme temperatures. Motorists should not proceed past Cunnamulla or Quilpie without adequate reserves of petrol, oil, water, and minor spare parts.*
>
> *Caveat viator.*

Indeed, let the traveller beware.

Only delirium can help her now.

There are no roads, but certain 'tracks' do present themselves on the Government Printer's stationery – dotted lines that meander vaguely then peter out. The translation of these markings from map to landscape is a psychic skill, in the exercise of which earnest map-readers may go astray and may wander into Outer Maroo.

Most are looking for opal.

All of those who find the place are lost.

Things come and go around Outer Maroo. They appear for a little season, then they vanish, and the red earth stretches to kingdom come *in secula seculorum, amen.* When I say vanish, I mean it absolutely. Finis, the end, full stop, amen and amen. People perish. Their habitations and their histories seem to leave no trace, though they do make an effort, they scatter messages. Relics abound, if one only knows how to look. In fact, Outer Maroo is thick with coded testaments, but the messages are legible only to those who can read the secretive earth.

Consider Inner Maroo, which, in the latter part of the last century, flourished as a town for about four years, but whose only present trace is a lacework of holes in the ground.

As for visions: oh yes, out here they manifest themselves, no question; then they dissolve, then they reappear. This is a simple fact, due to atmospheric conditions. A lake, for example, or a mountain range, or a certain cattle property with wide verandahs can all turn out to be illusions, but the illusions themselves are hard data, a scientific truth. I am setting this down because I am trying to understand my own difficulties and because I want some future reader to understand (if I am ever able to reach a future reader) why this disturbing story is sometimes fragmented and dispersed by shifting filaments of moisture in the upper air, and by variable atmospheric densities, and by rifts in time.

I want you to understand why the telling is complicated; why the facts may seem to float loose in a sequence of their own devising, much as a bunch of helium-filled balloons, their strings all released from the same hand at the same moment in time, and from a point, let us say, one mile upwind from you, will certainly not reach you as a cluster. Some will drift so high in upper thermal currents that you will be unable to see them, though they will nevertheless pass by. Some may brush your hand. Some will veer north or south and never reach you at all. Some will spin in contrary winds and come back to you, days later, from further on.

Time is a trickster, and so is space, but the air above an ocean or a desert is more devious than either of these. The air in such places is bent. Do you understand me? *Bent.* I mean that in all senses. The air is a card-sharp. The air is a conjurer who likes to juggle both space and time: the things themselves, that is, as well as your perceptions of the two.

You probably know this.

You have probably stood on a clifftop somewhere – on North Head, say, at the lip of Sydney Harbour; or on the scarp at Buderim, overlooking the Queensland coast – and you have shaded your eyes and looked out over the Pacific on a day that was as clear and sharp as a razor, and you have seen a ship on the horizon, with another ship, its identical twin, floating delicately above it, upside down. Both the real ship and its airy double may have been there yesterday; or perhaps they will be there next week. Somewhere in time and space, both ships are real; but not here, and not now, and certainly not upside down, though your eyes are seeing true. Similarly, in the desert atmosphere (of which, perhaps, you are less likely to have had personal experience), the shimmering outback air can present on the track ahead a man who passed behind you a day ago.

Any children's encyclopedia will give you explanations. There will be diagrams and definitions. *Mirage,* the editors will say, *is an optical illusion due to certain atmospheric conditions.*

Questions that interest me: What would constitute a true mirage? Are there sound mirages? When you hear a voice, do you ever really know who is speaking? Oyster heard voices, he said; where did they come from?

I have a hunch that stories such as this one are too common for comfort these days. They will get worse as the decade advances. They are breeding in the dank millennial air, they are multiplying like rabbits and not just out here, west of the dingo fence. In plain common sense, there are things it is better not to know because the knowing makes living too painful. If people choose to give themselves like moths to a flame, what can be done? There do not seem to be any precautions that can be taken. Nevertheless, nevertheless, the story has become a bushfire now; there is no stopping it. So. Too many foreigners found Oyster's Reef, that was how it began; and anyone who finds this place is lost.

Nevertheless there is a postal address, and occasionally, in spite of everyone's best efforts, mail gets through. Beresford's, in fact, has an overturned beer keg between hardware and home medications that is officially Australia Post, and an old envelope is thumb-tacked to one of the keg staves. The envelope is creamy yellow and curled at the edges. Within the nebula of a delicate tracery of fly spots drifts a pale moon of postmark that could be Melbourne (at any rate, the peaks of what must be an M are visible) and one can just make out an address that, having faded first into sepia, has moved on to a more delicate and elusive shade that could best be called a memory of fawn:

Ma Beresford
Outer Maroo,
Queensland 4480
(Bear NW of Quilpie and Eromanga, or SW of Longreach and Windorah, or E of Birdsville. Good luck)

Passing from pub to pub a long time ago – it must have been a long time ago – the letter left gossip like a trail of breadcrumbs in its wake. That is how the rush began, people say. Ma Beresford herself blames the second cousin who sent word of a family death. The death was of no interest to Ma Beresford, but the deceased, who had spent his childhood in western Queensland, left behind in the debris of his life a diary with a childhood listing of opal floaters found: dates, locations, colour and quality of fire, classification according to the typology of a young mind more fanciful than precise – *bloodburst*, *crazed fern*, *sunflash*, and other such categories. And there were childhood ravings about opal seams thick as a man's thigh and as long as the Barcoo itself. The second cousin, with no thought at all for the consequences, sent the dead man's diary on as keepsake and curio. Doubtless the letter had been steamed open and resealed many times along the way, and so some in Outer Maroo lay the blame squarely at the door of Australia Post. Others claim it was Oyster himself who delivered the letter, or intercepted it, or indeed wrote it, which would, I suppose, explain everything.

At any rate, it was to this same overturned yeast-reeking beer cask that Oyster's young foreigners would bring their letters and cards. Ma Beresford would solemnly weigh each item, dispense the requisite stamps, give a ritual three thumps at the ink pad, and then, aiding the official franking of envelope or postcard by adroit movements of her tongue between parted lips, would certify in indelible ink that the document in hand had been duly received by the postmistress of Outer Maroo. She would indicate the slot in the keg through which the letter should be dropped. At the end of the week, after business hours, and with due official security, the keg was cleared. The mail was sorted (by country, by state, by town), taped into bundles, and transferred to a canvas sack. Ma Beresford herself presided, though it was frequently young Mercy Given, working a couple of hours a day after school, who did the actual pulling of the drawstring rope, and who knotted the sack securely and affixed the Australia Post seal. Following these rituals, the fragile cache of fears and longings, inscribed in so many languages, was safely and permanently stored with all the other sacks – 'Till doomsday, if need be,' Ma Beresford told Mercy – in a small locked room at the back of the shop.

'Foreigners mean trouble,' Ma Beresford always said. 'Better for everyone concerned,' she said, patting the mailroom door in her sage and proprietary way, 'if this lot stay in Pandora's Box.' She was a woman of axiom and principle. Postcards, naturally, she read; but she would swear on the Bible, if need should ever arise, that she had never steamed open a single letter, not one.

Regarding foreigners, Ma Beresford had truth on her side, for there was no one in Outer Maroo who would deny that foreigners have meant trouble no matter where they came from: whether they were from Charleville or Quilpie, whether they were teachers from Brisbane or bright kids from Sydney or Perth, whether they were from the Murri camps that came and went along the riverbeds, or from countries where they speak another tongue: American, for example; or Greek, or Vietnamese, or Italian, or the poncey sucked-in bitter-lemon words the Poms use.

In the long run, foreigners are all much the same.

They are not us.

The arrival of any foreigner changes the map, and foreigners spell the beginning of the end.

Before the beginning of the end, before Oyster, when time still swam in its lazy uninterrupted way, foreigners came once in a blue moon and were either fêted or shunned. They trickled in, one by one, on bullock drays or in four-wheel drives or on walkabout. Or they might simply stagger out of the sun, raving and half starved, as Oyster did. Once or twice, there were camel caravans. Then Oyster came, and quite soon after, jeeps began to announce themselves in small red clouds. There were campers and squatters, and they kept arriving as the zeros on the calendar got closer; or at any rate that was the connection that Oyster himself made, and the newcomers shared his belief, and so disposed themselves for a certain kind of future, now upon us.

Ma Beresford herself, in those days, had no time for the year 2000. 'Some people see pink elephants,' she said, 'and some see zeros. Gimme a break. It's opal dust they've all got in their eyes.'

At any rate, there were people who came along the Birdsville Track from Coober Pedy, and there were people who came from Dallas, Texas, and from Oklahoma, and from Europe, and from God knows where and everywhere. Beside the road from Quilpie and from South Australia junkweed grew: the rusty stalks of abandoned cars and burned-out utes and stripped four-wheel drives; and all the drivers had dust in their eyes.

Opal. The word itself was like a charm. You could stroke a word like opal. You could taste it. You could swallow it whole, raw and silky, like an oyster, and then Oyster could reel you in.

There was, the rumour went, even more opal in the gnarled underside of western Queensland than could be trawled from the caverns of Coober Pedy or from Lightning Ridge. Seams of turquoise and starflash red must have run through the sleep of the fevered and of those drawn to hazardous quests. Psychics, given a handful of soil from a cattle station, could no doubt identify the run of a seam. Dreamers must have seen opalescent veins branching like creeks in flood, a dense tangle of them, a teeming capillary system of translucent wealth. At truck stops, people whispered of overnight fortunes. There was also, I think, brisk trafficking in metaphysics around the traps since it was widely believed that opal was not found by geologists, nor even, except sporadically, by fossickers, but by the dedicated, the single-minded, the pure in heart. It must be waited for, though in the right place, needless to say, and in the right frame of mind.

So there was opal and there was Oyster.

Those who were suitably receptive might have had a leaflet pressed discreetly into their hands on city streets in Brisbane or Sydney. These were handed out by Oyster's recruiters, and I used to have one that a backpacker, a young American woman, had given to me.

OPAL: THE VISION SPLENDID

Pure light and pure truth preserved in the womb of Mother Earth.

Opal is the Logos made manifest.

Prepare ye the Way of the Lord.

Join the seekers and ye shall find.

Contact Spiritual Quests Unlimited (phone and fax below)

Do you see what I mean?

Some pamphlets, less biblically inclined, claimed that opal was the ovum of the Earth Goddess, and there were occasional arguments, sudden and violent, I understand, on the Brisbane–Quilpie trains, between seekers of differing theological persuasions. There were persistent rumours of underground towns like Coober Pedy, new ones, their presence detectable by the sudden eruption of moonscapes. These were unmistakable, people said, and clearly visible from the air as colonies of white mullock heaps blistering the red earth, the white mounds being the only detectable sign of urban life. It is certainly true that Oyster's Reef looked like this.

The towns that were being gossiped about in the railway pubs bore names like De Profundis, Deep Thought and Pascal's Pit. Entering such towns without a guide was hazardous, the rumour went. People disappeared with no more ado than the sound of an indrawn breath. Abandoned shafts lay in wait for them, lured them, lapped at the edges of their desire for final truth. Without warning, they hurtled down toward the ultimate black opal of their dreams.

Certain kinds of people – tax inspectors, for example; government surveyors, reporters, Telecom linesmen, cameramen – seemed particularly prone to disappearance without trace. There was, in consequence, a quiet traffic in runic maps which travelled along the stock routes and outback pubs and came with a mantra: *ninety per cent of the world's opal supply*. And the pilgrims and seekers and map-buyers told it to themselves like beads: *ninety per cent ninety per cent ninety per cent, and only for the pure in heart.*

The stance of the national media (not readily obtained in Outer Maroo, I have to say) toward this ragtag brigade of prospectors was supercilious and was relegated to small filler items deeply buried. There was no evidence whatsoever, the respectable newspapers announced (though the tabloids told a somewhat different story), of any finds beyond agglomerates of worthless potch, and the occasional floater of value, and the not-commercially-viable fortresses of boulder opal. Queensland opal, officially, remained as obdurately inaccessible as ever.

But the pure in heart were not deterred. They took the train from Brisbane with a ticket to the end of the line: one thousand kilometres of fevered dreaming and spiritual exercises and bore-water showers. Everyone smelt faintly of sulphur. At Quilpie, they hitched rides on anything that moved and kept westward.

The outback, they murmured to one another.

The voyage out is the voyage in, they said. They exchanged secret signs, left hand to left hand, palm against palm, thumbs entwined.

Forty-eight degrees Celsius, they wrote wearily, proudly, on post-cards; or possibly, depending on postal destination intended, they wrote instead: *One hundred and twenty Fahrenheit at noon.*

And at night, they wrote, *it's freezing. Below freezing point.*

The difference between night and day in the outback is astonishing, they wrote. *Out here, everything runs to extremes.*

The Old Fuckatoo was extremely present, that was certain. The length of the drought was extreme. There were extreme degrees of animal panic about. There were too many foreigners, everyone said. There were far too many foreigners around.

And then one day, abruptly, there were none . . .

The stench, on certain days, was worse after that.

The drought continued.

The absence of the foreigners grew vast and oppressive and terrifying. We turned in on ourselves. We hunched into the smelly breast feathers of the Old Fuckatoo.

We were ashamed.

We were frightened; or perhaps, I think now, not so much frightened as living in a prolonged state of shock.

And now more foreigners are on the way . . .

Book I

Outer Maroo

We are talking about spirits, living spirits and Dreams and tribal areas . . . A lot of gudias [white people] talk about land as if there's nobody owning it underneath the ground . . . He can drill a bore . . . and make his roads with a bulldozer. But what happened to my tree here. I've got that tree here, I was born under that tree. That's my background in that tree. For so many years it was standing here, for so long . . . We are walking on top of our old people's bodies.

Noonkanbah: Whose Land, Whose Law?
Steve Hawke and Michael Gallagher

Last Week

Monday: High Noon

More foreigners are on the way.

In Beresford's, someone looks up and sees Digby's truck float into view, suspended out there (maybe still twenty miles off, maybe only two), shimmering at the yellow edges of its cabin and rocking gently on the swell of its own heat wave. Someone, one of the men, observing this in the middle of fence-repair calculations, lurches a little and lets a handful of nails leak through his fingers. The nails shuss back into the nail sack, *shik shik shik,* a shivery rush, metallic.

This is a sign.

Any sound can be a sign now, and everyone in Beresford's goes still. This is the way it is. Everyone watches, everyone listens, everyone disappears behind a vacant look that says *It's no use asking me, I don't know anything,* and the question on everyone's mind is: where will it end?

Well. It will end at Oyster's Reef, of course, where it began, we all know that, but *when* will it end?

Mercy has noticed that people cannot live in the ordinary way any more, drifting comfortably along without thinking, the way they used to. Hours used to flow into days and days into time just as smoothly as creeks sail into rivers and rivers to inland seas, or so people say, so books maintain, so Miss Rover – Mercy's former and only schoolteacher – claimed, and Mercy is inclined to believe that once upon a time these things were so. On certain days she can almost remember when there used to be a slick of water in the pale golden bed of the river and in the concave salt-pan crust of the Sea of Null.

But now it is no longer certain that B will follow A, or that rivers will ever flow anywhere again, or that the air will not smell of death, and so the people of Outer Maroo are wary, especially where foreigners are concerned, and Mercy can feel the anxiety fluttering around Beresford's like a bird that cannot find its way out.

At the soft pock of the falling nails, the spell settles on them all (they are familiar with it now, the way it drops like a mosquito net, suffocating). The clocks become loud, and each second takes twice as long to pass. In slow motion, women turn from the vegetable freezer and gaze out the window where the heat and the thick fragrance of corruption crouch like sluggish, malevolent beasts. Young Alice Godwin and her dreadful mother Dorothy are fingering a bolt of thistledown cotton, their hands full of the soft blue stuff, but the second they see the yellow mirage of the truck drifting in toward anchor, their fingers go slack and the bolt of cloth gallops off the counter and over the floor. Blue billows east and west, soft masses of it puckering at tea-chests, frothing over booted feet, pleating up against saddlery and sorghum sacks and tubs of rice. Ma Beresford is going to be furious, but Mercy catches her breath and shuts her eyes tightly to memorise the lovely rush of colour unspinning itself. She folds it away for safe keeping in those same dream niches where she stores the pinfire opal and the gem-seamed book-rich tunnels of Aladdin's Rush.

Visions such as these shimmer and tease and make promises and translate themselves little by little. When Mercy summons them up again and unwraps them, she feels lightheaded. She feels that soon she will be able to build a fence with them, no, not a fence, a wall, that soon she will have enough pieces of . . . pieces of . . .? – what are they? – enough pieces of these things that cannot be turned into darkness, these pieces of light, enough of them to build a wall, four walls, and the walls will be high enough and potent enough to contain everything she knows about Oyster's Reef, and there will be no windows and no door at all in this room that she will make, this shining bunker, but nevertheless she will put locks on the radiant walls and wrap them in polished steel bands which will flash back the sun, and all the darkness of Oyster's Reef will be contained within them, on the inside of the fortress, with no possibility of leakage whatsoever, and then Mercy will be able to walk away and will no longer have to know what she knows.

'Mercy,' Mrs Dorothy Godwin says sharply, irritably. 'Don't stand there in a daze, child, when strangers are coming. Help me roll up the blue.'

'Mum,' Alice Godwin says, 'I feel sick.' She presses one hand against her chest and holds the other over her mouth. 'Mum, can't we go before they get here?'

Alice and Mercy exchange a look of pure kinship, pure panic. Their helplessness is like the soft unravelled blue cloth, Mercy thinks; it connects them.

'We will go just as soon as we can, Alice.' Alice's mother has no time for weakness, not even in herself, although she is sometimes willing in her own case to grant extenuating circumstance. 'Don't talk in that *whiney* tone, child. Pull yourself together. We will go just as soon as we can.' Alice's mother slips several reels of thread into her handbag, a discreet gesture, and one that is executed with the utmost delicacy and grace. All the reels are in garish and impractical colours. It is a point of honour with her to steal nothing that could be of personal use. Honour flourishes in the town of Outer Maroo. Honour will compel Junior Godwin to drop in over the next few days, embarrassed, and equally discreet, to return what his mother took. Everyone knows this will happen.

Dorothy Godwin knows, and does not know, this. She has the gift of forgetting.

There is much to forget in Outer Maroo. In Outer Maroo, forgetting and honour are as crucial to survival as a good artesian bore.

Dorothy Godwin pushes the cardboard core of the unravelled bolt of cloth across the counter. 'Mercy, the blue.'

The blue streams silkily through Mercy's fingers.

The eyes of Mrs Dorothy Godwin move from face to face. Everyone watches everyone else, warily, eye to eye. Everyone understands that such mutual vigilance is necessary. Mercy thinks of a story in the school reader: the one of the little boy who kept his fist in the dyke all night. If anyone slacks in the hard communal duty of forgetting, she thinks, who knows what sort of inundation will drown the town?

Alice folds herself over her stomach and whimpers.

'Well,' her mother sighs. 'It can't be helped.'

No, people murmur.

What's done is done, they sigh; and any stranger would instantly conclude: here is a group of people bound by guilt; they dread, and constantly expect, retribution. Or, conversely: here is a group of innocent people dazed by awful circumstance; they know that the weight of evidence is overwhelmingly and unjustly against them; they wait haplessly for a harsh and wrongful judgment to be handed down.

'What's done is done,' Dorothy Godwin says.

As though a secret signal has been passed, there is an exodus, carefully unhurried, of Godwins and of several others who have recalled pressing business at far reach. Beyond the verandah, red dust and exhaust fumes plume around their idling cars. As soon as they have seen the new arrivals, they will leave, but they need to know who is coming. They need to take stock. After that, they will go.

But why is it, Mercy wonders, that they will all drive back to their cattle properties or their sheep stations or to their stake-outs in the opal fields, and not one of them will simply drive away? And why is it that from time to time, not often, certainly, but there has after all been a slow trickle of visitors since . . .

since . . .

. . . there has been a steady trickle of visitors in these past twelve months since Oyster's Reef disappeared . . . since people began to come looking for the missing . . .

So why is it that Jake Digby occasionally arrives with passengers, but no passengers ever leave with him again?

That thought catches Mercy off guard, and she breathes quickly and hugs herself in the manner of Alice Godwin. Jess puts her hand on Mercy's shoulder. 'Hush,' she murmurs, or seems to murmur. 'It will be all right.'

Everyone looks at Jess.

One of the men, laughing a little, relieved to have something to laugh at, says to Jess: 'I could've sworn I heard you speak, Old Silence.'

Jess looks at him without smiling and nods.

'I didn't *mean* . . .' Mercy foolishly tries to explain, but there really is no need. Spoken thoughts or unspoken, everyone has the same ones, and Mercy presses her crossed arms harder against her stomach and curls herself over her sickness till the feeling passes.

Jess touches Mercy on the cheek with the back of her hand, motherly. It will be all right, her gesture says, but Mercy fears that it means goodbye, that Jess is about to leave, that she will walk out of the shop, across the verandah, across the dust to Bernie's Last Chance, where she will be instantly absorbed by the washing of floors, or the making of steak and kidney pies, or the pulling of drinks at the bar, whatever Bernie needs. Then Mercy imagines, feverishly, that Jess will hang up her apron on the peg behind the kitchen door, and that she will walk away toward the Red Centre and disappear, as so many have disappeared. She clutches Jess's hand convulsively, and Jess does not let her hand go.

She can feel Jess's thoughts coming back to her through the pressure of Jess's hand. *It's all right*, Jess says. *I'm not going. And I know what you meant.*

What Mercy meant, what she *meant*, was not the obvious. Of course any passengers arriving with Jake cannot leave, that is understood. It is horrible, it is more horrible every time, but that is the way things are. The question is: why does no one else ever leave? – not counting Miss Rover, who was in a different category, a different category altogether, Mercy is quite clear about that. Miss Rover was very suddenly transferred, and in any case that was before things at Oyster's Reef got out of hand. Teachers were always in a different category.

Teachers never belong, people said. They come and they go.

From the small towns of western Queensland, they mostly go.

But why, Mercy asks herself, does no one *else* leave? Leave and not come back, that is; because obviously Mercy does not count the small convoys that go to Longreach or to Quilpie or to Brisbane to sell the opals and to bring supplies back: to bring food, beer, drinking water, drums of petrol, clothing, haberdashery, bolts of blue, supplemental fodder for the cattle and sheep until the drought lifts, spare parts for the tunnelling machines and the blowers, for the winches, for the hammermill mixers, for the augers, for all the grazier's and the opal miner's needs. No one wants supply-company men arriving unannounced, so people leave and come back, yes. They leave in fours: two trucks per trip, two drivers per truck; and they return in six, ten, fourteen days.

But why does no one simply *leave*, the way Miss Rover did, without looking back? Petrol rationing is one reason, of course; the fact that petrol is kept under lock and key. But even the people with access to petrol come back. Why? This interests Mercy, the riddle of what it is exactly that has glued them all together. At night she lies awake and ponders it. She constructs thought experiments and unravels them and follows their threads. Ma Beresford and Ma's Bill, for example . . . suppose they failed to come back from a provisioning trip, what then? Suppose they sold a whole shipment of opals, and kept the money, and bought airline tickets to Tahiti?

Suppose Mr Prophet failed to return from the sheep and cattle sales in Longreach or Charleville or Roma?

Or consider Mercy herself. Could she leave?

Suppose she were to climb aboard Jake's truck one day, suppose her parents permitted it, suppose the elders permitted it . . . well, of course no one would actively permit it, but suppose they were to turn a blind eye? Well, of course they would not turn a blind eye, but suppose she were somehow to sneak on the truck anyway, suppose she were to hide under a seat until Jake reached Birdsville or Windorah, and suppose she were then to hitch another ride east to Quilpie, and then take the train to Brisbane or to Sydney or to . . . well, to anywhere. The unlimited possibilities make her dizzy.

Could she do that? Anxiety drums against the underside of her skin. She tents her hands and presses her fingertips together and there seems to be a low electric humming in her veins like pins and needles, like hope perhaps, because the stunning thought comes to her that she could, she could, she could leave on Digby's truck, *technically* she could. And perhaps one day she will. She will, yes. She will fly through the window of Outer Maroo. One day. She will escape, possibly, in spite of so much evidence that there is only one way to leave town. In Mercy's case, an exception will be made. Something will happen. Any day now, perhaps today, someone not yet known to her will arrive in Outer Maroo, perhaps today on Digby's truck, and there will be a certain kind of light around this person which Mercy will recognise, and the stranger will look at Mercy in a certain way, and Mercy will look back, and the stranger will beckon, and Mercy will go to the stranger like a sleepwalker without a second's pause and without looking over her shoulder, the way people did when Oyster first arrived in town, but this will be different. This stranger will be as different from Oyster as day from night.

And Mercy will walk through the wall of fire, oh she has no illusions, nobody can have illusions any more, it is not going to be painless, but she will do it. In the twinkling of an eye she will be translated into her real self, the one Miss Rover saw, the one Jess sees and knows, the one which has always been smouldering and fizzing away somewhere under her skin. There are nights when the hum of this other life burns her fingertips and fills her lungs with so much heat that she has to breathe fast with short little gasps or she will faint.

But then again . . . maybe everyone in Outer Maroo lives by such lunatic hope?

And if she did leave . . . if she did get away . . .?

Mercy tries to imagine herself in Brisbane. She tries to imagine Brisbane: tall buildings, a river with water in it, grass that is green instead of brown, garden sprinklers, jacarandas. She makes herself walk beneath the jacarandas, a little ghost full of emptiness. No matter how she moves herself through Brisbane, fast or slow, by ferry along the river, by foot, by day, by night, Outer Maroo goes with her like a phantom limb. That is how it would be. That is how it would be for all of us, she knows. We would be like people who have had a leg amputated, or an arm torn off. We would not believe that the missing piece was missing. We would not be able to tolerate the absence. We would have to come back.

Nevertheless, Mercy would like to believe that possibilities she has not yet thought of could exist, in some other dimension perhaps. After all, could anyone have imagined Oyster before he came? Could anyone have imagined that day when Miss Rover stood on the verandah at Bernie's and made the whole town hold its breath? So Mercy marks time. She takes messages as they come, she saves little tokens of light. She lets blueness and the spill of soft cotton cloth fill her senses, she gives herself to the lift of them, she holds them, she breathes them out.

When she opens her eyes again, she must devote her attention to Digby's truck, which has at last arrived in the street outside, which is rocking into berth at the Shell petrol pumps in front of Beresford's, which is spilling out the newest shipment of foreigners. The foreigners float beyond the shop window, not yet fully tethered to the red earth, but twisted and pulled into thin wavery shapes by the haze.

Jake Digby is already on the verandah. He leans against the screen door, his strong sweat-and-whisky smell moving on ahead of him, and he pauses for a moment to make a space for the fog of himself within the hot bubble of the shop. Flies nuzzle his face and he bats them off with his Akubra. He lets the door slam behind him.

'Where's Ma Beresford?' he asks, looking around.

No one answers. Sometimes it takes whole minutes to readapt to the eyes of an outsider, even to one like Jake Digby who comes whenever there are people who insist on being brought, which is not often. The thing is: he comes and he goes. There is a great gulf fixed between Jake Digby and everyone else. In Beresford's, they suck on this knowledge and move it around in their mouths for longer and longer before they come upon the kernel of any word that can safely be spoken to Jake.

'She's gotta sign for the water,' Jake says. 'I brought ten fifty-gallon drums on spec. Reckoned you could do with 'em, but I gotta get paid up front, and she's gotta sign for 'em.'

Rivulets of sweat trickle from his hair and leave route maps in the dust on his face. He is wearing khaki shorts and heavy work boots and a less than clean singlet. He wipes the back of one hand across his forehead. When he lifts his arm, a gust of something like sweet flyblown fruit reaches Mercy and she swallows quickly and rests her hand on the spice jars behind her and concentrates on cinnamon sticks and thyme.

Everyone is watching the foreigners – there are two of them, a man and a woman – who stand swaying in the heat.

'Been on the road two days,' Jake says. 'Came all the way from Quilpie, with one bloody breakdown per day. Found this lot' – and he jerks his thumb back over his shoulder – 'at the Quilpie Railway Hotel. Been there weeks, apparently. Not travelling together. Don't even speak to each other hardly. You'd think they were practically at war. According to the lady there' – and here Jake indicates by a certain fleeting modulation of the voice that he is using the term in its generic sense, but with grudging respect, and that as far as city types go in general, and city women in particular, this one is a bit of all right – 'according to the lady, she asked to buy a ticket to Oyster's Reef, if you can believe where this cock-and-bullshit's got to, it's like bloody fairies, it's like Santa Claus, yer can't stamp it out. Well how was she supposed to know, eh? she's a Yank, she read it in the papers over there or got a postcard or something, it's gone halfway round the bloody world and back again, and some clever-arse joker in the pub told 'er she'd have to wait a few days, the line was unnergoing temp'ry repairs. And she believed him, see, well that's the thing about Yanks, innit? you could sell 'em Ayers Rock.'

No one laughs. It is all very well for people in Quilpie to make jokes. Quite apart from everything else, people in Quilpie think they are superior because the railway line stitches them to Brisbane. They act, so Ma Beresford's Bill has informed Mercy, as though you can hear the pulse of the whole bloody nation tick tick ticking in their precious Railway Hotel, in which you can buy the Brisbane papers, well *la-di-da*, and in which you can even buy unused paperback books and the *Australian*, and who would want to, could Mercy tell him that, when those toy boys in Canberra and Sydney don't know a Santa bull from a Simmenthal bull from bullshit, or an artesian bore from a fucking hole in the ground. Hell, any moron with a satellite dish can tell you what the Prime Minister said yesterday (begging Mercy's pardon, and the pardon of the whole Living Word congregation of which Mercy's father is the pastor, or used to be; begging the pardon of the whole bang lot of the Living Worders who believe that a satellite dish is the mouth of Satan, and television is his voice in your home), still, with honourable present company excepted, any dope in the pub who is watching the TV over the bar can wank on about foreign policy and the bloody arrogant French in the South Pacific, but it takes intelligence to know when to crop-dust for heliothis in the sorghum or for locusts in the fucking buffel grass. And even though at Mercy's house they pray for Ma Beresford's Bill . . . no, that was before; at Mercy's house they used to pray for Ma's Bill, that the Spirit of the Lord might put a burning coal on his tongue to purify it, nevertheless they always agreed that he was right about Quilpie, that wicked city.

'Well how was she supposed to know?' Jake repeats with a touch of belligerence, from which everyone understands that Jake has fallen for his female passenger hook, line and sinker.

'Yeah, Yanks are funny like that,' someone concedes, finding a voice, a safe thought. 'They'll believe anything you tell them.'

'But how could she have known Quilpie was the end of the line, eh?' Jake is warming to his subject, spoiling for an argument. 'I found out who the joker was. Gave him a little lesson in manners for his trouble. Should keep him quiet for a while, I reckon.'

Mercy is squinting, because the heat rearranges people. The two strangers are pleated diagonally like Japanese dolls, rice-papered, their heads stretched out into points that slant away to the right of their feet. When they move, the lines shift in slow motion, and new points form, new angles, new shapes. They rearrange themselves like coloured chips in a kaleidoscope. The woman puts out a hand to steady herself, and for a moment Mercy can see her clearly, but as soon as the woman's palm touches the flank of the truck, her mouth opens in shock and she goes out of focus again. She cradles her hand against her cheek and then blows on the pads of skin tenderly (Mercy can see two mouths, two hands) and looks around in a sleepwalking way. She is wearing sandals and a sleeveless white dress which comes halfway down her calves, and a floppy straw hat from which a crumpled ribbon trails. The hat, Mercy thinks, has been rammed into suitcases all its life. It is soft and durable, much worn, not fashionable, not a tourist's hat of the kind Mercy has seen in year-old *Women's Weeklies* that Ma brings back from Quilpie. It could belong to a cattle cocky's wife. The woman takes the hat off and fans herself. You can tell from the way she puts up her hands and does little tap-dance steps that she is not used to bush flies. Folded splinters of her arms whirr around her and she looks at her hands in a blurred way as much as to say: which pieces are me and where oh where have they brought us and what are we doing here? She smiles at the slow ballet of her hands much as a baby does, absorbed in its clever fingers and thumbs. Mercy can see a helpless kind of laughter rising in the woman, and recognises the hysteria that sits on the edge of sunstroke and dehydration. The woman turns toward the man, laughing, inviting him to share an uncertain joke.

But the man will have nothing to do with uncertainty. The woman's languorous amusement irritates him. He turns from her, frowning, and studies the road that runs to nowhere in both directions, assessing Outer Maroo's five public buildings: Beresford's General Store cum Farmers' Co-op cum Post Office Agency; the pub; the School of Arts hall, which once served, before dry rot set in, for all dances, wedding receptions, and wakes, as well as for the Country Women's Association and the Returned Servicemen's League; and finally the two churches: the Living Word Gospel Hall and St Chrysostom's, once Catholic, well, still Catholic, no doubt, *in secula seculorum*, but now unsafe, untenanted, collapsing under the weight of termite colonies, evangelical rivals, and soft rot. The stranger who came on Jake Digby's truck notes everything with the fierce air of a man taking down evidence. There is something about the mass of him, about the concentration of will, that causes his mirage selves to settle and coalesce. Even with the width of the shop, the window, the verandah, and the road in between, Mercy is mesmerised and can feel the pull of him.

She thinks suddenly, incongruously, of Gideon.

She does not want to think of Gideon. Oyster's Reef streams from Gideon like a vapour trail. She does not want to think of Gideon, though some bodily tic of the stranger perversely reminds her . . .

Is it Gideon, perhaps, for whom the man has come looking?

The man makes a decision and crosses the space of red dust and leaps lightly up the verandah steps without even looking to see what the woman is doing. For a moment his hand rests against the screen door, but then he changes his mind and rubs a space in the dust of the window instead, and peers through the grubby glass. He looks directly at Mercy and she holds her breath, although she knows very well, having done it often enough, that when you look into the murky shop from outside in the sunblind light, you see nothing but shadows.

The man himself is shadowy, framed by the smeared oval clearing he has made. He looks like a formal portrait, sepia tinted, from some other time. Mercy wants to memorise him for her private collection, to file him with the pinfire opal, and with Miss Rover's books, but she dare not close her eyes in case he vanishes. He has greying hair, once dark, and dark eyes. It will not surprise Mercy if the glass begins to melt where his gaze passes through it. Several tendrils of his hair, damp with sweat, fall across his forehead. His lips are not like the thin hard lips of men in Outer Maroo, but full and soft. Sensual, Mercy thinks. It is a word she has been waiting to use, longing to use, ever since she heard Miss Rover say it. Yes, *sensual.*

Mercy's own lips move responsively, shaping themselves toward something she cannot name, and it occurs to her that she could come out from behind the counter very naturally and cross the shop and check the levels in the grain bins below the window. She should do this, because it must be a couple of days since she has checked the grain levels, and he has not moved, the foreign man, he is still staring through the oval of rubbed glass. She knows he can see nothing except shadows, but at a certain point, when she is close enough, their eyes will meet . . .

'Maybe we could tie a string to 'er and pull 'er back down to earth.' Jake Digby is snapping his fingers, click click, in front of her face.

Mercy blinks at him.

'Thought we'd lost you,' he grins. 'Got our head in the clouds, have we, love? You gonna tell me where Ma Beresford is, or not?'

'Uhh . . . she's gone down to Brisbane with Bill,' Mercy says. 'With the two big trucks, for supplies. I'm minding the shop while they've gone.'

'You'll have to sign then,' Jake says. 'If you want the water.'

Mr Prophet says stiffly, 'Mercy can't sign, she's under age.'

'Suits me, mate. I'll take the bloody water back. Gotta be at least ten properties between here and Windorah where I can sell it for whatever price I care to ask. I'll just have a few beers and I'll be off.'

No, no, no, voices protest.

'Hot-headedness,' Mr Prophet reproaches, 'is not an asset in business, Mr Digby.'

'Is that so, mate?'

'A little patience, Mr Digby. With a little patience, we can come to an arrangement.' Mr Prophet always speaks, even when mustering cattle or supervising the winching at the opal digs, in what Mercy thinks of as his prayer-meeting voice. She believes he is not aware of this. His property is a hundred kilometres out of town, well served by an artesian bore, but the bore, alas, has a high sulphur content. Particularly high, most would say; so that, while the water on Jimjimba is fine for livestock, and for the washing of dishes, and even for the taking of showers (once one gets used to the alkaline slick on the skin, and the frightful smell), nevertheless it is not pleasant – decidedly not – for human consumption; although when rainwater tanks are empty, as now, one drinks what one must.

Mr Prophet speaks. 'Outer Maroo always needs drinking water,' he says. He gives the words such a mournful and delicate moral resonance that he seems to have indicated: *Thou art weighed in the balances, Jake Digby, and found wanting.*

Jake is impervious. 'I'm easy, mate. I just gotta be paid, that's all, cash on the barrel. This is me own initiative, and me own risk, a bit of extra business on the side, as close to legal as you'll get out here, and at a discount price some blokes would hock their mosquito nets for. But somebody's gotta sign, because I gotta have legal-looking receipts for the weigh-station johnnies and the tax man, and those blokes have a bad habit of cropping up when you least expect 'em on the other side of Quilpie. Once you hit the bitumen, in fact. The second the road surface improves, that's me rule of thumb, civilisation is down on yer like a ton of bricks.'

Mercy, startling herself, offers: 'I can pay you cash from the safe, Jake. That's what Ma Beresford would – She'd want me to.'

'I believe she would, Mercy,' Mr Prophet says. 'Nevertheless we do not look upon . . . *irregularities* . . . lightly, Mr Digby. We do not look upon . . .' In his mind's eye, perhaps, Mr Prophet looks upon the sulphurous bubbling of his bore-water outlet pipe. 'In times of drought,' he murmurs, 'we cast ourselves upon the Lord.' He closes his eyes. Perhaps the Lord confides in him. 'His Ways are not our ways,' Mr Prophet acknowledges. He clears his throat. 'This is the Lord's doing, Mr Digby, although you may well think you have come here of your own accord.'

The elders cannot help themselves, Mercy has noticed. They must always speak this way, it is like a disease. They reinfect one another at every prayer meeting and become incurable. Once Mercy was afraid for herself, thinking such thoughts. Now she lets them come and go. She lets them stay for a while. She holds them up to the light and examines them. If it were not for Ma Beresford and Ma's Bill and Miss Rover, if it were not for Miss Rover's hidden library, if it were not for Jess and Major Miner, how would she have known there was any other way to talk? And since there are these two worlds, one of which she could so easily have missed knowing about, how many others might there be?

Jake is scratching his crotch. 'I reckon I'm a bit surprised to hear that God is in on the water traffic.'

Mr Prophet smiles his sorrowing smile. 'In spite of yourself, Mr Digby, you are an instrument of the Lord.'

'Jesus,' Jake says. 'Gimme a break, mate.'

Mercy cannot blame Jake. She always wants to wipe Mr Prophet's smiles off her skin.

'Your blasphemy changes nothing, Mr Digby. I will sign for the water. Mercy is too young, her signature would not be lawful.'

'Yeah? So who's gonna know? A scribble is a scribble. I'll do it meself for that matter.' Jake makes a defiant flourish on the white form with a ballpoint pen. 'Don't know why I didn't think of it before,' he says witheringly. 'An old sinner like me.' He squints with one eye, and holds out his thumb like a measuring stick, assessing Mercy. 'Too young, is she? Looks just about the right age to me.' He runs his tongue around his lips in a particular way, and makes small animal sounds, and winks at Mercy. 'How old are you, anyway, my luv?'

'Do not answer, Mercy,' Mr Prophet says.

Behind his hand, Jake makes a face and rolls his eyes for Mercy's private benefit, and she presses her lips together to prevent a smile from escaping. 'What's this?' Jake says. 'Muzzling the witness? I call that buggering up the evidence, which is, I understand, against the law. Gonna have to report this, Mr Holier-than-Thou. How old are you, luv?'

'Sixteen,' Mercy says, blushing, complicit.

'And never been kissed, eh? Never been touched.'

Mercy wants to be on Jake's side against Mr Prophet, but she is unprepared for this remark and that is precisely the problem with foreigners. Any stray comment can turn out to be a hand grenade. In a second, all the air can be sucked from a room. The mosquito net can settle. Mercy's lungs feel as though they are stuffed with wet towels. She can see warning eyes all over the room. Panicked, she steps toward Jess.

'Hush,' Jess murmurs. 'It's all right.'

'You should wash your mouth out, Mr Digby,' Mr Prophet says.

Jake laughs easily. 'Bloody good idea. Just as soon as I get to the pub.' He winks at Mercy, not noticing the change in the silence, or perhaps choosing not to. 'Remind me to send you something belated for your birthday, darling. Something you won't forget for your sweet sixteenth.' Jake rocks his hips back and forth, suggesting promises, an arc of them, a trajectory. 'Just kidding, luv,' he winks. 'Got a daughter meself, and I'd shoot the donger off of any fancyman who laid a finger on 'er. Hey, let's get moving. Give us a hand, you blokes. I need help to unload the water.'

The screen door slams behind him.

Mercy, awash in confusion, watches almost everyone follow. She buries her face in Jess's shoulder. 'I have to go now,' Jess says. 'You'll be all right.'

Mr Prophet opens the screen door to let Jess pass. He closes it again, and looks back into the shop. The weight of his gaze is like a grey week of prayer meetings.

'The Lord be with you, Mercy,' he says.

She should say, she knows she should: *And also with you, Mr Prophet.* She tries to. Her tongue sticks to the roof of her mouth. The door squeals, sighs, lets in the heat, lets in the odour of dead and dying cows, bangs shut again.

He is a righteous man, Mr Prophet. Mercy tries to like him. He is, Mercy's father says, a man in torment.

Mercy can smell fear on him.

She is afraid of him.

The Lord be with us, she thinks nervously, from habit. But she no longer has any confidence that the Lord is anywhere at all.

This Week

Jess: Mapmaking

Now that the end of the world is upon us (the end of the world as we have known it in Outer Maroo), it has seemed to me sensible to start there, with the beginning of the end, just last week, the day the foreigners arrived. But beginnings and endings have always puzzled me. How can we tell one from the other, since they so inevitably swallow their own tails, their own tales? Here we go round the mulberry bush, forever chasing those two trollops, those two teases, those tarts, Start and Stop. Both the flash of the starter's gun and the finishing post are so dependent on point of view, they are so damned tantalising, that the very idea of pinning them down provokes.

Another damned photo finish, my dad, a great man for the horses, used to fume; and what he always meant was that someone standing somewhere else had cheated him out of fair winnings.

As for the spectacular photo finish of Outer Maroo, I am as troubled by the telling as by the tale, one person's termination point being another's brave new world.

Consider Ethel. She sits there, cross-legged in the red dust at the edge of the bora rings, smiling to herself, rocking gently backwards and forwards as though she hears singing and the rhythmic stamping of feet in the gidgee boughs. She has been putting the scattered rocks back where they belong, filling gaps in the circles and centuries. They have been here, the bora rings, for over twenty thousand years, it is believed; it is only in the past hundred, a hiccup in time, that indifferent graziers and the treads of their four-wheel drives have scattered the stones and have imprinted zippered scars across their sacred clay skin.

From time to time Ethel grins at me, and her teeth flash in her black face like stark white lightning.

'My mob chuckling up their sleeves,' she tells me. 'My mob been here all along. They been waiting for this.'

'I wouldn't have thought your mob were wearing sleeves.'

'Fuck off, Jess,' she grins. 'Whitefella Maroo been and gone once, and been and gone twice, and we're still here, my mob and me.'

She is waiting for a lost language to come back to her. She believes it will rise out of the stones. It will drift into her, into the place where words are made, with the smoke from the gidgee leaves. She pokes at her smouldering branches with a stick. She is waiting for a name other than Ethel to rise out of them, for the name she was never given but should have been, for the name history took from her. She is waiting to meet her other self. She is waiting for her name to settle into her cupped hands, knowing that it might not come from the smoke because there is no predicting the ways of the Old People. It might fall from a passing bird. The *Wandjinas* might bring it. It might slither over her arm. *She, the rock python* might set it down beside her. She waits.

'Reckon us Murris got the last laugh,' she says complacently. The Murris in their serried invisible ranks crowd around her. She sees them all. 'You just johnny-come-latelies, Jess. You and Major M.'

As for what is visible: there are only three of us left here; one Murri woman, and two of us johnny-come-latelies.

There may be more survivors, we hope there are more survivors, there will certainly be survivors out on some of the properties, there'll be jackaroos, some station hands, there may even be survivors in town, but we can only be sure of ourselves. For those few who got away before the end, in the opposite direction, toward Brisbane, we have hopes but no information. Everything depends on the wind, and on how it shifted, and on where their Land Rover was when it shifted.

There are three of us left on this side of town: Major Miner, Ethel and myself, camped out here among the breakaways. To the east, the bushfire rages like a mad thing, like a dragon unleashed. It bucks its tail and snorts and coils itself around boulders and trees and pushes its own wind systems from its throat. We can feel its hot breath. We can hear it roar and spit and blaspheme. If it so chooses, if the fancy takes it, it can lift its long neck and flick its tongue in our direction and translate us into white heat and into clear gaseous nothing. We could never outstrip it, not even with both petrol tanks full and Major Miner's foot to the floor. It is the Beast of the Apocalypse run amok.

This is the Day of Wrath.

I write because what else is there to do? I write against time. I write against the whim of the fire. If the flames pass over us, I would like a record, at least, to survive. This is a sort of primitive magic I'm engaged in, I recognise that, and I'm well aware that whatever I get written won't last nearly as long as the bora rings; but at least it will huddle safely under Cretaceous layers older than the first firestick. Inside the Land Rover's metal toolbox, hidden down one of the shafts, it will wait for the next millennium. In ten years, fifty, two hundred, when someone stumbles across the mine, all the opal will be crazed from the heat. The skin of the metal box will fall away in black flakes. The paper will be frail. Perhaps my writing will be stranger than runes.

Of course, this tinpot end-of-the-world with its one hundred k radius is not the first endgame for Outer Maroo. Armageddons come and go out here, like everywhere else, a dime a dozen all over the world: all of them horrific for those involved, all of them quickly forgotten. But this little end of the world has come early. It is ahead of schedule, this one; ahead of Oyster's prediction. This end of the world is a much more lower-case mickey-mouse affair than Oyster would have liked (set off by accident and ludicrous miscalculation) and it did not wait for the zeros to flip over. It would have hurt his pride, this explosive fuck-up. Oyster got the date and the scope of it wrong, though those are the least of his errors.

Speaking of which, speaking of the year 2000 . . .

But here is the problem: if that is the end point, where to begin?

How can I speak of Oyster's 2000 without grief? It is torture, this impotence; knowing that it is possible (not likely, perhaps, but possible) that people are still alive over there, inside the ring of the fire. There is nothing we can do. The heat beats us back like a blowtorch.

'I think it's quick, actually,' Major Miner says. 'Smoke inhalation and shock take care of things, I think, thank God.'

I want to believe him.

We wait. We watch.

I think of famous last words, of last year, of last week . . .

I can't make sense of time, particularly not out here where the First Ones speak to Ethel in lost tongues, where she hears corroborees from the last millennium, where the Old People sing of the ocean that used to lap these inland rocks, where the fire scorches yesterday and will burn into several tomorrows; but I do know that time does not run in a straight line, and never has. It is a capillary system, mapped outwards from whichever pulse point the observer occupies. I happen to know plenty about mapping. In another life, another time system, an earlier incarnation altogether, I was a surveyor and cartographer for the state of Queensland, Australia. I know only too well the extent to which maps are magic systems. I know all about the hocus-pocus of precision instruments and of time.

To put this another way, stepping into a story or constructing a map are much the same thing; and both are like tossing a stone at a window: the cobwebby lines fan out from the point of impact in all directions at once.

I began with the beginning of the end, one week ago. But of course, the end began long before that. Perhaps I should start one year earlier, with the event that was the indirect cause of the arrival of last week's visitors, an event crouched like a toad, loathsome, in all our dreams; by which I mean, of course, the abrupt and spectacular disappearance of Oyster's Reef. But I cannot bear to start there.

In any case, how could I start there, without explaining . . .?

So perhaps it is better if I begin two years ago, with that terrible day when Susannah Rover, as the town so carefully, so delicately, so euphemistically put it, was 'transferred'.

Or perhaps three years back, when she arrived?

Or I could begin more than a year before her arrival, on the broiling December day just before Christmas when Oyster himself arrived.

Surely that is the *real* beginning of the end?

And yet Oyster's coming looks so utterly different from this vantage point, knowing what I now know, than it did when he staggered into town, so different that I do not know how I can begin to reconstruct that day without misrepresenting it.

'What are you doing?'

'Oh God, Major! Don't *do* that to me.'

He has this way of materialising, Major Miner, this way of seeming simply to appear from fissures in the mesa where the veins of opal run.

'Sorry,' he says.

'I was tying myself in knots.'

'Join the club,' he sighs. 'Doesn't do any good, though.'

We both stare at the cavorting horizon where it leaps into red and orange peaks.

'I hate this,' he says. 'I hate it. Not being able to do anything. It drives me crazy.'

'I know. Me too.'

'What I don't understand is why I can't get Quilpie on the CB. Can't raise anyone anywhere. There has to be some stray trucker somewhere between here and Innamincka . . . but I can't raise a bloody peep.'

'The fire must interfere.'

'Shouldn't. I don't see how or why.'

'Anyway, no one would get here from Quilpie in time to do anything,' I say.

'No,' he admits. 'I'd feel better, that's all.'

'And what would they do for water?'

'I know,' he says. 'I know. But I would have done *something*. I'd feel as if I'd done something.'

'You did do something. We both did.'

'Yes. But the things we did . . .'

That is the trouble with complicity. It is so intricate; it is like a gigantic cobweb; it clings; you can never get it off; you can never tell where any one thread is going to lead.

'The things we did,' he sighs. 'The things we didn't do.'

'Yes.'

'You were writing.'

'A bit. Mostly thinking.'

'Old habits die hard. You're a compulsive mapmaker, Jess.'

It's true. He knows I'm trying to map the last four years. 'I've plotted the reference points,' I tell him. 'But I can't decide where to begin.'

He laughs. 'Yeah. That's a question and a half, for bloody sure.' He shakes his head, watching the horizon. 'Talk about depressing *déjà vu*. Reminds me of the fall of Singapore, fires everywhere, end of a whole way of life. You knew it was the end.' He studies the palms of his hands with amazement, as though the lines on them might offer some clue. 'I was nineteen years old and scared to death.'

He shocks me like that from time to time, reminding me how long he's been around. It's hard to think of him as an old man: all that energy, that quickness of movement, the wiry body, the agile mind. 'Can't believe how far I've come to get nowhere,' he says, his eyes on the flames; they show no perceptible signs of diminution, though there have not been any explosions for several hours. We think all the petrol supplies must have gone now, but there's so much tinder about: the saltbush, the acacia scrub, the wooden buildings. 'Hungry things, fires,' he says. 'You should've seen them eating up Singapore.' He brushes the back of his knuckles against my cheek, then lets his hand slide down my arm. He leaves it there. 'On the plus side,' he says, 'I've survived a few Armageddons and kept going. You could say I take ends-of-the-world in my stride. Almost, anyway. I suppose that's something.'

I look at his hand on my arm, the way the light catches the tiny hairs on the backs of his fingers. Odd, isn't it? how details snag the attention at the most inappropriate times. I study his wrist. It is sinewy; it seems to me both indestructible and frail. I find his hands madly exciting. I take both of them in mine, and lift them, and put his fingers, one by one, in my mouth. His breath smells ragged and sweet. And then suddenly we are in his cabin, in his tumbledown mining shack made of galvo and nerve, and we are frantic for each other, everything a blur of skin, legs, cock, cunt, breasts, buttocks, and where does all this hope, all this laughter, come from? We are famished, hungry as fire. We devour. We feast on each other.

Beginnings astonish me, the way they can rise out of ashes; and as for the histories of lovers, they're outrageous. They're like folk tales, they're like fantasies, with the embarkation ports of the two protagonists so often altogether incongruous and the crossing of their paths so random; not to mention the question of their ruthlessness, of their swimming through joy like heedless kids while the end of the world is taking place, fiddling each other while Rome burns.

The sheer tactlessness of starting over at such a time!

This is the sober truth: *In the beginning* is always now, and ever shall be, world without end, amen; and starting points are like so many cards to be shuffled. They change shape, they change in value, according to how they are dealt.

And here I am in the role of the dealer in the last poker game in Outer Maroo.

I deal Susannah's card because I can do that. The dealer calls. The sequence belongs to me. I deal Susannah Rover, who haunts me, who haunted us all, and who kept quite a few records herself, though they end abruptly.

Knock it off, Jess, she says.

I like to think of her like that, unbroken as ever, unbowed.

God, you were reckless, I accuse. I find I'm still angry with her. You were so damned foolhardy, I say. So bloody impatient. So intransigent. You can't change Australia in a day. You can't just barge into western Queensland and snap your fingers –

Yeah. Well, she shrugs, in that same old disarming way. *I've never thought that getting nowhere let anyone off the hook, that's all.*

I'm not sure this is any better than last week as a starting point, but it is the thing which presses most insistently against me. It happened about two years ago. Oyster and Oyster's Reef were still with us. Brian (Mercy's brother) was still with us. Susannah herself was still with us.

It was the day she was so suddenly 'transferred'.

Two Years Ago

1

'You can seek but ye shall not find,' Susannah Rover called through the screens. 'That's the rule around here, I reckon.'

She threw her words like a handful of stones at both the Gospel Hall and the pub. The faithful winced in mid-prayer and turned startled faces to the windows. Inside Bernie's Last Chance, in the bar, they stopped talking. The ceiling fans were old and noisy, but the men heard her.

'It's that nutty schoolteacher,' someone said.

'Twelve gates to the city,' she called tartly, 'and every last bloody one of them bolted shut. To keep *us* in and *them* out.' She had Outer Maroo's attention, and she paused to savour it. What she tasted, I suppose, was that kamikaze potency, fleeting, yet unassailable, of someone who has decided she has nothing left to lose. It went to her head. 'Even if someone were *looking* for this place,' she challenged (she spoke loudly and clearly; she seemed calm, and even disdainfully amused, but some inner stopper had blown) 'even if someone were determined to find this town, chances are they wouldn't. The odds are against them. The game's rigged.'

Miss Rover, come over, the children sang. There was still a school then, though there were never many children. There was never much of a school. Miss Rover taught in it more or less by accident, not quite officially, and not for long. She came, she turned things upside down for a year, she was transferred. Once upon a time the school was probably a pinhead on a map somewhere, in the office of some Director of Education in Brisbane. Probably the pin, or the map, or the office, or the Director of Education himself was somehow mislaid.

'I realise,' Susannah said, 'to be explicit, that for Outer Maroo the object is not to be on maps.'

From inside Bernie's, where even at midday you needed cat's eyes, came the shuffle of uneasy movement on bar stools. One of the men groped for a shutter, opened it, and stuck his head out the window. 'You are asking for trouble, luv,' he warned.

'Hello, Pete,' she said, tugging at the long black hairs on his arm. 'I'm over here.'

But Pete Burnett, leaning out from the dark inside, was sunblind. He thrashed about with one hand, searching, irritated to be at a disadvantage. By way of punctuating his confusion, and to gain a little dignity, he blew into the torpid air an amber spitball of beer and beer froth and phlegm. When it hit the hot verandah, it sizzled, and a tiny vaporous plume floated off it. 'You are really asking for it, Susannah,' he said.

'Missed.' Miss Rover studied the steaming gob of spittle on the weathered board and touched it with the toe of one sandal. She drew the liquid line of the Queensland coast with her foot. 'The object of maps hereabouts,' she charged, 'is to mislead. Even on the maps of the Government Surveyor,' she said, 'Outer Maroo is nowhere to be found.'

Is that such a terrible thing? Pete might have asked her. The seduction of nowhere is hard to resist, he might have said, if his feelings knew how to fit themselves inside words. Most of us, he might have said, drifted into Outer Maroo (population 87) for precisely that reason; though when he thought 'population 87' he was not of course including the Murri camps or Oyster's Reef. He felt that went without saying, and merely listened as everyone else did, uneasily. He sensed she'd been building up to this. He knew the secrecy and the rumours had been getting to her.

A storm was coming, everyone could smell it. Apart from Susannah's cold and foreign eye, her observing eye, apart from her sharp tongue (and they both made everyone edgy), apart from these, there was everything else: the drought, the stench, the carcasses, the dead cattle, the dead sheep, the Reef, the Old Fuckatoo, and the silences, the silences which Susannah kept refusing to respect. The town had been feeling eerie changes in pressure (barometric and social) for months.

The air pressed down, as it usually does, like a blanket; or, more accurately, like thick scorched sandpaper. We felt stifled. Heat rashes mottled and pricked us. Dust that was the colour of powdered blood slithered between the weatherboards and curled around the blades of the ceiling fans. Tormented wraiths of it danced through Bernie's, tapping this one on the shoulder, nuzzling that one's cheek, whispering black thoughts in our ears.

No one could breathe.

Susannah Rover leaned against the verandah rail. Not a man would have prevented her from entering the bar if she had chosen to; not physically. But the air would have changed, the mood would have changed. It would have changed radically. Susannah Rover knew this only too well. She had crossed those lines before. She had fronted up in her fair share of outback pubs; she had accepted as some sort of dangerous two-edged tribute the sudden crowding at the bar when she entered, knowing that the CB word would have passed like bushfire from road-train to truckie:

There's a sheila in a jeep heading west . . .

Yeah. Spotted her. She's a redhead. Well, sort of. Faded redhead, I reckon you could say . . .

That's strawberry blonde, you dickhead. She's got bedroom eyes, but. She left Cunnamulla twenty minutes ago . . .

Seen her, mate. Jeez, get a load of the T-shirt. Great tits, eh? She's reached Bingara . . .

She's pulling up, mates. She's parked the jeep outside the Queen's Arse . . .

She was familiar enough with all that: the boisterous warmth, the rough gallantry, the jokey sexual come-ons and their silky undercurrent of threat. She also knew what she lost once they let her in, once she got herself accepted as one of the boys: she lost that hair-fine line of fleeting deference to what she might say. In Outer Maroo, she had always hung on to her otherness. When the men were wary, jostling each other like cows at a molasses lick, they listened; at least for a minute or two.

'It's taken me a while to figure things out,' she said in her throaty voice. (Pete always associated the sound of it with the school bell, he told me; because of the way it carried, clear, and ripe, but with soft edges. She drove the most unlikely blokes to poetry, Susannah did. If Pete were translating sounds into taste, he reckoned hers would have been, by texture, the kind of viscous acacia honey that blooms in thick beads on the combs under the wattles, but with lemon juice added.) 'A lot of thought and effort has gone into keeping this town off maps,' she said.

More than she knew, in fact. Even more than she knew.

'If I were you,' Pete warned her, 'I would stop before I went any further, darling. I would go while the going is good.'

Miss Rover, you're done for, the children laughed, high-pitched, reading moods in the air, turning somersaults, chasing each other around the she-oaks and the tortured gidgee trees in a frenzy of the coming tumult they could smell.

Casually, as though she had just swung her bare brown legs out from under the mosquito net, as though she were still stretching and languidly pushing back the skein of sleep, Susannah Rover lifted some stray curls from her neck and twisted them up into her loose French knot. She kept her eyes on Pete, who kept his on the fluid lift of her dress. She baffled Pete, and excited him, and scared him, and she knew it. She smiled at him.

Mercy, who was Miss Rover's quietest and most diligent student, watched nervously from the lectern of the Living Word Gospel Hall across the street.

(*Mercy is my little fire opal,* Miss Rover wrote to a friend when she first arrived, which was only a year before she was transferred away. As it turned out, the letter never left Outer Maroo, and it was Mercy herself who showed it to me long after Susannah had gone.

> Takes the breath away, *Miss Rover wrote,* but only reveals her dazzle in certain lights and then you cannot imagine where her colours are coming from. Thirteen years old, going on a hundred, looks about ten because she's small or undernourished or something, innocent as a newborn in most ways, older than you or me in others. She's not allowed to listen to the radio or watch TV, and she's not supposed to read anything but the Bible, so she is positively ravenous for anything in print. After school, very furtively, she listens to my radio and watches my TV as though these acts were the most exotic sins. She constantly expects retribution of a fearful but unspecified sort.)

While Susannah Rover tugged at Pete Burnett's arm, Mercy's surveillance was intense but surreptitious, filling the margins of her book. She was reading aloud from the Scriptures. She had to stand on tiptoe to see the onionskin pages – it is a gift, people said, the way that child reads – and from her elevated position, balancing her weight against the crosspiece of the lectern, she could just see the verandah of the pub. Between verses she would pause and raise her eyes, seeming to glance at the over-excited children in the street. She strained to hear the conversation, to hear Susannah and Pete, but always and at once, into the valleys of her silence, sluiced the devout bubbling hubbub of the faithful. *Amen, amen*, the worshippers would jubilate (it was the daily prayer meeting, late afternoon, and 'jubilate' was one of Mercy's private verbs). The jubilators insisted that the tumble of their loud hosannas – *hallelujah* and *glory to His name* and *praise the Lord* – should bounce in the red dust and ricochet and mingle and compete with worldly sound.

> (Mercy leaps at new information of any sort like a famished dog for a bone, *Miss Rover wrote,* but she already has a headful of more weird knowledge than an alchemist. How many angels danced up and down Jacob's Ladder? She will know the answer, and will cite you chapter and verse.)

'For Chrissake, Susannah,' Pete said, as Miss Rover ran an index finger along his arm. 'Half the town's watching.'

'Outer Maroo is here,' Miss Rover said, pointing at her spittle map with her toe. 'Somewhere vaguely east of the Channel Country, and sealed off from the rest of the world.'

'The rest of the world can go to hell,' Andrew Godwin said affably, joining Pete at the window. 'As far as we are concerned.' He had to hold his Akubra at a rakish angle to keep from being blinded by the light. He did not have it on, but he doffed it anyway, and with a stylish flourish that brought it back to the shielding of his eyes. 'If you'll forgive me for being blunt, Susannah,' he said in a considered and gentlemanly way, 'you are even loonier than my klepto wife.'

'And here,' Susannah said, pointing again to Outer Maroo, 'right here at Bernie's Last Chance, in a little back room which is off limits to almost everyone, the king sits in his counting house counting out his money.'

'You've been drinking,' Pete said in a low voice.

'You are stark staring bonkers,' Andrew said.

'Counting out his money and his opals, and no doubt fingering his balls. And nobody knows where the money comes from, and nobody knows where it goes.'

For whole seconds, no one breathed. Sometimes, once a decade or so, a cyclone barrelling down from the Gulf of Carpentaria reaches Outer Maroo. For a day before, there is an unnerving stillness. All the air is sucked out of the town. And then chaos and flash floods are unleashed. Those are the seasons out here: drought or floods; with an eerily calm day of foreboding in between.

That is how it was in Bernie's that day, inside, and on the verandah, and across the street. Everyone was stunned into stillness, waiting.

You must understand two things about small outback towns: that gossip about almost everyone and everything is ceaseless and rife; and that certain things are never mentioned at all. There is a great gulf fixed between what may be verbally kicked around and what is absolutely taboo.

For example: everyone knew that Andrew Godwin, local grazier, husband of the eccentric and not-much-liked Dorothy, owner of Dirran-Dirran, whose hundred thousand acres stretched from Outer Maroo to beyond the Northern Territory border, was regularly casting his seed across the land: with various blonde and long-legged backpackers who all ended up at Oyster's Reef; with pretty little Josie O'Leary, his stockman's kid, who was the age of his own teenage daughter; and with Ethel, the Murri woman the Godwins kept on in the house when the rest of the Murris pulled up stakes and moved off to Bourke. And that is to name just a few. The sowing of the seed took place, as a rule, rather noisily, in a small room at one end of the shearing shed, and the sowing thereof could be heard by the shearers, a motley crew if ever there was one. They reckoned old man Godwin pumped faster than the click of electric shears. There were endless discussions on this theme in the pub, endless jokes.

Everyone also knew that Andrew Godwin's teenage son shot himself through the head (Ross, that is, his middle child; the one between young Alice and Junior, the same Junior who manages Kootha Downs for his dad, and who keeps returning what his klepto mother steals). Everyone knew Ross shot himself, and everyone had a fair idea of why, particularly since the poor boy was known to be crazy about Josie, whom his father was regularly racing. Not a word of this passed anyone's lips. Ever. That would have been crossing a line.

Susannah Rover herself crossed a line on Bernie's verandah that day. She spoke of something the whole town knew about, but she breached a taboo. Everyone knew that vast amounts of cash were changing hands, but nobody knew what went to whom. Everyone harboured suspicions. Everyone secretly believed that his neighbour received an unfair share. Everyone's hands were in the till, everyone was involved one way or another with Oyster's Reef, but no one wished to see it like that. They all felt soiled. They would all have hotly denied feeling any such thing.

Everyone also feared that the rush would spread, that more adventurers and seekers would arrive, that more division of the spoils would thus occur. This had to be stopped. More foreigners had to be kept out. The ranks of the chosen were complete, Mr Prophet urged; the one hundred and forty-four thousand, figured symbolically, were already within the fold, and the gates of the city should now be closed. The one hundred and forty-four thousand, Oyster demurred, as the Book of Revelation made quite clear, were chosen by a Will beyond man's reach and would gather themselves toward the Reef as that Will decreed. The finer points of theology eluded most, but no one wanted to give the opal traffic up. No one wanted to antagonise Oyster. Everyone constantly feared that a tax man, or a government surveyor, or someone from Mineral Resources, might show up. From the very first day, there were people who wondered under their beers about just what sort of government agent a schoolteacher might turn out to be.

Knowing nothing and being untraceable was everybody's goal, though no one mentioned such matters aloud; at least, not until Susannah put her foot in her mouth.

There was, naturally, a shocked silence.

Then there was hubbub.

Pete had been joined at the window by a goodly number of drinkers at varying stages of drunk. From her lectern, Mercy could see others muddling at the door, jostling for a view, spilling out on to the verandah and beyond, crowding the steps, shuffling their boots in the desiccated red earth. She could see Bernie himself, frowning, leaning against the etched glass panels that filtered sunlight to the murky inside. She could read possible retribution in the set of Bernie's shoulders. She fancied she could see Jess, Old Silence herself, but that was the child's overheated fancy because Jess was well back in the shadows behind the bar. She could see Susannah Rover, slight and defenceless, with all those pushing and shoving yobbos around her, a woman at risk. Nevertheless. How interesting, Mercy thought, that the men even stop drinking to watch her.

> (Mercy thinks I am the Keeper of the Tree of All Other Knowledge, *Miss Rover wrote in one of the letters that never left Outer Maroo.* I offer the delectable forbidden fruit. I'm the smuggler of under-the-counter ideas, the seducer, the sorcerer herself, I suppose. Heady stuff for a teacher, but dangerous. Can I magic my little apprentice out of this outhouse before I get us both in deep shit? That is the question. There's some pretty strange stuff that's passing for normal out here. I don't know if I'll be able to believe it myself once I get out, if I ever get out, so what good will it do to blow whistles? Who'll believe me?

As for the rest, the pay is not bad, coming as it does from the pockets of the three local warlords who hired me: two graziers, one of whom is also a terrible wowser (everyone calls him 'Mr Prophet', though I call him – privately, of course – Mr Brimstone, or Old Blood-and-Thunderguts); the third is the owner of the pub.

It's a weird combination. Why would a teetotaller team up with a publican, you ask? Good question. Why would two graziers appear to be involved in a private arms race? This town is one big riddle to me.

And the men are what you'd expect, but I make do.)

'Susannah,' Pete said huskily, opting for a different tone. He ran his tongue around his upper lip and fortified himself with more beer. 'Listen, sweetheart, you've got a touch of sunstroke, I think. Let's go for a spin.'

'On the other hand,' Susannah said, 'everyone knows where the opals come from, but does anybody know exactly what is going on at Oyster's Reef? Or how much cash is changing hands and where the cash comes from? Or what happens after the opals leave Bernie's back room?'

'For Christ's sake, Susannah,' Pete said, urgently. 'That's none of your bloody business, love.'

'*Then the Lord rained upon Sodom and upon Gomorrah*,' Mercy read, '*brimstone and fire from the Lord out of heaven; And he overthrew those cities, and all the plain, and all the inhabitants of the cities . . .*'

Please, Miss Rover, she prayed silently, pressing her fingertips and thumbs together. She could not tell exactly what she was frightened of. She prayed that Miss Rover would not look back at the cities of the plain, or at Oyster's Reef, because the hot shimmering air of trouble came off them like the air off a compost heap.

'*Escape for thy life*,' she read aloud, '*look not behind thee, neither stay thou in all the plain; escape to the mountain , lest thou be consumed.*'

Nevertheless there was a spirit of rebellion in Mercy which Mr Prophet had detected while under the strobe light of the Holy Spirit. 'Mercy,' he had said after prayer meeting one day, 'your mind is full of vain questions.' The palms of his hands were turned out toward Mercy and tilted up. 'They are spreading like a cancer in your soul.'

Mercy stared at the chemical stains and blotches on his upturned cattleman's palms, the cattle-dip and fodder-spraying burns, the incipient melanoma sores. She was full of confusion.

'Cast your questions upon the Lord,' Mr Prophet urged.

Mercy studied her own hands.

'I am praying for you, Mercy.' He said this in a kindly way. He was a man who wanted to be kind, she saw that. He was a man sandpapered by his own intransigent and passionate beliefs.

Mercy also prayed for her spirit of rebellion, as though it were a dangerous infection she had picked up, one that ebbed and flowed unpredictably. She was alarmed by its growth, though sometimes she indulged it and gave it free rein, as now, when her spirit of rebellion was secretly and quietly exuberant to see Susannah Rover standing there calm as a cucumber under the ferocious Australian sun, while a bunch of yobbos who could scarcely believe their ears hung on her every word.

A little bell with a clear and glorious sound pealed victory notes inside Mercy's head. I will jubilate, she said to herself. I will lift up mine eyes to Miss Rover . . . but then the thoughts shut themselves down abruptly in panic lest she had sinned against the Holy Ghost by blasphemy, the one sin that could never be forgiven, world without end.

'The existence of a town,' Miss Rover was saying, 'can be camouflaged by a map, but there are things you can't keep a lid on for ever. Sooner or later, they are going to leach their way out through this frangible soil and leave their mark.'

'For God's sake, Susannah,' Pete said angrily. 'We're not schoolboys.'

'There are letters and postcards being written and mailed,' Miss Rover said. 'You think you've stopped them getting out – oh, I know all about that; it took me a while, but I know. I could get very angry myself, Pete. About the letters, I mean. Only there's something I think you've all forgotten.'

'Is that so?' Bernie asked.

'Yes,' Susannah said, 'it is. Because the people waiting for the letters that never arrive get a message, don't they? They get a very loud message.'

The men made a collective sound and swayed a little, all together, like a bee swarm, spoiling for trouble.

'I'd say someone else is going to have the last laugh, mates,' Susannah said.

'*But Lot's wife looked back from behind him*,' Mercy read, '*and she became a pillar of salt*.'

'Leave her,' Pete said, apprehensively. He had pushed his lanky frame through the window, and climbed out with some difficulty. Now he made a rough and jokey claim to possession by draping an arm around Susannah Rover's waist. 'She's a raving loony, mates, take no notice.'

Mercy saw Miss Rover pick up Pete's arm as though it were a bit of saltbush that the wind had blown against her. She looked at it with a raised eyebrow, curious, but certainly polite. She held it away from her and examined it for another second or two, then she kissed it on the wrist and let it go.

'Now listen, Susannah, my dear,' Bernie said patiently, much as he might speak to a man who has had a few too many, 'I think you've forgotten who pays your salary. We're only asking you to teach our kids to read and write. That's all. Just stick to what you got hired for.'

'If it isn't Himself,' Miss Rover said, curtsying.

'She's been drinking,' Pete said. 'I can smell the gin. I think she smokes stuff too. I think she gets it from those fuckwit kids at the Reef.'

'As for reading and writing,' Miss Rover said, 'since you bring up the subject. The Murris can read and write, which isn't something you ever take into account. They can read this country like a book, and they've got their own bush telegraph. I think you can assume that the word is out and about on Oyster's Reef and on Outer Maroo. The *other* word, I mean. The word on what's really going on. I think you forget these things.'

'She's right,' Major Miner said quietly. 'It was asking for trouble to sink shafts so close to the bora rings. The Murris aren't going to keep quiet about it, and why should they?'

'They can talk till it rains again,' Bernie said, 'for all I care. And as far as I'm concerned, they're still Abos. They're not getting any fancy new names outta me. I been watching black faces whingeing on TV ever since I got the satellite dish. Finders keepers, I say.' There was a murmuring hum of assent from the drinking swarm, and Bernie warmed to defiance. 'Nobody gets free beer or free opal on account of a suntan round here. Not in my establishment.'

'Hear, hear.'

'You know where they can shove their sacred sites.'

'Look at what's happening in Cunnamulla,' someone called.

'Look at what's happening in Bourke.'

'We don't want any packs of feral black kids running wild around here, Susannah,' Andrew Godwin said, affably, reasonably. 'This isn't New South Wales. It isn't Bourke.' He smiled expansively. 'Hell, everyone knows *I've* got nothing against the Abos' – and we all thought of him fucking Ethel in the shed. 'If they have a legal case, there's the courts.'

'Anyway,' Bernie said, disgusted, 'they've got the attention span of five-year-olds. They've all lost interest and gone and buggered off to Bourke. Good riddance, I say.'

'If I were you,' Miss Rover said, 'I wouldn't congratulate myself on the sudden disappearance of the Wangkumara camps. I'd find it ominous, if I were you.'

Ooooooh, the men said, looking at each other and winking and slapping their sides. *The wonky-wonky camps*, they said. *The wonky-wonky men are gonna get us . . .*

'*Ominous,*' one of the men said, pushing his tongue against the inside of his cheek. 'We don't know them big fucking words round here.'

'Big words, big tits, and too big for 'er boots,' someone said.

There was raucous laughter.

'She's a bit too big for her boots, and she's barmy, but otherwise she'll do for a sheila,' a deep voice offered from out of the twilight of the bar. 'If she can just keep her nose out of other people's business. Bernie's right, Susannah. Finders, keepers. People gotta work for their bloody keep, that's the rule in this country.'

'Is that you, Bill Beresford?' Miss Rover called.

'Yeah,' he said, appearing at the door. 'It's me. You are lucky that most of us consider you one of the boys, Susannah, that's all I can say. And a bit touched, up top, as well.' Ma's Bill tapped on his forehead with one finger. 'That's how come you get away with murder, love.'

'Ah,' Miss Rover said. 'Now we get down to the heart of the matter. Getting away with murder.'

'Jesus, Susannah!' Pete said softly.

The men sifted opals in their pockets and watched her.

'Does anyone keep a head count out at the Reef?' she asked. 'Does anyone keep a pregnancy count? Does anyone know how many of Oyster's kids –'

'I wouldn't comment, if I were you,' Bernie warned.

'Knock it off, luv,' Pete urged. 'Hey, listen, I've got the truck. Let's go for a spin.'

'I think,' Bernie said, 'that you should apply for a transfer, Miss Rover. I don't really think we got that much need for a school after all.'

Miss Rover, come over, the children sang.

'And I think,' Miss Rover said, 'that you won't shut me up so easily. I think that you don't realise just how many messages are getting out. For example, a letter or two of mine went to Bourke with the Murris, which may be the long way round to Brisbane, but then again, it might be more expeditious than Australia Post.'

'Jesus,' one of the men said, seemingly casual. 'What big fucking foreign words she keeps in that slutty little mouth.'

'I think maybe she should wash her filthy tongue,' someone said.

'Maybe a few other private places, eh? She admits she's a *Boong*-lover. How many of those black bastards do you reckon she's fucked?'

'They're all cunts, schoolteachers. Always were, always will be. They all fuck you over in school.'

Miss Rover come over, the children shrieked, madly excited.

> *Miss Rover, Miss Rover, you've ticked off the drover,*
> *And here come the shearers to put you to bed.*
> *Here comes the swagman to chop off*
> *your your your your . . . head!*

'Listen to your own children,' Miss Rover said, 'Listen to what they know about you. Do you know what they know about Oyster's Reef? Do you know what they say?'

Mercy almost choked on a word from Genesis. She could feel her heart bucking against the Bible, and the lectern, soft with termites, shuddered.

'Words are maps, you'll find out,' Miss Rover said. 'Words are maps and they'll get –'

'Words'll get you into trouble, luv,' Pete warned jokily, a little panicked now, fighting to turn a hard edge in the air on its side. 'You're gonna trip on them and flip yourself arse-over-head. Better eat them.'

'I'm eating them.' Miss Rover reached down the front of her dress and pulled out a letter she had mailed from Beresford's a week earlier. She waved it in front of the men, then she began to tear the paper into little squares. One by one, she put them in her mouth and chewed.

'She's off her rocker,' Pete said. 'I'm taking her home.'

There was a skirmish, Pete pulling, Miss Rover resisting, the men closing the circle a little. There was a dreadful, mad, animal smell . . .

'You keep right out of this, Old Silence,' Ma's Bill warned.

'Jess!' Bernie said, like an order. 'For God's sake, stay outta this! You want to get yourself . . .?' and there wasn't much time, that was clear. These things are like bushfires. They can whoosh up out of nothing in a few seconds flat, especially when too much booze is involved, as it always is around here.

'Not even you can shut me up, Jess,' Susannah said. 'Enough is enough.'

'Listen, mates,' and there was a sharper edge of anxiety in Pete Burnett's voice, 'just ignore her. Teachers come and go. They come and go and change nothing.'

Miss Rover, come over, the children sang, turning somersaults in the red dust and laughing shrill high-pitched laughs.

> *You're done for, Miss Rover, your number's come over,*
> *and here come the squatters to chop off your head.*

'Words are like bushfires,' Miss Rover warned. She was high on something. She was high on having crossed the line. 'You can't stop them. And you can't tell where they'll end up.'

'You're a flaming nut,' Pete said. 'I bloody well give up on you. I give up.'

'I don't give up,' Miss Rover said.

She turned and saw Mercy through the window and waved the remnants of her torn letter, and before Mercy had time to think, she had raised a hand in salute, and Miss Rover put a word there and it burned.

'Thank you, Mercy,' Mr Prophet said tightly. 'You may sit down. And may the Lord inscribe His Word upon our hearts.' The congregation, as one, was transfixed, its gaze on the scene across the street.

'We will bow our heads in prayer,' Mr Prophet said, 'that the peace which passeth understanding may settle like a dove in every heart.'

Something brushed Mercy's heart and her wrist. It was the dove of Miss Rover's word and she closed her fingers round it and kept it in her fist where it fluttered violently and bucked about like a trapped thing.

Mr Prophet rose to his feet, lifted in the wind of the Holy Spirit. 'We will now sing a hymn,' he announced. 'We will sing "Onward, Christian Soldiers". Begin to play, please, Mrs Jones.'

'At the right moment,' Miss Rover whispered, 'you must set my word free.' She whispered this to Mercy quite clearly in her teacher's voice (so Mercy insists), between the first and second lines of the hymn. Mercy could feel her own heartbeat cavorting as wildly as the word in her hand. She started and turned around, but Miss Rover was not in the pew behind, only her brother Brian, with his eyes closed; not just closed, squeezed shut. She beamed his name at him: *Brian, Brian!* But she could no longer reach him that way, perhaps because he was four years older and was becoming strange to her, distant, moody, solitary, an adult.

Across the street there was a scuffle going on, nothing out of the ordinary, no more violent than usual, a few broken bottles and jagged shouts, it went without saying, but nothing that wouldn't blow over in fifteen minutes, Mercy thought. Nevertheless, she wished she could still see Miss Rover.

Miss Rover, come over, she prayed silently.

'Remember me,' Miss Rover whispered, clear as a bell. '*Promise.*'

Mercy turned around again, startled, and this time Brian watched her from wide sombre eyes.

'All my books and journals,' Miss Rover whispered from somewhere inside Mercy's head, 'are in the wooden press in the schoolroom. You know where the key is hidden. Keep them safe.'

I promise, Mercy said.

2

Mercy pored through Miss Rover's dictionary, word by forbidden word, sucking each meaning as she went. The taste was addictive. She licked words and polished them and held them up to the light. She set them down with precision, she set them down with the same kind of care that Bernie took when he and his underlings cut opal, or when they polished the rough stones, or when they bonded opal veneer on to potch. Bernie and his workers turned out flame doublets, lightning doublets, red doublet flash. What they made smouldered. What they made sold to tourists for a great deal of money in Brisbane.

Whenever it was possible, Mercy stole away to Aladdin's Rush, where she had hidden Miss Rover's books. There was a corroding iron ladder bolted into the main abandoned shaft, and she climbed down, carefully, into coolness. She had to keep a map of the tunnels inside her head, and she had to feel her way. Though she carried a torch, she steered by touch. So far, she had never been lost; she had always found her way back to the books. They teased Mercy and provoked her. She found them as fantastic as the Bible, and she began to fashion her own kind of doublet, to bond substances as different as onyx and opal, as incompatible as sandstone and silk: there was the Gospel Hall view of things, and there was the view from Miss Rover's books, and how was she to join them? How was she to contain both ideas at once?

Psalm 90, verse 9, she wrote in her diary. *We spend our years as a tale that is told.*

There's a tale that needs telling, Miss Rover said. She had been doing this quite often since her transfer. She would start up conversations and leave Mercy to write both scripts. I'm counting on you, Mercy, she would say.

> Once upon a time, *Mercy wrote in her diary,* not long before the year 2000, the people of a small town in south-west Queensland shaded their eyes and looked into the white of the sun. They saw something: a black speck, a bloodspot, a shape no bigger than the size of a man's hand at first. It moved toward them from out of the haze.

That is very fine work, Miss Rover said in her ear, and Mercy glowed, she preened, she flared on the sparks of her own words. Miss Rover told Mercy whatever Mercy needed to hear. You could escape if you chose to, Miss Rover told her. You could spread your wings.

'We could escape, Jess,' Mercy said to the tunnels of the Rush. 'We could leave Outer Maroo.' She wanted to hear the words out loud. She wanted to make them tangible. She wanted to see them visible, like a mirage, in the treacherous air.

This is where Jess has escaped to, the tunnels could have told her.

The walls of the Rush curved around Mercy, they folded her in. They were the colour of whipped cream, fluted like drifts of silk, and if she stood and stretched her arms above her head, she could brush the arc of the roof with her fingertips. On the other side of the roof, thirty feet above, the parched red earth broiled and cracked; but underground, in the creamy Rush, the air was cool. Mercy could feel the picked seams of where the opal used to be, she could feel the shimmering echoes of the blues and teals and greens, she could see the phantom tongues of fire.

Opal is amorphous silica, *she wrote in her diary,* with water trapped inside. The water and the silica diffract the light, and that is why colours chase each other on the skin of the stone. The water in opal is thousands of years old (Miss Rover said millions), so the past is locked inside it the way a meaning is locked in a word.

Aladdin's Rush is abandoned, it has been worked out, but opals still hide here. I have found three opalised seashells – from a million years ago, Miss Rover said, when Outer Maroo was under the sea. If that is true, fish have slithered and silvered where I'm sitting, and the great slow waves of the ocean floor have washed these walls.

That is the *long* history of Outer Maroo, Miss Rover says. She showed us photographs of the *plesiosaurus* that miners found at Lightning Ridge. It is the most beautiful thing I have ever seen, a great opalised fish that has swum through colour since the world began. It is older than the dinosaurs, she said.

Beverley Prophet told her father and he came storming into the school. It was his school. He owned it, he and Mr Godwin and Bernie, because they didn't want any of us kids from Outer Maroo to be sent away to Quilpie or Brisbane. They were afraid we would talk, I suppose. Brian and I should have been in high school, Toowoomba or Brisbane, Miss Rover said, but of course we don't have the money for that, and in any case Mr

Prophet says that everything we need to know is in the Bible. He read us the first chapter of Genesis, and told us that God made the *plesiosaurus* on the fifth day, and that no fish or any living creature existed before six thousand years ago.

'You mean God made the *plesiosaurus* on a Thursday?' Miss Rover asked, and he told her to watch her step.

My shells must know their own past. They are full of nothing but ocean when I hold them to my ear. I don't know what to believe.

I do know my father is embarrassed by Mr Prophet. When I asked him if we had to believe that the *plesiosaurus* was created on a Thursday, he said that the Bible speaks to each of us in its own mysterious way. We should leave the answers in God's hands, he said. Brian, my brother, said I shouldn't be asking these questions, Brian said they are not relevant, Brian said that Oyster says that time itself is the fossil from which the opalised future comes. Miss Rover said that Oyster is highly intelligent, but he still talks bullshit.

Brian said that Oyster says that Miss Rover could never understand the transcendental nature of interlocking time spheres, and nor could I. That was before Brian left us and went to the Reef.

I know it is less than sixty years since a Beresford, some older relation of Ma's, found opal floaters at Aladdin's Rush and built the house that is the oldest in Outer Maroo. That was in 1938.

But before that there was Maroo, a handful of miners and a few opal shafts in the 1870s. The miners set up camp and sank the first shafts inside a bora ring, not far from where Oyster's Reef is today. There was trouble. The miners blamed the Murris and there was a massacre of their camp. Everyone knows this. It's still a junkyard of bones out there, not far from the Reef. Some of Oyster's backpackers came and told Miss Rover one day, and she took photographs. She mailed the film to a newspaper in Sydney, but of course the letter never left here.

After the massacre, the old town, the town of Maroo, prospered on opal for three years, and then it was burned to a crisp. Everyone says that the Murris who escaped the massacre came back and did it. Everyone said the place was jinxed. That was in 1873. Maroo sank into the earth until Outer Maroo was built to the east of it . We call the oldest shafts, the 1870s shafts, Inner Maroo, because all that is left is holes in the ground.

Mercy closed her diary and leaned back against the curving wall of the Rush. She pressed her fingertips together. *Miss Rover, come over*, she wished, and she rubbed the old Aladdin seams, and *abracadabra*, Miss Rover's own journal rose like a genie from one of the cartons of books. The journal had not been regularly kept, and there were pages torn out, and the entries were very rarely dated, but for Mercy, the fragments were full of enticements. She cherished them. She read them avidly.

Outer Maroo. February.

Hotter than Hades. Lost world. Just getting here pretty amazing in itself; picked up in Quilpie, 2-seater Cessna, by local grazier, Andrew Godwin, a lecher if ever there was one. Blindfolded; security reasons, he claimed; real reason, in my opinion, an excuse to touch me up, plus kinky leanings. Landed on airstrip on his property.

Thirteen kids, all ages, in my school. They all come from another world. The kids at the Reef even more so; all utterly lost.

o o o

Oyster hears voices, he says. Two things are abundantly clear to me: Oyster is extremely intelligent, and Oyster is mad. Quite mad. No, on the second point I waver. I was absolutely certain of it on first meeting; but circumstantial evidence to the contrary keeps unsettling me. How can it be that these young backpackers I keep meeting, these seekers, these best and brightest who drift in from Brisbane and Sydney and Melbourne, from Europe and the States, how can it be that they are so drawn to him? What is it that draws them? Well, his eyes, I suppose, for one thing; though I find them chilling myself. Where do his voices come from?

o o o

Mr Dukke vanKerk, or Mr Prophet as everyone calls him, once ran cattle on the High Veldt, I've ascertained. He saw certain writings on the wall, however, and moved on to a prosperous ranch in Oklahoma. He even went to the trouble of becoming an American citizen. Then, social change threatening to catch up with him even there, he decamped again to the cattle haven at the end of the line. He owns 250,000 acres and is now a born-again Australian, passionately opposed, naturally, to any changes in the constitution or the flag.

o o o

Everyone seems to know, by osmosis, that Andrew

Godwin's middle son shot himself, and that Andrew is deeply mortgaged to one of those vast all-American hamburger corporations that own half of western Queensland and the Northern Territory these days. I learn these things from Pete when I push him hard for information; but he lets them out reluctantly. We don't talk about stuff like that, he says. It's not cricket.

That, of course, is partly superstition. Since the bottom fell out of the wool market, sheep people everywhere are madly scrambling to switch to cattle as fast as they can, just as fast as they can get their hands on Simmenthal and Santa Gertrudis and Hereford stud. All those big spaces on the map that used to ride on the sheep's back, as we all got taught in school, are letting the shearing sheds collapse and are turning to beef. Just about everywhere west of the Warrego is mixed now, sheep and cattle both, but some properties have managed the switch better than others. Nobody wants to jinx things by mentioning difficulties. So nobody comments that some American bank practically owns Andrew Godwin, hook, line, and ding-dong. That would be crossing a line.

o o o

All year, I have been writing and mailing letters at the rate of knots. Lost cause. Letters becalmed in doldrums as I recently found out by accident. Post Office, what a laugh. Everything goes into black hole.

Such original postal procedure, I must confess, has come as a blow, so have given up on letters, or rather, on mailing them, though still write them for reasons of sanity and calm. As for telephones, we do have them, though the servicing thereof is slightly bizarre, and a surf of static drowns all but a local call. Telecom linesmen and technicians do appear, but their vans have an alarming habit of combustion (the spontaneous variety, naturally: fierce sun, conducting metal, petrol tank; it must be faulty construction, people shrug; all these Telecom vans . . . they are probably Made in Japan).

So. There do seem to be reasons for concern, as every paranoid person believes. Are my scepticism and self-mockery reassuring proof? How could such proof be said to be reassuring? So it goes. I consign myself to this journal and hope it's just the extravagance of outback colours getting to my imagination. I've got a touch of the lurids, I tell myself.

I told Jess I was keeping a journal. We all keep journals, she said, whether or not we write them down. I don't quite know what to make of Jess, the way she only speaks when she chooses, which is practically never. What's all this silence for? I asked her, and she, very loudly, said nothing.

Why do I stay when I am afraid to know how this story ends? How do I think I would get out if I decided to go? I feel horribly pushed toward some grand and futile gesture. What more can I learn of Oyster and of Oyster's Reef and of all of Oyster's sad devotees that I will not regret knowing?

○ ○ ○

Once upon a time, a young teacher (make that youngish), for various reasons of which she would prefer not to speak, answered an advertisement for a private posting in western Queensland. She took the train to the end of the line for an interview in Quilpie. (Quilpie! She should have known. She should have known.) After that she found herself lost – which was exactly what she was looking for – in Outer Maroo, where the object is not to be on maps.

As for Oyster's Reef . . . the object is not only to be off maps but outside time. The Oysterlings await, with mournful eagerness, the big bang, the crustacean shazam, the end of the world, and – according to Oyster – trailing clouds of zeros shall it come. But then, if old newspapers are anything to go by, people began to lace zeros and events a decade ago, and here we are, still, in the final decade but not quite at the lip of the turn, with signs and portents whizzing by, so who can tell?

At any rate, the Apocalypse Kids have been arriving in droves, and most of those are still here. I think. I hope. When I say here, I do not mean in the town itself, though individual kids surface briefly from time to time, then vanish again. They always come into town in threes. They watch each other. I barrelled up to one such little trinity the other day and asked them why. The triangle is the most stable of forms, they said, and points in all directions to God.

Triangulation, I told them, is a slow and most painful form of death.

They did not even smile. They are terribly earnest. They live in the underground opal tunnels of Oyster's Reef. Everything runs to excess out here, including the drought and this ghastly and omnipresent smell of death. The Old Fuckatoo, people call it, and it is pressing us hard. The whole town seems drugged.

O O O

Time played its usual games with Mercy: it was not a line, not a circle, but a fog. Things happened, but it was difficult to fix them in a sequence. Her brother Brian, for instance, moved out to the Reef, she found it hard to be precise about when. And then Mercy herself, without intending to, went there briefly, but when was that? She was looking for Brian. She kept seeing her visit again, she kept seeing the Reef, it kept appearing to her, she kept seeing Brian, she kept seeing Susannah Rover . . .

What would constitute a true mirage? she kept asking herself.

'Jess,' she said, dancing around a question, and the usual rush of silence, busy, foaming, swirled around us. You could see the crests of questions coming in, and the murky undertow of answers rushing back. They roped and braided themselves, they were never still, they were always moving away, their speed was quicksilver, dangerous, they could never be grasped. They threatened to drag her completely out of her depth.

'Jess? If mirages are real . . .? I mean, *somewhere* they are, aren't they? So how would we know, Jess? I mean, if we saw something . . . if we thought we saw something . . . how would we know . . .?'

And how could she be encouraged to finish a question like that?

'Jess, I want to tell you . . .'

But mirages assailed her.

'Except I can't,' she said. 'I want to tell you what happened at the Reef, but I can't. I just can't.' She covered her face with her hands. Her sobbing was very quiet and came from a long way down; it was like old air bubbling out of a mine shaft.

*

'*Lord, make me to know mine end,*' Mercy read from the lectern of the Living Word Gospel Hall. '*Make me to know mind end, and the measure of my days, what it is, that I may know how frail I am.*'

She lifted her eyes from the page and looked out the window. Across the road, people loitered under the acacias with their hands in their pockets, or sat on the steps, or waited in an untidy line along the verandah. Mercy could see the lacework of their nervy intentions, the short shadows they made, the way the burning sun toyed with them, the way the red dust kept silting up their dreams. They were waiting for their turn. Their hidden fingers played with colour-shot stones. The blues and scarlets in the stones flashed like birdwings; they were never still. The people with stones in their pockets were waiting for Bernie. They waited for Bernie to weigh and assess and pay cash.

Less and less often now did the young foreigners come in from the Reef. When they did, they came in threes. Mercy kept watching for Brian, but never saw him.

Oyster no longer trusted Bernie, it was said, and vice versa. He had a new middleman now: it was Andrew Godwin, some whispered; Dukke Prophet, others claimed. Or maybe Ma Beresford? All gossip raged unspoken, a matter of raised eyebrows, pursed lips, the significant pause. Alliances were shifting, that was certain, but no one was quite sure how. There were more people who no longer trusted anybody else.

Below the reading shelf of the lectern, Mercy made O's with her index fingers and thumbs. *Miss Rover, come over*, she prayed.

She thought of asking the congregation: To what town was Miss Rover transferred?

Teach me to know Miss Rover's end, she thought of reading out loud. Teach me to know the measure of her days.

She could hear, as she so often did, Miss Rover's voice inside her head: the measure of days from any one event to another is determined by a slide rule, Mercy, and time is a trickster. So is memory,

Mercy thought. Miss Rover hovered like a cobweb, almost visible, and sometimes Mercy could feel the fine silky touch of forbidden ideas. But more often Miss Rover began to seem like a wicked tale she kept telling herself, a perverse tale, a tale that smelt of vain questions, a tale that spoke of a spirit of rebellion which was punishable by . . .

She made Miss Rover write her letters, though both of them knew these letters could never arrive. Miss Rover's messages were long and witty and irreverent and encouraging and full of all kinds of illicit knowledge, and they were beautifully written in intricate sentences that Mercy wanted to wrap in crocheted cotton handkerchiefs to tuck up her sleeve. She often read these letters to herself.

She did believe Miss Rover would post them, in spite of what they both knew of Ma.

It would be an act of faith.

Mercy thought of the actual messages, which she would never see, piling up in the Dead Letter Office in Brisbane, drawing attention to themselves, snaking whitely through the fascinated dreams of postal clerks until somebody, some day, opened them and read, because stories do insist on being known.

But how old will I be? Mercy wondered. How long will it take?

She lowered her eyes to the sacred text of the Psalms. '*For a thousand years in thy sight,*' she read, '*are but as yesterday when it is past, and as a watch in the night. Thou carriest them away as with a flood; they are as a sleep: in the morning they are like grass which groweth up. In the morning it flourisheth, and groweth up; in the evening it is cut down, and withereth . . . For all our days are passed away in thy wrath; we spend our years as a tale that is told.*'

'You've got your head in the clouds again, Mercy,' Ma Beresford said. 'You dream up too many tall tales.'

Why didn't you at least let Miss Rover's letters go out? Mercy wanted to ask her; why didn't you take them to Brisbane and post them there? Because, she would point out, the rules should have been different. An exception should have been made. Miss Rover was a Queenslander, she wasn't foreign at all.

'Yes she was,' Ma Beresford would say.

Or perhaps she would say: 'I don't remember any Miss Rover. You made her up, Mercy. It is crazy, the things you make up. You always have your head in the clouds.'

There would be reasonable grounds for this response. No one ever spoke of Miss Rover, who had vanished like the water from a creek; absolutely, that is to say, leaving behind her not even the sound of her name. For fear of such an answer from Ma, Mercy kept her questions locked in her fist. And so her days passed as a fitful sleep and as the grass which flourisheth (though only within the little sphere of an artesian bore and only on those properties which irrigate their scrap of lawn constantly) and then turneth brown and withereth under the relentless sun.

'Mercy,' Ma Beresford would say sharply, snapping her fingers, and Mercy would startle, lost. 'Major Miner is waiting to be served,' Ma might say. Or: 'Do you think you could serve Mrs Godwin, Lady Muck, if I'm not asking too much.'

'Sorry,' Mercy would say, embarrassed. 'I was . . . I'm sorry.'

'Head in the clouds.' Ma Beresford would tap her forehead with a finger.

'You must come and visit Alice, Mercy,' Dorothy Godwin said, 'before she leaves. I'm sending her down to boarding-school in Brisbane, I've made up my mind.'

'Yeah?' Ma was not impressed.

'I know what you all think. And Andrew is opposed, but you don't understand. This is no place . . . There are certain graces, you know, which can only be acquired . . .'

'Tell Alice I miss her,' Mercy said. 'It's been ages.'

'Yes,' her mother conceded. 'That school business, that frightful business . . . She's been too upset.'

'Tell her . . .' Mercy said, agitated, brushing words off her clothes, off the counter. 'Tell her . . .'

Mrs Godwin was flexing her fingers as though she had cramps, which always meant . . . 'Yes yes, yes of course. Yes?' she prompted. 'Yes yes?'

'Tell Alice . . .'

Mercy watched the fingers of Mrs Godwin touching things, reading their surfaces, sliding them into her bag. This happened in slow motion. It was beautifully done.

'And tell Alice . . .? tell Alice . . .?' Mrs Godwin pressed.

Mercy blinked. 'What?' she asked vaguely.

'You see?' Ma said. 'Hopeless. I blame the Old Fuckatoo.'

The Old Fuckatoo was roosting again. The drought continued.

A work roster had to be set up. By first light, before the heat and the flies, teams in Land Rovers had to drag the livestock carcasses further away from the town. The smell of death seemed to settle in like a permanent resident.

The Old Fuckatoo came and went. It came and drifted away.

Mercy drifted.

She watched for the young people from the Reef who came and went, who came and went, though less and less often, but when they did, Mercy sold them stamps, and touched the ink of their frailties with her hands, and drew the postal-bag drawstring of oblivion around them.

'How much does it cost airmail to Boston?' a girl asked. She had an American accent. She had bitten her fingernails raw. The other two Oysterlings, her watchers, were at the door. They hovered, picking up packets and putting them down. 'I'm Amy,' the girl said in a low voice, nervous. 'I recognise you. You were out at the Reef for a little while, but then you got away, I don't know how.'

Mercy could feel a softness starting at her ankles, and then spreading, and she knew that in a second or so she would dwindle into nothing, she would simply leak away, she would disappear through the floor like the last waterhole in a creek bed seeping into sand. No, she wanted to say. No, that wasn't me. She had to hold on to the counter.

'Well, I do know *how*,' Amy said. 'But I mean I don't know how you managed to –' They both jumped. 'There isn't just this postcard,' the girl said urgently, looking nervously back at the door. Her companions had let it slam shut and were on the verandah, but one of them watched through the glass.

Mercy tried to speak but had to gesture behind her instead. Her gesture meant: there's no one here except Jess, and you don't have to worry about her, she won't talk; but Ma Beresford's out in the storeroom and she could come in.

'Yes,' the girl said, flurried. 'I'll be quick. I've got these letters.' She rummaged in her handmade sack, the kind the people from the Reef often carried, rough spun, embroidered with peace symbols and with pentacles and with the dire number 666, which was the Mark of the Beast in the Book of Revelation, and which was cancelled out with a fiery cross; there was also the Opal of Great Price in its oyster shell. The girl took out a slim bundle of letters tied together with green tape. 'I haven't got envelopes,' she said. 'I haven't had a chance to mail them. I was in here once before and I don't know, I just had a bad feeling somehow from that woman, that . . . Ma Beresford, isn't it? I mean, she's not very sympathetic to any of us, is she? She doesn't like us. And there were other people here and I didn't want to ask for envelopes, you know, in case . . . because we're not supposed to send letters, we're not allowed, just postcards. So I've kept writing these letters and hiding them and waiting to mail them. There's not many, we never have time. The thing is, I have this feeling I can trust you, I don't know why. Well, because you've been there, I suppose.'

She looked at Mercy with intense pleading eyes, and Mercy's eyes, also pleading, looked back. *Don't*, Mercy's eyes begged. *Don't, don't, please don't ask anything of me, please don't count on me.*

'Because,' Amy said, 'do you remember that day . . .? at the Reef . . .? and Gideon was carrying you up the ladder to the meeting, and I was at the top waiting to go back down the shaft . . . – it was the purest chance, you know, that we met, it was Oyster himself who sent me, who told me to go back and get . . . – and anyway, at the top I took your hand and pulled and helped you out . . . and we looked at each other . . .?'

Mercy said nothing. Mercy thought she might faint.

'I knew at that moment,' the girl said. 'Because, you know, I'd been chosen too. I'm one of his Special Ones, so I knew. And I knew our paths would cross again. I don't know how I knew that, but I just knew. I knew everything would depend on you. It was like . . . I looked Gideon in the eyes, and I knew he knew it too. It was the first time I saw someone else out there *admitting* it to himself . . . that everything was, you know . . . that it was *crazy* . . .'

Mercy felt as though the air were unsafe. It was heaving. It was curling her into waves. She felt seasickness, air sickness, coming on.

'You remember?'

'I don't remember anything,' Mercy said.

'The address is on this bit of paper,' the girl said. 'If you'll put them into envelopes for me and mail them . . . only I can't pay you for the stamps, we don't have money, but I'll give you an opal, I'll give you two, I'll steal more for you if you want, but can you, you know, put them in the post one at a time so they won't be noticed or anything?'

The girl placed the little bundle on the counter and when Mercy did not move, she lifted one of Mercy's hands and lowered it on to the letters. 'I trust you,' she said. 'I count on you.'

Mercy could think of nothing to say. She picked up the letters and scanned the shelves and tucked them out of sight behind tinned spinach and tinned beetroot, which gathered dust.

'There's one more thing,' the girl said.

'No, please.' Mercy felt as though something were stuck in her windpipe, or in her lungs. She could feel herself turning blue.

'It's a photograph. It's not mine, it's Gideon's. Angelo's. Well, it was mine, it was my Polaroid camera, and a man took it for us, that man who lives out in the breakaways, the one who works boulder opal all by himself . . . he took it.'

'Major Miner,' Mercy said.

'But Angelo asked if he could have it,' the girl rushed on, 'because he wants – I mean Gideon, *you* know Gideon, that's Angelo's name out there – because he wants to send it to his father . . .' She pressed her lips together as though to hold back something that exerted a forbidden but inextinguishable pressure. 'I can't tell you the relief it was, after that moment,' she said. 'I mean, you can't trust anything you think after a while. Everyone acts as though everything is normal, and so you think . . . you ask yourself . . . you're afraid it's only you, that you're crazy, that you don't understand . . . and so you . . . and so you . . . you just stop thinking, really. But then suddenly you see in someone else's eyes, and it's such a *relief!* Since then, you know, secretly, we've used our real names to each other, Angelo and me. It's like, it feels like a stick of dynamite in our hands. Gideon and me, you know. You remember.'

No, Mercy thinks desperately. No. She does not want to remember.

'So could you put the photograph in an envelope for him, and mail it? He put his father's address on the back.'

'No, listen, please . . .'

The girl took one of Mercy's hands and put the print in it, face side up. Mercy saw Oyster, in white, in the middle, Gideon on one side, Amy on the other, and various others in a background blur.

'No, please,' Mercy begged. She did not want to think of Gideon. 'You don't understand.'

'You live here,' the girl said, lowering her voice even further. 'You must know the ropes. You must know how to get away.'

Mercy could feel her heartbeat shift rhythms: slow, then crazy fast, then a dizzy gap of nothing. She would have to ask. 'Did you know my brother?' she whispered. 'Did you know Brian Given? He wasn't there when I went. Gideon said he wasn't there any more. Do you know what –' She couldn't say it. She couldn't ask if Amy knew what had happened. She couldn't put it that way. You had to ask questions carefully. If you asked the wrong way, you could tilt the way the answer came back. 'Do you know where he is?' she asked.

'Where he is,' the girl repeated without inflection. She seemed to weigh the order of the words. She seemed to know what the question meant. 'No,' she said sombrely, 'I don't know. I didn't know a Brian. We have other names there.'

'Yes. His was Emmanuel, I think, but I'm not sure.'

'Emmanuel?' the girl said vaguely. 'No, I don't know. People disappear, you know. They just disappear. There are lots of stories. Some of us just . . . especially the Special Ones. I'm Rose of Sharon out there.' She put her hands over her eyes and ran her fingers up through her hair like a comb, then she held the hanks in her fists and twisted and pulled. Her hands trembled. 'Oh God,' she said. 'He was so kind at first, he was just like a father to me. "You're my little Rose of Sharon," he'd say, "my Special One," and I still wish, I can't help it, I still wish, when he sends for me . . . even though I *know* . . .'

Her body went slack as though the business of the letters and the photograph had used too much energy up. She chewed at her fingernails. She said dully: 'I'm Rose of Sharon out there. I may not even *be* Amy any more.' She looked at the beads of blood on her fingers, puzzled. 'I used to be Amy.'

Miss Rover Miss Rover, come over, Mercy pleaded urgently. *Miss Rover, Miss Rover, Miss Rover, Miss Rover . . .*

Amy leaned in close. 'We want to steal a car,' she said. 'Can you help us? I can give you two opals right now.'

Mercy's voice was lost in a swelling in her throat and she had to gasp and cough to get it out. 'It's impossible,' she whispered, her throat sore. 'It's impossible. It's . . .' – and then the sound freed itself, and came out in a rush – 'See, everything's strange now, everything's turned really strange since Miss Rover was transferred . . .'

That was so long ago, so terribly, infinitely far back. That was the Stone Age. That was before history began. That was nearly a year ago now.

'Angelo tried to talk a guy into helping us . . . the one who got you away from the Reef, what's his name?'

'Donny Becker,' Mercy whispered.

'Yes, Donny Becker. Angelo wanted him to take us, to make a run for it . . . but he's changed. He's too scared now, Angelo says.'

'It's not just that. There's nothing he would be able to do.' Mercy heard something, a footstep, and shoved the photograph down the front of her shirt . She spoke low and quickly. 'No one's allowed more than half a tank of petrol at a time, except, you know, Ma Beresford or Mr Prophet or . . . when they make their trips. So even if you stole a car, you couldn't . . . You wouldn't even get to Eromanga. Unless you stole Bernie's or Ma's or Andrew Godwin's – but that would never –'

'Help me steal petrol.'

'It's impossible. There's just the pump outside here, and the tanks on the properties.'

'Properties?'

'Dirran-Dirran, Jimjimba, the cattle properties, the sheep stations, Mr Godwin, Mr Prophet, and . . . you know.'

'No, I don't know.'

'Well, the graziers, the cow cockies. They get their petrol from the depots in Quilpie. They truck it back in forty-four-gallon drums.'

'Help me steal one.'

'It's impossible. They're always watching.'

'Who's always watching?'

'I don't know. Everyone. Ma Beresford, Bernie, Mr Prophet's people,

Andrew Godwin's people, the elders, *everyone*. I don't know who's watching. Everyone's watching. And Oyster's got people watching, I know he has.'

'Oh yes,' the girl said bitterly. She chewed her lip. Mercy could see that her nails were bitten raw. 'Isn't there a *policeman* somewhere?'

Mercy laughed. 'In Eromanga. But he's Bernie's cousin.'

'There must be a way,' the girl said.

'No,' Mercy whispered. 'There isn't. Except walking, and then you would die.'

'I'll walk, then,' the girl said quietly.

Ma Beresford came into the shop, and Mercy had a sudden coughing fit.

'I want to send it airmail,' Amy said calmly, putting a postcard on the counter. 'It's very important.' She rested her eyes on Mercy and smiled. 'Goodbye,' she said. 'And thank you for everything.' She nodded and left, but at the door she paused and turned. 'Goodbye,' she said again.

'Bye-bye blackbird,' Ma Beresford called, and after the door had closed she said to Mercy, 'What was *that* all about?'

'I don't know,' Mercy said. She bit her lip. 'They're all strange, aren't they, Jess?'

'Foreign,' Ma said. 'Whad'ya expect?'

She picked up the postcard. '*Dear Mom*,' she read aloud. 'Have you noticed that the Yanks can't spell "Mum"?

'Dear Mom,

Our life here is amazing. It is not at all what I expected. When you live in a community of perfect harmony, each atom in the group having its perfect function as each organ does in the body, then everything changes.'

Ma Beresford rolled her eyes. 'None of these foreigners talk sense. Will you listen to this, Jess!!

> 'We live underground, in the bosom of our mother the Earth, from which God our Father made us. It is amazing how cool it is in the tunnels where we work and sleep. But above ground it's like an inferno, around 120 degrees Fahrenheit. Out here, everything runs to extremes.'

'Rubbish. What rubbish,' Ma said. 'What's extreme about Outer Maroo, Mercy? It's only extreme if you're used to a different normal.'

Mercy could not comment, since Outer Maroo was the only normal she had known.

Later, much later in the day, when she dared to look behind the tins on the shelf, the letters were gone.

'Ma?' she asked tentatively. 'Did you . . . you know . . .?'

'What?' Ma asked briskly.

'I . . . Nothing. I lost something. I think I might have left some letters on one of the shelves . . .'

'Honestly, Mercy.' Ma Beresford tapped her brow. 'I don't know what gets into you, I'm forever finding letters you haven't mailed. But I always post them for you. They all get into the keg.'

'Ahh . . .' Mercy said.

She felt sick. She felt that she was going to faint. 'What's the matter?' Ma asked sharply.

'Nothing! Nothing. I just . . . they make me miss Brian, that's all.'

'Too many of them,' Ma said irritably. 'I'm sorry about Brian, Mercy, but if you go in for religion too much, that's what comes of it. They give me the pip, the whole lot of them. They can go up in smoke, for all I care.'

Last Week

Monday Afternoon

1

Alone in Beresford's, Mercy walks slowly to the empty window where the foreign man no longer stands. Instead she can see the bald spot on the back of Mr Prophet's head. He leans against a verandah post and shades his eyes, observing Digby's truck. Mercy puts her hand up to the cleared oval shape within the grime of the window glass, the space which the foreign man has rubbed clear, and lets her fingertips rest there. From memory, with her index finger, she draws the outline of his head. *Sensual*, she murmurs, savouring the taste of the word. She stands on tiptoe and presses her lips against the glass.

Through the oval, she can see the man again, the foreign man, on the far side of the truck, striding purposefully toward the pub (*striding*, she thinks; *purposefully*). She loves the way he walks. *Fluid*, she thinks. As horses move; as water moves. In Outer Maroo, men move awkwardly, as though the act of walking embarrassed them, as though they would rather be on a horse or behind the wheel of a truck. What amazes Mercy about the foreign man is the complete absence of uncertainty. There is no hesitation in him. Red dust rises in puffs around his shoes. He walks for all the world as though he has been in Outer Maroo before, as though he knows the place intimately, as though he knows and has always known exactly what to do. And there is something else, some sense of compressed energy. He will turn out to be one of the angry ones, Mercy thinks, and her heart misses a beat because the angry ones are such easy targets and are the first to go.

The man does not even pause on the verandah of Bernie's Last Chance, the pub that has never run out of beer, not during floods, and not during the longest drought of the century, which is what this is; they could all pin medals on their chests if they so desired, Ma Beresford says. The man does not so much as glance back over his shoulder toward the truck where he has abandoned the foreign woman. The dark behind Bernie's swing doors swallows him up.

Jess will be waiting for him there.

Later Jess will tell her – Mercy knows exactly what Jess will say – Jess will tell her it is because the man comes from somewhere else that Mercy feels these pins and needles in her blood. 'You think everything's magic that doesn't come from here,' Jess will say. 'But people are much the same on the coast, and everywhere else for that matter.'

'Excuse me.' Someone touches Mercy's shoulder.

'Uh!' she gasps, whirling around.

'I'm sorry, I didn't mean to frighten –'

'No, it's just . . .' She cannot quite believe that she has not heard the screen door. Head in the clouds, Ma would say. 'I didn't hear you come in.'

It is the foreign woman, the woman in white, the one with the battered straw hat and its crumpled ribbon, which Mercy now sees is chewed.

'I wonder if I –' The woman sways, and catches hold of one of the grain bins and lets herself slide down, leaning against it, until she is sitting on the floor. 'I'm terribly sorry,' she says. 'I don't feel very – it's the heat . . . I have a horrible feeling I'm going to faint.'

Mercy runs behind the counter. She takes an ice-cube tray from the refrigerator and reaches into the little cupboard below the till where Ma Beresford hides a flask. Back at the grain bins, the woman has not fainted, but has gone limp.

'Do you ever get used to such heat?' she murmurs. 'I suppose you must.' Her eyes are closed. She is curled into herself like a new leaf.

'Here,' Mercy says, pushing the unstoppered flask to the woman's lips. The woman gulps. Rivulets and tributaries of brandy spill down her chin. Mercy tips a handful of ice cubes out of the refrigerator tray and drops them down the front of the woman's dress.

'Uhh! ah! ah!' the woman gasps, leaping to her feet and shaking her dress violently. There is the rapid-fire sound of bullets as the ice falls through to the floor.

'I'm sorry,' Mercy says. 'But it works.'

At the sight of the woman dancing, lifting her dress away from herself with thumbs and index fingers, lifting her sandalled feet in quick tempo time, Mercy presses a hand over her mouth, and in spite of herself begins to giggle.

The woman's eyes widen with distress . . . and then, quite suddenly, with shared mirth. She begins to laugh, and Mercy laughs with her, sedately, but their twinned laughter takes on a life of its own, and it spins and spirals upwards and begins to twist faster and faster, like a thing separate from them, out of their control, and it skitters and dances and bends its funnel of hilarity toward them and sucks them into its vortex and they cling to each other, exhausted. The shop is an empty theatre of watchful but sympathetic things. Mercy and the woman lean against the grain bins and hang on to their sides and rub their eyes with the backs of their hands. Their eyes are streaming.

They are weeping with laughter.

And then, at some not easily discernible point, Mercy becomes aware that the woman is no longer weeping with mirth, but simply weeping. She is sobbing in a quiet, stifled way. Mercy bites down hard on her own fist, because laughter, rare though it is in recent times, always seems to her merely the brackish foam crest on a great wave of sorrow, a tidal wave, a wave that is pulling her down and will drown her like the wave that left her mother blubbering and coughing on the sand the time her mother was taken, in her mother's impossibly distant childhood, to the coast.

'I'm sorry,' the woman says at last. 'I'm sorry. This is not like me at all. I don't know what's the matter with me.'

'It's OK,' Mercy says. 'It happens to most people who come out here in the beginning. You get used to it. Would you like a cup of tea?'

'No, no, don't bother. I'll get one when I – I have to find somewhere to stay. Where can I stay?'

'There's only the pub,' Mercy says doubtfully. 'But it's not a – Ladies can't stay there.'

'*Ladies*,' the woman says in amazement, and with such a delicate air of derision that Mercy realises she will never be able to use the word again because it will taste too ridiculous on her tongue. 'And where do ladies stay, then?'

'Well, uh, they don't . . . We've never had . . . except in the beginning, you know, the young ones, and they all stayed out at the Ree . . . but not afterwards. I mean, not the ones who've come looking, we've never had a woman come looking, that's only been men.'

'Come looking,' the woman says slowly, carefully. She straightens her back against the keg stave and studies Mercy. 'What do you mean, *come looking*?'

'I mean . . . I didn't mean . . .' Mercy presses her hands together. *How could I have said that? How could those words have come out of my stupid mouth?* She opens her eyes very wide and shrugs. 'I just mean, you know, people get lost out here. They come looking for somewhere they can hitch a ride, to Windorah or Quilpie, you know. Or they come looking for opals. But only men.'

'I'm looking for someone,' the woman says. 'I've got a photograph.'

'No,' Mercy says. 'It's no use. Please don't show me.'

'Pardon?' The woman is startled. She frowns, concentrating, translating.

'I mean –' But Mercy can think of nothing to say. And then she can. 'You have to go back with Jake on the truck. You have to go and tell him now. *Please*. You *have* to.'

Dust motes, gold in the afternoon sun, dance between them. Now Mercy is aware of the yeasty smell of the grain, of the sharp tight stink of saddles and boots, of the fragrance of cinnamon, of thyme, of rosemary, all of them reaching her singly and in concert from the spice shelves, as though all her senses are on tiptoe, waiting, and the blue rush of the spilled bolt of cloth is like surf in her ears, and each white thread of the dress of the woman opposite is as keen and fine as piano wire and cuts Mercy's skin.

The woman is very still and observant, as a cat is observant, watching its prey. Without wavering in her terrible attentiveness, without lowering her eyes from Mercy's eyes, she reaches into her bag, shuffles her hand there, and brings out a photograph. She holds it out to Mercy. 'I am looking for Amy,' she says.

Mercy sees the shelves in Ma Beresford's swaying toward each other; she sees the walls tilt; she sees the floor lift itself like a wave. She closes her eyes. She breathes deeply. When she looks again, the room has steadied itself. She will not look at the photograph. She wonders why dust motes in sunlight always rank themselves in parallel lines. Is there no dust in the spaces in between? Could one adjust one's life like that, alter its alignments a little, nudge it on to a parallel track, a space in the clear? There were tiny steps that she, that others, might have taken months ago, a year ago, two years ago . . . and if they had taken them, how different things might be now. But how can one know in advance which landslide will be started or averted by the moving of a pebble with the toe? Can she apply to the woman's life the pressure of a fingertip? Can she lean against one day in the life of this woman just sufficiently to push her out of the gilded bar where frenzied specks of dust collide and crash, into the still space where nothing happens?

She puts her hands together and they feel papery in the parched air. She would pray if she could; but in the place from which God once capriciously inclined his ear, there is nothing but a scorch mark. Over her desolate praying hands, she looks into the woman's eyes. 'Please go out on the truck tonight,' she says.

'Why?'

'Because.' She rushes the woman with words. 'Because otherwise you'll be stuck here for months and you'll hate it. There's nothing . . . especially for a woman . . . and people are not very friendly to strangers.' Under the woman's gaze she falters. '*Because*. That's all. I can't tell you.'

'Do you understand,' the woman says gravely, 'that you are offering me the first glimmer of hope I have had?'

'There's no hope here,' Mercy says. 'Not in Outer Maroo.'

'I think of Amy as my daughter. She isn't, though for a number of years, she was my stepdaughter. But she's my daughter as far as I'm concerned. That is what she is to me. For various reasons, we are all that we . . .' She is studying Amy's photograph. 'It's curious how close hate and love are, there's just a membrane between them. Did you know that?'

'Yes,' Mercy says.

The woman's eyes flicker toward her with interest. 'You're young to know that.'

'I just . . . I didn't mean . . . I was just agreeing, just being polite.' The woman raises her eyebrows, observant, and Mercy feels compelled to add: 'Yes, I do know. I wish I didn't know, but I do.'

The woman nods. 'I'm not trying to pry.' She sighs. 'No matter what has happened to Amy, I have to know, do you see? My last letter from her was mailed from a place called Quilpie. I found Quilpie. In that last letter, she said she was heading further west, she was going to a place called Oyster's Reef. I've heard nothing since.'

'You see, there's no such place,' Mercy says urgently. 'It's like . . . it's like El Dorado. There's no such place.'

'Isn't there?'

'No. No, really. No, there definitely isn't.'

The woman lifts the photograph higher and Mercy averts her eyes.

'Have you ever seen her?'

'No,' Mercy says.

'You haven't looked.'

'There aren't any foreigners here.'

'You see,' the woman says quietly, 'I have already . . . When you don't hear for such a long time . . . you phone embassies, you read newspapers, you have nightmares, you phone police departments, you write pleading letters, you write threatening letters, and then you write nothing, you pray, you light candles, you go to tarot card readers, you lock yourself up with exhaustion, you just need to know. Then you make airline reservations. I have accustomed myself to the idea that the worst might have happened to Amy. But no matter what has happened, I have to know. I have to know. Can you understand?' She begins to repeat the words like a mantra, very quietly. 'I have to know, I have to know –'

'Please,' Mercy begs. She leans forward and places her hand over the woman's mouth.

The woman says quietly, slowly, looking Mercy in the eyes: 'I am staying until I know what has happened.'

A great sigh shudders through Mercy.

'So I suppose I should book a room in the pub.'

'No, you can't stay there,' Mercy says. 'You really can't.' She makes a sudden lunatic decision. 'You can stay at our place. We've got a room, now that Brian's . . . now that my brother's gone. I'll take you home with me, we don't live far. But I have to . . . first I have to close up the shop.'

Urgent energy possesses her. There is a blur of chores: counting the money in the till; locking it in the safe; fastening windows and doors. Then she is directing the woman into the battered utility truck. 'You have to climb in my side and slide across,' she apologises. 'The passenger door doesn't work.'

She tosses her head defiantly at the stir of interest in the street. As she starts the motor, Mr Prophet appears. He looks pained, astonished, but Mercy pretends not to see.

'Mercy,' he says reproachfully, leaning in through the open window, leaning close. Mercy roars the engine. She smiles at him, regretfully, setting the bulwark of noise in between. The door rattles.

'Mercy!' he shouts.

He puts one hand on the wheel, but the vehicle reverses itself violently, as though caught off guard by its own gear, and leaves Mr Prophet standing there, shocked, staring at his hand. 'Oh gosh, I'm sorry,' Mercy calls, but the truck ignores her and lurches skittishly into full forward leap.

'This is not wise, Mercy. The proper place for . . . *Mercy*!'

Mercy puts her foot to the floor, and the truck enters a cloud of red dust.

The woman looks dazed. After several minutes, she says with a kind of wonder: 'You're very young to drive. Especially like this. At what age do you get a licence out here?'

Mercy laughs. 'We don't bother with licences in Outer Maroo. We drive as soon as we're tall enough to see over the steering wheel.'

'What's your name?' the woman asks, coughing.

'Mercy Given. I'm sorry about the dust. It's better with the window up, even though it's hotter. It's a stupid name, I hate it.'

The woman smiles. 'Amy hates hers too. At your age, everyone hates her name. Mine's Sarah, by the way. Sarah Cohen. How –' But dust barrels down her lungs and she abandons herself to a coughing fit.

'Wind the window up.'

'Yes. Sorry.' When the coughing subsides, she asks, 'How old are you?'

'Sixteen.'

'Amy was only seventeen when she left home. She was only seventeen. But that was four years ago.'

Mercy accelerates. Already her bravado is seeping away. *What have I done?* She drives faster. The dust lifts around the vehicle like a red mushroom cloud. Mercy swings off the unpaved road and turns on to a track between stands of she-oaks and gidgee. Saltbush scratches the car. Ahead is a long low house with verandahs.

'Amazing,' Sarah says. 'It's like a tiny green oasis. How is that possible?'

'Bore water. See that pipe elbow sticking out of the ground, near the verandah? That's the bore. We only had to go down twenty metres, we were lucky. Ah . . . they are going to be . . . my parents, that is . . . they'll be a bit . . . We're not used to visitors. And lately, since all the trouble . . . I mean, the drought and everything. Everyone's nerves are shot. They are going to seem a bit shell-shocked, probably, a bit nervous. Please don't take it personally.' As she turns off the ignition, she says by way of warning: 'Um . . . my dad's the pastor of the Gospel Hall. Was, I mean. He used to be. There'll, uh . . . I'm afraid there'll be Bible reading and –'

Two sheepdogs, frenetically joyful, hurl themselves at the car. Mercy has to shout above the barking.

'There'll be prayer and stuff like that after dinner. Well, I shouldn't say prayer, not exactly, not any more, not spoken out loud anyway . . . *Exodus! Leviticus! Be quiet!* There was a split in the congregation, and my father was . . . *shunning*, it's called, *de-fellowshipped*, but they go through – *Leviticus! stop it!* – they go through the motions just the same. You can excuse yourself. They won't mind. They're not like Mr Prophet. *Exodus, you crazy –! Get out!*'

'It's all right. I love animals. What a jump!' Sarah reels a little, nevertheless, under the dog's boisterous greeting. 'Who's Mr Prophet?'

'That man who leaned in the window, who tried to stop – Exodus, out!' Mercy opens her door. 'He's elder-in-chief at the Gospel Hall. Well, he's set himself up that way.' Her manic energy is deserting her and going to the dogs. She feels weak. *What have I done? What have I done for the sheer pleasure of defying Mr Prophet?* She sees something, clear as a mirage, floating just above the bonnet of the car: three calves on shaky newborn legs, faces soft. They have the huge, luminous, puzzled eyes of animals born into the drought; they have the eyes of her parents; Sarah's eyes. She stares at them. She sees a bird of prey swooping down, the beak going straight for the eyes. 'Uh . . . look,' she says, 'maybe this isn't a good idea.' Her hands are shaking. 'Maybe I should take you back.'

'In fact, I won't mind at all about the prayers,' Sarah says. 'It's all extremely interesting to me, because of Amy's letters. I need to try to understand what drew her. It's a total unknown to me, all that, Protestant mysticism, I mean, though I'm familiar enough with *our* brand of it, Hasidic and Orthodox, Lubavitcher . . . As must be obvious to you, since I'm Jewish.'

'Jewish?' Mercy frowns, puzzled. She is distracted from the mirage for a moment and turns. 'You mean, like in the Old Testament?' When she looks back, both the calves and the bird have disappeared into a pleat in the air.

Sarah laughs. 'I wouldn't think so, no. I'm just your regular non-observant American Jew, though my sister has become ultra-orthodox and moved to Israel, which upset our parents even more than my marrying a Gentile.'

'I didn't know there were still Jews,' Mercy says with amazement.

Sarah stares at her. She presses her fingertips against her temples. 'What is that strange smell?' she asks vaguely.

'Ah, that. It's the Old Fuckatoo,' Mercy says. 'It's roosting again.'

2

Beyond the swing doors of Bernie's Last Chance, the darkness is thick enough to touch and smells of mushroom culture. Nick remembers the trays with their glass covers in his grandmother's cellar; the coolness, the sweet fungal musk, the pearled clusters of white caps pushing through the humus; he remembers the small alcove beyond the arch, where he had to lower his head, he remembers the cobwebs, the dust-crusted bottles of wine and ouzo stacked high, and behind them the damp stone wall, weeping slightly. The smell of Bernie's Last Chance is similar, a rich compost-heap kind of smell, yeasty beer slops, and body odours turning fungal, and mushrooms, and wine-damp, all mixed together, rushing him with vertigo and nostalgia. Here he is sliding backwards to that moment when he took his young son, his born-in-Melbourne fair-dinkum Australian son, three years old, back to the ancestral Greek village. 'That one will be in and out of trouble all his life,' his grandmother says, and there is Angelo clambering up a pyramid of bottles, fearless and self-destructive from the start, already searching for the pot of gold at the end of the wine cave, a mad light in his eyes, doomed before his first year in school.

Across twenty years the sound reaches Nick, the hum, like a murmuring of monks, at first just a low chant, then sonorous, rumbling, ominous, swelling, the bottles beginning to move. He can hear Angelo's scream. In the pub in western Queensland, instinctively, he lurches and flings out an arm and manages, somehow, to pluck his scrap of a son from the carnage in the nick of time. (The *nick* of time, he thinks, sardonic; that's me. This time too, he hopes, and mentally crosses himself.) The wall of wines sways like a sandcastle swamped in brine, it sags and dips and rolls, but miraculously, though the cellar is awash in rolling bottles, scarcely any of them break. They wheel and skid across the stone floor and Angelo clings to him, sobbing.

'You'll always have to keep your eye on him,' his grandmother says. 'Always. It runs in the family, it's in our blood.' She strokes Angelo's hair absently, her eyes focused on something not in the cellar, and he knows that she is back on the Aegean coast with her own brother, the one who drowned. 'Everyone loves the troubled ones,' she sighs. 'It's a gift they have. A trick.' She trails her fingers over Angelo's face. 'He has my brother's eyes and his mouth. He's going to break our hearts, this little one. Keep your eye on him, Nikos.'

Nick sometimes thinks, for minutes at a time, that he will die of anxiety for Angelo, whose soft little hands are so tightly clasped around his neck that Nick can scarcely breathe. He takes hold of the small arms and eases them away from himself. Angelo's wrists are as frail as bird bones. Sometimes Nick can feel his arteries kink and twist and flip themselves over with the anxiety that his son evokes in him, with the intensity of his desire to keep Angelo from harm.

'Perhaps if you are very vigilant, Nikos,' his grandmother says, doubtfully.

'Angelo,' he whispers in his son's ear. 'Angelo, do you want to play with my toy soldiers? Your great-grandmother still has them.'

Angelo stops crying. He considers. He smiles tentatively. Then he wriggles out of Nick's arms and begins to play with the scattered bottles, rolling them gently, smiling radiantly.

'No one can save them in the end,' Nick's grandmother sighs. 'Not those ones.'

'Heat got to yer, has it, mate?' Bernie asks.

'What?' Vertigo, dizziness, bottles raining down on him like skittles, Angelo's face, Angelo's needy eyes, Angelo's birdbone wrists: he has to brace himself against the whirling bar.

'Touch of sunstroke, I reckon,' Bernie says. 'Better sit down, mate.'

'Oh. She'll be right,' he says. 'Just need a drink.' He is relieved that the words have simply presented themselves without any volition on his part. Push a certain button; get an answer.

'Power's?' Bernie asks. 'Cooper's? Or good old Four-X?'

'Four-X. Yeah.'

His own brain astonishes him, the way it handles language; the way the different little file drawers up there hear things, process them, comprehend without translating, automatically click back a response in the right vernacular. Different microchips, he supposes; and wired to every one of the senses with phenomenal precision. Smell your grandmother's cellar, think in Greek; taste a mango, speak Australian; get bitten by mosquitoes or get a mouthful of bush flies, and you find yourself swearing in all the lurid colours of Queensland.

Once, a tourist, an American tourist, but a Greek American who had been born in the same village as Nick, had walked into his taverna at Noosa by sheer chance. Nick did not recognise this person, not consciously, and the visitor did not recognise him. They had been briefly at school together almost forty years earlier, for Nick had been a child when his parents left Greece for Australia. Nick and the man from his earliest years in school had not seen each other since. There was nothing obvious to trigger the memory, nothing to distinguish this visitor from twenty others at the tables round about, and the visitor spoke English with a strong American accent, and yet, without thinking about it, Nick found himself addressing the man in Greek, much to the man's surprise. And to his own.

'There you go, mate,' Bernie says, pushing a Four-X across the bar.

Nick can still see almost nothing in the darkness: only grey shapes and the dull gleam of the brass foot-rail against the bar. Maybe he has scorched the retina of both eyes. This would not surprise him after so many hours in that oven of a truck, on that baked red flood plain, under that barbarous sun, that brutal light. The light in western Queensland is like the light in an interrogation cell, he thinks with a quick sick spasm of recollection. He feels a violent twinge of claustrophobia, the military police bending over him, the cell light in his eyes. Why had he made that ill-timed trip into Albania? For a friend, yes; but perhaps also simply for the risk?

The thing about risk, he thinks: it's not just an aphrodisiac, not just a Benzedrine thrill, it's also the best painkiller known. So how can he pretend to be surprised by Angelo's life? (*It's in our blood*, his grandmother sighs.) Passionate mistakes, Nick broods, as in full-throttle passion barking up what is positively, absolutely, the wrong tree: that has been passed direct, a genetic liability, from father to son. Add to that the damned family myths, told over and over. Wouldn't they make Angelo feel obligated to self-destruct? Nick takes a mouthful of beer and is almost grateful for it. Almost. Beer, in his opinion, is little better than bilge water, but when in Rome . . .

Sensory memories are exhausting. They are as dangerous as sunstroke. They can prostrate you. He takes another grateful gulp of the vile beer. When in Rome . . . and when in Australia even more so, since tolerance for different norms is not high. He can imagine what might happen to a man who asked for a glass of ouzo and a bowl of olives in an outback pub. He closes his eyes tightly and sees a red network of rivers branching and circling, a bloodshot photograph, perhaps, of all the dry watercourses he has passed in the last few weeks.

When he blinks, he can distinguish Bernie's face up close, and further afield a watchful and silent circle: three men leaning against the bar, others at the pool table, others on stools near the shuttered windows. Not a sound, not a movement, all eyes on him. He wonders, for a moment, what it would be like not to feel foreign, *marked*. In Australia, it is not only a matter of birth. Nick has been in the country since the age of seven; Angelo was born here. I'd like to live without a hyphen, Angelo said to him once. Greek-Australian. It never went away.

'I would like a room,' Nick says, self-conscious under so many eyes, knowing his vowels slide out with a slippery mix of accents: broad Australian, which he thinks he has managed rather well in the brief and formulaic bar talk, and something foreign, an undertow of unplaceable sounds. But what really gives him away are the grammatical constructions. Every time. It is because, with his parents, he always spoke Greek at home. Even after a lifetime, the sentences can slip out with a wrangled formality, especially when he is trying hardest to be unremarkable.

'Where yer from?' Bernie asks.

'Brisbane,' Nick says tersely.

'Brisbane?' Tell that to the marines, the tone suggests.

Nick takes a mouthful of beer and says nothing.

'Brisbane,' Bernie says again, derisively.

'That's right, mate. More or less. North coast, to be precise. Noosa Heads. I own a small –'

'Before that, I mean.'

'Oh, all over the bloody shop, mate,' Nick says lightly. 'Born in Melbourne,' – it is only slightly a lie; only seven years out – 'yeah, started out in Melbourne. But after that, all over the bloody shop.' At least he has learned that much in Australia, how to play verbal cricket, how to deflect questions off the side of the bat, how to swim unseen behind words the way Australians do, so that interrogation slides away like water off a duck's back, no feathers ruffled, not his own nor those of anyone else. He can feel the air in the room shift, in fact. He can feel that a small wary space has been made for him. The right idiom, the right pinch of slang, the right pattern of intonation, these are like the right caress of Aladdin's magic lamp. *Open Sesame*, they say.

Not that being born in Melbourne would help all that much up here. It's *difference* that Australians hate, he thinks; Melbourne or Athens, they're much the same to people out here.

Bernie pushes a somewhat grubby sheet of paper and a chewed ballpoint pen across the counter. 'Fill 'er out,' he says. 'For the room. What's yer name?'

'Nick.' He prints just the four letters. He even thinks of himself that way now, especially at Nick's Taverna, classiest restaurant in Noosa Heads, serving Greek cuisine, and written up in *Places to Eat in Australia*. 'Nick McCree,' he says, and prints it in block capitals, since Nikos Makarios on a bar chit does not help matters anywhere, and certainly not between the Warrego and the Barcoo.

'Irish,' Bernie says, reading upside down, his voice dry. He raises his eyebrows and looks around the pub and pushes his tongue into one cheek. 'Irish. Now, who'd've thunk it?'

'Only on my father's side,' Nick says, unruffled. Reel them in on their own superstitions; hook them on their sanctities. The savage taste of the satire improves the beer. He feels better by the minute. (*It's in our blood*, his grandmother reminds. *Disasters flock and call to us like sirens, but one person in each generation has the luck of Ulysses. You have it, Nick. You will often be scorched, but never burned.*) It is absurd, he gives not a minute's credence to these family superstitions, but he has always, nevertheless, been sustained by a quite magical belief in his own luck and his own invulnerability. 'Never knew the bastard,' he says.

'Oh well,' Bernie offers uncertainly, and again Nick can feel the slight shift in the mood of the room. Absentee fathers are something they know about. Bernie wavers and then extends his hand. 'Bernie O'Donoghue. The room's not much chop, I'm afraid, but the tucker's good.'

Bernie does not ask what has brought Nick McCree to Outer Maroo, and Nick reads ominous meaning into the absence of the question. He feels his luck hesitate for a moment and turn a queasy somersault, colliding with the doomed fortunes of Angelo. Of course it is all nonsense, his grandmother's predictions. He can never shake their hold on him. He is made profoundly uneasy by the failure of Bernie O'Donoghue, publican west of nowhere, to ask what a man with a ridiculous Irish name and a Greek face and a faded Melbourne/Greek accent is doing in this fly-blown place. It is not as though strangers would wander into such a townlet every day. He can feel the unasked question like a tic at the corner of one eye. He can feel a pulse beating at his temples. He wants to push for the question to be asked.

'I'm on me holidays,' he offers, getting the wrong grammar carefully right. 'Fossicking around.'

Fossicking for what? he wants Bernie to ask, but Bernie is cleaning the counter with a cloth. Fossicking for information, he might answer Bernie. Or might not. Fossicking for whatever is hidden, he might say lightly. Fossicking for whatever it is you are covering up in this god-forsaken hole. No, these impulses are outright stupid because it is dangerous to show your hand in outback poker. There are altogether too many abandoned mine shafts round about, too many ex-army types with a thing about explosives and a craving to blast boulder opal from any stretch of ironstone rock, too many people with nothing to lose. At night the people with nothing to lose can hear the black tunnels cooing to each other: sing a song of opal, of nowhere, of oblivion; send us your foreigners, the strangers in your outback ports; send us your desert sailors, let them listen to our siren song.

He has gone too far. He has not gone far enough.

'Gotta be a better way of making dosh than running a restaurant in Noosa, eh mate?' he prods Bernie. 'Heard there's opal lying around out here for the taking.'

Bernie squints and holds a pint pot up to the murky light. He considers. He spits on the outside curve of the glass and applies his polishing cloth. He decides in favour of the larrikin and putative Irish father of Nick McDoubtful. 'Yeah,' he says. 'Cost you in sunstroke and dehydration, but.'

But. Nikos Makarios makes a note. Remember to throw in a few floating terminal *buts*, play your Queenslander card. Should have done it already.

'We get a few suncrazed bushies staggering in,' Bernie says. 'From time to time.' He lifts up another pint pot, squints, spits on it, applies his cloth. 'Sometimes they got a floater or two, and sometimes they got nothing but potch, and mostly they just got ravings about seams no one can ever find again. You wouldn't believe the number of fabulous finds that have been sworn to.' He laughs. 'Seams thick as a man's arm, and long as the drought. And never set eyes on again.'

'Like Oyster's Reef?' Nick says lightly.

In the mirror behind Bernie O'Donoghue, he sees all the heads turn, sees the stillness. The mirror is smoky amber. It is pocked with black spots where the silver backing has gone, blistered by dryness, scratched, chewed by insects. These irregular non-reflective spaces seem important to Nick. He can hear the silence of the watchers gathering strength. A man could walk into a bar and disappear, he thinks. He could fail to walk out again, and who would know?

He can smell the tension, the hostility.

Idiot, idiot, idiot.

He has thrown away the advantage. Was there ever any point in having the advantage? Did he ever, in fact, have it? Did they ever believe in a streak of Irishness in him? In spite of himself, he feels a prickle of pleasure along his skin. There is something in him that loves brushing up against danger, loves the feverish touch of her hot whore's body. And he believes in his luck. He believes he is immortal.

Bernie busies himself with a tray of glasses. 'Heard that one, have you? Must have gone halfway round the bloody world, that tall story.'

'I read it in the *Sun*, but,' Nick remonstrates. 'Some journalist bloke who said he'd been there.'

Bernie lifts his eyebrows. 'Yeah,' he says. 'Read all about it. Werewolves in Brisbane, flying saucers in Alice Springs.'

'Some journalist bloke from Melbourne,' Nick insists.

'Melbourne,' Bernie says, rolling his eyes. 'That'd be right.'

One of the men leaning against the counter shifts his feet, and twists himself toward the visitor. Nick stares straight ahead, watching the mirror behind the bar. The man has eyebrows like unkempt brushes that meet the downward droop of his curls. Nick imagines them scraping the rim of the Akubra that the man has placed on the bar. He has the face of a beautiful boy grown middle-aged, grown both sly and slack, gone prematurely to seed. Cow cocky, his body language says, speaking the easy sprawl of entitlement. At the forward peak of the crown of his Akubra there is a hole, about two inches in diameter, jagged at the edges – as though rats, or some inner obsession perhaps, have chewed their way out from his hair. Beneath his ferocious eyebrows, his cow cocky's eyes are ferret-bright.

'Where's the sheila?' he asks.

Nick turns from the mirror and stares at him.

'The sheila on the truck,' the man says. 'The looker. The bird in the white dress.'

'Got yer eye on 'er, eh, Andrew?' Bernie laughs. 'Got the old shearing shed in mind?'

'Gave it a thought,' the man says.

Nick inscribes a circle on the bar with the bottom of his beer stubby in order to ward off her perfume, but wisps of it, like fog, appear from nowhere and eddy under the edges of this manoeuvre. He can see her shoulders, the soft skin puckered slightly against the white straps. She reminds him of his wife, his ex-wife, now why is that? She reminds him *generically*. She reminds him of the image he had (so wildly wrong) of his ex-wife when he married her. He feels angry. People like that, people like her (the woman on the truck) and his ex-wife (as she seemed to be) and Angelo, they should be locked away in isolation wards. They should be quarantined. There is something dangerously infectious about them. They get themselves into trouble too often, and their indifference to their own fates makes too heavy a demand.

Everyone is looking at him, apparently waiting for an answer.

What was the question?

'Eh?' he says blankly, meeting the cow cocky's eyes.

'The sheila, mate. Where'd she get to?'

'Beats me, mate,' Nick says. 'Don't even know her name.'

'Bloody waste of a truck ride from Quilpie,' someone offers, and everyone laughs. The laughter is raucous and does not quite cover several ribald suggestions.

'You been here before?' the man demands, studying him intently.

'You must be joking.' Take the offensive, Nick thinks. They recognise that. They respect that.

'Coulda sworn I'd seen you,' the man insists.

Nick thinks, with a lurch of excitement: he is remembering a family likeness, he sees the shadow of Angelo's face. Nick brings the tips of his index fingers together, separates them, touches them again. His fingers are steady.

'Maybe I got a double, mate,' he says. 'They reckon everyone has.'

'Don't *mate* me in that poncey accent, mate.'

Nick stays loose and lets the idea of molten steel run through his veins. He lets the steel cool and harden. He has never backed off a fight, though he considers fights stupid and tedious. He used to box. He still plays rugby. He is not as fit as he would like to be, but he expects to come out of any fight as the winner. Of any fair fight, that is.

'Maybe you have a relative,' the cow cocky says. Private-school accent, Nick notes; but one that has gone loose at the edges, silted up with too many years of outback dust. Nick flicks one eye toward the mirror without turning his head. They are all waiting. 'You have any relatives keen on opal fossicking?' the cow cocky presses.

'I have not had the habit to observe,' Nick begins, and would like to spit on his stupid tangled words. Damn these grammar-book constructions, damn them, these old patterns that seep up because he is really nervous now, excited, on the brink of something. There is no question, now, that he has found the right town. He gulps at his beer. 'I don't keep tabs on my relatives,' he says, levelling out, surfacing into Queensland vowels. 'Not worth the trouble, and practically none of them in this country anyway, as far as I know. Well, yeah, a handful in Melbourne maybe. But most of me mad dad's crew took off to America from what I can make out' – he's talking too much, he has to stop – 'from what I hear on the family grapevine, that's where they went, New York, their loss as far as I'm concerned, don't know what they're missing, eh? they're all so busy trying to strike it rich over there.' Talking too much, talking too much, for God's sake, stop.

'The luck of the Irish,' Bernie says drily.

'Yeah,' Nick says. 'The bloody luck of the Irish. I'll drink to that.' He raises his stubby. He sweeps it in an arc, embracing the room. 'To the luck of the Irish.' He drinks, but no one responds. No one moves. Without conscious decision or volition, he finds himself adding: 'As for me, I'm gonna find Oyster's Reef and get rich as sin. Gonna haul in opal by the tonne. I'm counting on me fucking Irish luck.'

Bernie is absorbed in polishing a pint pot. After several long seconds, he says, 'You're gonna need it, mate.' He reaches back and seems to be placing the glass tankard high in the mirror behind the bar, but turns out to be signalling someone. 'Jess'll show you the room,' he says.

Jess materialises out of the gloom. It is not clear to Nick where she comes from. She is simply there, waiting.

Jess is stillness itself, Nick thinks, though he has the sense of something coiled, waiting to spring, under the placid mask of middle age; something sleek and sensuous, like a female tiger.

Bernie says, as though speaking to someone slow-witted, or hard of hearing, or both: 'Upstairs, Jess. The room with the sink. And show him where the dunny is, OK?' To Nick he says (tapping his forehead): 'Old Silence, we call her. Don't take it personally.' To Jess he says again: 'Don't forget to show him where the dunny is.'

Jess gives no sign that she has heard. She seems to Nick to be suspended in a vacuum, floating, waiting for a button to be pushed. Everyone seems unnaturally still to Nick, though it is possible, of course, that the problem is one of perception and that the receptor nerves in Nick's eyes and ears have gone into slow-motion cycle, or perhaps the nerve paths to his brain are partially blocked. Receptor nerves: would that be right? he finds himself wondering heavily. Where would he have picked that up? Why does he have this lethargic sensation of being underwater? Everyone is watching. It must be the heat. No one can afford a wasted movement.

Someone over by the window says: 'They've finished unloading the water. Himself is on his way, Bernie.'

'Right,' Bernie says.

Jake Digby pushes disturbance ahead of him, there can be no doubt of this, since Nick can feel the soft buffeting of his approach fill the room and push against his skin in little shock waves. Something has definitely tampered with his sensory system, revealing, for example, the electric currents of anxiety in fizzing gold, like a run of sparklers, from head to head. Jess seems closer to his bar stool. He has the odd sensation that she is smiling at him, though in fact her lips are in a straight sombre line. He wonders if it is possible to be drunk on only two beers. Possibly; if one is seriously dehydrated from the desert air. When he slides off the stool, Jess nods and turns and he follows her.

On the stairs, she turns and winks.

Or perhaps he imagines it.

Last Week

Monday Evening

Beneath her fingertips, the texture of the gingham tablecloth speaks to Mercy of sorrow. She can feel anguish in the slender rolled hem. Each tiny impeccable stitch against the pad of her thumb has a history. To such labour Mercy's mother now gives herself with passionate concentration, stitching and knitting , stitching and knitting, washing, ironing, cleaning, cooking, as though sufficient attention to detail on the smallest domestic grids might shift alignments elsewhere, might rectify something in the larger scheme of events.

'Let us give silent thanks,' Mercy's father says.

Into the heavy silence, the clock on the mantel chimes. Mercy can feel the weight of her father's inability to pray pressing down on the dining room. The word for his face, she thinks, is ravaged. She tastes the consonants carefully: *ravaged.* They carry within themselves the sound of storms, the exhaustion of storms weathered. Yes, it is a good word, the right word. In a mysterious way, the exact word can slightly and momentarily ease her anxiety.

Mercy studies the face of Sarah, whose eyes are politely closed, but whose lashes flutter a little against the curve of her upper cheek so that the pupils under the eyelids seem skittish and busy. Light and shadow dapple the room. The setting sun fills the sky with brash orange and floods the verandah and falls through the open doors and across the table and splashes the soft skin of Sarah's hands. The hands are tightly clasped, the knuckles white. Is Sarah someone else who wishes she could pray? Mercy wonders.

Perhaps not. Perhaps not. *A regular non-observant Jew.* What would that mean? Perhaps, like Miss Rover, Sarah would see prayer as a cowardly avoidance of responsibility and action.

A belief in powerlessness is seductive, Mercy, and so is belief in a Higher Power. They both let one off the hook too easily.

Since her departure, Miss Rover has taken up permanent residence as a sniper inside Mercy's head. There are other snipers. There are the irreverent and earthy voices of Ma Beresford and Ma's Bill. And the voices of the elders. And others, and others. Mercy is trapped in the crossfire. Also there are the clamouring voices of books, Miss Rover's books and her father's library, what used to be her father's library, two different worlds. Is all this listening so exhausting for everyone, or only for Mercy? She feels like the conductor of an orchestra full of musicians who have run amok; they play discordant instruments; they have set up permanent and competitive rehearsal inside her mind.

She follows the spill of light that flows over Sarah's wrists and multiplies itself in knives and forks and white plates, and laps at the hands of Mercy's mother, hands which are also clasped, but slackly, with the trust of a child. Her mother's face has the kind of repose available only to the very young, the very innocent, the very old, and to those who have suffered a stroke. Which, in a way, Mercy thinks, her mother has.

'Amen,' Mercy's father says.

'Amen' – a soft echo from her mother.

Her mother rises and goes to the kitchen. When she opens the oven door, a blast of heat seems to displace all the air in the house. The filmy curtains at the windows lift and preen. Beyond them, wind-chimes peal softly.

'It seems so strange,' Sarah says, 'to eat hot food in this heat.'

'Does it?' Mercy is immediately interested. 'Why?'

'Oh, I just mean everything's so different. I'm not very good at managing so many differences at once.'

Managing so many differences at once, Mercy thinks, with an inner stir of excitement. So Sarah suffers from the same disease. A bond exists, and it must be that Mercy has sensed it from the first moment when the foreigners shimmered into view. Perhaps it was telegraphed from nerve to nerve. Perhaps Mercy is blood relative to all who are strange, and alien only to the people she knows.

Mercy studies the wraiths of the words that float above the table-cloth, that skirmish with the knives and forks, that ribbon their way between the chairs. She watches them drift up into the sticky spirals of the fly papers. *It seems so strange to eat hot food in this heat.* It seems so strange that anyone should find this strange. Mercy can feel pins and needles of excitement along her arms. How obvious, and yet how electrifying to find that there are vantage points from which she, Mercy, is *foreign*. She wants to look at the dining room, to look at her parents, to look at herself from Sarah's eyes.

'Climate seems to me a much bigger difference than language,' Sarah says. 'I find myself *amazed*, really, that we speak the same language . . . that we *seem* to speak the same language . . . I find myself wondering if we do. It must make you think quite differently, to live like this. To me this feels like living in an oven. Amy wrote that the nights are sudden and cold, but they aren't, they're burning, and I can't seem to, I can't seem to . . .'

'That's only in winter,' Mercy's father says, 'that the nights are cold. From December to March, they are just as hot as the days. In July, they go below freezing.'

'How . . . how awful. That's even more . . . I can't imagine such extreme changes in twenty-four hours. I can't follow the logic of climate here, the rules all seem haywire. I can't seem to . . .'

Mercy watches her closely. She is not only speaking of climate. I can't seem to get it right, her eyes say, and I can't afford to make mistakes. You have information. I sense that there are things you know. I sense that you have answers to questions I can't bring myself to ask. Not yet. Not before dinner. Not before I have time to adjust to the heat. Not before I have time to prepare myself; in case, after all, you know nothing; in case, after all, you do.

And what of the other man on Jake's truck? Mercy asks her silently.

She imagines she sees the impact of her thought in the flicker of Sarah's eyelids. She sees the image of the man rise into Sarah's mind.

'There was someone else,' Sarah says drowsily. 'Someone else waiting in Quilpie, and on the truck.'

Mercy feels dizzy. Perhaps she thinks up the world. Perhaps she really does. Perhaps she *could* think it up. Perhaps she could make it come out right, if she concentrated, if she worked out the story ahead of time, if she could get to the ending before anyone else did, before it happened, if she could change it. She would only have happy endings.

'The heat didn't seem to bother him,' Sarah says.

Mercy closes her eyes and sees him in the shadowy pub. What questions is he trying to ask at this moment? She sees him filling up space in Sarah's mind, she is sure that Sarah can smell the sharp sweet odour of his skin, that when she runs her tongue across her lips, just as Mercy herself is doing at this moment, she can taste the man on the truck, she can taste him again as she tasted him fleetingly on the road, two hours west of Eromanga, say, when Jake swerved over saltbush clumps and the two passengers were thrown against each other. There is an earth smell to the man with the sensuous lips, and his sweat is slightly sweet, and his weight, so unexpected and violent, makes her (makes Sarah, makes Mercy) feel faint. Mercy presses the back of her hand against her lips. Her hand trembles.

She thinks, with a sudden intense hunger, of Donny Becker: of the time he put a lizard down the front of her dress; of the time, in prayer meeting, when he touched her leg, when he ran his hand, as though by accident, along her calf. Mercy can feel a flush of heat from ankle to knee. She knows Donny Becker can scarcely read, but he climbs in through the window of her dreams and she teaches him. She teaches him to lean in close across the pages until their tongues touch, and she feeds him words that way, like a mother bird to her chicks. I'll give you everything I know, she tells him. You don't know anything, Mercy, he tells her; you need looking after.

She knows that Donny Becker always wants to touch her. She knows she wants him to. She knows he knows that.

There are other things that she somehow knows. Perhaps Oyster was right about the fruit. Perhaps it *was* from the Tree of Knowledge, when he made her eat, though already by then she never believed anything Oyster said. The delicious forbidden fruit, he said, and made her eat, and made her eat, and you will be as God, he said, and you will know all things, forbidden things, and secret things, and the secret desires inside the minds of others, just like me, Oyster said, just as I can see the hungers inside your mind, little Mercy, and inside your body, I can see your thirst for the Living Water that I can give, and your hunger for the fruit of my Tree of Knowledge that you long to eat, and she said no, you are wrong, no, I don't, but she had to eat and drink, Oyster made her, and perhaps after all he told the truth, though it made her vomit so much at the time. Perhaps she has truly eaten the fruit of the Tree of Knowledge and now knows all secret things and the hidden thoughts and desires of other minds. Perhaps now she will never be able to un-know forbidden things.

Perhaps she will die from the weight of them.

She closes her eyes. She can see the foreign man and Sarah in the train before it leaves Brisbane. The train waits in the station, they are in the same compartment but at opposite windows. She sees the way they ignore each other, the way they are so aware of each other's presence that Sarah can feel the kiss of his shirt, pure cotton, like a brush of lips against her forearm, and he can smell the talcum powder between her breasts and can taste the skin of her shoulders. It is interesting the way they both know that they are stalking the same answers, the steel wheels on the railway lines chanting the questions, past Roma, past Charleville, pushing west to the end of the line. Quilpie. They both carry letters postmarked Quilpie. They both reread these letters privately, they both see wraiths on the street, they both ask questions, apparently innocuous, at the post office. They are conscious of each other's letters and questions on Jake's truck, though they rarely look at each other, rarely speak. Sarah is aware of the man throughout the journey, and even before she boards the train in Brisbane, just as Mercy would have been.

Mercy has a new theory: that people who wake suddenly, breathless, from terrible freefalls into black space, these people give off signals like radio towers, they give off a certain aura, a force-field perhaps. Their force-fields collide. In dreams they swim in pools of dark water, bottomless, and they meet one another down there. They know one another.

Mercy lowers her eyes to the hem of the tablecloth and presses the tips of her middle fingers against her thumbs. *Now I am Sarah*, she says, concentrating, and here she is looking out of the corners of her eyes at Mercy, a strange child, and here she is thinking of the man's hands – what is the man's name? she really has to know his name – but if she is Sarah now, and she is, she wills herself to be Sarah, then she must certainly already know the man's name, though she has forgotten it, and she must concentrate, even if all she can see at the moment are his hands, she is thinking of his hands, of a certain quirky gesture he is given to, a gesture he made on the verandah at Beresford's and on the road as he strode down to the pub. The gesture is not infrequent. He will bring the tips of his index fingers together, just for a second, then point them outwards, then touch them again, then point them outwards and shift them, up, down, east, west, juggling them slightly, weighing directions. He is completely unaware of his movements, she is certain of that. He is assessing directions, but he is not lost, not floundering. He will take all possible directions by the throat, Mercy sees that.

All the way from Brisbane, she – Sarah, that is – has wanted to place her cool hands against his wrists, and Mercy too wants to close her fingers lightly around them (or are they Donny Becker's wrists? They shift and change) and she has wanted to let his compressed energy buffet her. She runs the tip of her tongue around her lips.

'Donny,' she says.

Her mother looks at her, and then at Sarah. 'I hope it will be all right,' her mother says, suddenly frightened. 'Charles? I hope they won't –'

'Nothing can happen,' he says soothingly. 'The dogs –'

'Yes, of course,' Mercy's mother says, relieved. 'The dogs. Of course.'

'He's a strange person,' Sarah says. 'Intense. Moody. He seemed indifferent to everything. The heat, the flies, the dust, Jake, me. Everything. His name's Nick.'

Nick. Mercy holds the name gently between her palms, out of sight, beneath the tablecloth. At certain angles, it reminds her of –

No. She will not think of Gideon.

She sees that something in Sarah sends up protective barriers against the name. She sees that Sarah does not trust a man like that, a man who sends out powerful messages to your body before he has so much as spoken to you. She has a radical distrust of men like that.

She does not like him. She does not want to speak to him. She has avoided him. She can taste him on her lips.

Mercy's mother returns to the table with a casserole, cradling it in her hands and using her apron of thick soft towelling as shield against the burning pot. You would think it was a baby being carried with such tenderness, or perhaps this occurs to Mercy because of the swaddling bands of white cloth. Did her mother carry Brian that way once, did she cradle Mercy in the hollow of her apron, tied to her body, to herself? Yes. Probably. With the same voluptuous absorption in the task. Her mother, committed to denial of the flesh, earnestly deaf to all private desire, nevertheless knows the language of the senses instinctively. Everywhere Mercy directs her eye or her ear there are contradictions so great that she cannot understand how the fabric of the world contains them. If she were to hear the air turn boisterous with the sound of ripping, the sound of life tearing itself apart at the seams, she would not be surprised.

Mrs Given lowers the pot on to a trivet. With one apron-wrapped hand, she lifts the lid and a fragrant curl of steam rises like a will-o'-the-wisp and floats across the table. 'Sarah?' she murmurs.

'Yes. Thank you, Mrs Given. It smells wonderful.'

'Vi. Please call me Vi. Everyone calls me Vi, though it's not my real name. It's short for Vivian, but that's not my real name either. That's funny, isn't it? It's just a name a teacher kept calling me at school by mistake, she mixed me up with someone she remembered from somewhere else, and the other children thought it was a great joke and so they called me Vi to tease me and then everyone else did for the rest of my life, isn't it strange? We're so pleased to have you with us, Sarah. It's lovely to have visitors again, isn't it, Charles?'

Mercy's father smiles, but the smile does not reach his eyes.

Vi dips her ladle into the casserole and gives herself over to the absorbing blend of colours and textures: the chunks of beef, the dear little carrots that Ma Beresford brings back, bulk frozen, from

Brisbane, the translucent pearl onions, the green splinters of freeze-dried parsley. It is puzzling to Vi how sorrow and evil slip through such a dense net of goodness. She does not understand where they fit, or how there is room for them in the world.

'It's very hot,' she warns Sarah, apologetic, proffering the steaming plate. 'I'm sorry I can't make you a salad but we can't get fresh vegetables out here, you see, otherwise I'd . . .' She pauses, the plate wavering in the air between them. 'Maybe if I used the tinned beetroot? Yes, I could do that, and the tinned beans, would you rather? since you don't like hot meals?'

'Oh no, no, really . . . I mean, I do,' Sarah says. 'It's just, where I'm from, Boston, we associate hot dinners with winter nights, snow outside, that sort of thing, so it's just unusual for me . . . but everything's unusual, isn't it, when you move from one culture to another –'

'Snow.' Vi repeats the word with wonder, her ladle poised in mid-air. 'Is it like the frost in the refrigerator?'

Sarah laughs, startled. 'Yes, I suppose so. Well, not exactly. It's softer. More like . . .' She frowns, concentrating, lifting her hand as though snow were drifting from the ceiling where the dark spiders watch quietly. The spiders distract her.

'I can't imagine.' Vi shakes her head, her eyes dreamy. 'And falling out of the sky. It's so strange to think of it. Sometimes when the dust storms are very bad, or when I'm defrosting, I open the freezer and put my cheek against the ice. It prickles. It's a lovely feeling.'

'Vi,' her husband says gently. 'The casserole.'

She looks at him vacantly, smiling. 'Did you say something, Charles dear?'

A terrible mournfulness shadows his eyes and draws down the edges of his mouth. He has to struggle against the pull of it to speak. His lips smile. 'The casserole,' he says again, patiently.

Vi studies the dish, focuses, lifts another plate, dips her ladle. 'Boston,' she says, as though the word were an exotic vegetable that must be tasted slowly and meditatively. She is caught again, suspended in mid-action, waiting for the flavour of the word to seep into the casserole steam. 'Boston. It's in America, it's near New York, isn't it? Imagine someone from Boston in our house. Isn't it strange? And what could have brought you all this way to western Queensland?'

'Well, actually,' Sarah says, and blood rushes to her cheeks, 'my daughter did. My stepdaughter.' She clasps her hands and presses them together. Mercy sees the wrists of the man on the bus, feels his volcanic questions, which are also Sarah's, pressing up against Sarah's larynx. 'She was backpacking around Australia and she sent me a letter from Quilpie. But since then –'

'*Mum*' Mercy stands, knocking the edge of the table . . .

'Vi, dear, the dinner's getting cold.'

'. . . you're dripping gravy on the tablecloth, Mum.'

'Oh dear,' Vi says. She rests the ladle in the dish and licks one corner of her apron. She dabs at the dark splash that is bleeding in filaments along the gingham threads. 'Isn't that curious,' she says, pausing, 'the way it's spreading.'

'Let me serve, Mum.'

'It *is* faintly ridiculous, hot meals in this climate,' Charles acknowledges. 'But we're still so hopelessly British in our habits, that's the reason, Mrs, ah . . .' He smiles fleetingly and nods at Sarah to compensate for his inability to address her by her first name, the only one he has been given, but the use of which is unthinkable for him. 'We don't even notice that it's inappropriate. Thank you, Mercy, that's plenty. You can sit down again. I think your mother would prefer to do the serving herself.'

A small tic kinks a muscle in Mercy's cheek. She presses her lips together and concentrates on the ladle and counts silently. One, two, three, the ladle is an old one, white enamelled, six, seven, and the chips in the enamel have interesting shapes, nine, ten, especially with the eyes half closed, thirteen, fourteen, small black silhouettes of animals, a camel, a book, Miss Rover, Donny Becker's hands, the beautiful foreign eyes of Nick at the window of Ma Beresford's shop. At the count of thirty, she lowers the ladle into the dish again and pushes it slightly towards her mother, who continues to observe the slow-spreading stain with fascination.

'Why does it spread like that, in straight lines?' Vi asks. 'It's like spokes coming out of a square wheel.'

'It's a phenomenon called bleeding,' Charles says. 'Mercy, sit down, please. It adheres to the principle of conduction. All fluids are conducted along the available structural channels of distribution. Thank you, Mercy.'

Mercy glances at Sarah. Sarah's eyes rest on Charles momentarily, startled, curious, translating, then she lowers them politely. She is absorbed by the tendons in her hands, the way they push through the skin like ramparts. Her hands ache. She unlocks them and flexes her fingers. She puts the tip of one index finger in her mouth.

Mercy continues to watch her covertly, ready to bridle at any intimation of mockery, ready to leap to parental defence. Her father's fingers drum themselves on the table, a tattoo of tamped-down anguish and irritation, habitual. Mercy thinks of picking up her plate and pressing it on the drumming fingers, pressing, pressing, she is almost crushed by the energy of her desire to do this, she can feel the force of it, pressing until the fingers are pushed right through the table, silenced. She imagines the splintered hole in the table, the smashed plate. She can actually feel the shards in her hands.

She is awash in a familiar exhaustion. She experiences it as a terrible lassitude of the body, but the sensation also presents itself visually: there are two currents of rushing water, black cold floodwater, sweeping down dry tributary arms of the Barcoo, hurtling towards a confluence at Cooper's Creek. Mercy is flotsam. She is split in two. She is swept along both watercourses simultaneously. The speed of the rushing water is incredible. At the confluence, at the moment of collision, a great column of black water throws itself up like a tidal wall. Mercy's two flood-swept selves smack into the wall as though hitting concrete. There is nothing but darkness. All the water of the Barcoo flood plain explodes and annihilates itself in mist.

Mercy hangs on to the edge of the dining-room table. She cannot breathe, but the secret of surviving is doing nothing, feeling nothing, hanging on. If she counts slowly backwards at this point, she can reverse the flow of the flood, and now she has found something to hang on to, a spar, the loving stitches in the tablecloth, each one perfect, each one a promise that will save her from drowning. The tidal wave recedes, recedes, has receded, the flood flows backwards towards the quiet source of the Barcoo.

Storm warnings: yes, she must be more attentive. She has to train herself better, be more absent, immerse herself more completely in details as her mother does, anchor herself beyond the highwater line of flash floods, one of whose unstoppable watercourses is the racy pace of Mercy's blood when her father speaks to her in that particular way, in that tone of voice, or when he parcels out the world by the Laws of the Medes and the Persians, an immutable system, beyond challenge, received by direct private pipeline from God.

The other current, the cross-current, is her constant anxiety for her father and her mother, the sense she has had for as long as she can remember that she has to protect them, that only she stands between the harsh world and her parents' vast and frightening innocence, which was as terrible as Brian's had been.

'*Conduction*,' Vi says earnestly, as though all is now clear. She runs her fingernail along the stain on the cloth, tracing its quills. 'So that's why it has spokes. Charles knows everything.' She smiles complacently, reaching for the ladle. 'Sarah? Ah no, I've served you already. Mercy, two ladles or three? Charles's father was a schoolteacher in

Sydney, that's where he gets it from. My brothers said I was marrying an encyclopedia, but they were just teasing. They admire him, really. They've always been a bit scared of him, I think, that's why they used to make fun of him.'

Sarah says: 'It's sobering, travel. The way it shows us our own ignorance.' She makes an arrangement on the tablecloth with her fork and the bread-and-butter knife. 'Amy said that in her letters. She travelled all around Asia first, lived in a Buddhist monastery, then an ashram in south India. Nothing is ever what you expect, she said.' She swings the fork away from the knife, inscribing a circle. 'People living out here . . . I had a certain image of my own, you see, and you are not what I was expecting, Mr Given. I thought, you know, roughnecks, cowboys, that sort of thing. But of course to be a rabbi, a clergyman I mean, you would have a college education, so I'm simply revealing –'

Mercy's father winces. 'No,' he says.

'– I'm afraid I'm simply revealing the awful scope of my ignorance,' Sarah says. 'I hope you'll forgive my foolish and limited –'

'No,' he says roughly. 'As a matter of fact, no. Not with us, it's not required. *For it is written* . . .' He pauses, discomforted by old habits. 'Our people stand by the Bible.' He clears his throat. '*For it is written, I will destroy the wisdom of the wise, and will bring to nothing the understanding of the prudent* . . . Well, that's what we . . .'

'My sister's children talk like that,' Sarah says. 'Always quoting the Torah. Well, they're not children now. My nephew's in the army, the Israeli army. My niece is in New York, she's joined the Lubavitcher sect, I expect you're familiar with them?'

'Ahh, no,' Charles Given says, embarrassed. 'I'm afraid I haven't . . .'

'It's Hasidic, a sort of extreme, a sort of fundamentalist – Not so different, I think, from the groups that Amy, my daughter, got involved with . . . a Jewish version of the same phenomenon.'

Charles Given sighs. The palms of his hands absorb him. 'I'm afraid my knowledge is very limited. I never went to university, Mrs . . . er . . . I'm just an autodidact.'

'Sarah.'

'Pardon?'

'My name. It's Sarah.'

'Ah. Yes. I'm afraid I didn't catch your surname.'

'Cohen. But please call me Sarah.'

'And, ah, well . . . Mine is Charles.'

'You are an interesting man, Charles. And extremely well read.'

'No,' he says, 'no, I'm afraid not.' But he is caught off guard. He is embarrassed by his own pleasure. He is, in fact, almost overwhelmed, like a schoolboy who has just won a prize and been singled out at assembly, in the presence of all his peers. He is torn between self-consciousness, a rush of pride, and the fear of coming retribution from certain quarters after school. Charles Given blushes and cannot speak. Mercy can hardly bear it.

'Books,' her father says, tries to say, with much throat clearing, 'books have been my weakness, I'm afraid.'

'An admirable weakness.'

'Not everyone thinks so, Mrs Cohen.'

'Really?'

Vi says, apparently inconsequentially, 'The Tower of Babel, men who thought they knew as much as God, you know. I do agree with Mr Prophet that the Bible is all we need, but it was wrong what he did. It was a dreadful thing to do to Charles.'

'The stew is delicious, Vi,' Charles says. 'As always.'

'You don't think I put the carrots in too soon? I think they're softer than they should be. Brian likes them crunchier, doesn't he? Our son Brian,' she explains to Sarah, she begins to explain. 'Our son Brian . . .' Her voice trails off.

Mercy and her father exchange a look.

'Mercy,' he says stiffly. 'Mercy . . .' – beseeching her, needing any formula, anything neutral, anything meaningless.

But words stick in Mercy's throat.

'Mercy,' he says, harsh with effort. 'It would be a good idea if you made the tea for your mother.'

Mercy nods. When she scrapes her chair back, it falls over. 'Sorry,' she says. 'Sorry, Dad. I'll get it.'

In the kitchen, she devotes herself to details, she lets the details make as much noise as they please, the whole clanging orchestra of them, let them clash, let them rise in crescendos, the fragrance of the loose tea-leaves, the dimples in the battered pot, the high polish, the curved surface, the reflections, her moon face elongated, the texture of the tea-cosy, hand-crocheted, the whistle and steam of the kettle, the roiling boiling water like a river in flood. Her mother is right. Hang on to the details, the details may save you on drowning day. The details, the divine details, her blessings upon them, are so noisy they can block out all the rest. The talk in the dining room, for instance; a background murmur she cannot hear.

When she returns with the pot and milk and sugar on a tray, her mother is saying: 'I remember when Brian was very little, he was standing on the verandah one night and looking at the moon, it was full, and you know, Sarah, the nights are very clear and they can be very cold out here, and we have millions and millions of stars, the heavens are wonderful, aren't they? They say you can't see nearly as many stars in the city, I can't remember what the reason is, Charles will know . . . it's funny, I lived in Brisbane until I was ten years old, you know, and then my father was transferred out to Longreach, which is outback but still a town, so I've lived in cities and towns, but not for a very long time and it seems like a dream now, I can't really remember what it was like.' She laughs a little. 'They are sort of like heaven for me, cities and towns. I believe in them, I believe that Brisbane is still there, but it doesn't seem very real, you know. Of course I know it is, heaven I mean, much more real than Brisbane. I always think I can remember standing in the garden in Brisbane and seeing the stars, but I expect it's just part of my dream. When Brian was little, he used to try every night to count the stars. He used to write the numbers down in a book. I remember this one night when he was staring at the moon and he said: "Mummy, does God switch it off every morning?" Isn't that lovely?'

Sarah says, 'Moments like that . . . memories of our children . . .' She presses her right hand against her mouth. With her left hand she lines up her fork with the white squares in the gingham cloth, squinting a little, making the alignment precise. She moves the salt shaker, and then the pepper, on to the same axis, intent. 'They're overwhelming, aren't they, the memories of little things?'

Vi is suspended in sudden knowledge. 'Your Amy . . .?'

'I'm sorry,' Sarah says. 'I'm not myself. It was when you mentioned the moon.'

Vi reaches over and places her hand on Sarah's wrist. Sarah stares at it. The two women seem to exchange information through the surfaces of their skin. They seem to discover all that they need to know about each other.

Mercy's father puts his head in his hands.

Mercy prays. *Please, God*, she begins, from sheer habit, but no, she will not. *Miss Rover come over*, she thinks urgently instead. But Miss Rover whispers, as she always does: *Powerlessness is seductive, Mercy. You must think for yourself and act on your own.* And so she wills, in her own right, with her own force, that no one will speak. She wills that nothing will be said.

'Your dinner,' Vi says to Sarah. 'You've hardly touched it.'

'I had this sudden . . . it was so vivid I could smell the lilacs beside the porch . . . Amy would have been ten or eleven . . . it's a difficult age, isn't it, to have lost one mother already, to feel very uncertain about your father . . .? And then Amy and I, we never quite knew how we should . . . first I was her schoolteacher, then suddenly I was her stepmother, it was complicated. Amy herself engineered it, actually, and what was strange . . .' She watches Vi's automatic reach for the casserole dish and so she extends her own plate, she permits Vi to add another scoop of stew to her almost untouched meal. 'It's delicious,' she says. 'I'm sorry I'm not feeling very . . . It's the details, isn't it? Details that get stuck in the mind, they're so potent, they're like concentrated essence of the past. One drop, and a whole era mushrooms out, all these sensations you'd forgotten –'

'Yes,' Vi says, excited. 'Yes. That's exactly how it is. I remember Brian was wearing a little white shirt I'd made him, and brown pants . . . I'd cut down an old pair of Charles's, do you remember those, Charles? They had a very thin black stripe in them, you could hardly see it, and Brian used to say it prickled his legs. And he used to ask Charles, "What's prickle? What makes prickle, Daddy? Is it the hairs on my leg and the hairs on the pants playing tickle?" The questions that boy could think up.' She shakes her head in fond wonder. 'What was that book, Charles, that he used to want you to read to him? Over and over, he knew the whole book by heart.'

Charles looks at her sorrowfully. 'Vi,' he pleads.

Mercy thinks that their lives have become like that children's game where the ringleader pretends the wind has changed. Each time the wind changes, everyone has to freeze, an arm in mid-air, a foot in mid-step, a mouth open. Everyone understands, even Sarah understands, Mercy can see it, that it is better to say nothing.

'Yes,' Vi says, 'yes, you're right. I'm sorry, Charles, it just keeps . . . Oh Mercy, you've made the tea, that was lovely of you. Could you? Thank you, darling.' She reaches for the tray which Mercy pushes toward her. 'Aren't these lovely?' she says to Sarah, leaning her cheek briefly against the gaily coloured tea-cosy. 'My mother crocheted this. You can't get them now for love or money.' She pours tea, deploying cups and saucers with soft urgency. 'What *was* that book, though? Where did we put it, Charles?'

'Vi,' he says, despairing. 'Vi, my dear.'

Mercy thinks: there is the fact that talk can change nothing. And there is the need to talk bearing down like a river in flood, unstoppable.

She watches Sarah. She can feel the pressure of words rising in Sarah, can see them pushing against Sarah's throat. Then she can see Sarah's thoughts on a screen inside her own head. More and more often, lately, this has been happening, quite suddenly, against the inner surface of her eyes. It is not a good sign. It frightens Mercy. It's because I think too much, she tells herself. It is because I read. It is because I have eaten of the fruit of the tree of knowledge.

She sees the taut wrists of the man on the bus. They remind her of Gideon's wrists, as Gideon handed her to Donny. She can taste a question in her mouth. She has it on the tip of her tongue. Instead she says flatly, without intending to: 'In the Living Word Gospel Hall one day, they took all my father's books from his library and threw them into the fire. They tried to burn Miss Rover's books too, after she left, but they only got a few. I saved them, I hid them. Nobody knows. She was the last schoolteacher we had here.'

Sarah pushes her plate away.

'You should have left,' Mercy says sadly. 'I told you. You should have hidden on the truck.'

'No,' Sarah says quietly. 'I am doing what I should be doing.'

Is Mercy doing what she should be doing?

She sees the beautiful eyes of Nick at Ma Beresford's window. She sees the ballet of his index fingers. He will take all the possible directions by the throat, she thinks.

And so will Sarah, she decides.

And so will I, she promises herself.

This Week

Jess: Old Silences

Out here, silence is the dimension in which we float. It billows above us like the vast sails of galleon earth, ballooning into the outer geography of the Milky Way; it washes below us where the opal runs in luminous veins; it stretches west as far as the shores of the Ice Age, with nothing between then and now but rusted and powdering rock. If I strain my eyes, and shade them from the terrible glare, and stare east across the silent tongues of fire and the crumbling red elevated plains toward tomorrow, toward the dimly imaginable Queensland coastline, I go on and on and on seeing nothing but a silence so profound that it roars in my ears and pummels me and makes me feel seasick.

The silence of the fire, from this distance, is particularly eerie, though I can imagine it snapping and crackling and pistol-whipping Bernie's and the Living Word where there is nobody left to hear.

What is the sound of one verandah post falling in a ghost town?

I find it difficult, out here among the breakaways, out here in the country of mirages and salt pans and lost languages, to separate the notions of time and space and sound. They seem interchangeable. The words for them seem arbitrary, but also slippery and fluid. Perhaps, for example, it is another town, and not Outer Maroo, which burns; or perhaps the fire has burned itself out, and what we are still seeing are spirit flames, the mirage of a conflagration.

It is impossible, from this vantage point, to pin down where time ends and where space begins and how one might possibly describe the sound of the silence of either one (because there *is* a sound that silence makes in the inner ear and under conscious memory and along the arteries and lymph glands and on the skin, a sound like a heartbeat, like a drumbeat, like the feet of dancers in a corroboree, like time passing, like the wind blowing across thousands of miles of bare rock). It seems to me, out here, that time and space and sound are merely functions of one another and that they are related as solid and liquid and gas are related. They sneak across their own boundary lines, and their separate states coalesce at this vanishing point where I sit, like Robinson Crusoe, among the breakaways.

The 'breakaways'; 'breakaway country'; I say the words aloud because that might be a way to explain how the sound of my voice, bouncing about like a skipping stone, becomes part of the geography, and draws this space into the particular shape of my thought, and gives it a slot in time which I presume to label as the time of my life.

Funny, that. *I am having the time of my life.*

I am un-having it. I am breaking away from all my pasts out here where the landforms cut loose and take off like wild brumbies.

In the very idea of 'breakaway country' there is an implication, purely verbal, of an event in time, of some particular incident that took place, before which there was a stable and appropriate state of the land, some outback norm of worn-out worn-down elevated flatness, from which these sudden mesas and harsh ravines were and are a deviation. They are *deviant*. 'Breakaways', we surveyors labelled them, shading them in on government charts. The breakaways, you could be forgiven for assuming, were headstrong: they were land with a rebellious and adolescent streak.

Certainly they make movement and progress (toward what? for what purpose?) more difficult, for us, for opal fossickers, for Ethel's mob, for explorers, and most certainly for surveyors, and so we marked out the problem with words as much as with instruments, we hammered in a few verbal stakes. It is very personal, very judgmental, this language of the makers of maps. *Deviant landforms,* we say, and by implication: here are the moral boundary posts, running sometimes parallel, and sometimes not, with the dingo fence.

The breakaways themselves are impassive. They have receding brows and ridged feet held demurely together in front of them like the Sphinx. They brood in silence. They watch over the bora rings, those mazy circles of stones placed here who knows how many millennia ago? There are gigantic rings and small ones, and rings within rings, a paisley surface, complex, a great corroboree ground and meeting place for five tribes. Absences in their ghostly thousands thrum against the skin of red clay like a pulse. They are all gone into lost centuries, gone into the dark history of Inner Maroo, gone to Bourke, gone to Innamincka, gone to Cunnamulla, gone.

Inner Maroo is down there among the bora rings, a square-pegged system of lost round holes within the wrong circles. Oyster's Reef, which I cannot quite see from here, is also there, just on the far side of that bluff that looks like a giant man crouching. That is *Lungkata*, Ethel tells me. He was killed for stealing emu eggs. You can see the spear scars – those deep vertical grooves, those ravines – on his flank.

'He was one of the Wangkumara mob, *my* mob,' she says.

Her mob is still with us, all around us, and was, and ever shall be. She can feel them, she says. She can see them. They talk to her, those First Ones. I have an image of them sitting around smoking gidgee leaves, chatting, giggling together in that low rolling way, chewing charred goanna strips. Last week, last month, last year, she communed with them. She knew what was coming. This town's been sung, Jess, she warned me. The writing was on the walls of the breakaways, she reckoned. The days of Outer Maroo were numbered (not that I needed to be told), and she could wait. She could afford to wait. She could smile to herself and simply wait.

And now her waiting days are done; and here is the Old Fuckatoo come home to roost.

I can see the glow of that great bird of prey brooding over the town. The ex-town. The town could never quite be seen from here, but its transfigured self, Aurora Maroovialis, floats above it like a spirit ship above its twin: refulgent, the sunset of Outer Maroo, the pure idea of Oyster's City of Light.

Though anyone can (*could*) walk out here from the town in a couple of hours, the breakaways are not visible from Outer Maroo, screened as they are by the slow rolls of the land and by scruffy shawls of acacia, mulga, gidgee, and stunted gums, all of which the fire is now busily slurping up. A ferment of migration surrounds me, swift and silent: kangaroos, wallabies, snakes, lizards, birds: the rats leaving the sinking ship.

Emus, a pair of them, pick their awkwardly delicate way out of the scrub, beaking at insects, necking the low trees, heads moving in concert with such weird dreamy grace that they seem to be engaged in a *pas de deux* all on their own: two balled-up furry little birdskull ballet dancers, nothing but eye, gliding atop their long-legged necks. And now my scent reaches them. They stand stock still, shocked. They draw their long necks up to full outrage. The necks begin working in panic, and the delicate legs keep time, dancing a few steps this way, a few steps that, frantically indecisive about their line of flightless flight. The birds look both comic and poignant. I count to twelve before they finally decide on a direction, their feathered skirts bouncing like tutus.

The strange is normal here.

Ethel is singing now, a low crooning sound of quarter-tones, of no tones, of tones from an unknown scale.

'This place has been sung, Jess,' she says complacently, for the Nth time. 'This place has been and gone before, and now it has been and gone again. You done for, Jess.'

'Good riddance,' I say. 'I been wanting to shed this skin.'

Ethel laughs and shakes a finger at me. 'Snake lady,' she says. 'Maybe you'll be Jackamara woman next time, Jess. But Outer Maroo's been and gone.'

The Second Coming and the Second Going, I think, and the bushfire is going to burn until kingdom come.

My kingdom has come, Oyster said.

My name, said someone else, *is Ozymandias, kings of kings . . .*

Out here, where the lone and level red sands stretch as far as the eye can see, I feel as though I could be the sole and final reference point for the very idea of dates and maps and language, such poignant ideas, all of them, such brave little stratagems, at once so frantic and clever and ridiculous in their attempts to get a foothold on chaos. They are like candles lit by the devoutly desperate in a church. I should know: ex-novice and ex-mapmaker, both; ex-government surveyor. That time of my life (the surveying time) ended unexpectedly and very suddenly. I could pinpoint it on a map with my geodimeter if I still had one. The geodimeter emits light waves that hit topographical obstructions and bounce back to the watching eye which measures: and here is the exact location of the translation of Jess Hyde from one incarnation to another: a summer night, more years ago than I wish to recall. I could take my spirit level and set up my plane-table on its tripod, and I could shade in the landforms of death and rebirth very precisely: at Roma, cattle-trading town in central Queensland, a few driving days' east of where I am now; a day of seismic collision, of incompatible strata meeting head-on and buckling and violently giving way.

Not for the first time in my life; not by a bloody long shot.

I look at these various bits of my self and my history, all of them floating about me, all simultaneously correct and present and buoyant (time being, as it seems to me here, the warm bath in which I am immersed; though that is a crazy image, *bath*, in a place where the idea of water is a shimmering trick on the empty salt-panned bed of the Sea of Null). But here they are, like so many soap bubbles drifting by: my gypsy childhood; the convent years (oil and water, those two). And here I am, later, with government trappings and expensive equipment, no wiser, always trying to map my way backwards to the fateful fork in the road.

Out here, there can be no illusions: whatever calibrated surveying instruments and theodolites may say, all the tables and taxonomies and charts are flickering *wishes*, nothing but tapers signifying a desire to impose order on the ungovernable, signifying an undying and touching faith in magical thinking, which is what mapmaking is. Here is Hercules, spooning out the ocean with his shell; and here are the rest of us, dipping into the sloshing wake of random violence, galaxies, deserts, city states, continental plates run aground, world wars, childhood, droughts, nebulae exploding, cups of tea, parents, teachers, surveying instruments and charts, flags, nations evolving and devolving, ancient hatreds, ancient fears, ancient passions ceaselessly renewed, apocalyptic fantasies, millennial dreads, city by-laws, earthquakes, inundations . . . here we are parsing and labelling and taking topographic readings and turning on the radio and looking at our clocks and making love.

Making love . . .

'I love the way you laugh,' Major Miner says, 'when you come,' and it's like all the stoppered years popping like a champagne cork, I can't stop, I'm rolling over and over and over, green grass and wattles and the hillsides of childhood, the railway embankments, the silver lines flashing and flashing and I'm bound like an arrow for the promised land.

'My dad,' I say, gasping, and gurgling after my dizzy voice, 'my dad was a . . . dad was a . . .,' and the Major is laughing too, it's infectious, the way my dad's laughter was. You couldn't stop them once they got going, those ganger crews. 'My dad was a railway ganger,' I gasp. 'He used to take me . . . he used to let me ride . . .' and I can feel the rush of the trolley again, the bliss of it, the see-saw squeak of the ganger's drive-handle, the men pushing, sweating, singing, swearing, laughing, cursing the blisters, cursing the relentless up-and-downing, adoring the speed, the trolley swallowing the straight silver lines and spitting them out again behind, the sheer rush of it, the heaven of it, the wild mad funnel of laughter that whooshed us along.

'My dad and my mum,' I say, 'were utterly disreputable. We were railway gangers, railway gypsies, we lived on the run.' I adored them. I adored those untrammelled days. It seems to me now that we passed our days and our nights in laughter, but of course there was violence too, and shouting, and fights, bottles broken, bottles thrown, and singing, and hunger and booze and cheap greasy food, and the telling of stories, and fights, and love. They thumped me and hugged me. I had bruises and kisses, I suppose, by equal dose. I was happy. I loved it, I loved it. I loved the way love unrolled his swag in those makeshift camps and passed the bottle and the fags around, I loved the body warmth, the singing, the men and women rolling and humping under blankets, the campfires, the billies boiled, the stolen jumbuck barbecued, the drunken sleeping all in a heap.

Major Miner says, wondering: 'I never once heard you laugh in Outer Maroo.'

No, I think. No.

'It's too far back,' I explain. 'It's too hard and too far to get back there. All the bridges were blown up.' Until now, for some reason. Until him.

The gangers' camps are on the other side of self-consciousness, before I understood social disgrace, before I had been reclaimed, saved for school, cleaned up in the convent, before I had been introduced to shame.

'My clothes were always filthy, and stiff with sweat,' I tell him. 'Hard as a board. I was a dirty little ruffian.' Maybe that was the shortcut the senses took: the sweet sweat of love, the delectable, leathery, mining-and-explosives fug of Major Miner's skin. I stroke it, I nibble it, I bite. 'You're so delicious,' I tell him, laughing again. 'My nut-brown man.' I was so happy in those dirty sweaty days. So happy. 'I almost never get back there,' I sigh. 'Not even in dreams. It's too far. Except with you.'

I was a little savage, people said; a saucy little six-year-old tart with wicked eyes. 'Be careful,' I warned Major M. 'I was the sort of kid your mother warned you about. You never know what you might catch from me. I'm a risk.' I smoked. I swore like a man. From time to time, I had lice in my hair. *Don't touch her*, other parents warned. I knew what fucking was; I saw it all around me every night, the bodies heaving and whooping with joy beneath a blanket, the stars above. Afterwards, my mum and my dad would let me crawl into the hot sweaty space between them. They covered me with kisses. The brown grass pricked me through the groundsheet. The cover was stiff with love.

'God, you're wild. You're wild,' Major Miner laughs. 'You're like a young girl, a wild child.'

'You're done for, now,' I warn him. I'm hungry, I'm starving, I can't stop. 'Kiss of Death, that's me. You're marked now.' I'm afraid of waking, afraid of not finding my way back. I want to stay dirty and dank, I can see the flash of railway lines, this is where I belong. 'My true colours,' I gasp. 'They're indelible.'

'Hallelujah,' he says. 'Hallelujah, glory, and amen.'

I can't stop laughing.

We're disreputable, I think, with the world burning down. No tact. No respect for social conventions. Just like my disgraceful mum and dad.

'What are you laughing at?' he asks, laughing too.

'My mum,' I splutter. 'The first time they tried to take me away. The way she mimicked them, the way she . . .' It's like whooping cough, this mad kind of mirth. It spirals into a place where no oxygen is. It leaves you blue. 'The way she . . . the way she . . . and the way they . . . They were ladies from the CWA. They wore *hats*!'

'Ssh,' he says. 'Sshh . . . you'll choke.'

'And *gloves*!' I gasp. '*Gloves*!'

'Shh.' He cups his hand between my legs, gently, as though stillness starts there. This is where peace begins, his hand says, and the lovely smell of him is all mixed up with railway lines and dirty sleeping bags and the tang of brown grass and burrs.

'She told them to fuck off,' I say, soberly. 'She put a billycan lid on her head, like a smart little hat. She said: "My kid's worth ten of your frilly daughters, and she knows more than any kid who goes to school." She held her sheep-gutting knife in front of her. "You'll take her over my dead body," she said.'

I can still feel the rush of it, the triumph, the way they shuffled backwards like scared ewes. I saw the names they called her in fizzing lights, like skyrockets. Slut. Floozie. The Whore of Babylon. 'Whore of Babylon yourself,' my mum said, indifferent, brandishing her sheep-gutting knife. They were magic words to me, every one of them; abracadabras; open sesames. I would flash them in whispers like scimitars, like flaming swords. I would say them like prayers. I thought the railway ganger's life was very heaven.

'We were free as wild wallabies,' I say. 'Free as brumbies.'

We were feral. We were untamable.

I knew that I would always be safe; that I would only have to lay about with my sheep-gutting word. *Whore of Babylon*, I would say, and enemies would curl up at my feet.

'But you *were* taken away, weren't you?' Major Miner says. 'In the end?'

In the end.

In the new beginning.

Over their dead bodies, more or less. And taken too far to ever get back.

There was a dream I used to have, a nightmare: two sets of railway lines, two gangers' trolleys, neither one of them equipped with brakes. I am on one of them, pushing, pulling, pushing the see-saw handle. The other trolley passes like a meteor. 'Jess!' they call, whipping by. 'Dad!' I scream into their slipstream. 'Mum!' But we are racing further and further apart at the speed of light.

I play jacks on this headland, on the lip of my private mesa. I've been doing it for years, walking out here, taking my totems out of their hiding place, putting them back again. I amuse myself by tossing and catching three objects, all found within a stone's throw of where I sit: one is a fossilised mussel shell, its butterfly wings perfect and intact and touching each other with the delicacy of two hands folded in prayer. Inside the carapace, I suppose, is the crouching mussel (possibly opalised, but I cannot bring myself to break open the flawless shell-halves to see); also inside, no doubt, is a petrified memory of the time when an ocean washed this rock. The second object is a long thick sausage of ossified dinosaur shit; and the third is a beer can, crumpled, its four Xs bleached faint in the sun. More than once, out here, I have laughed out loud, and then huddled, appalled, at the dreadful sound of my laughter bouncing back from the silences.

Time is a joke, I think. It rushes by like a railway ganger's trolley and goes nowhere. It makes no sound.

Out here, there is almost a kind of menace to the silence, which is not so much golden as burnished with a frightening immensity. There is always a fine rufous mist in the air . . . no, not mist, moisture being one of the many absences, but the air nevertheless has the appearance of mist, the particles of red earth lifting themselves in thermal updraughts, drifting, wisping about like rust, floating down again, coating saltbush and gidgee, coating the mind so that ridges of thought become visible, showing up like welts or like maps drawn with a finger on a dusty ledge.

The vastness of the silence frightens all of us, I think. Everyone feels compelled to make a mark on that silence, to fill it with evidence of passage. That is why people have always clustered in railway gangers' camps, or in Bernie's or in Beresford's or in the Living Word. They are making noise: joyful unto the Lord, etcetera, or merely comforting, or merely raucous. They do it to reassure themselves.

They are also impelled to give voice to the things they must not speak of in public. Taboos, that is to say, ferment; taboos insist on being broken; they become compulsions; people need to scream them in secret. Nuns whisper them into the pages of their missals and in confessionals, and sometimes to the young girls in their care. The people of Outer Maroo tell their cattle . . . *told* their cattle. They told their sheep, they told the rocks, they told the mine shafts, they told the sky. Or they talked to me. Sooner or later, they all talked to me.

It is a curious thing, a self-imposed silence, the way it invites confidences and revelations, and the way it reveals some deep-seated belief that the mute are also deaf, and are possibly stupid, but are certainly innocent, and are a safe repository for secret things. Most people in Outer Maroo, I think, saw me (or rather, saw Jess Hyde, which is not quite the same thing) this way. Old Silence, they said. They thought of me as they would think of a wall or a boulder, or perhaps as a rock cavern in the breakaways: hollow, receptive, capable of the infinite absorption of sound, a black hole that gave nothing back.

This suited me.

It is, in fact, accurate.

I think of myself as a black hole whose visible edges are Old Silence. She was a sort of getaway outfit, a costume I stitched together hastily and stepped into one night in Roma, the only way out of a dead end.

Something happened. What goes around comes around. Here we go again, I thought dumbfounded. Where did it get me, all this measuring and marking and mapping my way back to what was lost? Where does a circle start? and where does it end?

I wanted to step off the treadmill.

I wanted to go off on a tangent.

I wanted to find the vanishing point where the parallel railway lines met, and I did find the one thing that my parents and the Sisters of Mercy had in common.

Like all of them, I went into Retreat. Silence swallowed me.

Sisters of Mercy. I haven't thought of it before, the rich irony; and yet they *are* kin to Mercy Given (as well as being absolutely not).

'Was it by force?' Major Miner wants to know. 'When they took you, I mean. Legal injunctions, police, that kind of thing?'

'Believe me,' I say, feeling queasy, 'this end of the world is nothing compared to that one. For me personally, I mean.'

It was just as fast and violent, just as mad, just as bewildering and accidental: a drunken fight, a knife or two, and how could it be? but it was, apparently it was, apparently my father had killed a man he thought of as a drinking mate. 'I'll kill you, you fucking arsehole,' he screamed, as witnesses testified. He could never remember later what the fight was about. 'But I loved the fucking bastard,' he kept saying. 'I loved the stupid fucker.'

It was his unstoppable, garrulous, tale-telling self that did him in.

I'll kill you, you fucking arsehole.

Findings: Intent to cause bodily harm. Intention to kill. Malice aforethought. Life sentence.

'He could never even tolerate a *tent*,' I tell Major M. 'He hanged himself in his cell. And then my mother . . .' Superslut in the billycan hat, the Invulnerable, the Whore of Babylon, my mother curled in on herself like a child and grieved unto death. 'The shock, and the booze . . . they locked her away in Goodna to dry her out. She was in and out, in and out, between Goodna and the gutters after that.'

'And so the nuns got you,' he says, stroking me.

'At least better than the CWA.'

'Poor Jess. How old were you then?'

'Seven.'

'You must have hated them.'

I didn't in fact. I loved the sweet order, the cleanliness, the sung vespers, the smell of books and learning, the contemplative silences, the headstrong intelligent women behind demure veils.

'In a funny way, you know, they were like my mum. The other side of the coin. You couldn't push them around. They would tell the Bishop to fuck off, though not in so few words, it goes without saying. And they doted on me, so of course I doted on them.'

I was the spoiled darling of the convent, just as I had been in the railway gangers' camps; but an absolute abyss ran between my two worlds. There was a rift valley down the middle of every waking thought and every dream. I knew two different languages, one for railway gangers and one for nuns. They seemed to me to have not a single word in common.

Once a month, one of the Sisters (one of whom I was particularly fond) would take me down to Brisbane by train, and we would visit my mother in Goodna. 'We pray for your mother, Jess,' the Sister would say, and I would want to strike her. My mother doesn't need praying for, I would want to shout. She's worth ten nuns.

I would have to get away. I would have to lock myself into the toilet on the train.

Once, my mother, drunk, stinking, her clothing torn and unseemly, showed up at the convent in Roma, and then I knew shame. I also knew I would scream at any nun who looked at her with pity or with reproach. My mother was quite silent. She just stood there on the verandah, weeping, and I stared in horror at the puddle which appeared on the boards between her legs. It seemed to get bigger and bigger, it kept flowing, silently, leaking away between the boards. I thought I would drown.

After she left, I ran away for a day, and hid myself, solitary, in a culvert under the railway lines. Sometimes, just after a train had gone by, I would lie on my back between the rails, my hands folded across my breast.

Motion sickness could cripple me.

I dreamed always of trains without brakes.

I felt like someone on a ganger's trolley between one galaxy and another, always alien, my trolley tracks roller-coastering themselves into knots. There were always two of me, on parallel tracks, going in opposite directions, speaking two different languages, thinking incompatible thoughts out of different sides of my head.

I think that was when I first felt the lure of *nowhere* as of some irresistible force, as the end of the line where my life was rushing, the ultimate terminus sucking at me, waiting for me to jump all the tracks.

And then it happened, as suddenly and stupidly as it had happened to my dad, in the dark alley outside a pub in Roma. One summer night, there was a man with a knife, a man on my own surveying team, a man I fancied, a man I knew had the hots for me. He could have got what he wanted by asking, but he didn't want to ask.

'You want me, Jess, don't you,' he said, a statement, his voice slick with booze.

'Three guesses.'

'Yeah, you want me. Just what you been needing, Boss Lady' – low drunken laughter, the knife at my throat – 'what you been longing for.'

It was the laughter, I think, that triggered things; and the knife; and the fact that he was right. The Furies visited me, there was more blood than seemed possible, and the knife was in my own shocked hand. The blood puzzled me. I skated on it, slipped, lay beside him on the wet red road. I held his head in my arms. 'I just wanted to fuck you,' I whispered, 'you stupid beautiful oaf.'

Not even his eyelids moved, but the bloodied mouths in his chest made a sucking sound, they spoke, and after that I didn't want to speak at all. There was too much that I didn't want to say. At that precise moment, I stopped being Jess Somebody Else, Jess who was heckled and jekylled by the bad joke of life. I pulled on the baggy costume of Jess Hyde and I fled. It was months before I read in a newspaper that he wasn't dead at all. Surface wounds, the papers said. Women can't do anything right, he joked, which is why they shouldn't be boss ladies on surveying teams.

Fuck you, I thought.

And here I am at the terminus, beyond the end of the line, with the town of Outer Maroo and its dirty little secrets in the palm of my fizzing mind.

'Make a fist,' my dad used to say, shadow-boxing. 'You gotta get them before they get you, only way to go.'

'Life is a bugger and then you die,' he told me. He swooped me up like a bird. He danced me round, breathless with laughter. 'So pump the trolley, me ganger boys, and let 'er rip! On with the show while the going's good.'

'You're a wild thing,' Major Miner says. 'What are you laughing for now?'

Because the going's so good, I would say if I could just catch my breath.

The going's so good I could mend the world. I could put it back together again like a jigsaw puzzle. *Whore of Babylon*, I could say, making a fist. *Abracadabra.*

And Major Miner's mouth is on mine, and I am lost, and have found myself again.

Last Week

Tuesday

You can tell when people are dreaming, Mercy thinks, standing silent as a cat on the verandah, watching Sarah through the film of lace curtains and mosquito net. Sarah is sleeping late, as though drugged. It is fear, Mercy thinks: the fear of answers. She wants to know and she doesn't want to know. Mercy understands avoidance. She does not want to see the photograph of Sarah's daughter.

Sarah moves restlessly through a dream. Sometimes she speaks. On Sarah's eyelids, Mercy sees a flutter of shadow and harsh gold, where the sun, which lacks all delicacy by this hour, pushes its burning finger through lace and net, and sears what it touches. But there is also a counter-play, a counter-movement, from the underside of Sarah's eyelids: a dream pecking at the shell of her sleep, working its way into the world.

When she wakes, Mercy thinks, I could take her to Aladdin's Rush. When Sarah sees the books, she will understand, she will know that whatever could have been done was done.

Ah, but was it?

Perhaps, at Aladdin's Rush, Mercy will be able to answer her own questions as well as those, both asked and unasked, of Sarah. Perhaps she will be able to tell Sarah, not everything . . . no, not everything, that would not be possible . . . but what Sarah most needs to know.

Spirals of superheated air twist out through the verandah railings and rise toward the sun. Mercy feels herself swaying in the lift of them, being floated towards the Rush. She feels lighter than air. She can hear a sort of merriment in the dust motes, scudding around her. She touches her lips with her tongue and thinks of Jess watching over Nick, who makes her think for some reason of Gideon, *no*, no he does not, she refuses to think of Gideon, but she can safely think of Donny Becker who got her away from the Reef, and who pressed himself against her in prayer meeting once. She asks herself why so often lately it is as though her body runs away with her thoughts. She will see lips that move in a particular way, or eyes of a certain colour, and it is as though they were the lips and eyes of all the imaginary young men she has ever dreamed about, it is as though they turn on fizzing currents that run from her head to her breasts to the damp hot place between her legs. She is flushed and excited, she wants to take the whole world into herself greedily, she wants to embrace trees, cows, sheep, the sun, Donny Becker, she could dance, she could fly, but then just as suddenly she is tormented with shame because that must have been what Oyster saw, what he knew about her, this greediness, this wet heat, and if that . . . if that is what . . . and then she feels ill and confused. She fears she may be one of the whores of Babylon, much spoken of from the pulpit of the Gospel Hall, those painted women who think lascivious thoughts and whose fate, like that of Jezebel in the Old Testament, is to be cast from windows into outer darkness and eaten by dogs; and yet even so, she resists believing that the bright spinning thing that skips in the air when Donny Becker looks at her *in that way* . . . she will not believe it is evil.

From time to time, she can feel on her skin a possibility of change in the weather.

'Mercy,' her mother calls sadly, wearily, from a verandah chair.

Mercy shivers. The rising currents of warm air drop her suddenly. 'I'm coming, Mum.'

'It's lovely to have you home for lunch,' her mother says, but she says it with that air of disproportionate gratitude that Mercy finds so burdensome of late. Her mother has changed the scale of things, so that minute details will billow out like spinnakers and threaten everyone's balance. 'Is Ma Beresford back?' her mother asks nervously. She believes that a return to right order in any one particular might help in some incalculable way to level out again the pitch and toss of their lives.

'No. This afternoon, I think.' Mercy sits in the chair beside her mother. 'There was only me this morning. But no one came in, so I closed the shop.'

'No one came?'

'No,' Mercy says.

'Oh.' Her mother reaches out a hand that trembles slightly. 'That means . . .'

What does it mean? Mercy wonders. She strokes her mother's fingers gently, as though they were bruised. Perhaps it means that Mr Prophet's miners and stockmen and jackaroos, or else Andrew Godwin's, or possibly Bernie's stonecutters and grinders and polishers, are huddling somewhere, out at the new shafts or at the pub. Perhaps decisions are already being made, lots drawn. Perhaps the accidents that seem to happen so mysteriously, so speedily, whenever foreigners arrive . . . perhaps such new accidents are already on their way? Or perhaps it means nothing at all. Perhaps it means that since everyone *fears* that decisions are being made, out there somewhere, by someone unknown, then everyone stays out of sight. Perhaps accidents happen because everyone, tense as tripwire, stumbles into them.

'It doesn't mean anything, Mum,' Mercy says lightly, or she

attempts to say lightly, though she fears her mother can read anxiety merely from the surface of her skin.

'It's hard to breathe,' her mother says.

And yes, the Old Fuckatoo is roosting again, closer and more fetid than ever. The look in its eye is not basilisk, any more, Mercy thinks; not neutral. Since the Reef disappeared, it has not been possible to predict what the Old Fuckatoo might do. There is a mad, evil glitter in its eye.

'It doesn't mean anything, Mum,' she says again. 'There are just days when no one comes in, that's all. Usually I stay there anyway. I stay and talk to Ma or Ma's Bill. Or I just stay by myself and think. I like the shop when it's empty. Or else I go and talk to Jess.'

'Did you see Jess today?'

'Yes,' Mercy says. And then, because it is really another question that her mother is too fearful to ask, she says: 'Nothing's happened. Jess is keeping her eye on him. She has some jobs lined up for him, she reckons he's safe as long as she keeps him busy where she can see him, in Bernie's shed.'

'Yes, yes, oh yes, that's safer. Otherwise . . . yes, heatstroke, and who knows . . .? They have to stay inside, Sarah too.' Vi puts her hands over her face. 'Of course, you were right, Mercy, it was the right thing, to bring her here . . . you couldn't leave her, but I wish . . . I just wish . . .' She looks around vaguely for something mislaid. 'She told us his name, I think, but I can't –'

'Nick. He'll be all right, Mum.'

'Oh, yes, he's safe with Jess. Nobody would dare.' Her mother looks along the veranda to Sarah's room. 'She's slept all morning.' She clasps and unclasps her hands. 'I wish Charles hadn't had to go out,' she says. 'I wish he'd stayed home today.'

'He couldn't, Mum, not with old Mrs Dempsey dying, he had to go. He'll be all right.'

'That Telecom man,' her mother says fearfully, and begins to cry. 'That one who wasn't Bernie's cousin . . . the time he came.'

'That was an accident. That was an accident pure and simple with the telephone cables.'

'Where are the dogs?' her mother says, sitting forward. She calls to them. 'Where are they? Why don't they come?'

'Mum, you know they go off after rabbits. They'll be back.'

'I have this feeling,' her mother says, 'I just have this *feeling* that Brian will telephone today.'

'Oh, Mum.' Mercy presses her fingertips and thumbs together. She closes her eyes. *Miss Rover, come over.*

'Don't you often get that feeling?' her mother asks. 'That he is trying to phone?'

Mercy often gets the feeling that she is trying to phone Miss Rover. She dreams that she dials a Brisbane number, and Miss Rover answers and says *Hello? . . . hello? . . . hello?*, and Mercy shouts, but the line always goes dead, and the operator always says *We regret that your call cannot go through at this time, we regret that your call, we regret that your call, we regret certain difficulties, we apologise for any inconvenience and we suggest that you send a letter instead.* Mercy tries to write a letter instead.

'It could be from anywhere,' her mother says. 'From Mount Isa, or Darwin, wherever he managed to hitch a ride. You know how Brian daydreams, Mercy. You know how he loses track.'

Mercy always makes Miss Rover watch her when she begins to write something in her head.

'We *know* he was already gone before the end,' her mother says in a low earnest voice. She is speaking to herself. She is engaged in passionate debate. 'We *know* he wasn't there then.'

Mercy is always sitting in the classroom after school when she writes her letters. She is setting all the details down.

'*Two foreigners came*,' she begins, '*and the weather began to change.*'

'That is excellent work, Mercy,' she makes Miss Rover say.

'*Two more foreigners have come*,' she writes. '*There is something different about them. I do not think it will be so easy to get rid of them. I think the weather will change.*'

When she opens her eyes, Sarah can feel the dream slipping away like a silk cloak from bare shoulders. She clutches at it, or tries to, but a hopeless languor afflicts her fingers, and the dream slithers just beyond reach. For a second she sees Amy's face undulating in its folds, and she can feel Stephen's hand again, just for an instant, on the nape of her neck. She can see Amy watching them, singing a little song of incantations under her breath, holding her fingers over her eyes in a magic pattern, or perhaps weeping, her face pale, her nose bleeding, and there seem to be postcards, a waterfall of them spilling from Amy's mouth, spinning towards Sarah's hand, fluttering away between Sarah's fingers which perversely refuse to hold anything in spite of the fact that there is something crucial written on the cards, and Sarah did have one in her hand not long ago, she is sure of this, because she can see fleetingly and intermittently backwards into the folds of the dream to where she knew what was written on the card, yes, she can see herself standing there smitten with a sudden radiant understanding of everything, and it is extremely urgent that she catch hold of the silken edge of that moment and pull it back, that she merge again with the Sarah-self in the dream, who is no longer quite in focus, who is getting fuzzier and softer, but who reaches out helpfully with the postcard, offering it, and perhaps it is not too late, because Sarah-outside-the-dream can almost touch her own outstretched hand, she may be able to catch hold of the card, she may be able to read it again, it brushes her fingers, but no, it's too late, it's too late, the card and the entire dream have gone, drifting over the shadow line, falling away into the neverwhere between her slack index finger and thumb.

One more failure to snatch Amy out of her blank spaces. Sarah can hear the bell that tolls missed connections, an endless clang, measuring off bad timing, wrong turns, ineptitude. This latest blunder is catastrophic, although fortunately the catastrophe seems to be following the trajectory of the dream, dwindling in magnitude at high speed like a falling star until there is nothing left but a pinpoint of regret. It is possible after all that Amy has simply gone backpacking onwards to Darwin, or rolling westward like a wave on her inner sea, her knapsack stuffed with postcards and nowhere to mail them since Quilpie. So she mails them instead from sleep to sleep, knowing Sarah will stay attuned. Perhaps in Sarah's next dream the postcard will be delivered.

Or it is possible, after all, that the postcard was not even intended for Sarah. It is entirely probable that the card was addressed to someone else, to Stephen, for example; or to the man with the unnerving blue eyes whom Amy had met somewhere between Brisbane and her fate; or to the other one, Gideon, who had become Amy's friend.

> He calls himself Oyster, and Gideon is his right-hand man. They have leased the mining rights to an opal seam from some cattle farmer (graziers, they call them here). There's a strange system in Australia, I don't understand it. People don't really own their own land, they only own the surface of it, the top eighteen inches, or something. The federal government owns any minerals under the surface. So if oil or opals are found on your land, you do not have the right to stop someone mining them. They have to pay you royalties for going through the surface of your land, but that is all. It's very strange. As you can imagine, it has led to a lot of friction with Aboriginal people (in Queensland, they call themselves Murris) who do not want mining companies on their land, but have no power to prevent them. As for Oyster, he has come to some private arrangement with the grazier.
>
> I met Gideon by chance on the beach at Noosa, on the Queensland coast. No, not by chance. I don't believe in chance any more. I believe all these connections are

meant to be: you and me, Sarah. You and Dad. Me and the guru at the ashram in Pondicherry, the one who sent me here. We were walking on the beach in India one day, about ten of us, looking out at the Bay of Bengal, and suddenly the guru turned round and touched me on the shoulder and pointed out over the sea. The reef is calling you, he said. Go.

I was upset. I was happy in his ashram. I didn't want to leave. But now I understand why. I thought he must mean the Great Barrier Reef, so that is why I came to Queensland, and that is where I met Gideon, who took me to meet Oyster. But this is the amazing thing: Oyster's opal mine – and he runs the mine as a commune, everyone shares the work, and the commune uses the money to spread the gospel of peace – his opal mine is almost as far inland as you can go, but he calls it his Reef. I almost fainted when he told me.

Can you imagine how I felt, Sarah? It was like a bolt of lightning. It was the same way I felt years ago, when I was a little girl, and I took you to meet Dad. I just knew, somehow, that this was meant to be. I believe every detail of our lives has a purpose. I believe we are interlinked with every other soul on earth. We have to listen to the sighing of the earth, Oyster says, and to the message of the sea. God is everywhere, and we are in the Last Days. A thousand years are as a day in the sight of God, and the Day of the Earth has reached the evening of its last thousand years. I believe that, Sarah. You can hear it in the message of the sea. You can hear everything when you meditate. I often hear you, Sarah. I keep you and Dad in my thoughts. You don't need to tell me what he did, and when, because I already know. He

> has already given himself back to the universe, I know that. Oyster explained to me that I haven't lost him. He is already part of the New Heaven and the New Earth.
>
> We will all be part of it soon. At the dawning of the year 2000, Oyster says, all that we know shall pass away, and the New Age will begin. Oyster has intense eyes of the most unnerving blue, and when he looks at you, you feel as though he can see your thoughts. Gideon is his partner. It is Gideon who goes out into the highways and byways to recruit workers for 'the vineyard of the Kingdom of Heaven' as Oyster calls it. It isn't just a cooperative opal mine at Oyster's Reef; we will be living in a new way. We will be preparing for a new heaven and a new earth.

Perhaps the postcard in Sarah's dream was intended for Oyster or Gideon. Its message may indeed have been important for the addressee, but as for Sarah-outside-the-dream, she can dismiss such little losses with detachment.

She certainly feels detached. She feels as though she is floating slightly above the bed. Her room shimmers with light that is excessively bright, and there are small spinning discs, or more accurately red circles, hollow, bleeding into yellow at both their inner and outer edges. She would have to describe them as miniature flaming circus hoops. They float in all directions, and collide and coalesce and part again.

It seems important to recognise this landscape of spinning lights, but Sarah cannot think where she is. She can feel the edges of a great pool of dread lapping at the room, at the bed, at the sheets, at this filmy thing . . . what is it? She seems to be inside a cocoon. There are folds of net spilling out of some point above her, enclosing the bed, and just beyond the pleats of the net are the wavelets of dread. She has a sense of marshes, and of backwaters that twist and mislead, and of treacherous quicksand traps, and of salt pans . . .

Salt pans?

Sarah inspects the words with curiosity. They are new to her, and yet she seems to know what they mean: shimmering stretches of deception across which she will have to find stepping stones. The salt pans are part of the puzzle, part of the labyrinth, but she has read somewhere, she cannot remember where, that a foolproof recipe exists for escaping a maze. If one takes every turn to the left, and *only* turns to the left, eventually one will be free. Can that be right? But what does she do if three left turns lead to a dead end? Go back one turn? There must be another rule she has forgotten.

Nevertheless she must begin. She swivels her eyes to the left. Where is she? She can rule out her apartment in Boston because there is no horse-chestnut tree beyond the window. She senses movement, and has a vague sense of people crossing and of traffic sounds, much thinner than usual, a single vehicle, perhaps. The vehicle coughs and purrs and misfires and falls into silence. Perhaps she dreamed it. Now she can hear nothing, see nothing, beyond the window.

The window must be open, or perhaps there is no glass, because the lace curtain keeps lifting very slightly, even though the air seems hot and still. Beyond the lace, there is a thin wafer of greenness, and beyond the green, something red and burning hurls against the house a light of such intensity that the curtain has become more or less invisible, has become a radiant membrane between what is on Sarah's side of the window and what is beyond. She blinks several times and now it seems to her that she can see her classroom at the school in Boston, the children's drawings on the walls, and Amy, mutinous, glowering, with her sheaf of black sketches.

'What are these, Amy?' she asks.

'They're for my birthday,' Amy says. 'I'm seven today.'

'And it's the birthday girl's turn for Show and Tell. Tell us who gave you your present?'

'I gave them to me. I made them.'

'I see,' Sarah says. 'Happy faces. Smiling for your birthday and floating like bubbles on a fizzy birthday drink.'

'They're not smiling for my birthday. They're smiling because they can fly away wherever they want to,' Amy says scornfully. 'They're balloon people, that's why. That's their heads floating on strings, and that's their bodies down there. They leave them behind. They don't feel anything. They can fly wherever they want.'

'Ah,' Sarah says.

'*I'm* a balloon person,' Amy explains.

'Can we all fly with you on your birthday?'

'No,' Amy says. '*My* balloon people fly so high it's freezing up there, and they have to wear mittens.'

'Ah yes,' Sarah says. 'I can see their mittens.'

'I'm a balloon person.'

'Yes, you said. Is that why you took everyone's mittens from the locker room?'

'I didn't,' Amy says. She scrunches her drawings up into a ball and throws them into the wastepaper basket. 'There aren't any balloon people,' she says witheringly. 'People can't fly.'

'Why don't we get all the mittens out of your locker and give them back to everyone?'

'Except my father,' Amy says. 'He's a balloon man. You could fly with him.'

Sarah turns restlessly, and bats at the mosquito net and the sun, and here is Amy bringing Stephen on a string. He bobs about at the window, ballooning, eddying this way and that. He has magic marker eyes, perfectly round, unnaturally wide and bright, with glowing black pupils and lashes like rays of the sun. His mouth is curved like a banana, but when he twists on his string and shows his about-face, the banana is turned upside-down.

Stephen eddies and dances in the currents of white light, and Amy tugs his string and smiles and hands the string to Sarah. 'Hold him tight,' Amy says, 'because he keeps on flying away.'

'He's not my balloon, Amy,' Sarah says.

'Yes, he is,' Amy insists. 'Mummy doesn't want him, and he doesn't want her either, he doesn't want to go flying with her any more. He has lots and lots and lots of balloon women, but I don't like them. I want him to fly with *you*. See?' And now Amy has Sarah on a string, and she ties the two strings together and lets them go. The Stephen and Sarah balloons bounce against each other and lift and twist and touch and bounce. Amy catches them again, and tugs them through a restaurant door.

'I'm Amy's teacher,' Sarah explains.

'What I specialise in,' Stephen says, 'apart from mathematics, that is . . . May I say that I am mesmerised by your eyes?'

'Amy is a gifted child,' Sarah says, 'and extremely intelligent, but I worry about her. She withdraws into herself. It's as though, even when she is talking to me, she is absent.'

'Yes,' Stephen says absently, staring into Sarah's eyes.

'All her drawings are in black crayon,' Sarah says. 'She never uses any of the other colours. It's disturbing, don't you think?'

'Not particularly,' Stephen says. 'Her mother's an artist who works with charcoal a lot. Who abuses charcoal, I'm tempted to say, although all that smudging seems to appeal in grotty little third-rate galleries in Harvard Square. Charcoal, of course, is not the only substance her mother abuses.'

'I think Amy feels abandoned.'

'We both need someone,' Stephen says. 'Amy and I. We've both been abandoned. Her mother's gone off to live with ten people in an artists' commune, not one of them sane, in my opinion.'

Amy draws on the paper napkins. She draws three balloons with their strings tied together in a bow. She encloses them all in a little house.

Stephen takes Sarah's hand. 'Will you come and have dinner with us tomorrow?'

'Well,' Sarah says, losing her way a little in Stephen's eyes. 'Yes. All right.'

'I'm writing a book,' Stephen says, 'about the relationship between fractal curves and irregular mathematical sequences and art. Does the Lorenz Attractor mean anything? Or the Mandelbrot Set?'

'Ahh . . . I've heard of them,' Sarah says. 'I think.'

'I've just got the photographs back,' Stephen says. 'The experimental artwork. For the book plates. They're quite stunning. I'll show you if you're interested.'

'Yes,' Sarah says, uncertainly, though it is Amy whom she does not want to lose sight of. She can feel the riffs and syncopations of her heartbeat as the child floats away into the margins of photographic plates and over the page.

'Amy!' she calls. 'Amy!' She is riffling pages, careening through fractal muddle, straining for the string of Amy's balloon.

'You lost him,' Amy accuses, just out of reach, drifting skywards. 'You let go his string.'

'It's the Lorenz Attractor,' Sarah says, watching the twinned swirling strings spiralling into the sun. She holds her arm over her eyes, but the light makes them water, it burns, and Amy is in danger, flying too close to the fire. Remember Icarus, Sarah warns. She grapples with the mosquito net. She cries out.

On the verandah, Mercy and her mother startle and hold themselves still. Mercy knocks over her chair as she rises. Is it possible that she is running when her feet feel like leaden weights?

'Sarah?' she asks through the window, breathing fast. 'What's wrong?'

'I didn't, I didn't,' Sarah says.

'Sarah?' Mercy calls. 'Is there someone –?'

She checks herself. She can see there is no one else in the room. *(Fear is just another form of superstition, Mercy; we breed it ourselves, we make it ourselves in our minds; we can unmake it.*
I know, Miss Rover. I know. I know I can people a whole country or a whole book with my mind. I know I can make you come back. I know perfectly well it's impossible for anyone to reach the house unseen. I know I can make Sarah safe.)

'It's OK, Sarah,' Mercy says. 'There's no one here. Just us. You've been dreaming.'

Sarah opens her eyes and blinks. 'Amy?' she asks.

'No. It's me, Mercy.'

'Why do you always run away?' Sarah asks. 'Don't you understand . . .?'

Doesn't Amy understand how precarious the balance is? Amy counts on Sarah, but Sarah herself steps like a heron across quicksand. If Amy sinks, Sarah fears she may lose her own footing. Sarah wants to take her by the shoulders and shake her. Don't you see? Don't you understand what you're doing?

Sarah closes her eyes against the light and covers her face with her hands. The glare is so fierce she can see the network of veins and the blood flowing through them. She can see tiny bubbles and whirlpools and the brackish capillary dispersal into deltas and the foaming push of the floodwater arteries at her wrists. In between all this busy bloody canal traffic, her flesh is translucent, and she sees, through the luminous membrane, her body's present anchorage. It is Stephen's cottage in Maine, though this is odd, because she cannot remember another time when the light in the cottage has been so intense. No doubt the fierce heat is responsible for this opaque film that covers everything, for the fuzziness, for the lack of clarity. She can actually see more clearly with the pillow over her eyes.

Behind the pillow and against the underside of her lids, the images sharpen. Now she has her bearings: salt pans, the cottage, the lake. She dips a paddle over the side of her bed, and strokes, and feathers the tip, and makes her way through the mosquito net and then through the window and on to the porch. She steps ashore and walks from room to room.

The cottage is deserted.

There are various signs of Stephen's presence (his plaid jacket behind the kitchen door, a small pile of books and scribbled notes on the bedside table), but none of the signs is recent. She leafs through the notes beside the bed. Most of them are mathematical equations, unintelligible, but she finds one containing words:

That passed the time.

It would have passed in any case.

Yes, but not so rapidly.

She stares at the note. She feels edgy. The words are part of the riddle of unease. She can smell something musty in the air, the trace of absence. She must have arrived on a day towards the end, and even as she thinks this she can feel a horrible agitation in her body, something that starts at her fingertips, something icy which advances like pins and needles, dispensing shivers. She huddles under the sheet, pulling it higher. The End. She picks up another small ball of paper and unravels it. *Endgame*, it says. She feels colder. Experimentally, in the hope of effecting some sort of exorcism, she says aloud, 'I am frightened of endings. I am frightened of finding out how things end.' Somehow the admission eases her panic slightly. Of course, she realises, it is the end that she has been sensing, it is the end that has been lapping at the hemline of her sheet. The cottage smells of that time of dread when Stephen has begun to absent himself more and more often, when he is devoting himself to the mathematical computation of his vanishing point. Negative reality, he calls it.

She can hear loons calling from the lake, pure and plaintive, each note falling on to the porch like a soft wet ball of leaves. If Stephen were to emit some sound from wherever he is – in his office at the university, or in his parked car, or simply leaning against a fallen tree trunk in the woods, perhaps – his voice would sound the same, it would reach her in the same way.

She wanders out to the porch where the swing waits with her book and marker just as she left them. She rocks gently back and forth, back and forth, reading, waiting. Around her the air is ominously still. She is conscious of the heaviness that precedes a violent summer storm. She can feel the air sucking at her skin, pulling her body towards what is going to happen.

There is a kind of melancholy that is almost indistinguishable from peace, she thinks. It arrives after one has given up the notion that there is still something one could do to alter the course of events. One surrenders. One gives oneself over to the seductive drift of helplessness. She supposes that this is really exhaustion, but it is strangely pleasurable. She is without anchor now, as Stephen has been for some time, and yet who could have believed that would be possible? She had aligned herself with absolute safety, she thought; she had married into WASP fortresses, all the New England bulwarks and Episcopalian guy-ropes of respectability buckling her in.

She is without anchor now, as Stephen has been for some time, as Amy has always been. She can understand, almost, what lures them.

Even before she hears the roar of the car, she is aware of the disturbances it sends ahead of itself: the flocks of birds rising, the squirrels chirruking panic down the line; and then of course the muffler, deafening in its absence, and the soft tympanic counterpoint of bushes slapping against the metal flanks. Sarah braces herself for the tug of war: of Amy ravenous for consolation; of wolfish Amy, ferociously unreachable, holding all comfort at bay. Nevertheless, in spite of herself, she feels hope. Amy is coming. Amy keeps coming. Amy, perhaps, believes that Sarah can break the spell. And Sarah, not Princess Charming but the wicked stepmother herself, has to hack a way through the thorns and unspell the spell and wake up the damaged sleeper. She has to convey to

Amy that it is possible to survive both the age of seventeen and the dreadful onset of the awareness of parental imperfection and frailty. I did it, she wants to tell Amy. It can be done. (And perhaps it can also be undone; Sarah is never sure. Her sister and her sister's children have done it differently, with equal uncertainty of lasting success.)

Amy's car spits back the woods, lurches across the humps of exposed granite in the clearing, ploughs through unmown grass, and brakes hard up against the verandah railings. Her driver's licence is recent, and she is drunk, still, with this heady new access to power underfoot and at the tips of her fingers. Her car is a sports model, not quite old enough to be vintage, but certainly sufficiently used to have attained a good brash age of defiance. Various parts of the vehicle are missing, and Amy flaunts these gaps like trophy flags, especially the thunderous proclamations of the space where the muffler used to be.

Amy cuts the engine, and a sudden shocking silence fills the air. She slams the car door.

'Where's Dad?' she asks lightly, thumbs through the belt loops of her jeans. She gives a credible performance of indifference, but only fleetingly. Without the armour of her car and the protective mechanisms of noise, her defiance seeps away like air from a slow puncture. She turns her back, looking through the trees towards the lake. She does not wait for an answer, but runs down the slope towards the dock, scooping up a handful of pebbles as she goes. She skips her stones, one by one, across the skin of the water. Sarah watches the light catch the whirr of their spinning passage, and sometimes hears the soft plash as they disappear. After she has skipped her last stone, Amy throws herself down at the end of the dock, flat on her stomach, and stares at her image.

Sarah looks into nowhere, waiting. She is grateful simply for the presence. We could live like this, she thinks; we could be silent and with distance between us, but at peace, each knowing the other safe. That would be enough.

Restless, Amy swings herself into sitting position, pulls off her shoes, stands, and dives into the lake fully clothed, neatly and quietly as a just-caught fish slipping back off the dock. The green surface of the water closes over her and is sheer as glass. Nothing breaks the surface, no ripple, no sound. Seconds lap softly against the shingle and pile themselves up. Birds call, but otherwise the silence is as loud as Sarah's heartbeat and thuds against her skin. She can hardly breathe. Too many minutes have piled up. Something is wrong. She runs down the slope to the dock. 'Amy!' she calls, stumbling.

'Yes?' Amy says, pulling herself out from under the dock. There is just a small, sucking, slapping sound. She hooks her arms over the mildewed boards.

Sarah breathes raggedly. She sinks down on to the dock, her legs trembling, and rests her hand on Amy's wet arm, but Amy is as slippery as lakeweed. 'Please don't do that to me,' Sarah says. She stares at the quicksilver place where their two reflections coalesce and dissolve. It is myself I hold on to, she thinks.

'Where's Dad?' Amy asks quietly.

'I don't know.'

Amy disappears, then knifes out of the water on the opposite side of the dock. She hoists herself up, pleats and unpleats her body, and walks back up to the cottage, swinging her hips, and peeling off her sodden clothing as she goes, dropping it piece by piece behind her. On the verandah, she huddles in a deckchair, naked.

Sarah follows.

'You let go,' Amy says dully. 'You didn't hang on to him.'

'No,' Sarah says. 'You can't hold anyone against his will.'

Amy's eyes flash with anger. 'How do you know it's against his will? Sometimes people can't say what they want, they just *can't.* Sometimes they have to say the opposite of what they want.'

'Yes, I know. But you still can't hold someone who won't let you hold him.' Or her, she does not add.

'You didn't try.'

'Perhaps that's true. Perhaps I'm tired of trying.'

Amy stares out over the lake. 'So you're leaving us,' she says flatly. 'I knew you would.'

Sarah says nothing.

'He's probably fucking some graduate student,' Amy says, working up anger again. 'They're probably having it off on the sofa in his office at this very minute.'

Sarah watches Amy trying to convince herself. It is as though Amy hopes that sufficient rage exercised on his behalf might push her father back into a manic phase. On the other hand, it is possible that she is not aware of how critical things have become.

Amy raises her voice, panicky. 'And it serves you right. You don't even fight. You don't even try to hold on to him. That's what you get for taking advantage of how lonely he was when my mother left.'

Sarah is surprised by a fleeting urge to laugh. A memory of dazzle brushes her: Stephen as meteor, Stephen ascendant, Stephen as the man who always got what he wanted and who never took no for an answer, Stephen as perpetual motion machine . . . Who could have guessed how fragile, how tissue-thin, that costume was?

Amy pushes out her lower lip. 'My mother knew he'd never stay with you.'

In fact, Sarah thinks wearily, sadly, as your mother would have known very well, and as we both know, Stephen, quite simply, cannot stay. Anywhere. With anyone.

But then again, memory is so cunningly selective. Stephen moves from tick to tock and back again, but not regular as clockwork, not at all. He immerses himself, appropriately, in the mathematics of chaos. He swims in the fissures of existing logic, he dives into the great crevasses where paradigms shift. From time to time he fails to come up for air. This may be personal quest as much as academic discipline. He is trying to unravel the equations of his fractal life. In any case, not even Stephen himself can predict when his tick will turn to tock, and certainly not that delicate point when his pendulum will pause and quiver and reach again for the other end of his arc. Who knows if any given swing can be weathered?

Amy, possibly, erases the tocks. She is careful not to remember them.

Without forethought, and without intending to speak aloud, Sarah says: 'Before your father . . .'

'What?'

Before Stephen . . . Yes, there was such a time. There must have been; though recovering it is like reading old teaching notes for a history lesson. Time is elastic, a function of the mind, Sarah knows this well enough. Even so, it is astonishing how far back ten years can stretch.

'Well?' Amy challenges. 'Before my father?'

'Before your father, I was your Grade 2 teacher. And now you're about to go off to college.' Sarah smiles. Maternal pleasures and anxieties keep catching her off guard. 'Four acceptance letters! When are you going to let us in on the big decision?'

'That's for me and my father to discuss.'

Sarah puts a hand up to her cheek, as though she has been hit with a stone. She notes that the paint is peeling again on the porch railings and decides that she must scrape them down tomorrow and coat them with sealant.

'And what about you?' Amy demands. 'Where are you off to?'

Sarah thinks there is enough sealant left in a can in the garage. She must check tonight, in case she needs to buy more.

'What about you?' Amy says, agitated.

'Does it matter?' Sarah shrugs. 'I suppose I'll move on.' *Afterwards.* She almost says it, but stops herself in time. *After whatever is going to happen, happens.* 'Before your father,' she says, 'I was a bit of a wanderer.'

'A wanderer.'

'You'll always have my address and phone number.' She is afraid of appearing to make demands that will scare Amy off. 'If you want them,' she adds.

'A wanderer. Before my father, you slept around, you mean. And now you'll do it again. Like a slut.'

'That's a silly word, Amy.'

'Didn't you.' Amy does not inflect her voice. 'Before my father.'

'Not so much.' It's curious, Sarah thinks, to see an image of yourself in someone else's frame. 'But that's one way of putting it, I suppose.'

'And they never stayed with you.'

'I think I never let them.'

'Anyway' Amy says, 'you made one big mistake.'

'I don't regret anything.'

'Fuck you,' Amy says softly. She walks naked the length of the verandah and back again. She sits on the steps and hugs her bare legs up against her breasts. 'If anything happens,' she says, 'I hold you responsible. I want you to know that.'

There can be no doubt, Sarah thinks, that cataclysm sends out shock waves in advance of a strike, and that those who are about to be most closely affected can sense the vibrations just as surely as a delicate seismograph can detect earthquakes before they arrive.

'If anything happens to *whom*, Amy?' Sarah asks quietly.

Amy begins to weep, at first silently. Her body is hunched over, forehead against her knees, her shoulders move as though she were swimming to save her life. Strange sounds gurgle from her throat, louder and louder. The sounds of drowning, Sarah thinks, but she does not know how to offer comfort without offering offence. She moves from the porch swing to the steps and sits beside Amy without touching her.

'It's nobody's fault, Amy,' she says. 'Not his, not mine, not your mother's, not yours, not the fault of any of the other women, not his research. It's like having cancer. Or like being damaged in a car crash. It's just one of those rotten things that happen.'

'It's *not*. It's not like having cancer. He can *do* something about it. Why doesn't he stay on his medication? Why?'

Sarah sighs. 'It's part of the condition, unfortunately. He believes he doesn't need it.'

'What about us?' Amy sobs. 'It isn't fair.'

'No.' Tentatively, Sarah touches Amy's long hair. 'It isn't fair. Especially to you. I'm so sorry, Amy.'

'Don't touch me,' Amy says. 'Don't you fucking touch me.'

Sarah feels immeasurably tired, far too tired to move away from Amy, to move back to the porch swing. The loon floats its long plaintive note across the railings. Sarah feels that after whatever is going to happen has happened, she will need to sleep for a year or so, like Rip Van Winkle, and then she will wake up and perhaps she will be again the person she once used to be. The past ten years will be erased. Her life will continue as though those years had never been, and she will have slept off the dangerous burr of attachment.

'I've decided I'm not going to college,' Amy says abruptly. 'I *had* accepted Wellesley already, but I cancelled and got the first term tuition refunded direct to me, not that Dad will notice. I've bought a round-the-world ticket with the money. I'm not hanging around waiting for him to decide whether to off himself or to win the Grand Slam of Mathematics. I'm going to India first. I've got a charter flight that leaves next week.'

She stands and walks down the steps and keeps walking. Sarah feels dizzy with panic. 'Your towel,' she calls stupidly, snatching it up and running after.

Over her shoulder, Amy says evenly: 'I don't want to know what happens. You can write if you want, on condition you never tell me what he's done.'

'Where will I write to?' Sarah asks.

'Post offices. American Express offices. Wherever. If you want.'

'Of course I want.'

'I'll send you postcards,' Amy says. 'If you want. So you'll know which country I'm going to next. And which city.' She is already at the end of the dock when Sarah reaches it. A pale gold light, faintly green, falls down through the leaves and spills from her shoulders, flowing down her back and over the curves of her buttocks, to puddle like wings at her heels. 'I have to take off,' she says, poised for flight, poised for diving, but not moving.

Sarah can feel, with a certain amount of dread, the sticky future, the burrs of obligation, the rush of protectiveness spreading like a contusion below the skin. Love is a virus, she thinks fearfully. It lurks around like malaria. Just when you think you are extricating yourself, just when you think you are cauterised and ready to leave, it resurfaces. Once you've been infected, you're never again completely free. It's a lifetime condition.

'Don't let go of my string,' Amy says in a little girl voice before she dives. There is scarcely a sound. Sarah sits on the end of the dock and watches the sleek white body underwater, smooth as milky opal shot from a bow. She shades her eyes and waits for a break in the surface. She waits and listens. Beneath her she hears a soft slapping against the pylons of the dock and she lies on her stomach and hangs over the edge, but sees only a water snake. 'Amy?' she calls. But there is no sign of Amy beneath the dock.

Sarah scans the unruffled skin of the lake, and the clumps of bushes and low-hanging trees that lean into it here and there. She waits. Amy is a strong swimmer and a secretive one. Perhaps she has grown gills. Perhaps she is watching Sarah from the reeds. Sarah waits until she hears the thunder of Amy's car thrashing its way back through undergrowth towards the road.

'Amy!' she calls, bounding up the slope, stumbling and slipping. 'Amy, wait! What day do you leave? What flight?' There is so much furniture in the way, and the verandah is the wrong way round. 'Stop!' she calls. 'Stop the car, stop!'

'Sarah, Sarah,' Mrs Given says, fluttering. 'They've stopped. But we don't know who they are.'

'I do,' Mercy says. 'I know the trucks. One is Donny Becker's ute.'

'I can't see Amy's car,' Sarah says, blinking.

'Donny's working the new mine out at Jimjimba now,' Mercy says. 'The other truck's Tim Doolan's. It's always parked outside the pub because he does opal-grinding for Bernie.'

Sarah sees a battered utility truck, more or less white, and a rust-corroded faintly blue Mazda at the far end of the Givens' drive, at that point where the bore-water-nourished oasis gives way to red earth. Dust is shifting around the tyres, and exhaust fumes fart upwards at intervals in blackish tufts. The cars are idling side by side, facing the house.

'Where are the dogs?' Mrs Given asks. 'Oh, why don't the dogs come? What does it mean?'

'I'm going out to talk to Donny,' Mercy says.

'Mercy, no!' Her mother clutches at her. 'No. We will stay on the verandah and pray. The Lord will protect us.'

Mercy extricates herself as gently as she can. 'We don't need the Lord's protection, Mum,' she says drily. 'Donny and I are good mates. He's probably come with a message from Ma Beresford, she must be back by now.' Mercy's tone is festive. She could be setting out to catch goannas again with Donny. 'Maybe you should make Sarah a cup of tea,' she says, over her shoulder.

'Oh where are the dogs?' Mrs Given moans. 'What does it mean?'

Mercy can see the men talking to each other through the car windows as they wait for her. Left foot, right foot, she has never realised how long the driveway is, Donny Becker would never hurt a fly, left foot, right, once he caught the most beautiful lizard that either of them had ever seen, quite tiny, with dark flashes of blue, like opals, on its scales, and he gave it to her, he put it into her two hands and his fingers brushed all the way up to her elbow and the lizard ran after his fingers, tickling the length of her arm and over her shoulder and slithering under her dress and between her breasts. She shrieked with embarrassment from the tickling, and Donny reached in and caught his lizard by the tail and took it out for her. But Mr Prophet saw them and they both had to confess at prayer meeting, and the whole congregation prayed that the works of darkness and of the flesh be cast out of them. Another time, in prayer meeting, Donny was next to her in the pew, and he ran his hand along her leg and no one saw. Mercy asked Miss Rover if she knew why everyone at the Living Word believed that God didn't want people to touch each other. Miss Rover laughed and said: 'I believe you will work that out for yourself very quickly, Mercy, in that sharp little mind of yours.'

The soft crunch of Mercy's sandals on the drive says Miss Rover, come over, come over and help me, I am trying to set it all down like you did, I am setting my left foot down, then my right, I am setting everything down. Miss Rover, come over, don't let them see I'm scared, do not let Donny Becker and Tim Doolan see that Mercy Given is frightened because she can smell in the stillness of the air that something is not quite right, that something is definitely wrong, do not let them see that Mercy Given's hands are beginning to tremble very slightly, because Mercy knows that fear is simply something she has made up, and she is going to unmake it, and she is determined to write the short history of Outer Maroo quite differently, she is going to change the ending, she is going to make it come out right, and that is why Mercy concentrates on her feet. She watches the bull ants scattering in paisley swirls around her sandals, she sends them into a frenzy with each step, they stream away from her like sprays of jet. She could lose herself in those mazy patterns, she could hypnotise herself.

'G'day, Mercy,' Donny says.

'G'day, Donny. G'day, Tim.'

Tim nods and says nothing.

'What do you want?' Mercy asks.

'Hop in,' Donny says. 'I come to take you back to Beresford's, Mercy. Ma wants to see ya. She's back.'

'Why didn't she telephone?' Mercy asks. She steps up to the driver's door of Donny's ute. There are beads of sweat above his upper lip. His suntanned arm, resting on the window frame, is almost touching her. She is very aware of the distance between her lips and his arm. She thinks of kissing it. She knows he wants her to. She can smell his pleasant Donny smell. His eyes rest on hers the way they did when he gave her the lizard.

'How come Ma didn't call me?' she asks.

'All the telephone lines are dead, didn't you know?' Donny swivels his eyes away and stares down the drive uneasily. 'Hop in, Mercy. We gotta go.'

'Why's Tim here?' she asks.

Donny shrugs. 'He was on his way to a stubby race.'

Tim gets out of his car and stands behind her. 'Get in, Mercy,' he says impatiently. 'My fan belt's gone. Gonna have to leave my heap here, and come back. We're both going back with Donny.'

'My dad keeps spare fan belts,' Mercy says. 'Only he's got them in the car, and he's out at the Dempseys'.'

'Shit,' Tim says. 'What's he out there for?'

'Because Grandma Dempsey's dying.'

'Shit,' Tim says.

'OK,' Donny says, suddenly animated, relieved. 'That's that, then. Get back in your car, Tim. Let's go.'

'Doesn't make any difference,' Tim says. 'That foreign woman's there, isn't she? That's the main thing. Get in, Mercy.'

'No,' Mercy says, her heart thumping loudly. 'I'm going to go back into the house to phone Ma first.'

'No, you bloody aren't,' Tim says. 'Because all the bloody phone lines are dead, we already told ya.'

'I don't believe you.' She touches Donny's arm with her fingertips. 'What's going on, Donny?'

'Nothing,' Donny says, not looking at her.

'We bloody haven't got time,' Tim says, grabbing her and pushing her towards the passenger side of Donny's ute. She kicks and struggles. Tim gets in the car, dragging her with him. 'Let 'er roll,' he yells at Donny, but Donny is staring through the windshield, paralysed. 'Will you give 'er an almighty jolt and get 'er rolling?' Tim yells.

'Let's call it off,' Donny says.

'Are you crazy? And what'll happen to us if we do? Ram the car, you fucking idiot.' Tim is gasping with the effort of pinning Mercy's arms. He knees her in the back and Mercy feels something like a ten-tonne bruise at the base of her spine.

'Mercy, I'm sorry!' Donny yells. 'I'm sorry, Mercy, I got no choice. It'll just be a fire, that's all. They'll get away.' He reverses at high speed, manoeuvres, accelerates, and drives straight for the back of Tim's car. There is a jarring crunch, and the empty car starts rolling slowly down the slight incline of the drive towards the house.

Time changes then. The air changes. The light changes.

Something strange happens in Mercy's ears. Everything goes silent. Everything floats in slow motion.

Mercy can see the intention ballooning in front of the windscreen, poised there like one of those floating balls of incandescent white light that drift from roman candles, she sees it hanging there, sees it in the rolling car, sees it in the anguish on Donny's face and in the leer on Tim's.

'No one'll get hurt, Mercy,' Donny is shouting. 'It's just to make her leave.'

'Teach your father a bloody lesson,' Tim snarls.

They are all three of them curled up and pressed against the dashboard from the collision, and now whiplash descends on them as a slow ballet. As they recoil, soundlessly, weightlessly, Mercy twists herself from Tim's pinioning arms, reaches for the door handle, launches herself into air. She rolls and rolls. She is one complete ball of pain and gravel-rash. Her mouth is full of dust and she is watching the number plate on Tim's car as it rolls towards the house.

'No!' Mercy screams. 'Miss Rover! Jess!' she screams, instinctively calling on the most powerful forces that come to mind.

She can feel almighty strength rushing into her from somewhere, she rolls on to her feet and then she sprints. She lunges at Tim's car, hangs on to the rear bumper and lets herself be dragged.

'Mercy, no!' she hears Donny yell. 'Run for it, Mercy, run!'

But the car is trundling sluggishly now, and Mercy can afford to let it go, and she springs up, and sprints alongside it and wrestles with the door handle and scrambles in. She is halfway down the drive, she can see her mother and Sarah on the verandah. She pushes the gear lever into reverse, and roars back out the gates. She swerves past Donny and presses her foot to the floor. Donny's car turns in a skirl of dust and chases her. She is heading for nowhere. She is heading west, where nothingness is. Fifty, sixty, eighty, one hundred kilometres per hour. Donny's car is gaining all the time. One hundred and twenty. One hundred and twenty-five.

She feels a wild and utterly fearless elation, and for the first time in her life understands the lure of stubby races, those outback death-meets where drivers guzzle an entire slab of beer stubbies while racing (right hand on the wheel, left hand holding the stubby, foot to the floor). The hummocky tufts of saltbush and the spiky bushes send the cars into orbit.

There are no tracks on the way to nowhere.

Anyone who reaches the finish line alive is a winner.

Have Donny and Tim been drinking? She cannot remember noticing if she smelt anything on Donny's breath. They are closing in on her, drawing alongside. Are they going to ram her? She's just ahead again, she can feel the hot breath of their car engine on her neck. At one hundred and thirty, she opens the door, hunches her shoulders, and hurls herself from the car. She rolls and rolls. She feels sandblasted. She feels as though someone has set her body on fire and is smashing her head with rocks.

She is dimly aware of a massive explosion, then another, and of a great ball of fire. Her ears sing a long high sustained note. Blackness comes up out of the earth to meet her.

Wednesday

Pointillism, Mercy thinks. That might be the right word for the pinprick swirls of dried blood. She has an earth rash on all exposed surfaces and on many unexposed ones, and touches herself gingerly, but each point of contact feels like a branding iron. Her thoughts swirl like smashed embers and scorch where they fall.

She keeps wishing again for the blank space that swallowed her one second after the explosion. There was no pain in that place, and no thinking. It was like black water. She longs to return there; she leans into the sweet currents of nothingness; she feels dizziness, nausea, a great racking wave of grief welling up. But just as she is gratefully swooning under, it passes. She is high and dry, stuck with consciousness.

Pointillism, she thinks fiercely, and for a moment the burning sensation that she wears like a body glove is soothed, but only for as long as she can hold the vowels inside her mouth. This is a word that invites exploration, a melodic word that wants to be sung as a brief falling phrase with sharp consonantal tips, though she is not at all sure of the pronunciation which is not explained in *Dictionary of*

Great Paintings of the Western World, one of Miss Rover's books. The illustrations in the *Dictionary* are not large and the paragraph on each painting is sometimes puzzling, as, for example: *La Baignade* by Georges Seurat (1859–1891). Mercy can see the heading, but has to turn pages in her mind to read off the entry, second from the top right-hand side.

> *One of the best known works of pointillism; that is, of the application of thousands of small dots of colour to the canvas. Looked at closely, the small dots of paint are apparent. From a distance, they blend to convey luminosity.*

Mercy holds her arm at a distance and squints until the dots of dried blood blend. From this angle, blurred through her lashes, her arm is undeniably shimmering, her arm has a certain . . . how would she describe it? . . . she would have to say her arm has a certain luminosity, yes – another word she so rarely has a chance to use in Outer Maroo. But suppose she had been born somewhere else? some place where Oyster had never closed everyone in on their shameful secrets? – in Brisbane, say; or in Boston; or in a village in Greece like Nick; and such hitherto unthought-of possibilities now tease and absorb her: the puzzle of where people happen to get born, and the difference this makes to their lives, and to the way they think. And what of the pointillist spikes of Mercy's thoughts about yesterday? Mercy's thoughts about yesterday do not bear thinking about, and she will not think them.

There are places where people think only in colour, in Paris, for instance, where Seurat and the Pointillists lived. Mercy imagines the pleasure of talking to painters, *painters*, and she has to pause and let her mind veer into a detour of amazement to ponder the idea of people who might say in Beresford's, over the fencing wire: 'Well, yeah, I'm a painter actually, been painting since the drought got serious,' and might say it quite casually, in the way that other people said, 'I'm a drover, mate; been taking cattle from the Top End to the Brisbane Yards since before the Year of the Flood.'

Mercy believes she would be more at ease in a world of people who think in colour. She tries to imagine Seurat and his friends in a pub in Paris. Mercy is there surreptitiously, out of sight, drying the glasses for Jess, keeping well below the windowline in case Mr Prophet or one of the elders passes by. She can see Seurat leaning on the bar with his foot on the rail, which happens to be the spitting brass image of the foot-rail in Bernie's.

Seurat is talking to Jess, '. . . working on several studies,' Mercy hears him say, 'at the moment,' he says, and he is watching the way the light falls amberly through his beer, 'of the Sea of Null,' he explains. He does not talk with motionless lips, as people in Outer Maroo talk, nor with a heavy nasal drag. Far from it. Mercy knows exactly how he would speak because she has heard on Miss Rover's radio, and on Jess's radio, the kind of voice that painters have. Seurat speaks beautifully, the way announcers do on the BBC World Service, except of course in French, '. . . hope to capture the luminosity of salt pans,' he says, 'with grains of white.' He has flecks of light in his eyes, and the white-hot sun, which pushes itself like peppershot through Bernie's blinds: '. . . why I'm salting my canvas with spots,' he explains, 'though one can never truly pinpoint light.'

Jess smiles and says nothing, and Mercy floats, the golden light bears her up, and Monet is there too, a little like Nick perhaps, and he leans across the bar from the facing page of the *Dictionary*. 'For luminosity,' he says, and he is pushing his empty stubby across the bar, 'I find smudging works better. You'll never capture the haze,' he says, 'and you'll never capture mirages with your method.'

They are both of them, Seurat and Monet, washed in mauve and gold light, and through the windows of the pub, through the translucent parchment of the blinds, the red earth is strangely thick with wild poppies that have bloomed in the wake of a cyclone, and inside, where the light is softest, waterlilies float in the puddles of beer on the floor, and the face of Donny Becker floats there too, reflected and golden (not yet erupting into soot and rockets of flame), but when Bernie comes out of the back room and takes more stubbies from the fridge, Mercy finds that she cannot stop Ma's Bill from butting in with some stupid smart-alec remark. *Hey, Seurat*, he will say (Mercy knows he will have to put his tuppence-ha'penny-worth in), *hey, Seurat, you're dotty, mate*!

That is the trouble with Outer Maroo.

'A real painting,' Miss Rover said, back in classroom days, back when Mercy mooned over her books after school, back when Miss Rover was still there to answer questions, 'is as different from those postage-stamp prints as a real kiss is different from reading about one.'

'Oh,' Mercy said, thinking of Donny Becker's hand on her leg in prayer meeting.

'Most of those paintings, for example,' Miss Rover said, 'are huge. They are not done on flat paper, but on canvas stretched tight on a wooden frame. An actual painting is vibrant with texture. You can't just look at it passively. It grabs you by the scruff of the neck.'

From memory, Mercy projects the little square of *La Baignade*, enlarged, on to the canvas of her mind. The boy on the green bank, in red swimming trunks, dangles his legs in the water. He is full of sharp points and spaces. He turns and looks at Mercy in a particular way, a *luminous* way, so vibrant that she cannot resist the urge to touch him and finds herself caressing the blue bolt of cloth from which Alice Godwin's mother ordered ten metres. She presses her lips against Ma Beresford's cash register. She sees that the boy has Donny Becker's eyes and lopsided mouth, and also his freckles. I am fishing for lizards, he says. If I catch one, I'll give it to you. She can feel his hand on her breast, but when he grabs her by the scruff of the neck and kisses her, he has the eyes of Gideon and of Nick. The moment his lips touch hers, he goes up in flames. Seurat was right, Mercy thinks, breathless. People are full of flashbulb spots and blank spaces.

According to the book that smoulders away in Aladdin's Rush, Seurat's painting hangs in its full size, as its real and dot-dotted self, on a wall in Europe somewhere. It is difficult to believe in Europe, but Mercy makes an effort to take the continent's existence on faith. After all, it requires just as much effort to sustain her belief in Aladdin's Rush these days, and everyone knows that Aladdin's Rush exists, everyone knows where it is, though no one dares to go there any more, and undoubtedly it has grown more fabulous since visits became too dangerous. Mercy embroiders it, perhaps. Perhaps she has added books to its secret store. The world is made of shifting points of sand which blow about and regroup themselves.

Seurat was right.

At Beresford's, no one asks Mercy what happened to her face. No one comments on the pointillism of her arms and legs. No one mentions that the phone lines are dead. No one mentions Donny Becker or Tim Doolan. When someone disappears, Mercy has noticed, they drop from Outer Maroo as a star falls through space. They leave no mark. The air closes over them. You are never quite sure if something happened or if you imagined it or if everyone imagined it at once.

She closes her eyes and sees Donny's bronzed arm on the door of the car. She remembers she thought of lurching forward a little, so that she might accidentally brush his arm with her lips, and now it seems to her that she can remember the taste of his skin. She can see his swollen veins, the way they run from elbow to wrist like the Macdonnell Ranges or like the Olgas on a relief map, and she can see the soft rust-gold pelt that she once felt against her own skin in the very shadow of the prayers of the faithful. Perhaps Donny twisted towards her, brushing aside the points of light, and whispered something in her ear. Maybe he said: *We could have one hell of a bang, Mercy.* Or possibly: *I'm delivering sparklers. I've got a long one especially for you. The luminosity has to be seen to be believed.*

She has his voice in her ear like a trapped mosquito: *Mercy, I'm sorry*! . . . *Run for it, Mercy. Run.*

Ten times an hour she hears him behind her. *G'day, Mercy*, he says, and grins. But when she turns around it is someone else. How is it possible, she asks herself, for people so suddenly to cease to be? It is not logical, it is not possible. How is it possible for people to do things you cannot believe they will do, that they themselves, perhaps, cannot believe they are doing or would ever do? We only know a few pinpoints of someone, Mercy thinks. We don't know the spaces in between.

The spaces in between make Mercy dizzy. She is falling again, there is no bottom to this fall, there is nothing to hold her up.

She turns pages frantically in her mind.

> *The Pointillists studied refraction. They made a precise distinction between an object's intrinsic colour and the colour it acquired from the light. They studied the interplay of one upon the other.*

Donny Becker grows brighter and brighter, but where did his white light come from? Who painted him shamefaced in front of the congregation? As God is my witness, he said, I gave her a lizard but I wanted to touch her. I had impure thoughts in my heart.

Who painted him into a car with a target address?

Who watched all his intrinsic colour disappear into radiance and into shooting oranges and reds?

Mercy leans on the counter at Ma Beresford's and sees herself reflected in its dull sheen as scarlet flypaper. She unfurls her sticky self to the world, she hangs from the ceiling by her bloodied, blackened feet. She draws flies to herself and when they touch her, *pouff!*, all their private colour goes up in smoke, and she is hurtling through dust again, she is crawling back, dragging herself, limping along towards her house . . .

She sees her mother again, she sees Sarah, she sees the verandah bucking about her like a kite, she is crawling back into yesterday, her hair singed, her body blackened, her ears behaving strangely and singing a long single high note that hums on and on and on . . . She is sitting in a deckchair and the world is Seurat-spotted, the world is a Monet fog of ochre and blue, the world floats about her like a dream.

'This is shock, Mercy,' Sarah says (that was yesterday; yesterday, late afternoon). Sarah is dabbing iodine on her skin. 'Believe me, I recognise it, this unnatural calm, and this drifting off into another world. This is just the first stage.'

Was that only yesterday?

It is strange, Mercy thinks, the way time can behave like the Indiarubber Man, the way it can stretch itself out to infinity, the way it can shrink. Yesterday . . .

Clipping the singed ends from Mercy's hair, Sarah talks on and on, as though she is afraid of silences, as though questions without answers might loom up through any of the gaps in her voice. It could mean, Mercy thinks, that Sarah is in a different stage of shock. You have to brace yourself, Sarah says, for the next stage, which is rage. And then there'll be shame, and the sense of yourself as evil because you never meant to kill them. And there'll be times of total panic, the panic you postponed. It'll come back and swamp you, Sarah says. You'll hardly be able to breathe.

'I know about this,' she says. 'Believe me, I know. It'll help if you tell us what happened.'

'It was an accident,' Mercy assures Sarah and her mother. 'It was a stubby race, and they dared me, that's all. It was the speed and the hot sun. It made the petrol tank explode.'

It *could* have been that, Mercy thinks. It could have been, it could have been. She would prefer this explanation. She thinks it must have been an accident. She begins to embroider this theory, she begins to make it her own.

To her father, hours later, she says nothing when they stand side by side, silent, alone, on the verandah in the dark. The planets dip by them. They stare at millions of stars.

'That was a brave thing,' he says gruffly.

The Milky Way wheels overhead.

'There's the Southern Cross,' he says.

She knows that he means: the sign of the cross watches over us, all this is in the palm of His hand, His ways are inscrutable.

She wants to pound against his chest with her fists in exasperation almost as much as she wants to protect him from threat. He seems to her now like someone in a paper boat in the middle of floodwaters. Only his belief in the boat keeps him from certain inundation. Mercy cannot bring herself truly to want to argue the illusion out from under him, because what would happen to him then?

'I found the dogs, Mercy,' he says very quietly. 'Both dead. Hit by a car. Don't tell your mother.'

'No. I won't.'

'I fear,' he says quietly, 'there'll be more . . . accidents.'

The silence seems deafening to Mercy, and thick and soft like a blanket. It stretches itself out and flaps around them, muffling thoughts that neither of them want to hear. She keeps feeling dizzy. She keeps feeling blood seeping wetly from her limbs. Her skin is still on fire. The painkillers are like cottonwool packed around her ears.

'I think,' he says, clearing his throat, 'that it would have been seen as a . . . as a further provocation on our part, inviting Mrs Cohen here.'

Of course, it would have been, it would have been. By everyone. *I wanted to provoke Mr Prophet.* The sudden awareness of reckless criminal intention winds Mercy, shocks her. But just the same . . . he is a sad kind of man, Mr Prophet; a man twisted out of shape by the pull of his own barbed-wire beliefs. But is it possible that Mr Prophet . . .? No. Mercy cannot seriously believe this. Mercy cannot seriously believe that any one human being could wish to engineer the death of any other, she cannot seriously believe that Donny Becker . . . *No one'll get hurt, Mercy . . . Run for it, Mercy, run . . .* Mercy has no idea what to believe. Deaths must emanate, mysteriously, from the Old Fuckatoo, yes, that must be it; or from evil thinking, from Mercy herself, for example, who has carelessly wished to provoke; from heedless, reckless, provocative, whorish, Jezebel-ish Mercy, who harbours sinful thoughts in her heart.

'I'm sorry, Dad,' she says, in anguish. 'I should have thought of you and Mum.'

'No, no, no. It was the right thing to do. I didn't mean that at all.' He gestures up at the stars. 'Our comfort and our strength, Mercy, is that we are each accountable only to God for our actions, and after that, whatever is going to happen is His will.'

Mercy has to hang on to the verandah rail. She closes her eyes, giddy, and waits for the buffeting torrent of irritation to pass. She asks in a low bitter voice, almost steady: 'Everything that has happened has been God's will? All of it?'

'Evil comes from man's failures, Mercy. Not God's.'

'Dad, I still feel dizzy – I have to sit down.'

'Yes, oh, of course –' And she leans on him until they reach the wicker chairs. His touch feels like glue. His God feels like a vast viscous stickiness. Wherever you step, God is already there. Mercy scrapes her feet, one at a time, against the rung of the chair. Around her, desert creatures make their ticking night sounds. Do they all find tracks that make sense? Mercy wonders; does the sticky sap of desert grass hobble them? do they burrow through the red dust in fear and trembling, always afraid of being lost, of being crazy, of being guilty of doing nothing, of being guilty of rash and heedless acts that breed death? Do their thoughts go round in useless circles?

'I blame my own failures in particular,' her father says heavily, 'for what has happened in Outer Maroo.'

'Dad –'

'I have failed my own son, above all.' Mercy has to avert her face. She listens with heightened concentration to the rhythmic pillowy thumping of a small covey of wallabies. She sees the syncopated arcs, shadowy, against the acacias. She counts fourteen of them. She can feel the drumming of their powerful hind legs in the boards beneath her feet.

'I leave things too late, Mercy,' he sighs. 'I'm slow to see evil. I believe in original goodness, I suppose. It's a heresy.'

They watch a possum, beady-eyed, on the verandah rail. It stops, stock still, aware of them, then vanishes into the dark.

'Just the same, I had a premonition at the Dempseys'. I tried to phone Brisbane. I dialled police headquarters, and got through.'

She turns towards him, astonished.

'The person who answered thought I was a crank. And of course the line was fuzzy, you could hardly hear, but I did explain. West of Quilpie and Eromanga, I said. And then the line went dead.'

'Yes. Everyone's.'

'It is a judgment on me,' her father says. 'This helplessness.'

'Dad, for heaven's sake.'

'Goodnight,' he says wearily, and goes into the house.

'Goodnight, Dad.'

And now Mercy is someone whose skin and whose thoughts are blacker. They still scald her. They blister. They begin to fester and weep. She is someone who sees herself in the dull sheen of Ma Beresford's cash register, embroidered savagely with pointillist sores.

She is someone who dreamed of touching and kissing Donny Becker, whose freckles were like shadows on the sun, and who once gave her a lizard, and who may or may not have tried to kill her even though he did not want her dead.

Mercy is someone who killed Donny Becker.

Mercy is someone who wants to sob till the end of time.

Mercy is someone who understands less and less, the more she learns.

Mercy would love to speak to Ma Beresford, who is back again, or to Ma's Bill of this, but Ma and Bill have rules that are infinitely elastic and infinitely strict. Nothing shocks them. You have to roll with the punches, they say, and moping is utterly out of bounds.

'Now, Mercy,' Ma says, motherly but with a warning frown when Mercy strokes her burning and Seurat-stippled arms, when Donny Becker swims in her mournful eye. 'Now, Mercy,' she says, 'accidents happen, and there are plenty more fish in the sea. Take your woebegone face out of here for a while, and sit out the back.'

Mercy takes her woebegone face and waits at the back door of Bernie's. She is looking for Jess. She peers in cautiously at the door of the back room where Bernie sits by his precise and delicate scales, weighing stones, holding them up to the light, assessing colour and pattern and fire. Already, at the grinding and polishing wheels, someone new has taken Tim Doolan's place.

'What the hell are you doing here?' Bernie asks, looking up suddenly.

I've got two opals, Mercy thinks of telling him, that a girl from the Reef gave me a long time ago, over a year ago. But then she remembers that she never accepted Amy's opals, though they weigh like blood weights in her mind.

'If you're looking for Old Silence,' Bernie says, 'she's out in the shed boiling sheets.' His eyes rest on Mercy's body-swirls and on the bruise-blue smudges, the purple clouds of tattoo. 'Can't you cover yourself up?' he asks crossly. 'You look like a bloody Maori.' He speaks as though Mercy is guilty of something obscene, gross bodily carelessness, perhaps, or self-abuse. 'If I might give you a bit of advice, young lady, I'd take a leaf out of Jess's book. Silence is golden.' He shakes his head at her in irritation. 'You look like you're dolled up for a corroboree. Don't go anywhere near the bar, or you're gonna give the blokes heartburn, you're giving *me* heartburn just looking at you.'

Mercy stares at him. She remembers Miss Rover on the verandah of his pub, the last day before she was transferred.

Who *is* Bernie? she wonders. Where did he come from? What would disturb him?

'What are you staring at?' he asks.

Nobody knows where the money comes from, she thinks. *And nobody knows where it goes.*

'Scoot!' Bernie says, and he jerks his thumb over his shoulder towards the shed.

The shed is of corrugated iron, it breathes out and breathes in, exhaling heat and steam from the copper, inhaling Mercy. She bats at the hot fog with her hands until she sees Jess folding sheets. 'Jess,' she says, 'oh, Jess,' and gets folded into Jess's arms and the fitted corners of a double sheet. Jess folds and folds and for the first time Mercy weeps and Jess rocks her and strokes her damp hair. 'He gave me a lizard,' Mercy sobs. Jess puts a finger against Mercy's lips. She does not try to stop Mercy's tears, but croons something deep in her throat. Weep into the washing water, her crooning says. Weep on to the sheets, wrap them around Donny in your mind, and then you can brush his skin with your eyelashes while he sleeps. She sets Mercy to stirring the wet sheets in the copper with a wooden pole until she is sweat and tears and steam.

Mercy thumps at the sodden mass of bedding with her stirring stick and turns and turns until there is a small funnel in the middle of her cauldron. Jess adds a potion of washing blue, and together they watch it bleeding into the water, inking the rippled dip of the hollow, climbing its whirlpool sides, turning the sheets mysteriously white, then whiter than white. Jess bends the considerable weight of her shoulders behind a second pole and turns and turns. This is the magic trick, Jess's body says. This is the secret. You keep stirring until all the painful questions go up in motion and fog.

Double, double, toil and trouble, Mercy thinks, seeing Donny Becker's face folded into white and washing blue, seeing his eyes and his lips, seeing Jess's reflection and her own in the spinning galaxies of sheet.

When shall we three meet again? the water asks.

When will Donny Becker and Tim Doolan and Mercy Given meet again at the end of a driveway?

'Jess,' she falters in anguish. 'How could *Donny* . . .? How could anyone make someone like *Donny* . . .?'

Hush, Jess's body says, stirring.

'But to *me*, Jess? To *me*.' Ultimately it is this, perhaps, that has so shaken Mercy: that Death has had the effrontery to breathe on her, that he has walked up to her and looked her in the eye and smirked. It must be a mistake. It must be a misunderstanding. Mercy has had sufficient intimations, before this, of the feral stench of hate. Hate is a hot beast, a mad dingo, a feral pig, the Old Fuckatoo, she knows that, she has smelt them all skulking around Outer Maroo for years now, especially for the last two since Miss Rover left, and especially, especially since the Reef disappeared; but it has never truly entered her head before that the beast might mark out Mercy Given as prey. 'To *me*, Jess,' she says, dumbfounded. 'To *me*.' To Mercy Given, sixteen years old, with so many books not yet read, so many lips not kissed, so many arms that have not brushed against hers.

Jess puts a steamy hand gently over Mercy's mouth. Hush, her hand says. You are alive, your parents are alive, both the foreigners are still alive, it could be worse.

The living float around Mercy like points of light, and so do the dead. She and Jess wrap them in the sheets.

Thursday

In Beresford's, people come and go. Junior Godwin comes bearing gifts in a brown paper bag. He sets his Akubra on the counter and stares at Mercy. 'My God,' he says, appalled. 'What happened?'

Mercy shrugs. 'There was a car crash, and someone's petrol tank blew up.'

Junior rakes his fingers through his hair, agitated. Mercy notes that he does not ask whose car was involved. She knows he is afraid to find out. 'Oh my God,' he says. 'I hadn't heard. I've got a new bull out at Kootha Downs, Mercy, got him at the Roma sales, a real beauty, a Santa–Hereford cross, Hannibull, we call him, sweet-tempered as a lamb. And all my best breeders are coming on heat at once.' He speaks breathlessly, like a schoolboy on the headmaster's mat. 'I've been working till I'm ready to drop.'

'It wasn't any of the cars from Dirran-Dirran,' Mercy says. 'None of your father's men.'

Junior Godwin swallows. He wipes beads of sweat from above his lip with the back of one hand. 'Thank God,' he says. He seems winded, and fans himself with his Akubra, crushing the brim in his hand. He pushes the paper bag across the counter. 'I think everything Mum took last week is here, Mercy, but if anything's missing –'

'Yes,' she says. 'Don't worry about it. Is Alice OK?'

'Oh Mercy,' he sighs. He strokes his Akubra in a frantic kind of way, as though this might soothe his young sister. 'Poor Alice. She's staying with us, with me and Delia. We had to get her away from Dirran-Dirran, from Mum, you know. I'm taking her out mustering with me, it's the only way to keep her mind off – She's a different kid on her horse.' He spins the Akubra on one finger, energised by a new idea. 'She'd love to see you, Mercy. You could come back to Kootha Downs with me now if you like.'

'No, I don't – I can't. I don't think I can leave right now. More foreigners have come, did you know?' It is actually possible, Mercy thinks, that Junior does not know, that he is unaware, though for anyone else in Outer Maroo, the question would be ridiculous. It is amazing, however, what Junior manages not to know. He lives in another dimension, with only cattle, horses, bulls. 'One of them, the woman, is staying with us,' Mercy says, 'so I can't – And our dogs. Something happened to our dogs, so I have to –'

'No, no. Yes, I knew there were visitors, that's why Alice had another bad turn.' He puts his elbows on the counter and buries his head in his hands. 'She's having terrible nightmares again, Mercy.'

Is there anyone in Outer Maroo who does not? Mercy wonders.

'And all the phone lines are down again,' he says, as though this has a bearing on Alice's nights.

'Yes.'

'What happened to your dogs?'

Mercy shrugs. 'Dead.'

'Shit,' Junior says. 'Oh shit. Shit, Mercy.' He punches the crown of his Akubra. 'Cows and bulls are the only sane people I know.'

'Yeah. Give Alice my love.'

'Yeah,' he sighs. 'Yeah, I will.' Absent-mindedly, he picks up the brown paper bag that is stuffed with Dorothy Godwin's purloined items of haberdashery, and leaves. Halfway to the door, he turns back and sets it on the counter again. 'I'm glad you're all right, Mercy,' he says. 'I'm glad no one from Dad's –' He swallows. 'It's the drought, you know. It's the drought that's done this to people. The bloody Old Fuckatoo. Anyway, thank God you weren't . . .'

'Yeah,' she says.

Voices come and go through the screen door at Beresford's. From across the road, Mercy hears the hallelujahs of the Living Word, she hears the prayers of supplication and jubilation, she hears the thunder of Mr Prophet's voice. It is the time of the afternoon prayer meeting, which Mercy no longer attends.

'There were, in the days of the Israelites,' Mr Prophet thunders, has so often thundered, both before and after Oyster, before and after Miss Rover, before and during and after so many prayer meetings that Mercy cannot be sure if she is hearing him now from across the street, or hearing him with her inner ear, and she cannot therefore tell if the text refers to anything present and particular or not, 'there were those who did not as the Lord commanded. We read,' he says, 'in the Book of Leviticus, chapter 10, that *there went out fire from the Lord, and devoured them, and they died before the Lord. And their remnants were shown to the people as a warning of the wrath of God.*

'Let us remember,' Mr Dukke Prophet warns, has so often warned, 'let us remember the fiery power of the Lord God of Hosts, lest we offend against Him in thought or deed.'

And their remnants were shown to the people, Mercy thinks, and pieces of Donny Becker fall as brimstone, as burning rain.

Somewhere in Aladdin's Rush, she remembers (though how can she be sure what she is remembering and what she is making up, given that what she thinks she is remembering is so much more fantastic than what she thinks she has made up), somewhere there still exists, or has been imagined, a box of Miss Rover's notebooks and journals. *Remnants*, an essay by Susannah Rover, she remembers; 'the sort of thing I want you to do with the set topics,' Miss Rover says.

'A taste for subversion,' she says, 'is a useful skill. It's important to turn ideas inside out, Mercy: to look at the linings, the underpinnings, the hidden seams. Unpick them with satire,' she says. 'See what happens.

'Take *Remnants* for instance,' she says, 'a typically meaningless "set topic" dreamed up by some curriculum consultant in Brisbane. Very likely the curriculum consultant has just spent her lunch hour at a remnants sale in David Jones'. She wants a perky little essay about tables crowded with coloured squares, something impeccably written, mannered, shot through with verbal silk. But we have more leeway in the private schools, Mercy, especially a private school like this one, so well endowed.' She pauses to laugh and cannot stop laughing. 'So very dubiously endowed, and so very exclusive,' she says at last. 'That's our advantage,' she says. 'We can be disreputable. Spread your wild wings. Invent. You can tell the entire bizarre truth if you set your mind to it.'

Mercy is startled. 'But inventing isn't telling the truth,' she objects, 'and that's a sin.'

'Ah, sins,' Miss Rover says. 'There are some very inventive sinners in Outer Maroo. To write about them, you'd have to be as fabulous as the Bible, don't you think? You'd have to invent a secret code like the whale who swallowed Jonah for the Oyster who swallowed a town. Of course no one would believe you, but the record would be there. I think you could do it, Mercy, if you let your imagination take off.'

But what is the relationship, Mercy wonders, if the Pointillists are right, between the intrinsic colour of a certain event and the colour it takes on when what you remember is all muddled up, or when thinking about it makes you frightened? If we invent things and write them down, is it like killing a goanna in one of the outer paddocks where the bulls are kept? The dead goanna brings the ants and the ants bring a snake and the snake bites the jackaroo's leg and the jackaroo dies and then the bulls snort and get restive and spook the cattle and the cattle are never mustered because the jackaroo is dead so they stampede and break the fence and head for the Red Centre and turn feral.

If an essay lies in a box somewhere, in an abandoned opal mine, does it ferment?

Mercy sees herself sorting through boxes and finding a battered carton crammed with blue-covered foolscap sheets. She leafs through them for 'Remnants: a brief history of the relationship between the outback and the automobile', by Susannah Rover. She turns pages in the Aladdin's Rush of her mind.

REMNANTS
by Susannah Rover

1. Breakdown

When a car breaks down in the outback, the place where it stalls is its tomb. It will never be towed to anywhere else. The outback is littered with metal skeletons which blister in the sun and corrode and rust and slump into the earth. If the hulks are beside a major tourist route, where fleets of King's and Australian Pacific coaches bring the comfort-loving air-conditioned intrepid tourists, they will eventually receive a dignified burial sponsored by the Shire Council and the State Government. From time to time, the candidates for burial are the tourist coaches themselves.

2. Burial

At irregular intervals, either mystically or electorally determined, the local and state governments, mindful that outback tourists are romantics, send forth convoys of bulldozers and earth-moving equipment. These roll along the Mitchell and the Capricorn and the Warrego Highways, ploughing under the charred frames of former automobiles. The tourists, who come with preconceptions of space kept pure and untouched by human muddle, pay handsomely to have their preconceptions kept intact. What archaeologists of the next millennium may surmise, uncovering so many steel ribs and chrome tibia and fibula, we can only guess at.

3. Beyond the Black Stump

Of course, beyond the range of the Mitchell and Warrego Highways, anything goes. It is beyond all economic sense for any petrol station to tow. It is outside the bounds of viable economy to own a tow truck. As the Royal Automobile Club of Queensland makes quite clear, minor spare parts should be carried with the motorist at all times. If a problem arises for which a motorist is not equipped, he can radio for help on his CB. If he cannot radio for help, he has been extremely foolish, and will have to pray, or die of dehydration, or both. If he has radioed for help, eventually (though no one can promise how many hours or days he may have to wait), someone will come out to collect him and drive him back to the nearest town. If the motorist thinks his mechanical problems are relatively minor, he may arrange to take the requisite spare parts and a qualified mechanic out to his vehicle, though this is costly. Qualified mechanics are not easy to find; unqualified ones are available, but charge higher.

4. Remnants

When the motorist gets to his car, he will find it charred because the heat of the sun on the metal frame will have ignited the petrol tank. It is important to remember that midday temperatures are often around 50 degrees Celsius. If the motorist has been lucky enough to have his petrol siphoned off by a scavenger before the midday heat, he will find that his car has been stripped to the axles by the same, or by other, recyclers. This is always neatly done, both inside and out. Tyres, hubcaps, wheels, mirrors, numberplates, aerials, all engine parts, radio (naturally), steering wheel, seating and springs will be taken. The metal frame will be left in good condition, generally unmolested, but as the cost of towing will be higher than any possible reimbursement from a wrecking company or scrap-metal firm, the motorist should pronounce a blessing on the remnant and leave.

'Let your words fashion shapes unpredictably, Mercy,' Miss Rover advises; 'as mirages do.'

'Yes,' Mercy says. 'I do.' She leans into the lost afternoons, listening to forbidden radio. 'You mustn't idolise the ABC and the BBC World Service,' Miss Rover warns. 'They're formulaic, really. Spread your wings and fly higher than that.' But Mercy does idolise them, especially now that she can only hear them in her head. She spreads her wings and flies back to them, to all the illicit and crackling shortwave afternoons, all the lambent bell-like FM tones, all lost to her now; all the lovely voices, all the crisp ideas, they are all gone into the world of static.

It was the absolute confidence of those voices that so fascinated Mercy. There were so many different ways, she saw, of being certain you were right: there was her father's quiet way, and Oyster's way, and Mr Prophet's way. And then there was the way of the voices on the radio, which was just as certain, and just as dogmatic, but different. This is the truth, their tone said calmly, and no intelligent person will dispute it, but we will still be quite polite and only discreetly supercilious if you are not sufficiently well informed to believe us.

'When you write,' Miss Rover says, 'I want you to use your own voice, Mercy; the one you use to ask me your unnerving questions.'

'What is my voice like?' Mercy asks, surprised.

Miss Rover laughs. 'Original,' she says. 'Because your kind of innocence is so weird, Mercy, and you don't even know it. John Locke would have loved you.'

John Locke. Mercy estimates that she heard of more unknown things in a day from Miss Rover than she would ever live long enough to look up in Miss Rover's books.

Miss Rover laughs. 'Mercy,' she says, in the particular tone that signals a huge and private joke, 'you'll need to update *Remnants*. You'll need to write a second draft. You'll have to throw in car duels, ten-stubby races, apocalypse utes, the whole shebang.' She goes on laughing, and then suddenly turns quiet. 'I have a horrible feeling, Mercy, that I'm going to do something grand and pointless and irrevocable quite soon. I'm not going to be able to stop myself.'

The big bang, the Oyster gang, the whole shebang, Mercy thinks, leaning against the cash register in Ma Beresford's. She still gets a singing in her ears, and popping sounds, she still gets the flashes of Tim Doolan's car going off, then Donny's. Lightheadedness comes and goes. Her pointillist limbs itch and burn.

In Beresford's, though business is not brisk and time passes languidly, people do come and go, buying spare parts and dried parsley and bull bars and roo bars and cotton cloth. BERESFORD'S BULL BARS REALLY DO BUMP BULLS, reads a hand-lettered sign. Pete Burnett needs a fan belt for his auger. Jess is buying sacks of potatoes and grain. Mr Prophet is buying leather boots.

'Pete,' Mercy says in a tentative and foolhardy moment, 'do you remember that day Miss Rover was transferred?' She is surprised to find she has said this. Pete lurches as he turns to look at her, and tries to catch hold of one of the shelves, and then in mid-turn something odd happens to him, or perhaps it happens to Mercy, perhaps something slows down the messages to her brain. At any rate, Pete seems to wince and hug himself as though shot, then to finish his turning infinitely slowly, sleepwalking, sleep-turning, his arms weighted with lead. His eyes are alarmed. 'You remember? That day she'd been drinking a bit,' Mercy says, 'and she called you out on to the verandah at Bernie's.'

Jess lifts a sack on to the counter.

'Hello, Mercy,' Mr Prophet says. His voice is always gravelly and bronchial, conveying benediction from a great height. He appears to notice nothing unusual in Mercy's appearance. He appears not to notice Pete Burnett. 'I've been meaning to tell you that we've missed you.'

'Hello, Mr Prophet,' Mercy says. 'You saw me on Monday.' She holds her breath and counts to three. 'Before I got dressed up for the corroboree,' she adds flippantly.

There is a momentary flicker of shock in Mr Prophet's eyes, but it dwindles into something expressionless. 'I mean that we have missed you in the House of the Lord, Mercy.'

'It was the day the foreigners arrived,' Mercy says.

'Your guest is welcome too, of course,' Mr Prophet says. 'In the House of the Lord.'

Mercy thinks of telling him that Sarah is Jewish, but decides against it because the meaning of this is still mysterious to her and she has not yet raised the subject with Sarah. It was not a topic Miss Rover ever touched upon. It does not appear to be covered by Miss Rover's books. Of course there is a wealth of information in the Bible, and Mercy is very familiar with it, but Sarah has said that she is not at all like the Jews in the Bible. Mercy is nevertheless still tempted to mention the matter because intuition tells her that Mr Prophet would be disturbed by the information, and such a prospect is pleasing to her, is almost irresistibly pleasing; but this temptation is typically reckless and sinful, and indeed dangerous, on Mercy's part.

She climbs on the stepladder and takes down boxes of R.M. Williams boots. 'What size, Mr Prophet?' she asks.

'I understand,' he says, 'that there was some trouble with stubby races near your place.'

'No,' Mercy says. 'I don't think they were stubby races.'

'It's a terrible problem, young men and alcohol. And the Lord sometimes has harsh and fiery ways to call a community to repentance. In the Day of Judgment, the Bible tells us, only a Remnant of the faithful will be saved.'

'I think these size tens will fit you,' she says.

'I hope you will be in the Remnant, Mercy.'

'Do you?' she asks, surprised, looking up from prodding his foot through the leather. She touches the bruises and gravel rashes on her arms delicately. 'Do you really, Mr Prophet?'

His eyes waver, and it occurs to Mercy suddenly that he is as frightened as everyone else, that he has to stave himself into the armour of biblical texts every morning to keep himself upright and safe.

'The world is full of evil, Mercy,' he says. 'Full of the forces of darkness.' He is sitting in the chair Ma keeps for the trying on of boots, and his fingers grip the thin wooden arms. His fingers are white, the knuckles almost blue. 'It is like a canker, Mercy. It is everywhere. It is in the government, in the schools, in godless schoolteachers who poison our children's minds. It is in the goods which come to us from Brisbane, it is in the outside world bearing down on us. We have to raise up the standard of the Lord, we have to raise money for the armies of God, we have to arm ourselves against that Last Day when the gathering forces of the Prince of Darkness –'

There is a sharp pistol crack of splintering wood, and Mr Prophet, shocked, stares at the dagger of chair-arm in his hand. He blinks, disoriented. A bead of blood swells on his index finger and runs slowly towards his wrist.

'Mr Prophet,' Mercy says awkwardly. He looks so pale that she wonders if he is ill. She reaches for his hand. 'You've grazed the skin,' she says. 'Wait, I'll get –' She goes to the shelves of home remedies and takes ointment, a box of Band-Aids, a bag of cotton puffs. 'Give me your hand again.' It is the gnarled hand of a cattleman, leathery. She notes the dark scaly blotches on the skin. 'If Beverley wants me to read stories to her again,' she says, full of compunction, 'I could come out and visit one evening.'

Mr Prophet withdraws his hand. 'Thank you, Mercy,' he says, though she has the impression that the words are like pieces of wood in his mouth.

'She must get awfully lonely out at Jimjimba.' Beverley, she means, who is eight years old, and who has been rescued from the godless life of school. 'Tell her –'

'Mercy, that's very –' Something that is perhaps intended as a smile crosses his face, though the muscles of eyes and mouth go tense. '. . . kind,' he says. He grimaces. Softness frightens him, Mercy sees; he translates it as weakness. He looks at her sorrowfully. 'You see, Mercy, if a cow or a sheep is diseased, it is not a kindness to leave it living, is it? It is not a kindness to let it suffer, and to let infection spread through the herd. You understand that, don't you?'

Poor Beverley, she thinks. Poor Mr Prophet.

'We cannot let Beverley be contaminated,' he explains, in a tone which Mercy supposes he means to be gentle. '*Come ye out from among them, saith the Lord, and touch not the unclean thing.* That godless schoolteacher, Mercy, has turned you from the path of righteousness in ways you do not even realise. And then there are those who erect their pride in learning,' he says, delicately studying his boots, delicately avoiding direct reference to her father, 'into an obstacle between themselves and God . . . All this is the cancer of sin, Mercy.'

Mercy says as evenly as she can, indicating the blotches on his hand: 'You should have those cancer spots looked at, Mr Prophet. At the hospital in Roma when you're there for the cattle sales. You should have them removed.'

Mercy is conscious of Pete Burnett and of Jess at the edges of the room, but no one moves. She has the odd sensation of being on a slow swing, Beresford's drifting and dipping under her. She feels queasy. The Old Fuckatoo is brooding close, his fungal stink wafts along the aisles, they may all run out of air, Mercy thinks. The silence seems to be endless, though Mercy supposes that only seconds pass.

'There is a spirit of rebellion in you, Mercy,' Mr Prophet says sadly. 'We are praying for you.'

Mercy can feel a sudden throbbing in her arms, she can feel her spirit of rebellion beating its wings, she can feel the same dangerous thing that beat in her as she revved Tim Doolan's car to one hundred and thirty and jumped. She understands, suddenly, what Miss Rover was drunk on that day on the verandah at Bernie's, that day of her transfer, she understands what kept her so apparently lighthearted, what kept her so calm. It is an unnatural calm, Mercy knows that now. It is a dangerous calm. It is something one feels like a shimmer on the surface of one's skin. Mercy knows from the way Pete Burnett is looking at her that her eyes are glittering. It is even possible, she thinks, that this is what was happening to Oyster when his blue eyes burned, when he mesmerised anyone who looked, and the thought that she and Miss Rover and Oyster might all have something in common brings on such a shock of nausea that she tastes a thin bitter liquid in her mouth. Even so, she cannot apply any brakes. What is most dangerous of all about this glittering shimmering state is that it pushes up inside her like a cyclone and she cannot resist.

She lifts Mr Prophet's foot into her lap and kneads his ankle and instep, pressing the soft leather, assessing the fit. She bends forward over his leathered shins and looks up into his face. 'Are you praying for me the way you prayed for Donny Becker?' she asks.

At the edge of things, Mercy can see Pete nervously wiping the back of one hand across his forehead, but she does not blink, she does not drop her eyes from the face above. Mr Prophet goes still in the manner of someone who has just been slapped in the face. He withdraws his foot from Mercy's lap and stands. He raises both hands, palms open, fingers extended, high above his head. 'Lord,' he cries, as though in anguish. 'Lord, how long?' His closed eyes are raised and he addresses a presence beyond the ceiling. 'Lord,' he implores, 'with the Psalmist I cry unto You: Remember the reproach of Thy servants . . . Remember Thine enemies . . . wherewith they have reproached the footsteps of Thine anointed.'

Like the coming of rain – of which Mercy, like everyone in Outer Maroo, has fantasies – Ma Beresford arrives from the storeroom with a carton of tinned pineapple resting on her stomach like a misshapen child. She breathes heavily from the effort, and the carton slips a little in her arms. She lets it slide to the counter and bends over it and rests her head against it for a second. Perhaps it is the horizontal perspective, Mercy thinks, that lets Ma see the scene differently.

'You look very silly like that, Dukke Prophet,' Ma says. 'Put your hands back in your pockets where a man's hands belong, or else give me a lift with this stuff. I got rules here, and no carrying on with the Lord in public is one of them.'

Dukke Prophet flinches and seems to wake from a trance. So does Mercy. There is just a membrane, she thinks, between one world and another. When you pass through that membrane, the meaning of everything changes. Gestures, words, thoughts, emotions: none of these things are translatable. On one side of the membrane, Mr Prophet is powerful and dangerous; on the other side, he is ridiculous;

he is just a pathetic old man as frightened of the world as anyone else. But is it not possible, Mercy asks herself, that he is both of these things at once?

Is Mercy the only person in Outer Maroo who moves back and forth across the membrane? She envies Mr Prophet and Ma Beresford who know only the language of one world, who see only one way. As for Mercy, who knows too many languages, but is at ease in none of them, she feels exhausted. Perhaps I will blow apart into little pieces, she thinks. Like Donny.

Mr Prophet lowers his hands slowly and picks up his hat. 'Tell your father,' he says to Mercy, 'that we are praying for him also. The Lord saith that he who is not for us is against us. Remember that, Mercy.'

Yes, she thinks. I will.

'Tell your father that the Spirit of the Lord is pressing me. God will hold out an olive branch, but He will not be mocked. It will be a sign, Mercy. Whether the Given family returns to the Living Word with a contrite and humble spirit, and seeks to be re-fellowshipped, or whether the Given family keeps itself at a stiff-necked distance, you will give us your sign, and that sign will not be overlooked.'

Mercy watches him look vaguely at his old boots, laid neatly to one side. He cannot seem to remember why they are there. Only Ma Beresford bustles about as though everything is as normal as ever. Jess, still and silent, watches Ma. Pete Burnett has not moved. He holds the fan belt in his hands and stares at Mercy, who stares at Mr Prophet, who stares at his old and new boots.

Friday

When he sleeps, Major Miner is always in tunnels. He always has explosives in his hands. What moves him is that musty fragrance, subdued, loamy, faintly sweet, faintly rotting, of nitroglycerins in dark enclosed spaces. If he feels the walls of his tunnel, he can tell immediately where its weaknesses run, he can press his ear against the rock and hear the soft hum of restive fault lines and feel them shifting and stretching and resettling themselves. He is aware of them as a pulse against his finger pads. They vibrate in his inner ear. Geological planes, meeting and overlapping, send out signals: long sonic pips which he decodes. The sedimentary layers give off mellow notes which are blurred at the edges, and he can detect undertones both throaty and plaintive that remind him of oboes. He does not know where these reading skills come from – they are like a sixth sense – but he knows that his quirky affinity with wombats and roots and all things that feel their way in the dark is a dubious blessing. It is as though he had been born with a deformity, a useless extra, something quite shameful and best kept hidden, but one which can be made to yield up a double-edged sideshow value akin to that of the circus careers of a calf with a dangling fifth leg or a woman thickly matted with pelt from head to toe.

When sleep closes in on Major Miner, the walls of his dreams breathe and sigh. Often, too often, he is huddled down in bunkers or latrines. There are bombers overhead. Singapore falls and falls in the present continuous. Sometimes he is crab-walking, sucked-in, flattened, through vertical fissures in rock, and he feels like the soft centre of a sandwich. He expects constantly to be eaten. Bridges, or the steel lacework of radio towers, soar above him, eagle-beaked, and their pylons send down clawed talons; the talons grope for him. Ear against the rock, he can hear the thick bass notes of their foundation stumps. He feels for the intimate crevices, the vaginal folds, where he will slide the gelignite.

At other times, the sky seen through cracks is vast and empty and painfully blue and full of a fierce white light that sears his eyes, and he curls gratefully into his burrow, sunblind, hypersensitive in the dark. Along the walls, and pendant from the arced ceiling, he can feel the cobwebby nap of roots, the infinitely fine delta-ends of them (or are they in fact the beginnings, the alpha hairs where the very idea of the tree begins?) The roots feel like cornsilk, like angelhair, like the cloudy outer fuzz of silkworms' cocoons. This is where opal sings to him its siren song, and he could be at Coober Pedy, or Andamooka, or Mintabie, or Lightning Ridge, or at Yowah in western Queensland – he has worked all the fields since the war, he is a junkie, opal has him in thrall – or he is beyond all those known fields, beyond west, beyond anywhere, he is in Outer Maroo, and then he presses his whole body against the earth and his heartbeat sends out a signal and a signal comes back, and so it is that opal and the Major commune like two fax machines whistling to each other, cooing in their upper electronic registers the way they do in the latest high-tech deals of Andrew Godwin and Dukke Prophet with foreign gem-brokers; and then the capillaries of glittering, colour-jangled, water-spiked silica sing to Major Miner like choirs of angelic children, their plaintive voices descant, otherworldly, and pure.

He knows how to reach them. He can part rockface from rockface like a lover, gently, to expose the glowing smears of boulder opal unblemished. He was trained in explosives. The calibration of detonation velocities is his speciality, he can calculate *brisance* to the fineness of a hair, he can tame ammonium nitrate, the truly wild one; he can make it jump through hoops at his bidding; he knows exactly how many grains of inert desensitiser will slow TNT and cyclonite to slow burn.

In Singapore, not long before the cataclysm and the capture, one of his mates in the explosives unit had gone reclusive and oriental. It was fatalism, Major Miner thought; a way of preparing; and not, in the Major's opinion, the best way. They were both junior officers; Major Miner was nineteen, his friend twenty-one; they were both little more than frightened kids. His friend had taken to reading Confucius and the *Tao Te Ching* and Chuang-tzu. He told Major Miner the story of Prince Wen Hui's cook. Prince Wen Hui, touring his kitchens one day, admired his cook's flawless ease as a butcher. Beneath the cook's hands and beneath his blade, the carcass of an ox seemed to fall apart, neatly segmented, as though it were made of softened butter.

That is amazing, Prince Wen Hui exclaimed. What is your method?

I have no method, the cook said. I follow the Tao.

A good cook, he explained, needs a new cleaver once a year. He cuts. A poor cook needs a new one every month. He hacks. I have used the same cleaver, O prince, for nineteen years, and it has carved up a thousand beasts. That is because I see nothing with my eye, but instead, with my whole being, I give myself attentively to the mystery of the body of the ox. Then I let the blade follow its instinct. It finds the secret openings and the fine spaces between joints. I cut through no joint, Your Highness, I chop no bone. The ox falls apart. I clean the blade and put it away.

'This is a story that Chuang-tzu told,' Major Miner's friend said.

That is how it is with explosives, they both agreed. It is a matter of listening to the rock with the body and the mind and the sixth intuitive sense, and then the mountainside parts itself from itself in a slow and exquisite ballet.

'We could survive prison camp by this method,' his friend said.

'We could *avoid* prison camp,' the Major fiercely amended.

'But *if* . . .' his friend said. '*If*. It would be a way to survive.'

'A way to escape,' the Major argued, annoyed.

'Escape and escapism are not the same things,' his fellow junior officer said. 'We have to be realistic. We have to be honest.'

The Major could feel anger rising within him like a fever. 'It is not dishonest,' he said, 'to know in one's bones that one will never be unfree.'

'Ah,' his friend said. 'That is not exactly the question. Freedom, ultimately, is an inner condition. But we have to be prepared. When the worst happens, and in war it often does, the Tao is a way to live, a way to survive.'

'Perhaps,' Major Miner murmured, though of course he had not yet become Major Miner; he had a different name then; he was not a Major at all, he was still a minor. He was not even Minor Miner, he was Minor Somebody Else, but it no longer seems to him relevant to remember that name. It belonged to a different life.

As for the junior officer with Taoist leanings, whose name, in the profoundly ironic way of things, was Robert John Blow – and who was known in the intimate circles of the army's blasting clique as Joe Blow – as for Joe Blow: he did not live to see prison camp, but died *en route*, messily, of bayonet hacks, his butchers not cutting with the principles of the Tao on their minds. After his death on the day of the fall of Singapore, the day of capture, Joe Blow entered Major Miner's head like a slow-smouldering mix of nitrates and sodium chloride. He took up residence there throughout the years in the camp. He brought his Chuang-tzu story with him. And Major Miner did in fact move through gaps between brutalities, he did shelter in the interstices of camp starvation, he did survive in the wafer-thin chinks of possibility until peace broke out.

Often and still, Major Miner hears Joe Blow's quiet and hesitant voice; it is like a very long, very slow fuse with a punch at the end of it. He hears Chuang-tzu in the rockface of Queensland. He listens for fault lines. For years, also, he would listen to the stresses and the sudden pressure changes and the growling burn of his gelignite. He would fit the blade to the opening. He would marry the sounds.

Then his hearing became even more acute, his whole body became an ear. He could scarcely tell where his own vein ended and a vein of opal began. Like Prince Wen Hui's cook, whose blade never needed replacing, he ceased to require explosives. News of opal came to him at the speed of visible light, at high inaudible frequencies that burned in his inner ear. He owed this extension of his listening range to Bugger Harvey, another old loner out in the breakaways, a bushie, a fossicker, an old soldier, an opal man; and he owed it also to the Murris who camped in the riverbeds and who were the Bugger's mates.

Major Miner knows that the universe is full of noise. He knows that the black void of space between stars is neither black nor void nor silent, but luminous with radiation and thickly washed with waves of sound: with short waves and with long waves and with waves of a frequency far too high for the human ear. For a while, after the war, after the explosives unit, he remained in the engineering corps. He monitored vast saucer antennae in the outback isolation of Woomera, and he knows that a babble of sound, a constant hum of galactic static, reaches earth without pause from deep space. This hum is received at numerous global sites (usually military, sometimes academic), wherever there are listening satellite ears that can pick up the tight ribbon-pleated wavelengths that are shorter than radar. He who hath ears to hear, the Major knows, can pull messages from the air. And so it does not surprise him that there are opal rushes, that suddenly a whole regiment of listeners – Bugger Harvey and the Murris, for example, followed so quickly by Oyster, and then by Oyster's fey and growing crew – it does not surprise him that they begin to tune in suddenly, like a line of Telecom Australia repeater stations, to the sweet piccolo call of hydrated silica cells densely packed: that mother of all prisms, that hard-rock disco-beat diffractor of white light, the black opal.

The buzz of all those foreigners arriving, all that opal excitement in the air, is still with him, even though his dreams have turned dark again and all the young foreigners have gone. He sleeps in his shack in the breakaways and the seams that run beneath him sing a high descant lullaby, but then darker notes interfere, and he smells Singapore burning, smells the bamboo cage and the latrines, smells the Old Fuckatoo.

He wakes with a cry, uneasy.

He remembers how the worst things happened just before the end, when the captors sensed the turning of the tide. He can smell that same madness in the air now. He could smell it at Bernie's last night, the way it came off Andrew Godwin like a sweat, the way it rose from the hunched bodies in the bar like the stink of unwashed clothes. It was because the foreigner, Nick, was drinking with them.

Early morning sun fingers the floor of his shack, and the ladders of white light streaming through chinks in the galvo roof all seem to him to lead downwards, only down. He hears the dark note again, the bass one that sang in his dream. It rides in on the dust motes, and all his senses stand on tiptoe. The sound is distant and faint, but he reads it. Andrew Godwin's Troopie, he thinks, and sits bolt upright. He can tell from the way the burr of the motor reaches him that the truck is not moving towards the opal fields, but away from them, towards Outer Maroo, towards Bernie's Last Chance, which he had seen Andrew leave just a few hours earlier, at a wee drunken hour of the night. And now it is barely dawn.

Major Miner is not comforted.

He needs someone to talk to, he needs to report the Singapore smell, the madness smell, and what it means and what might be done before it is too late, but the need itself frightens him. For so long now he has found it easier to confide in rocks and sky than in people. He is a loner. In Bernie's, where he shows up perhaps once a month, he can spin small talk on cattle and opal and the drought, especially once the lubrication kicks in, but his talk skims across the surface of his life. He does not go for the talk, he goes for the silences. Jess's silences. For a few years now, he has taken to believing that some indefinable connection exists between himself and Jess. He watches her hand on the brass lever when she pulls his beer and then sets it on the counter in front of him. Before she quite lets go, he reaches for the glass. Occasionally they brush fingers, usually not, but always there is that second when both of their hands are on the glass. Though she never meets his eye, he has come to invest that particular moment with power: he thinks of it as the point where the transmitter waves kiss the force field of the receiver. He has taken to fantasising that their two silences commune with each other like opal seams giving off high sonic pips. He has never wished to risk putting his theory to the test.

Now his compulsion to talk is driving him into his clothes, though he fumbles and trips. He can think of only two people to whom it might be possible to say what he wants to say, to whom he might be able to explain: Charles Given and Jess.

He finds that his truck has decided on Jess.

By Friday, the Old Fuckatoo is nesting down so heavily on Outer Maroo that it is difficult to breathe. Bush flies, always bad, are worse. Black balloons of them kite about in thick little swarms. The breakaways, upside down and bent out of shape, float on the wrong side of town, rust-red, bleeding into the pale sand of the riverbed, a mirage full of horribly ominous symbolism, it seems to Jess.

She thinks the whole town may self-combust at any moment; that the sun and the methane gas will tango together; that *kaboom*, Outer Maroo will go up in smoke. She thinks everyone senses in the bones that the secrets cannot be sealed up any longer.

Everyone's nerves are shot.

Everyone fears (or hopes) that another accident is arranging itself.

When Jess climbs the stairs to the guest room in the early morning light, she fears the accident has already arrived.

The aroma of thick black coffee trails behind her like a plume. It curls under and over the tray, and ribbons about the slim packet, tied with green tape, that she has tucked between the bowl of sugar and the cream. She waits for the fragrant smell of morning to slither under the door of the only occupied room.

There is no response to her knock.

She knocks again, loudly.

From sheer anxiety, she leans her shoulder against the closed door and it gives way, and she sees the body through the cloudy folds of the mosquito net. The way it hunches so unnaturally under the sheet makes her feel ill. She does not know what she does with the tray, but she finds herself pulling handfuls of gauze from under the mattress in sudden frenzy. It's too easy, she thinks, for anyone to climb a post to the upper verandah and get in. Whoever has been here has tucked in the net very tightly, with a clear intention to deceive.

The body turns out to be a duffel bag under the sheet.

She stands there staring at it stupidly, not sure if this is good news or bad, and then she hears the low growl of a four-wheel drive moving slowly to keep its noise down. She lurches through the french doors on to the upper verandah, a rash move, because the boards have been soft and termite-ridden for years. Her foot goes through in one place, between studs, and pain shoots up her leg, so she backs up carefully and leans against the wall. She strains her ears: Andrew Godwin's truck. She watches the bare red thoroughfare, and at first sees nothing but stillness and the last stars, and then, in the dawn twilight, she can just make out the thick square shadow moving slowly, black against black . . .

She waits for it. She waits until it gets so close it is out of her line of sight. Then she goes back through the doors.

She hears the purring sound, the soft fart of parking; then silence; then the creak of the verandah below, and the low squeal of the door to the bar. She thinks of going downstairs, of confronting Andrew there, but decides to wait. She hears footsteps, quiet as a cat's, on the stairs.

The bedroom door opens and closes soundlessly.

Nick slides into the room.

'What the –? For God's sake, Jess,' he says, startled.

She glares at him. Relief makes her furious. She has got seriously out of the habit of voicing her thoughts, except to certain people, but she has a speaking eye. Where the hell have you been? her eye says, and she feels incredibly, disproportionately angry, she feels rage, she feels for all the world as though she were a frantic mother, or a teacher on a school trip who has had a student go dangerously astray or almost drown – because somewhere between her first and second knock at his door, her will to get the foreigners safely out of town has hardened into an intention as ferocious and single-minded as that other blind force that is busily arranging bad chance.

Nick sits on the floor and leans back against the foot of the bed. 'I'm a bit shaken,' he says, 'by what I've seen during the night.'

You were supposed to see nothing but your pillow, Jess glares.

She wants to hit him. She has to squeeze her two hands together, and all her interlaced fingers show white and red. She presses them against her stomach but she cannot keep her voice down there, she cannot stop it from rocketing out. 'You have no idea,' she says explosively, 'how dangerous, how incredibly stupid –'

'Well, Jess!' he says, raising both eyebrows, 'you spoke!'

'You've made me,' she says tightly. 'You stupid bastard.'

He laughs. He reaches for the coffee on the tray, stares at it, puts it down again.

'Oh Jess,' he sighs. He talks in a rush. 'I know this place is crazy. I knew it would be. I knew Oyster would pick a place exactly like this, a place like this was tailor-made for Oyster, it was probably mutual passion at first sight. And I knew Oyster was crazy because Angelo has such a talent for self-destruction, he's gifted at it, and because I met Oyster once, and because I've read a dossier on him that would make your hair stand on end, so I wasn't expecting sanity in Outer Maroo. But even so, this place is a bit of a shock.'

The kind of silence that is full of incredulity and anger and grief spreads between them. It rises out of Nick and fills the room. He gets lost somewhere inside it, and reappears on another of its tracks.

'Oh Jesus, Jess,' he says, looking at the floor, 'I want my son.' His voice has gone strangely small and vulnerable, like that of a schoolboy offering excuses. He is placating somebody, not Jess, pleading. 'I'm not going to ask you what's happened, because I want to believe they've just moved on, they've moved into the red heart, or that Angelo's . . . I want to believe . . . I just want one more minute with him.'

And then Jess realises that part of her anger is because she knows she is going to be required to tell him, eventually, even though he is holding that moment off just as fiercely as she is. And she understands simultaneously, and with blinding clarity, that the whole town smoulders with so much anger toward all foreigners, particularly toward those who come looking, because everyone owes them explanations, because everyone is going to be accountable for their grief.

But we didn't do anything, everyone wants to say, aggrieved.

And Jess can feel the sick echo of that: *We didn't do anything.*

Aye, there's the rub.

That is precisely where complicity lies.

Nick is festooned all around with the filmy tail of the mosquito net, and he pulls great dollops of it toward himself and twists it into a thick rope and hugs it. 'I just want to tell him it doesn't matter, whatever he's done, it doesn't matter. Whatever group he chooses to join, you know, if that's what he . . . I just want to tell him that.'

He stares into his coffee.

'Fathers,' he sighs. 'Why are we so bloody hard to please, so bloody *slow*?' He gives his net rope another twist. 'I'm such a stupid pig-headed idiot,' he says.

Now that she can keep her eye on him, Jess lets him sit there and bleed remorse into the folds of the net. Join the club, she could say to him. She lets him twist the gauze rope around his arm and untwist it and tie it in knots.

'I knew before I got here,' he says, 'from bits and pieces Angelo said . . . He came back and forth a few times, he was the *recruiter*, he was apparently Oyster's right-hand man.' He rolls his eyes savagely. 'I suppose you've met him, my son, I mean, but I don't want to know, I don't want to hear a word against – not that you could say anything I haven't said myself.' He's made the net into a tourniquet without realising it, and he examines his arm, bright red and turning blue, and relishes the pain. Jess knows about that kind of relief. When the throbbing starts, he unwinds the net. 'He'd show up at Noosa again, on and off. Unpredictably.' He stares into the net and sees unpredictable times, sees Nick's Taverna, classiest restaurant on the Sunshine Coast, written up . . . etcetera, sees Angelo back from the Reef.

'I knew that any town that went to so much trouble to seal itself off from the world . . . you're not even on the Government Surveyor's map, did you know?'

Jess knows only too well.

'Even properties are on that map. Every single cattle and sheep station in western Queensland is on that map, but not –'

'Not Dirran-Dirran,' she says. 'And not Jimjimba. Not even Kootha Downs, though Junior Godwin wouldn't care one way or the other.'

Nick blinks. 'Well,' he says. 'There you go. I knew a town like this was going to be full of lunatics, but I'm still shaken by what I've seen.'

What Jess can't believe is how much she didn't see. Evidently. And she is not used to missing anything at Bernie's.

'How did you get out of here without anyone seeing you go? How the hell did you get hold of Andrew Godwin's truck?'

'How do you know it's Andrew Godwin's?'

'That's a stupid question to ask anyone in the outback. We know the soundprint of anything on wheels the way you recognise the face of someone you know. How did you get it?'

'I borrowed it. Without asking, I must admit.'

'You're a maniac.'

'Andrew Godwin's a maniac.'

'He will be when he finds a truck missing, and then finds it back in town.'

'But he'll have no idea who took it, will he?' Nick says. 'He won't believe anyone *could* have whisked it out from under his nose.'

'By a fairly simple process of deduction,' Jess says drily, 'he's going to figure it out.'

'He's invited me to work in his mine.'

'Oh yes, I heard him. If you're foolish enough to go, I suspect it'll be the last ladder you'll ever climb down. A lot of bad luck will happen, do you know what I mean?'

Jess had watched them, Andrew and Nick, drinking in the bar the night before. She had kept her eye on them, she had watched them buying round after round: a bull-ring routine, an elaborate game, the way they circled each other, the way each tried to get the other drunk, discussing cricket, discussing rugby, discussing politics, discussing cattle and opals, discussing restaurants in Brisbane and on the coast, discussing politics, opals, and opals. Nick had tossed Oyster's Reef, the two words, on the table once too often, Jess thought. He was a careless gambler. He placed the words down casually, recklessly, as though they were trumps. Andrew had ignored them each time. It was a high stakes game.

'I heard you say goodnight,' Jess accuses. 'I saw you go upstairs.'

'Yes.'

'Just after midnight.'

'Was it?' Nick raises his eyebrows. 'I'd lost track of time.'

'And Andrew didn't go till after one.'

'Ah.' Nick smiles. 'By then I was hidden under a tarp in the back of his truck.'

Jess feels sick at the thought.

'I climbed out on the verandah and slid down a post.'

'You're crazy.'

'Not as crazy as Andrew Godwin.'

He tells her about the drive out to Dirran-Dirran, 80 kilometres of unpaved road. 'Not very comfortable on the floor of a truck,' he says, 'with a driver in advanced stage of drunk.' He feels his ribs and buttocks gingerly. 'Picked up a few bruises on the way.'

'Count yourself lucky that you got off so lightly.'

Nick laughs, then turns sombre. 'Yes,' he says. 'I know. Believe me, after what I saw, I know.'

He sees again the hangar in which Andrew parks the truck: the half-dozen Land Rovers, the tractors, the drills and winches, the small plane, and something else: racks upon racks of rifles, semi-automatics, automatics, machine-guns. An armoury.

'I mean, there must have been about a hundred of them,' he tells Jess. 'It shook me.'

Jess realises how one forgets, in a place like Outer Maroo, what is normal and what is not. There are certain kinds of homegrown craziness that one barely registers.

'It's only mad,' she says sardonically, 'if you're used to a different normal. There's a roaring traffic in army surplus stuff in the outback.' She spreads her hands to dissociate herself. 'Cow cockies always buy big, whatever they're into. It's for when the government, or the Aborigines, or whoever, comes to take their land.'

Nick rolls his eyes. 'It reminded me of Albania, an army interrogation centre where I spent a few horrible nights. I'm sure there were weapons you can't buy in Australia.'

'Could be. Planes come in low from the north now and then. They've both got landing strips, Dirran-Dirran and Jimjimba.'

'I feel queasy,' he says. 'I feel as though I must have stepped into some other planet. West of Quilpie somewhere.'

'Yeah, you did.'

'At about the same spot where I thought I saw surf on the Sea of Null.'

'Yeah. Probably. Somewhere round there.'

'What are the planes for?'

'Opal deals. And maybe other kinds of traffic, who knows? Buyers come down from Singapore and Indonesia. No one knows what Andrew Godwin or Dukke Prophet or Bernie are doing with all that cash. That's what got Susannah Rover asking questions. That's what got her into deep shit.'

'Who's Susannah Rover?'

'Don't ask.'

'I *am* asking.'

Jess sighs wearily. 'I can't bear to tell you. I still don't understand how you could have got away with Andrew's Troopie, he would've *heard* –'

'Luck. He was pissed as a bandicoot, walking round fondling his guns, and all of a sudden he grabs a semi-automatic and hops into a different jeep, a sporty little thing with no roof, and goes roaring off into the night, blasting bullets. He couldn't have heard a thing.'

'Another roo and emu hunting spree,' Jess says.

'He'd left his keys in the Troopie's ignition, so I just took off.'

'Well, now you know he's not a good man to cross. Just don't go down a Dirran-Dirran shaft.'

'Thanks for all the helpful advice.'

'Please,' she says, 'do yourself a favour and leave, just leave, just –' And then she is radiant with a sudden idea. 'In fact, now that you've stolen Andrew Godwin's truck, you've hit the jackpot. You've got a Troopie with two, maybe even a third, reserve tank. You've got enough petrol to get to Quilpie. You can drive out to the Givens now, before anyone's up around here, and collect Sarah, and you can both get away.'

'But I have no intention of leaving,' Nick says, 'until I find what I came to find.'

Jess feels heaviness settling on her. 'You may want to kill the messenger,' she says. She picks up the little packet from the tray and offers it. 'What you want to know is in here.'

'What is it?'

'Letters,' she tells him. 'Letters that were mailed, but never sent. You may have deduced by now that the postal and telephone services round here are irregular, to say the least. Don't try to read these now. Don't read them here. Read them when you're back on the map.' He stares at her, and she says uncomfortably, 'It's a pathetic enough handful. Three were given to me to mail by kids I didn't even know, and I saved them from oblivion. The others were given to Mercy by Sarah's daughter, and I managed to rescue those from Ma's eagle eye. You can give them to Sarah when you're safely . . . None are from your son, I'm afraid, but you'll get the picture. Read them when you're safely on the road.'

'I'm not leaving, Jess,' he says. 'Until I hold my son, or find out where he is, or speak to his grave.'

'I feel,' Sarah says, 'as though I'm living on the moon. I feel as though I'm trapped in a bad dream. I feel I can't . . .' She presses her hands, open and flat, against the Givens' breakfast table, and pushes herself slightly away as though testing once reliable laws. 'I have no energy,' she says wearily. 'The heat . . .'

'Let us give silent thanks for a new day,' Mercy's father offers. 'Let us pray.'

Even the nerves in his eyelids, Mercy thinks, and whatever tiny muscles operate such frail flaps of skin, are engaged in warfare. The skin of his spirit, she thinks, looks like my skin, blistered and scabbed. She can see the wasting of his frame, the way the flesh hangs slack on his arms, his knotted wrists, the way the bones push through.

Her mother's face is upturned, intense, and a tic in her mother's cheek bleats at the ceiling fan as towards a parent inexplicably harsh but still trusted. She appears, in fact, to regard some invisible point beyond the fan with the obsequious adoration of the abused child. She expects further punishments. She will not resist them. Her eyes are closed, but they flutter and tremble, and there are tears on her cheeks. Her hands are clasped tightly together, and Mercy imagines that the tiny fingers of herself and Brian, as infants, are somewhere in that web.

Sarah stares open-eyed but blankly through the window, where all that can be seen are the verandah posts, the pathetic scrap of irrigated garden, the bloodshot sky. She struggles against the obligations of politeness. Very soon now, Mercy thinks, all Sarah's questions will insist on being asked.

The clock on the mantel ticks into the interminable quiet.

'Amen,' Mercy's father says at last.

And Sarah, struggling to be courteous, rushes the table with words: 'I guess it's totally American of me, but I cannot comprehend this *passivity*. Fear I understand, but fear should galvanise one, fear energises, fear in wartime, for example, leads to heroism, it's well established. But fear that cringes in a corner, paralysed, is degenerative, it's disgusting, it's craven, it *festers*, it's more dangerous to the victim than anything his attackers can –'

Totally American of me, Mercy thinks, setting it beside that other puzzle piece: *I'm just your regular non-observant American Jew, though my sister's become orthodox, which was more upsetting to our parents* . . . or something like that. She is constantly daunted by how many things she does not know.

'I don't think,' Mercy's father says carefully, 'that we could describe Mercy's intervention as passive. With the car bomb, I mean.'

Mercy is alarmed by this violation of the unspoken rules in front of her mother. 'That was an accident,' she says. 'The petrol tank –'

'Oh God.' Sarah holds her head in her hands. 'Why is everyone play-acting like this? Mercy, if this was war, you'd have a Medal of Honour.'

Mercy swallows. 'But it wasn't anything, it was just a –'

'What is happening?' Sarah asks in a low voice. 'What is happening? Why won't anybody *say* anything? Why won't anyone tell me what has happened?'

'Because of shame,' Mercy's father says. 'Because of grief, Mrs Cohen. Because of complicity.'

Mercy's mother is holding herself so still that Mercy is afraid she will shatter in the way that delicate fossilised shells fall apart from the heat of the sun. She says urgently: 'I'm going into Beresford's now. Sarah, would you like –?'

'Yes,' Sarah says firmly. 'I would.'

Below his left eye, Sarah sees (her own right eye pressed against the sliver of light between two weatherboards in the kitchen wall), there is a small imperfection, the faint brown stain of a birthmark, which seems to her to offer a delicate and tantalising suggestion of vulnerability, of some secret inner layer which is kept armoured over by the confident pronouncements of his body, the way he walks, the way he frowns. Or perhaps it is simply evidence that the fizzing intensity he gives off was there from the start, or from before the start. Perhaps he hurled himself dangerously from his mother in his impatience to be Nikos, Nick, to be his own invention.

Mercy is pressed up against Sarah, and from Mercy's narrow angle of vision, the stained eye looks smudged, slightly out of focus, defenceless, as though it has sustained an injury but has learned to compensate for it. Donny Becker had pale freckles on the soft skin at the edges of his eyes. She imagines putting her lips lightly against Donny's closed eyelids, as lightly as a butterfly settling there, and her breathing turns ragged and she kisses the wooden battens of the wall.

Jess taps her on the shoulder, and when Mercy turns, startled, embarrassed, Jess gives her the plate of steak and fried eggs. 'Take it to him. He's had his coffee, but he hasn't eaten yet.'

Nick looks up as Mercy enters the dining room. Sarah watches from the crack in the wall. Mercy bites her lip, and her feet suddenly behave as though they do not belong to her. She is conscious of Sarah watching.

'Is that for me?' Nick asks, and she nods. She wishes he did not have Gideon's eyes.

He takes the plate from her, salts it and peppers it, and begins immediately to eat with single-minded attentiveness to the food. He lifts each egg with his fork and examines its underside. He prods the toast with one finger. The steak he cuts to see if it bleeds. Everything meets with his cautious approval. Minutes later, when he glances up, he and Mercy are both startled that she is still there. He frowns.

'You work at Beresford's.' He pulls out one of the other chairs for her. 'Talk to me,' he says. 'Would you like some coffee?'

'Jess says you won't leave, but you have to leave. You have to take Sarah and go.'

'Ah. Why?'

'Because I don't want you to die,' she says in a low voice, desperately.

His eyebrows lift slightly but his eyes do not move from hers. They regard each other gravely, intently. He reaches up to touch her cheek with his index finger. 'I won't,' he says. 'That's a promise.' But they go on staring at each other, not moving. 'My son,' he says quietly, 'my son Angelo has your kind of intensity. Your kind of curiosity.' He says something in Greek, and she feels as though she knows what this means. 'I hope it doesn't get you into trouble,' he says sadly. 'How old are you?'

'Sixteen.'

'A child,' he sighs. 'Angelo is twenty-three but he's also a child.'

'And you?' she asks boldly. 'How old are you?'

'Old,' he says, with a short bitter laugh. 'Too old. But very stubborn.' He is studying her face, absorbed. 'So you don't want me to die. I take it there's been a bit of a death epidemic.'

He waits for her response and she lowers her eyes. 'Am I the only person outside the know?'

'And Sarah,' she says.

'Sarah?'

'The other one. She came with you on Jake Digby's truck.'

'Oh, her.' He nods, and goes on nodding, smiling savagely, absent-mindedly forking bacon into his mouth. 'But apart from the two of us, everyone else knows what's going on and what happened at Oyster's Reef?'

Mercy studies the network of cracks in the Formica tabletop. If she closes one eye, she notes, and squints with the other, the cracks could be a map of the tunnels at the Reef.

'I brought Sarah to see you,' she says, rising abruptly, knocking over her chair.

Nick is not going to look at her. His allergy to vulnerability is too high.

'There are some letters,' he says gruffly. He fishes the bundle out of his jeans pocket. 'Jess gave them to me. Some from your daughter, apparently. Look through them and take what you want.'

She is so still that he has to look, just to see what she is or isn't doing. She is very pale. He can see the beads of sweat above her lip. He looks away.

'Just give me a minute,' she says, in a low voice.

'Sure.'

'It's . . . it's a shock.' She bites the back of her hand, she blinks very rapidly, she is swallowing sounds. 'It's too . . . it feels final. I don't want a last will and testament. I want *her*.'

'I know. I can't look yet either.'

He doesn't mean to do it, he is angry with himself for doing it, but he reaches across the table and puts his hand on hers. They sit there not looking at each other.

○ ○ ○

Major Miner is at Bernie's kitchen door.

'Jess,' he says, awkwardly.

Jess finds she is suddenly clumsy with the coffee pot. There has always been a bar counter between them, a line drawn. She prefers to keep boundaries set up.

'Can I come in?' he asks.

She nods and shrugs at the same time, to indicate indifferent courtesy. She gestures with the coffee.

'Yeah, sure,' he says. 'Don't mind if I do.'

But her hand is not steady, and she manages to slop coffee into the saucer and across the tabletop. Not that he notices. He begins pacing around the room. 'Jess,' he says, with an explosive sort of energy. 'I'm sorry to take liberties, and you'll think I'm mad. But I get these forebodings.' He circles the table, jerkily, like a feral dingo in a pen. 'I don't dare ignore them,' he says. 'It's a prisoner-of-war thing. You pick up moods from the air.' He keeps pacing. 'You're a good listener, Jess. I always feel I can trust you. You make me feel safe to let off steam.'

Jess sits down, or rather perhaps, sinks down, into one of the chairs at the table. Major Miner keeps pacing.

'I pick up auras,' he says. 'I don't even know how I do it. Sounds, smells, tensions. I felt it the day Susannah . . . and the day the Reef . . . and this week again. Everything is about to blow, I can feel it. It's going to be ugly –'

'I know,' Jess says.

'It's going to get out of control, and we have to get the two foreigners –' He stops pacing suddenly, between the great cast-iron wood stove and the refrigerator. 'Jess,' he says, amazed.

'It's my day for speaking,' she says drily.

Very carefully, he pulls out a chair and sits down opposite her. She is grateful for the line of the table in between.

'We're in luck,' she says. 'We've got a chance. They're both in there, in the dining room. And outside, Andrew's Troopie is parked . . .'

'I saw. I heard it this morning. That's why I came in.'

'Nick stole it. Not a smart idea, *but*, on the other hand, it's got a full reserve tank.'

He is still stunned to hear her talk. He is only half listening to what she says, and she can see a little smile running around his lips, and it disconcerts her. She has to turn away from him.

'There's only one way to get them out of here,' she says, 'and that's to promise to show them the Reef.'

'Yes,' he says heavily. 'That has to be done, I suppose. I'd rather not be the one to do it.'

'It has to be you,' she says. 'But you don't have to do it today. What does have to be done today –'

'Get them out of here, yes. And hide the Troopie in the breakaways somewhere, till they get a chance –'

'They won't leave until they've seen the Reef,' she says. 'Not Nick, anyway. He's stubborn.'

'But the woman? Do you think it's a good idea . . .? I mean, the shock is going to be . . .'

'Yes. I don't know. They both have a right, though. I think she'll insist too. But for now, can they camp out with you?'

'They can stay in the shack. I'll doss outside. No one'll think to look for them there.'

'Take them in Andrew's Troopie. I'll drive out later in your truck, so you'll have it. You can bring me back in.'

'Right,' he says. 'Right. Jess?'

'What?' she says.

They study each other, the table in between.

'Don't look at me like that,' Jess says.

'Why not?'

'Take them,' she says, turning away. 'Quick. Before anybody comes.'

Saturday

How it begins: like a hunger on the surface of Dorothy Godwin's skin. Redness appears at her wrists and then gallops. The itch is excruciating. She has to roll in grass, at express rates, and Ethel is watching as usual, let her watch, what difference does it make? Dorothy would like to scrape herself with steel wool.

It's because of the foreigners, she knows that. And now Andrew has invited the man to visit the mine, she doesn't know what Andrew can be thinking of, she told him that. I know very well what I'm thinking of, Andrew said, but then *abracadabra*, his Troopie vanished. And now the foreigners have done likewise, or so Ethel says. That is the word in town and along the CB trails. This might be a good sign, it might be bad. It might mean a propitious accident has arrived, it might not. She can see Andrew is jumpy too, because of the Troopie. Andrew thinks it might mean that the Murris are back. And the phones are all down, an ominous sign.

That is what has brought on the attack.

The rash is made worse by this smell, this rotting everywhere, the

Old Fuckatoo roosting again. The stockmen drag the carcasses off and burn them but the echo of the stench just hangs there. The wind keeps bringing it back. She has to roll across the scratchy scarifying hummocks of saltbush, mouth full of red dirt, and ants all over her legs and in between, the bull ants, the biting ants, every little crease they get into, but they do not help, no, they do not, the saltbush helps for a second or two, but only that, and what no one understands, certainly not Andrew – though Ross used to, Ross, her tender, her middle son, mourned for, yearned for, Oh Ross, Ross, my poor baby, You've coddled him, Andrew always raged, you've turned him into a sissy, oh she knew Andrew would take him away from her sooner or later, the bastard, the bastard, one way or another, she knew he'd win. I'll make a man out of him if it kills me, Andrew vowed. And if it kills *him*, for that matter.

It did.

I'm a dead man, Ross printed neatly on the note he left behind. *P.S. Dead men tell no tales.*

I hope you're satisfied, she said to Andrew at the funeral.

And then, after Ross, for a little shining moment there was Oyster, and *he* understood, he knew about hunger, Oyster who stepped out of the sun one day, a miracle, and who always and only wore white, and who – oh God, now she can feel the blisters inside her legs, on the underside of the skin, she can feel them galloping up the soft inside of her thighs – Oyster who came to her and touched her and who had a gift of stillness and peace in his hands and who –

Stillness. What would that be like?

'I am a healer, Dorothy,' he said. 'I have the gift of healing.'

And he did: an extraordinary shimmering thing, strange and beautiful, like a mirage of still water in the desert: the Sea of Null, wet and shining from shore to shore. It reminded her, Oyster's gift, of something from school in Brisbane, from history lessons, from medieval times, the Kynge's Touch or the Kynge's Evil or something like that, when people would bring the halt and the lame and the peasants with scurvy and rashes and plague, and the king would touch them and they would be well, and yes, Oyster could do it just exactly like that. His eyes. He just had to look at her, he could touch her with the milky blue behind the lashes – there was something a little strange about his eyes, a little frightening almost – or she could touch him, she needed only to brush the cuff of his loose white sleeve, she was like that woman in the Bible, the one with *an issue of blood* who touched the hem of Christ's garment, and *straightway the fountain of her blood was dried up; and she felt in her body that she was healed of that plague*. Oyster recited the verses. Thy faith hath healed thee, he said, and she would be moist again just from the way he said it, ready for him. Whenever, she promised him. Whenever.

He knew the Bible by heart. The Bible seeped from the pores of his sweet-smelling skin, but naturally Andrew was jealous, not jealous perhaps, that was not exactly it, though Oyster did have a way of making everyone want him all to themselves, which went both ways, it must be admitted. Oyster wanted exclusive rights. Nevertheless. It was not so much that Andrew was jealous in the usual and obvious sense, but he was uncomfortable with the religious aspect of Oyster, the Armageddon and Second Coming stuff, and reciting reams of the Bible by heart, which did, without question, put Oyster more into Dukke Prophet's faction, more under the thumb of Dukke Prophet, that sanctimonious crook who was tapping the Godwin water table for his bore, and tunnelling under Godwin boundaries in his mines, and creaming off more than the agreed share of opal brokers and arms dealers with that bigger airstrip and that high-tech satellite dish that guided the planes under radar, flying in low and illegal from the Gulf of Carpentaria and Indonesia. (You would think Jimjimba was a bloody military base, Andrew said, furious, competitive, hating to be outdone.) Yes, she understood that, she agreed with Andrew on that, she could not blame him on that score, even though it meant that Andrew began to want to get rid of Oyster, maybe not Andrew himself, she is not saying that, she is not saying Andrew lit the fuses, although there are moments when she thinks perhaps he did, but that is not the crux of the question, the crux of the matter is that Andrew wanted to keep Oyster entirely for himself, he did not want to share him with Dukke Prophet, that Pharisee, that money-changer in the Temple, that horrid and dangerous man with the slick of Bible verses all over his greasy hair, or with Bernie, or with Dorothy, or with anyone else, and so after a certain point, he wanted Oyster gone, yes, in the end he did, in the end, almost everyone did, everyone wanted Oyster gone – and so what there is nobody left to understand, since Ross so violently and suddenly departed, since Oyster returned to the mirage from whence he came, is the fierceness, the rigour, the sheer self-punishment of the steps to which Dorothy immediately submits herself, at the earliest sign of redness at the wrists, in her attempt to stop the hunger of her body from escalating into sin and into theft.

No one appreciates this. No one gives her credit.

And yet, God knows, she tries.

Do they think she enjoys being called a kleptomaniac? Not that the opinion of anyone in Outer Maroo matters: riff-raff from Irish potato famines, drifters, wreckage from World War II and Korea and Vietnam, schoolteachers, shopkeepers, holy rollers and evangelicals, the small pickings of the social scale. She should not waste a moment's concern on what they think, since what they think is of no consequence whatsoever, but then, ultimately, that is what she cannot abide: the lack of respect from people too ignorant to know that they do not have any warrant whatsoever to pass judgment.

And so, yes, it does bother her that no one appreciates that she has never, not ever, not once, simply yielded to the first twinge of hunger without having tried every delaying trick in the book. She negotiates with herself. She pleads. She bullies. She reads the words of the Old

Testament aloud to the boundary fence: *For, behold, the day cometh, that shall burn as an oven: and all the proud, yea, and all that do wickedly, shall be stubble . . .* She experiments with every other remedy she knows.

These devices never work.

They make her ravenous. They only intensify the famine.

And there will be Ethel watching, just standing there, stirring something on the kitchen stove, or dusting the mahogany sideboard, or polishing the silver, and looking out the window, staring, just staring, as though she were watching the spinifex growing, or the sky hanging there, just staring with that terrible effrontery of someone who will not deign to react. Or she will be sitting out on the verandah peeling potatoes, the whites of her eyes like milk in her black face. Let her watch, the old sphinx. What difference does it make? Dorothy and Ethel have pretty much already seen everything there is to see about each other. They have pulled each other's babies out and cut each other's cords. They have thrown dirt in the graves of each other's sons.

'Please do not delude yourself that I don't know who the father is,' Dorothy said at one birth. 'Please do not pretend that I don't know what goes on in the shearing shed. I've hidden there and *watched* you, you slut, with your fat black thighs splayed open.'

'There's a lot has gone on in shearing sheds, I reckon,' Ethel said, 'since olden times. Since back before the last beginning of this place. There's a lot I wish you could've hidden and watched. A lot of boss cockies always done what they want in shearing sheds.'

'I hope you have relatives in Bourke or Cunnamulla or somewhere,' Dorothy said, 'who can take this one off your hands. Or we could make arrangements if you'd prefer. The mission school at Cherbourg or Woorabinda.'

'My grandma was shot in a shearing shed,' Ethel said. 'My mother saw. She was hiding under a pile of fleeces and she was shaking so hard, the pile began to fall, but she stayed hid. Otherwise they'd've got her too.'

It used to be that when the itch came, Ethel would smoke Dorothy with gidgee leaves. A calm would fall out of the smoke and gather Dorothy up. The itch would escape.

'It's what the Old People always did when we were kids,' Ethel said. 'Anyone died, anyone sick, that's what they did. Happy smoke.'

But she does not bother to smoke Dorothy any more. She just watches.

Let her watch. What difference does it make?

And so, after everything, and only ever as a last resort, Dorothy unsheathes the gin from the soft earth under the verandah, where she hides it from Ethel, and she takes a few medicinal shots, and then she gets the Land Rover out and she points it towards Outer Maroo and Beresford's, and on the way she calls Pete Burnett on CB.

'Pete,' she says huskily. 'It's Dorothy Godwin. Andrew says to let you know he's at the New Reef today, and he needs to see you. It's urgent.'

In pain, the itch scalding her, shredding her, she waits for the static to settle. She waits, she waits, she can scarcely contain herself. One of these days the rash will eat her before she can feed it, she knows that. She guns the engine, she puts her foot to the floor, the needy red dust spumes around her. She holds the CB transmitter tightly as she drives. Her hand shakes.

'Calling Pete Burnett,' she says, gasping a little because of the way the rash branches over the lining of her lungs. 'Calling Pete Burnett, Pete Burnett, Pete Burnett.' She is beginning to hyperventilate now. He has no idea, Pete, of the agony a few minutes' thoughtless tardiness on his part can cause.

His voice scratches through the static, thank God. 'Pete Burnett,' he says. 'Receiving loud and clear.'

'Oh thank God,' she says, rather unwisely. 'Um, Andrew needs you, it's urgent. He's at the New Reef, and he says he'll be out there till –'

'Right,' he says. 'Opal?'

'Opal,' she says. 'Potch Point. Personally, I won't be there. I have to go into Beresford's for something.'

'Right,' he says. 'Over and out.'

And now she can begin to reassemble her elegant self, because she can be elegant. Her real and essential self is calm and elegant, as well as unfailingly gracious, courteous – though also, of course, in certain situations, when it is appropriate, she is polite but distant, as in dealings with domestic servants and Aboriginals, whom they are now supposed to call Murris if you please. Well, she said to Ethel, you won't get any newfangled word for what you are out of me; and what you *call* me, Ethel said, doesn't make one scrap of difference to me, Mrs Godwin. There is something about Ethel that provokes her. There is something about Ethel that brings out a side of Dorothy that is not her true self.

Her essential self is elegant. She was made for silk and lace parasols. She used to be, in fact, disturbingly beautiful, and perhaps she still is, but certainly she used to be, used to bewitch, she used to have such a reputation as a beautiful woman that all the eligible sons of the richest cow cockies around, every property from the dingo fence to the Northern Territory border, would drive a few hundred miles for a single dance. She was, earlier in life – it seems altogether another life now – but she was, in that earlier life, the belle of balls from the Isa to Charleville. Oh Charleville. She remembers with particular clarity that cloud of *peau-de-soie* satin and seed pearls and the streamers and the ballroom floor at Corones Hotel, beautiful Corones, pride of the outback, pride of the west, with its grand oak staircase and its marble floors and its leaded and stained-glass windows, and the graziers in black silk jackets and black bow-ties, and all the sheep money, all the photographs of prize merino studs on the walls, all the elegance, all the diamonds and pearls, when Australia still rode on the sheep's back, and click went the shears, boys, click click click, and the money rolled in, and the wool flecks flew, and the fleeces won prizes and went into bales and were trucked down to Brisbane, to Brisbane . . .

And they would all go down to Brisbane for the Royal Brisbane Show, and for showing off to one another the blue ribbons, the prize wethers, the prize studs, the prize bulls, the engraved débutante invitation cards, the diamond engagement rings, the parties, the balls, and Andrew Godwin, reckless and handsome, who danced only with her until dawn . . .

That was before the bottom fell out of the wool market.

That was before all the properties had to add cattle to the sheep if they could manage it, if they could possibly sink bores deep enough and build turkey-nest holding dams high enough. That was before the multinationals, the hamburger people, the Coles and McDonald's people, that was before they all began pulling the rug out from under the individual grazier.

And then there was opal, which has changed everything and saved the day, she supposes, if one is speaking only of money. But the soul has dropped out of things. Elegance has gone from the land.

For mining is *grubby*.

A grazier has class, but a miner? A miner has none.

These days people may think she is mad, oh she knows what they think, but they know nothing, they have no idea of the losses, they have no inkling of the complications in her life, they do not even remember that it was *her* land, her family property that Andrew married into and threw away, *her* birthright that he gave over to American hamburgers, American banks – and the itch is bothering her again now, she wants to scream, she has her foot to the floorboards, and people have no idea that she went to one of the most elite boarding-schools in Brisbane, that she won prizes, *academic* prizes, her mother had to beg her to disguise the fact in case she lost Andrew, what a catch, what a serve-herself-right catch-of-the-day Catch-22 *that* turned out to be, people in Outer Maroo have not the remotest idea that in actual fact Dorothy Godwin's logical and intellectual powers are as refined and intricate and precise as the complex arrangements of silica cells in opal.

What she steals in Beresford's, for example.

But to be honest now: could she seriously expect anyone in Outer Maroo to be sensitive to the nature of her choices, to the fine moral gradations involved? She is a woman of principle. For a start: she will never take anything of personal use. For another: she will steal nothing edible. Also, because she is fiercely patriotic: nothing that is wholly processed and packed within Australia. (She reads labels and fine print assiduously; she steals foreign, especially American.) And she will steal nothing blue – even though that might mean, as it did only recently, that day the foreigners arrived, that she had to pay an exorbitant and utterly ridiculous price for a bolt of fine cloth to make Alice a going-away dress, because she is determined, whatever Andrew might say and might try to do, and whatever act of reckless courage it might come to involve on Dorothy's part, hijacking one of the gem brokers' small planes for example, or just screaming off across the western plains with Alice and herself in the Troopie, whatever it takes, she is determined that she will whisk Alice off to boarding-school in Brisbane, whatever that may mean for Outer Maroo, and she really cannot see why it should matter, it certainly has nothing to do with Alice, poor lamb, nor with herself, although there is undeniably this sense of general contamination, this moral stench, it is like a toxic gas in the air, but all the more reason to get Alice out of it now, and whoever heard of a boarding-school that sent investigators out to a grazier's property, for God's sake. Boarding-schools know where their bread is buttered, especially these days. There would not even be any need to mention Outer Maroo. When Dorothy herself went off to school, her address was 'Dirran-Dirran, Western

Queensland, via Quilpie'. If that was good enough for Dorothy, it would serve for Alice too.

'*Via Quilpie* is not the kind of risk I want to take,' Andrew says.

'What rubbish,' she says. 'We're not even going to mention opal, which in any case would be a social liability for Alice. When I was in school, miners were down there with stockmen and shearers and Aborigines, *lower*, in fact. Lower. Alice will say "in sheep and cattle" as any well-bred grazier's daughter should.'

'That,' Andrew says, exasperated, but patiently, night after night as to a slow-witted child, 'would be playing right into their hands. That would be giving them a trump card on a silver platter. They could take her hostage.'

'Who could take her hostage?'

'The government,' Andrew says. 'You don't have any idea how critical things have become for the primary producers. You have no idea. You live in a fool's paradise, Dorothy. There's already been a siege at a property near Cloncurry. They sent in the *army*.'

'That's because those people refused to pay their taxes. They were asking for trouble. But the government doesn't even know about Outer Maroo, and no one here pays taxes on anything, so where's the risk?'

'That's what the graziers thought up in Cape York Peninsula,' Andrew says. 'They thought they were off the maps and off the edge of the world. You can't even get to them by road, you can't even get there by four-wheel drive, for God's sake. You've got to fly in. And has that protected them? No. The government ups and takes their land. Someone in Canberra signs on a line and that's it. All this bowing and scraping to world opinion and the United Nations, all this Indigenous Peoples crap, all this stuff forced down our throats by Canberra, I mean Oyster was absolutely right about that, even Dukke Prophet (and I hate the guts of that holier-than-thou crim), but he is right about that: it's in the Book of Revelation, it all adds up, the

Beast and the Whore of Babylon, there's no question they are the federal government and all these World Thought Police organisations: give us a break. The greenies, the Abos, the unions, all these communists, they've got the government over a barrel. National Parks, Land Rights, I tell you they are coming to take our land and we have to be ready, and I'm certainly not giving them Alice as a pawn in their game.'

If things are so bad, Dorothy thinks, that is all the more reason to spirit Alice safely away. 'If we are going to lose Dirran-Dirran,' she points out, 'then it is essential, *essential*, that Alice have proper social –'

'They'll take Dirran-Dirran over my dead body,' Andrew promises. 'There'll be a siege that will make them think twice. I'd like to see the Queensland police and the Australian army face up to my arsenal. We'll go down fighting, I can assure you of that. We'll leave them nothing but scorched earth, that's a promise.'

And Alice will not go down with the property, but will make a proper dêbut with engraved invitations, Dorothy thinks. That's a promise too. If Brisbane is too much of a risk, they could send her to Melbourne, Presbyterian Ladies College, somewhere like that; get her married to one of those nice Scotch College boys that live in immaculate little terrace houses and never rock boats unless they have their feet and their bank accounts safe on dry land. They could even send her to Europe, if necessary.

Are you crazy? Andrew wants to know. Does Dorothy have any idea of the kind of information you give over to government computers when you have to apply for a passport and buy an international airline ticket and fill out departure forms? Does she want all their private business spread out naked for every sleazy little federal bureaucrat to masturbate over? That is exactly why, he explains patiently, they hired a teacher and set up their own private school.

And look where that got us, Dorothy tactfully refrains from saying.

We are interviewing again, Andrew says. We will find someone more suitable.

But Dorothy privately vows that Alice will go to a proper school. What is the point, she wants to know, of making these vast amounts of tax-free money out of opal and then not being able to send your daughter to the best school money can buy?

The point, Andrew says, is to be ready. The point is to be prepared for the battle that is coming. Does she, for example, have any idea how much all these kalashnikovs cost? Does she have any idea of the difficulties and the costs of smuggling them in? That is the point of making money: to be ready.

'Ready for Armageddon?' she asks drily.

Because she must admit, although she always found the words of the Bible in Oyster's mouth seductive, she never seriously lumped him in with the evangelical types. He had too much class. The Bible was poetry on his lips. She never had a sense that he himself took things with the heavy literalness of Dukke Prophet; she felt there was a certain lightness to him; she felt that other things mattered more to him . . . though there was no question that the year 2000 loomed large in his mind. Privately, she supposes, she always interpreted that in a metaphorical sense.

And so, perhaps, does Andrew. Armageddon? he shrugs. If that's what Oyster and Dukke Prophet want to call it, he says. Personally, he doesn't care what it's called, but there's no question in his mind that the federal government has unpleasant things in mind for the year 2000. It is a watershed year. We know what's behind the republic, he says. We know what's on the politicians' minds. As far as Andrew is concerned, the coming battle is about graziers keeping their land.

My land, Dorothy says.

Ours, he says, frowning.

He is willing to join forces with Dukke Prophet to save his land.

He's willing to concede that a worldwide conspiracy is afoot. In a last all-out pitched battle – and that is what's coming, make no mistake – one takes reinforcements where one finds them. As for the religious dimension, it doesn't affect Andrew one way or the other. But if they, Andrew and Dorothy Godwin of Dirran-Dirran, lose their land, it will be the end of the world, right enough.

And Junior? she asks.

Junior! he says, lifting up the palms of his hands and rolling his eyes, because Junior and Delia live in a different time zone on Kootha Downs. They live in a different age. They do not live in Outer Maroo and never have, though they get their supplies from Beresford's like everyone else. No one knows what to make of Junior, who sticks stubbornly and totally to cattle though everyone knows there are opal seams as thick as rock pythons on his land. Junior is not interested. Junior studies cattle the way Oyster studied the Bible. He crosses Santa Gertrudis and Herefords with Simmenthals, he breeds out this trait, he breeds in that, you would think his cows and his bulls were fine crystal. He paid $9,000 for a bull at the Roma saleyards last year.

'Nine thousand dollars!' his father says.

'It's an extraordinary bull, Dad,' Junior says. 'Not just weight and body form, but the servicing capacity for the cows is phenomenal. And temperament! That's not easily come by in a bull, it's the X factor, as you know very well, but when it comes to servicing time, I can't even calculate how big a plus it is. This bull – I call him Hannibull – is so sweet-tempered you can walk up behind him and pat his bum.'

'What a lot of bull,' Andrew snorts. 'Do you know how many kalashnikovs $9,000 would buy?'

Junior and Delia look at each other and lift their eyebrows. They live in the clouds.

As for this permaculture thing: fanatics.

'I would never have believed I'd raise a communist,' his father says.

'If this raping of the land goes on, Dad,' Junior says peaceably (and that is one of the most infuriating things about him, the way he never loses his calm), 'it won't help much to have an arsenal. The land will be degraded down to rock. It won't support a blade of grass or a living thing. And yet the Murris were here for forty thousand years, through drought and floods, living off the fat of the land. I don't understand why it's taken us so long to learn from them. It's really quite simple to practise drought-proof farming.'

'Of course,' Delia says sweetly in her steel-trap voice, 'when you use sound farming practices, when you don't overstock, when you accept that there is a perfectly intelligent way to live with drought conditions, you do have to give up your $60,000-a-year drought relief from the government.'

'That is one of the few decent things this bloody government does,' Andrew says. 'I never thought I'd raise a bloody communist.'

It's because we let him go to Gatton, he tells Dorothy. It's those university types. Communist farming, Dukke Prophet says. Look what it led to in South Africa. This is one of the issues on which Andrew concedes that Dukke has a point. Dukke Prophet has shown Andrew how the telltale number, 666, the Mark of the Beast in the Book of Revelation, the number of Satan, shows up over and over again in the catalogues at Gatton: course numbers, telephone numbers, the place is saturated with it. Not that Andrew needed magic numbers to tell him there was something wrong with farming that wanted to turn the clock back to the bloody Aborigines.

'Junior has been brainwashed,' Andrew says.

'Junior is Junior,' Dorothy sighs.

'Mum,' Junior says sorrowfully, reproachfully, resigned. 'What are you doing?'

And here she is, she's arrived, she should have noticed because as soon as she slips something into her bag, the itch goes. It is amazing that she was so busy thinking, so involved with the futures of her children, that the calm could have slithered over her skin again without her noticing. She rubs her forearms: the surface is smooth as silk.

They are in Beresford's, haberdashery, her favourite aisle.

'What have you put in there?' Junior asks in a low voice.

'What are you talking about?' she says, because this is the amazing thing: even though she gets this electric buzz, this really quite delectable feeling, a wonderful on-top-of-the-world rush of joy . . . yet she is never conscious at the moment of doing it that she is doing it. That is part of the thrill: getting home and finding out what she has taken. It is like being a child on Christmas morning, or like buying a sample bag at the Ekka, the Brisbane Show. What will be inside the wrapping?

And the other astonishing thing is to find that her hand always follows the rules. She does not plan, and yet she has never taken anything of personal use. There is a profound moral system at work even when her mind is on holiday. She is reassured by this.

She believes Junior understands.

'Mum,' Junior says gently, very quietly. 'Why don't you just put those thimbles back now, and save me a trip to Potch Point?'

Well, he knows the answer to that. She also understands what he believes he has to do, she does not condemn him, although Potch Point has suffered in consequence. Potch Point is not the place it once was.

'Junior,' she says. 'I think Alice should come home again. I want to send her away to school. We have to get her out of this place.' She drops her voice and leans close. 'Have you noticed that the stench is getting worse, no matter what precautions people take? The whole town is smelling rotten,' she says.

'Alice is much happier with us, Mum. I really don't think –'

'Junior,' she says urgently, remembering Pete. 'I have to go. Give Alice and Delia my love. Tell Alice I'll come for her next weekend.'

Outside, as she starts her car, she can see Dukke Prophet through the window of the Living Word. He has his arms in the air, he is calling down God. She does feel quite confident that God, whom she thinks of as a Churchie or a Brisbane Grammar Old Boy, she does feel confident that God would find Dukke Prophet very tiresome.

She catches a glimpse of Jess and the foreign man, no, not the foreign man, it is Major Miner. Interesting, she thinks. She remembers that no one is quite sure where the foreigners are. Perhaps she should get Andrew to check out Major Miner's shack.

She feels the queasiness in her stomach that Alice felt when the foreigners arrived. If strangers keep showing up looking for people, and they have to accept that this will happen, that this will go on happening, how will the smell ever lift? Where will it end? Because there is no way back now; there is absolutely nothing anyone can do. It is horribly regrettable, but the greater good has to prevail in such cases, and she will not relax again, and Alice will not relax, until suitable precautions have been taken and the problem of the foreigners has been, as it were, laid to rest. Perhaps it has been. Perhaps it already has.

She can see no sign of Pete Burnett. She is late.

She drives like a cyclone on the loose.

But when she reaches Dirran-Dirran, there is no sign of Pete there either. He is not at Potch Point, which is Andrew's supercilious term for the shed where her things are stored. The shed is over the first shaft that Andrew ever drilled, the shaft that yielded nothing but potch – worthless opal, opal without any play of colour. The mine was dubbed Potch Point, and was backfilled. The shed was built over it. Dorothy adds two dozen thimbles, neatly arranged, to one of the pigeonholes. She prints out a label and dates it. In its way, her collection is a kind of diary, carefully organised.

Where is Pete?

When he comes, she will show him things she has never shown him before. She will show him watches and jewellery, things she took years ago in boarding-school: things she has never of course worn, and never coveted, because they were not to her taste. And she will show him larger, more poignant things, symbols of operations that were extremely difficult to execute when she was a student in Brisbane. For example, the road signs: MEN AT WORK, STEEP GRADIENT, CURVES AHEAD. There is a STOP sign as tall as she is and she leans against it, her cheek in the hollow of the O. I am so lonely, she tells it, I could scream. The S stands for scream and she will . . .

There is Pete's car, thank God.

'I thought you weren't going to,' she says. He has lost weight lately. His skin seems to hang on him, faintly grey. He looks haunted.

'Sorry,' he says. He smiles but the smile does not reach his eyes. 'It's not easy any more.'

'It's this awful smell everywhere,' she says, full of concern. She touches his cheek. He smiles again and strokes her hair absently.

'Shall I unroll the mattress?' she asks.

'Sure,' he says.

But they just lie there, looking at the undulations in the corrugated iron roof. Great hammocks of cobwebs dip towards them, heavy with dust.

She says in a small voice: 'You don't want me any more.'

'Oh Dorothy,' he says gently, taking her hand between his. 'It's not that. It's not that.' He sighs heavily. 'I don't want anything any more. That's the trouble. I've tried, but I cannot think of anything I want.'

'They've gone,' she says. 'They've disappeared. It's going to be all right. The Old Fuckatoo will fuck off.'

'I can't sleep any more,' he says, 'but I have nightmares anyway.'

'It's all these carcasses,' she says. 'It's the drought. If we had rain, it would wash the smell away.'

'I keep smelling her perfume,' he says.

'Pete, she was asking for it.'

'Do you know what they did to her?'

'She was asking for it. Face it, Pete, Susannah Rover was a shrew. She was a troublemaker, and she strung you along for one hell of a ride. Forget her.'

'I don't mean *then*,' he says. 'I don't mean that day at Bernie's. I can almost live with that because I did try to stop it. I did everything I possibly could. But I don't mean that. I mean afterwards. After they had kicked her to death. Do you know what they did?'

'Pete, please. What good does it do?'

'*Do* you? Do you know what they did?'

'What difference does it make?' she asks dully. She can feel the rash starting again, she can see the redness at her wrists.

'They took her to one of the old shafts at Inner Maroo,' he says. 'They had a feral pig in the shaft.'

Dorothy scratches frantically at her arms. 'I think –' she moans. She can feel the blisters lining her throat. 'I think I'm going to be sick.'

'So there is *nothing* left,' Pete says. 'Nothing at all. No bones, no clothing, nothing.' He reaches for a cobweb and pulls it down. He smears it over his face. 'Except her perfume,' he says. 'Her perfume is everywhere.'

Sunday

The black flies are so small and quick that sometimes they pass through a web like grapeshot, tearing it, and then a part of the spider-lace goes slack. It sways and drifts. Its sticky filaments grope about like lost streamers. The entire punctured web folds in on itself, a slow-motion parachute collapsing.

At other times, the black flies are caught unawares, especially by new webs not yet picked out with red dust, or when the flies perhaps are simply at cruising speed, or are coasting on a thermal down-draught, their wings idling. They trampoline into the nets, stretching them, and are catapulted back, but never quite far enough or fast enough to break the adhesive embrace. An airquake ensues.

In the Living Word Gospel Hall, Mercy watches the convulsions in a webbed theatre slung across the side aisle. Five flies, in assorted stages from outrage to shocked apathy, are wrapping themselves in soft death.

Mercy is here as a sign. She wants to know what is being said. Around her, people pitch themselves against the heat and dust and torpor and the sticky cobweb of sin. They clap their hands and sway to the music being belted out of a small, asthmatic bellows organ. They are seated closely packed on the wooden pews, and they lean into the words, listing sideways, left to right, then a hesitation, and back to left again, and the slipping sliding motion of the bodies gives the pews an odd look of racing eights bending competitively, though Mercy is not supposed to be thinking such worldly thoughts, *Miss Rover Miss Rover come over,* and here is Mercy watching sinful television again. That is Cambridge, Miss Rover says, I saw the racing eights one year, the first time I went to England, because there was an Australian rowing for his college, and it's important, Mercy, to look back here from over there, because only then can you fully appreciate the satire of the Henley-on-Todd regatta in Alice Springs, for just one example, and Mercy struggles to be over there looking here, or to be in an illicit television screen looking out, or even to be in Alice Springs where sprinters dress up as boats and compete, fleet-footed, on the dry riverbed, though one year, Miss Rover says, the regatta had to be cancelled on account of water flowing in the Todd. Mercy struggles to be watching from anywhere else, her eye on Outer Maroo, dipping her paddle in red dust and coxing for her pew, the rowers clapping and singing their way through the fifteenth round of a gospel chorus, sweeping themselves through the gates of the New Jerusalem and into the upper registers of spiritual climax.

The flies struggle to the same percussive beat, they wager the turbo panic of their wings against the give of the webbed trampoline. It is never a fair contest. The flies die, Mercy suspects, of exploding hearts. She would like to release them, except that she has an irrational fear of cobwebs.

Sweeping through the gates of the New Jerusalem,
Washed in the Blood of the Lamb . . .

From the pulpit, Mr Prophet directs the singing.

Far from the convulsive centre of the web, apparently uninvolved, the spider watches, gentlemanly. It grooms itself and licks its delicate feet. Perhaps it is giving thanks: a grace before feasting. It owns a property, Mercy thinks. One hundred thousand acres at least, good artesian water still running strong despite the drought, and who knows how many head of cattle and of sheep? It can afford to wait. In the spider world, it wears R.M. Williams boots and Akubra hats. There are opal stake-outs on its property and abandoned shafts for unwary flies.

One guy-rope of the web runs from the boss at the end of the pew in front of Mercy, where Beverley Prophet sits. Beverley is eight years old, the daughter of Mr Prophet's young second wife, and has her left hand cupped around her bible. She sings along with everyone else, and sways a little in keeping with the others seated in her pew, but she also writes as she sings. Her bible serves as laptop desk, and she shelters behind the bulwark of her left hand a piece of paper on which, with her right hand, she makes green-crayoned marks.

Beverley Prophet has a soft urchin face, not entirely plain, especially not when she smiles, and wispy brown hair which she wears in plaits that spiral into corkscrew curls below blue ribbons. She wears a pink cotton dress. She wears black patent leather shoes with buckled straps (ordered by catalogue and picked up in Quilpie by her father), and white socks with lace edging. A section of lace has torn loose and trails subversively. Whenever she twists sideways, which she does from time to time in order to glance furtively over her shoulder, Mercy can see her smocked bodice and the winking pink of satin-stitched rosebuds. There are interesting terracotta smudges of dust, and streaks of blackish red that represent, Mercy supposes, the remains of squashed flies.

Beverley finishes her green message and folds the piece of paper meticulously, moving the tip of her tongue between her lips to get it right. She does not turn and present her smocked dimples and puckers to Mercy, but regards the pulpit with beatific concentration. Behind her back, below the lower rail of the pew, she extends a rigid arm and offers her closed fist which rests in the bunched pink of her skirt, buttock-high.

Mercy drops her chorus book.

She leans forward to pick it up from the floor and takes the note. 'Your father's watching,' she whispers into Beverley's shoulder.

The huge web has five guy-ropes that Mercy can see, and perhaps many more. She wonders if there are ever turf wars between spiders, webs running into each other between windows and aisles, passing through each other perhaps, interlocking. One of the guy-ropes disappears up into the rafters and the silvered galvanised iron of the roof. There have been, from time to time in the history of Outer Maroo, hailstorms against that roof: never rain, at least not in Mercy's memory; just pellets of ice the size of ping-pong balls, or even larger, making havoc and thunder. Mercy remembers the time that hail fell exactly at the hour of afternoon prayer; and how they all went shocked and quiet beneath the doomsday din; and how, into the eerie silence that followed the storm, Oyster stood in the pulpit and said that the Seventh Angel had spoken, and there had been shouts and tumult, but Mercy does not want to remember all that, she cannot bear to remember. Not now. Not while Mr Prophet has his burning eye on her, not while the endless cyclic singing of the chorus is beginning to peter out, and the sermon is beginning to peter in.

When Mr Prophet speaks, Mercy notes with habitual and awful fascination, there is a little fleck of white that lines the inside of his lower lip. Against her will, she observes the way it gradually thickens. It reminds her of the brackish tideline inside empty beer glasses at Bernie's. She imagines Jess wiping a dishrag across the inside of Mr Prophet's lip. She imagines the soggy corpses of minute insects and flies from the bar countertop being deposited under his tongue. She tries to imagine how Beverley feels when her father comes to her bedroom to kiss her goodnight. Does Beverley make a kiss with her own lips as she waits, pushing the soft flesh out, holding it ready, expectant? Or does she lie in bed pretending to be asleep, with the sheet pulled over her face? Mercy ponders this. If she were Beverley, what would she do? She supposes she would reluctantly kiss her father. She supposes that if she were Beverley, she would not even notice that line of foam.

'Hallelujah,' booms a voice behind her.

'Amen, amen. That is the truth, Dukke Prophet.'

'The Word of the Lord. Praise His name.'

'And He shall come again,' Dukke Prophet says, 'and He will speak to the nations,' and will He speak in an accent like Mr Prophet's, Mercy wonders? – faintly American, with those strange vowels underneath that must be South African, and other notes that are broad Australian but which nevertheless sound as though Mr Prophet is all the time making an effort to sound Australian. The cobwebs drift, the words drift and scorch, '. . . the terrible flame of the Day of God's Wrath, that refining fire,' why is he so in love with fire? Mercy wonders, watching his words fizzing from the pulpit like little straw knots soaked in gasoline: '. . . a message from the secret place of the Most High . . . for the Sanctified, fire is not a destroying flame, but a *purifying* . . . For it is written, *He shall try them with a refiner's fire.*'

Detonations of joyful assent break loose around Mercy like firecrackers. Beverley presses the back of her fist against her buttocks and flexes all her fingers, wavelike, in a signal. Have you read my note yet? her fingers demand, and even her fingers speak Australian because Beverley was born at Jimjimba Station. Mercy wonders if Beverley feels foreign out there and whether she sometimes has to be translator, sifting accents for her father, smoothing out the vowels of stockmen, shearers, opal miners, jackaroos.

Mercy, by way of showing affection, brushes the inside cushions of Beverley's fingertips and thinks of fire, listening only to the edges of Mr Prophet's words, for both girls, raised from infancy in the noisy inner courts of the Lord, take as little notice of godly hubbub as those who live opposite railway lines do of trains, and usually Mercy would climb down into Aladdin's Rush, below the bluster of pulpit and congregation, and leaf through her books, or she would commune with Miss Rover, or she would surface and study insects on the walls of the Living Word and the patterns of nails in the floorboards and the play of light and the spinal knobs at the napes of necks bent in worship and the relative greasiness of one head of hair compared to another and the way some people rock and others shake and some roll on the floor in holy laughter and some are afflicted by weeping. She has become a dispassionate cataloguer of ecstasies, though today she thinks of the classifications and sub-systems of fire.

She thinks of petrol tanks ablaze, of exploding cars, of infernos in mine shafts, of the fire of the Holy Spirit moving like a Zippo lighter in sin-struck souls. Even tongues of fire, of sacred fire, she notes, speak in predictable vocabularies and in certain limited ways. She notes that Mrs Johnson, for example, always tips back her head until it rests on the top rail of the pew, and she makes a trilling sound with her tongue as though she were straining not to swallow it; that Mr Murray, on the other hand, has a habit of catapulting his body forward from the waist and slapping his hands against his thighs and shouting *Hallelujah hallelujah hallelujah*, but Mercy thinks of fire and of Brian. *Brian, Brian*, she whispers urgently, backwards across the two years since he left, further back into childhood, and his eyes gleam, and he holds up his fingers and flashes them twice behind his chorus book and they are playing it again, the old guessing game: how many times during one praise meeting will Mr Murray shout his hallelujahs out? Brian bites down hard on his fist, Mercy stuffs her handkerchief into her mouth, they both splutter and shake with squashed-down mirth, they pray for forgiveness, for Brian yearns to be purer than light, to be a spotless soldier of truth, and Mercy too, sometimes, mostly, except why do Ma and Ma's Bill and Jess and Miss Rover and all of the people who don't come to prayer meeting, have to be cast into outer darkness, it doesn't seem fair, simply because they have never been washed in the Blood of the Lamb, which is something Mercy has imagined since about the age of four, very vividly and horribly, and she is grateful that she has apparently already washed herself in the Blood but fortunately cannot remember doing it, or perhaps she hasn't really done it, perhaps she is not really saved after all, perhaps she will be cast into outer darkness too, which might not be so bad if Miss Rover is there and Mercy can look at her books, though Brian has certainly done it, but all those thoughts were years ago, years ago, and Brian has since marched on into battle and up into light, while Mercy . . .

Mercy is probably guilty of almost everything that cannot be forgiven, and she always has been. She cannot keep her thoughts pure. She cannot even hold her attention on a single spider because now he has disappeared and there are seven trapped flies, and when did the new ones arrive?

She is addicted to tangents.

You're too earnest about everything, Mercy, Miss Rover says, used to say, though Miss Rover always seems to be around because Mercy can never stay in one time zone either, she is always bouncing between future and past, the present never stays around her for longer than the blink of an eye though she tries to stay there, she does try, she throws out anchors but they never hold, she tries to get off at the station of Now, she pulls the cord, she tells the conductor, but the train is always express, it never waits. A wandering mind is not something to be ashamed of, Miss Rover says. It's an asset. The great artists and inventors could all be led astray on tangents at the drop of a hat. It's a good sign. It is even – though I hate to poach on your father's territory, and

I feel pretty bloody ridiculous making any sort of comment whatsoever on the dubious concept of sanctity – but it is even said to be the mark of true saints that the tiniest details can distract them. They see God in the distractions themselves, they see Him in the most minute details. They see infinity in a grain of sand.

Saints. The people with golden saucers stuck to their heads in *Dictionary of Great Paintings of the Western World*, and every last one of them Catholics, some of whom, it is true, might be saved in spite of themselves, this is acknowledged in the Living World Gospel Hall, at least in the opinion of Mercy's father, though probably not in the opinion of Mr Prophet, yet even Mr Prophet will acknowledge that *some* Catholics will be saved because it is not the fault of individual Catholics that the priests stop them from reading the Bible themselves, and it is not their fault that the Pope is probably the Antichrist and is also the Beast described in the Book of Revelation, but just the same, Mercy thinks, it cannot be considered reliable information to know what Catholics have to say about saints and their wandering minds.

'We believe in the sainthood of all believers,' Mercy tells Miss Rover doubtfully, dutifully, at the age of thirteen.

'*We*,' Miss Rover says. 'But what about Mercy Given? When she is thinking for herself, what does Mercy Given believe?'

Mercy Given believes that thinking is a minefield. She thinks thinking is like climbing down a deep abandoned shaft full of picked-out opal seams and of dangerous gases that wait for a match to be thrown in. She finds Miss Rover's cache of knowledge to be as seductive as opal tunnels that lead to who knows where but possibly never come out into daylight again. She finds knowledge itself to be inexhaustible and exhausting. She is not at all sure, any more, what she believes.

Beverley Prophet twists restlessly in the pew in front of Mercy, and casually, inadvertently, breaks the guy-rope of the web. The spider reappears out of nowhere, hunched down to half-size, and sprints up a single thread to the roof. On Mr Prophet's lip, the foam line has crested a little, and tiny pieces of spume detach themselves and fly into the congregation. Mercy is uncharacteristically alert, listening intermittently, gathering clues. Under cover of her chorus book, she unfolds Beverley Prophet's note.

DEAR MERCY, it says in wobbly crayoned capitals. ITS GOOD TO SEE YOU AGEN I MISSED YOU I AM TROOLY SORY YOUR FARTHER IS 666 I WISH WE CUD FEED THE LIZARDS TOGETHER AFTER CHURCH BUT IM NOT ALOUD ANYMORE LOVE BEVERLY.

'Like Shadrach, Meshach and Abednego,' Mr Prophet spumes on. The Book of Daniel, Mercy hears . . . the fiery furnace. The Living Word Gospel Hall feels like an oven, and the blades of the ceiling fan, turning slowly, urge her to sleep. She watches them, drowsy. Her eyes circle in to the nub of the fan. She feels drugged, but struggles to focus.

'As it is written,' Mr Prophet spittles, '*Nebuchadnezzar the king was astonied, and rose up in haste, and spake, and said unto his counsellers, Did not we cast three men bound into the midst of the fire? They answered and said unto the king, True, O king. He answered and said, Lo, I see four men loose, walking in the midst of the fire, and they have no hurt; and the form of the fourth is like the Son of God.*'

'They have no hurt,' Mr Prophet shouts. 'They – have – no – hurt! Hallelujah!'

Amen amen amen, rabbles around them.

'I see four men loose,' Mr Prophet calls, jubilant, the foamy tideline on his inner lip cresting and breaking, 'I see four men loose, walking in the midst of the fire, and they have no hurt.'

Amen amen.

'Brothers and sisters, God speaks to us in signs. He who hath ears to hear, let him hear. Walking in the midst of the fire, I say unto you. *And they have no hurt!*'

Amen amen hallelujah.

'The redeemed of the Lord,' Mr Prophet shouts, jabbing his finger at the congregation, 'wherever they may be, may walk in the fire without hurt. The blessed saints, the pearls of great price, yea, even the redeemed of Oyster's Reef, they have walked in the fire without hurt.'

Amen amen.

'The one hundred and forty-four thousand,' Mr Prophet says, coasting, reining back into peacefulness his jubilation and his frenzy, 'which is signified by the four men loose, the precious living jewels of Oyster's Reef.'

Amen amen.

Mercy cannot believe her ears. Fires are unhappening themselves, reefs reappear, guilt vanishes like clouds that bring no rain.

'And who,' demands Dukke Prophet, 'who was that fourth man, whose form is like unto the Son of God?'

He leans forward and whispers to them. 'It is Oyster,' he says. 'He is set apart. He has sent a message. Those whose hearts are pure shall never die.'

Some people laugh and some weep. Some fall to the floor and clutch at the legs of others.

'Even so, dearly Beloved, the forces of darkness have not prevailed, for the Angel of the Lord was standing at the gate of that inferno, and he was pointing the way, and behold tunnels of which no one had known opened themselves and led into safety. And Oyster and all the redeemed, the truly redeemed, radiant as pearls, shining like opals, pure as the clearest clouds after a storm, they wait for us . . . They tarry out there, brothers and sisters, like Jesus himself, who went out into the desert to pray.

'They have a message for us and this is the message:

'Behold the times of the Great Tribulation are upon you. The powers of the Prince of Darkness are sent to try you. The forces of

Mammon, and the forces of the State Government, and the forces of the Federal Government, and the forces of the Department of Education and its teachers who brainwash our children, invasion, they say, blaspheming the memory of discoverers and explorers, of good Christian men who lived in the fear of the Lord . . .

'The *invasion* of Australia, they say, but when this land was *discovered*, my brothers and sisters, when this land was discovered in 1770, it was claimed in the name of God,' though that was long before Mr Prophet was an Australian citizen, Mercy thinks, and the way you can tell he is not Australian, Miss Rover used to say, whatever his documents say, and whatever passport he carries these days, is by the way he wraps himself in the Australian flag, and by the way he flies the flag above Jimjimba, because whoever heard of an Australian who needed to do such thing?

'And it is in the name of God,' *the name of Gaahd*, Mr Prophet thunders, 'that Oyster calls to us to resist the forces which blaspheme and mock and disregard . . .' and Mercy tries to disregard the flecked white words, the spray of spit, the American/South African accent, the calls of Oyster, the pieces of Oyster that are caught in the webs of her mind, his eyes, his hands that touch, the fruit of knowledge that she had to eat, the unpleasant yeasty swollen overripe fruit of bluish red, *no, I don't want to*, and again again, she is sweating, she feels sick, she cries out . . .

'The Spirit of the Lord is moving among us,' Mr Prophet says, and amens and hallelujahs clatter about Mercy like hail.

Beverley swivels a little in her pew to see if Mercy has read her note, to see what is the matter with Mercy whose face has gone deathly pale. *Are you OK?* she mouths. 'And how shall we identify the false prophets among us?' Beverley's father demands. 'How shall we know them, when Satan himself, as the Scriptures warn, can come disguised as an angel of light?

'Be not deceived by those who show a humble and contrite spirit, be not deceived, my brothers and sisters. For many there be in sheep's clothing who inwardly are ravening wolves.'

There is a rumbling as of muzzled wolves from the congregation, and Mercy can feel the hairs on her arms and legs lifting, standing on tiptoe, as though waiting for a car to roll down a driveway to a house.

'How shall we know these false prophets, brothers and sisters?'

Tell us, Brother, voices on all sides urge.

'I will tell you,' Mr Prophet says. ' Ye shall know them by their actions, and by the secret signs that the Lord has given us. For the 666, the Mark of the Beast in the Book of Revelation, the Number of Satan, the 666 will show itself . . . and I ask you to examine your memories, brothers and sisters.'

A murmur, a hum, moves through the pews. Mercy can feel something like wet towels inside her lungs. When Mr Prophet breathes out a word like *books*, he breathes fire; where the sparks fall, trouble flares. Books give off the scent of Miss Rover. They have the rank charred smell of her father's library. She fears that she herself is giving off the stench of printed pages and of the tunnels of Aladdin's Rush.

'I ask you,' Dukke Prophet spumes, 'to think of the ways in which God speaks. I ask you to ponder the Divine Mathematics. I ask you to consider the ways in which the Lord of Hosts uses numbers to send us messages and to advise us of His will.'

Mr Prophet closes his eyes and raises both arms above his head. Someone begins to hum. Another takes up the burden of tune. Words break out, *washed in the blood*, there is a detour, *of the Lamb*, into song, into singing, into washing, into blooding, words are going round and round in Mercy's head, six rounds that Beverley sings and Mercy counts, six rounds of the chorus, each one washed, each one wheezing from the organ, and the pews are racing eights, leaning this way, leaning that, Mercy is dizzy, she is ill, she is going to be sick, in the blood, in the sweeping, of the New, *aaaaaand* . . .

'Sing it again, my brethren, sing it, sisters, one more time . . .!'

. . . and they are sweeping through the webs of the New Geometry, and now Mr Prophet is flashing a numerology of fingers, three on his right hand, three on his left. Six, six, six, he flashes, then he waits. Six, six, six, he signals again.

'I ask you,' he implores, eyes closed, the semaphore of fingers held high, 'to think of the numberplates of cars that you know, yea, even of the cars of those who present themselves as servants of light.'

Mercy tries to concentrate. She blinks and squints and strives to settle her wandering eyes on Mr Prophet. His edges are spiky and shifting, Mercy is feeling dizzy, she is possibly going to be sick, but Mr Prophet is talking about cars, something terribly important about cars, and through the window Mercy can see them parked outside, all wearing their thick overcoats of dust, all the cars and trucks and utes of the Living Worders who have driven in from cattle stations and sheep stations and opal stake-outs, who have driven 20, 50, 150 kilometres, about half the population of greater Outer Maroo, faithful souls to sing the praises, to listen while Dukke Prophet preaches cars, and so here is Mercy counting off cars like sheep, counting off the cars bought in Quilpie or Longreach, here they trundle, floating by her with their numberplates, God speaks in numbers, Mr Prophet says, and who is Mercy to argue, for all the cars arrive with plates but no one bothers to keep them in Outer Maroo. Here are the people discarding them, and here are the metal plates, clankety-clankety-clank, marching by Mercy's heavy eyes, rank by numerical rank, here are the people trading them in to Ma Beresford. There is Ma and Ma's Bill (though not inside Gospel Hall, of course, not in the sanctum of the Living Word where they are nevertheless prayed for, they are much prayed for, the day of their salvation being always confidently expected), so there is Ma and Ma's Bill, and there is Dukke Prophet himself, all stockpiling numberplates, and there they go to Brisbane or Toowoomba, or to the sheep sales in

Charleville, the cattle sales in Roma, using a different numberplate each time. There's less trouble that way, Ma says. We don't want a bunch of foreigners thinking they've got our number, do we now?

And now Mr Prophet has something very troubling to show them, and he is asking them to draw their own conclusions, he is grey with sorrow, yea, he is pulled down almost to the grave with sorrow, and he lifts a numberplate and holds it above his head.

Mercy squeezes her eyes tightly shut, then allows a small splinter of light to enter in. She sees the 666 MDX, she is impressed with Mr Prophet, he is such a good weeper, he is such an outstanding sorrower, Mercy cannot help but agree with herself that he is brilliant at what he does, he is so good at sadness that she herself is feeling miserable, she is feeling a deep ocean swell of sickness, and he found, my brothers and my sisters, this damning object under the Gospel Hall, under this very building, under the vestry, under the very room where the pastor spends his time in Bible reading and prayer, and in these latter days, brothers and sisters, it is Dukke Prophet himself, the humble voice crying in the wilderness, who occupies . . . but it was not , oh no my brothers and sisters, it was not . . . not the one who cunningly tried to hide the numberplate . . . that was someone who came before . . . and Mr Prophet is asking them to ponder in their hearts the meaning.

Mercy can feel the little scuffles of the wind of soft gaspings, of supplications, of the murmured pleas to the Almighty for guidance, and what does MDX stand for, brothers and sisters? Perhaps Mercy is the air, the swaying body of the hot still air of the room which Mr Prophet is jabbing with his finger, in which he is poking holes, at which he is stabbing because M stands for Man who has vaunted himself, puffed himself up in earthly wisdom, for Man reading worldly books instead of the Bible, turning aside from the wisdom of God and leaning towards the wisdom of Man and climbing the Tower of Babel to his own destruction.

And what does D . . .? Mr Prophet swoons to them, he sweeps them into the new, he swears it stands for the Devil who lurks within the puffed-up prideful, *pray for them* who trust to worldly books, who twist and turn the Holy Word to their own devising, and X is for Christ re-crucified, nailed there over and over again, placed last, crossed out of the reckoning.

Mercy sees how the spider is busy remaking the web that Beverley Prophet, so casually, broke. She watches the nimble parcel of legs slide down a new guy-rope and then swing like a pendulum between window and pew, anchoring streamers. Phrases attach themselves. Mr Prophet is reading from the Book of Revelation, chapter 13. '*And I stood upon the sand of the sea, and saw a beast rise up out of the sea . . .*

'And the beast . . . maketh fire come down , my brothers and sisters. *He . . . maketh . . . fire . . .*'

Something swings loose in Mercy's memory like a black bat, the smoking tunnels, the roasting flesh, she feels desperately sick, it is urgent and she rehearses how, in a minute, she will stand and walk down the aisle and out the door and then she will run to the clump of she-oaks . . . The congregation sways a little and turns pale. People weep. Mercy presses her arms against her stomach and hunches over.

'*And he causeth all,*' Mr Prophet thunders, '*both small and great, rich and poor, free and bond, to receive a mark in their right hand, or in their foreheads: Let him that hath understanding count the number of the beast: for it is the number of a man; and his number is Six hundred threescore and six.*'

Mr Prophet is leaning over the pulpit, a sad father, he is gentle with his wayward children, he knows they have questions: who is the beast? and who are those sent among us to administer the mark of the beast? and how long until that moment when the trumpet shall sound and the Second Coming . . . and the Day of Judgment will announce itself . . .

And let there be no mistake, Mr Prophet warns. '*If thine hand offend thee, cut it off,*' he reminds them, '*for it is better for thee to enter into life maimed, than having two hands to go into hell, into the fire that never shall be quenched . . .*'

Let no one mistakenly think, he thunders, that it is Christian kindness to hold back, to spare the wicked . . . *If a member of the Body of Christ offend thee, cut him off, pluck her out . . .*

How long, O Lord, how long? Mr Prophet implores.

And how long before Mercy's sickness will be fully upon her, before it will rise up into her throat and announce its coming? Perhaps if she concentrates on being down in Aladdin's Rush, perhaps if she pretends she is alone, perhaps if she makes Miss Rover sit beside her, perhaps then it will go away but why does she not simply get up and walk out, not walk, no, because it may very well be necessary to run, why is she afraid to do this, if only she could put mind over matter, if she could think the sick feeling away, because she *is* afraid, knowing they will all look at her and there will be a terrible silence, and then they will pray for her, *Amen, sister*, and the Devil will leap horribly from her throat in the form of vomit . . .

Rejoice, rejoice, Mr Prophet will say, because the evil is departed from her. The sins of the fathers are visited upon the children, but this child has been saved, the evil has leaped from her body, rejoice, rejoice, o my people.

Mercy sways and moans and holds her hand against her mouth. She wants to keep her evil to herself. How horrible to be prayed for, how horrible to be approved of by Mr Prophet.

Or perhaps he will say: *If Mercy Given offend thee, cut her off . . .*

Mr Prophet is patiently, lovingly explaining, decoding the beast who is sliding to the very core, sneaking into Outer Maroo by satellite dish though not in the homes of the godly where television, praise God, is not . . . but through the length and breadth of this country turned godless and gone whoremongering after . . . and the beast, it seems, is the godless government in all its manifestations . . . its Prime Minister who, significantly, serves the Pope, the Antichrist, the same Prime Minister who wants to twist history, to sink the country in a godless republican sea . . .

Mercy is adrift in the god-thick sea, she will get quietly to her feet in ten seconds, she will move to the end of the pew, she will walk meekly and unobtrusively, perhaps she will run, she will count to ten and then . . . and the ten horns of the Beast are the departments of the State Government, especially its Department of Education . . . and its teachers, its tax collectors, its maps, its roads, its tourist buses, all the forms of impurity and danger sent to tempt, to spy, to corrupt, to soil . . . but the end is near, the end of which no man knoweth the day nor the hour, as saith the Scriptures, but many signs, many prophecies, suggest that the *year*, and hath not Oyster warned them, though Mercy definitely cannot wait for the year 2000, she rises, she can feel a cold sweat from forehead to feet, her legs feel like water, she will have to will herself down the aisle, there is something rising in her throat with the force of a newly sunk artesian bore, it is urgent and irresistible. Mr Prophet points his fiery finger, but Mercy runs down the steps and across the packed red gravel to the spindly cluster of she-oaks where every one of Mr Prophet's words leaves her mouth in a thick rush of grey.

Something strange is happening to the light. At one corner of her eye, the livid disc of the sun clenches and unclenches but its rim is tearing loose and its centre is swooping into darkness as though a total eclipse were taking place. Pieces of Dukke Prophet's voice come loose also, black soot drifting . . . sun turning to darkness . . . moon into blood . . . judgment judgment judgment handed down.

How cold Mercy is, holding herself up with the she-oaks, no, not cold, burning hot, or perhaps both at once. She seems to be travelling between Cold and Hot as though they were separate and distant countries. She is moving at dizzy speed, too quickly for the vehicle of her body. It vibrates. Its wheels seem to be out of alignment. Its brakes have failed. Someone must have turned a hose on it because everything feels damp.

Mercy presses her clammy forehead against the trunk and stares queasily at the mazy rabbit tracks around her feet, the land's worst enemy, Miss Rover says, in spite of myxomatosis especially introduced, in spite of government death warrants, millions of them rabbiting on, breeding resistance, burrowing in, riddling the outback with holes. The entire bloody country will cave in one day, Ma Beresford says. The rabbit tracks merge and dissolve. It's late, Dukke Prophet cries, it's late, and the Day of Decision is at hand, and Mercy watches a rabbit surface and listen, nose twitching.

The rabbit quivers in sunlight, it gives off fear, it gives off a fog that Mercy enters, a strange new state, and a wonderful undulating calm is beginning to settle on her like a silk cloak dropped from the sky.

Oh dear, oh dear, the rabbit says, I think you are going to black out, and Mercy does not feel at all surprised to hear it speak because on the last day there shall be great signs and wonders, and also, Miss Rover says, the secret of the most subversive books is that the author never acknowledges, by so much as the tremor of an eyelash, that anything out of the ordinary is taking place. Remember that, Mercy. It is also the secret of con men like Oyster. That is what is frightening about them.

Oh dear, oh dear, the rabbit says, we shall be too late, we shall miss the end of the world.

Mercy clings to the trunk of the gidgee tree. She hears her name called.

She is dimly aware, on her left, of Jess. On the shadowy verandah, Jess is waving her arms, she can hear Jess's voice . . . 'dehydrated . . . sunstroke . . . going to faint if we don't . . .' and the percussion of feet.

On her right, Beverley Prophet is also running, 'Mercy Mercy, Daddy says we'll take you home . . .'

But Mercy is mesmerised by the paisley swirls of tracks in the dust. She is transfixed by the luminous eyes of the rabbit. Help me, she implores. She is swooping towards it in a sickening arc. The rabbit-hole widens and widens.

Miss Rover come over, Miss Rover come over, she calls.

And in another moment, Miss Rover reads, *down went Mercy after the rabbit, never once considering how in the world she was to get out again.*

Book II

Oyster's Reef

Surely some revelation is at hand;
Surely the Second Coming is at hand . . .

And what rough beast, its hour come round at last,
Slouches towards Bethlehem to be born?

W.B. Yeats, *The Second Coming*

1. Oyster

What we cannot forgive is the fact that we were seduced.

We cannot quite believe that we were all taken in by Oyster – at least in the beginning – and we cannot accept it. We cannot forgive ourselves. No. That is not quite right. Because we are embarrassed and even frightened by our gullibility, and because we are instinctively self-protective, and because we are cunning and devious and desperate in all the ordinary ways, we have come up with many different reasons for forgiving ourselves, but we cannot forgive Oyster. Dreams visit us in which, retroactively, we see all the signs and portents, all the early warning signals that we blithely ignored at the time. We were seduced because we wanted to be, and we do not forgive Oyster for that.

When he stumbled into town – it was just over four years ago, a few days before Christmas, at 2.23 one afternoon, a trivial piece of information perhaps, but a detail that happens to be fixed in my memory because I was behind the bar in Bernie's as usual and when I saw the stranger with the swag and the rifle on his back limping past the window, I looked at the clock as though it might give me some clue – but it was still the doldrum stretch of baked heat, when nothing is supposed to move. The pub was in a state of torpor, drowsy with stockmen and roustabouts and a few opal diggers (Major Miner, for example, was there; and young Donny Becker, I definitely remember that). They had all just had lunch and were sleeping over their beers. It was the listless hour, the hour of mirages, and for a moment I assumed I was witnessing an optical illusion.

Then there was a palpable sense of shock that it was possible for someone unknown to be out there, just beyond the verandah railing, without having given any advance warning whatsoever: no oncoming hum of a car engine, no cloud of dust, no whisper picked up in Quilpie or Charleville on supply trips that some drifter was in the region. More than that, more disturbing than that, was the fact that he was approaching from the west, from the broiling heart of the country, and not from the direction of Quilpie or Eromanga. Now it is true that there is a road of sorts, a track of sorts, from Birdsville; and there is another, of sorts, from Innamincka; but the four-wheel drivers who tackle these routes are rare, and this visitor was on foot.

His rifle slipped from his shoulder, and he grabbed at it, making a clatter, and there was a feral stir of watchfulness and unease, the kind that a stranger evokes as surely as a match strikes fire. Everyone moved out on to the verandah, a wary swarm, and the stranger stopped and looked at us.

He was like an apparition, insubstantial. He was like a mirage.

I think we did not really believe our eyes.

He was quite strikingly beautiful in that disturbing way of people who seem to hover in the androgynous border zones.

His clothes were loose-fitting and white – they seemed to be made of sailcloth, at least the loose pants and even the white canvas boots did, though the tunic was of something softer and finer. And then there was the blood, ghastly against the white pants, a great clotted sweep of it, dark and still moist, on his leg. We were all riveted.

He swayed a little, as though he were about to faint, and the weight of the swag and the rifle almost pulled him off his feet, then he steadied himself by catching hold of the verandah railing, and he smiled. When he spoke, his voice was low, and we had to lean close to hear, so that there was an aura of intimacy from the start, or there seemed to be, and we had the impression that we were being invited to hear momentous secrets.

This suited us.

He is one of us, we thought, relaxing a little, for nobody lives in a place like Outer Maroo unless he has things to hide (certain private details to bury, certain details to flee), and these hidden matters are so legion that they populate the desert spaces quite thickly, they sigh and leer and whisper and flaunt themselves, they fill sleep with a crowd of witnesses, they appear and disappear and reappear in such a way that even after a fugitive has safely reached nowhere, even after he has preened himself on his absolute exit from the map of his life, he will never feel secure. He will never feel adequately isolated. At night, he will hear the soft slither of the past: all the people who have observed him even momentarily in his flight, who have registered him, perhaps, who have mentioned his passing to someone else, who have read an item in a newspaper and looked at him (or her) and knit their brows together, thoughtful; all the people who know something, or who *might* know something, all sending out messages (a word, a raised eyebrow, a newspaper clipping) and in dreams a woman like me, for example, or a man like Major Miner, can see these messages seeping into the water table, drop by slow distant drop, leaking from memories and locked files on the other side of the decade, of the country, of the world, seeping into the great subterranean places where all the waters and all the memories meet and wash together. A man with a past to hide can hear the soft plash of evidence far below him, a thin but detectable stream polluting the Great Artesian Basin, bubbling and roiling away down there, its temperature increasing under pressure, its will to erupt growling and growing. It is biding its time. It is waiting to blow. It is waiting only for a new bore to be sunk, a new vent, a new opening, and then it will announce itself in a savage, showy, scalding explosion.

People who flee to nowhere are always waiting for retribution to catch up with them.

What is different about the Oysters of the world (so I realise now, though I did not understand it then) is that their dreams are untroubled. What I do realise now, at this moment, is that I am instinctively sliding away from reliving the moment of Oyster's arrival, embarrassed by the recollection of it, by the impact on all of us (on me too, I might as well confess it), by that indefinable but calculated aura that held us in thrall, and for which we will never forgive him – though the Oysters of the world are indifferent to the giving or withholding of forgiveness, they care nothing for recrimination or blame. Their dreams are untroubled. They do not expect to be caught. They never consider that what they have done merits censure. Perhaps they were adored and over-indulged as children; perhaps any mischief brought applause; perhaps they pushed at the edges of this unstinting adulation, looking for limits, and found none: when they tortured mice, say; or when they shoplifted; when they lured other children into danger, or dared them to lie on railway lines, promising safety . . . perhaps a mother or a grandmother smiled fondly and absent-mindedly and said: Isn't he a little devil? Isn't he a larrikin? Perhaps an ambitious but often absent father (a man of political power? a military man?) tousled the cruel little head and said approvingly: That's my boy. We men don't let the world push us around.

Or perhaps it was the opposite. Perhaps the absolute absence of endorsement or appreciation or affection of any kind rendered them unnaturally indifferent to the opinions of others, and therefore quite unaware, quite unable to gauge their impact on their prey.

I don't know, I don't know.

I do know that people like Oyster walk inside a gigantic shadow of themselves and that they are entranced by the play of that shadow on the wall of the world. I know that they must have an audience to watch the flickering theatre of their lives. They must. What, after all, would be the substance of a shadow with no one to see it? But they always *do* have an audience, the Oysters of this world, because they believe in their bones that they are above the common ruck of men and of laws. It is an article of faith with them. They make rules for others to follow, they themselves being exempt. They know they are chosen, and the calm certainty fills them with an intense white light. Moths are drawn to it.

Afterwards, in Outer Maroo, we told ourselves (that is to say, I believe each person told himself, went on telling herself, in secret; we have not often discussed the matter publicly in recent years, and especially not in this last year since the Reef disappeared; since then, needless to say, the matter of Oyster has become the ultimate taboo), we told ourselves that we had known immediately and instinctively that there was a certain kind of stink to Oyster, of a variety we knew all too well, though just how recent the blood reek was we did not guess. We forgave this stink because we were unable to scrub it off ourselves; because we thought it made him one of us; because, to put it bluntly, we thought it meant he was not a threat.

That, I think, is what made everyone susceptible.

But this is hindsight. This is hindsight.

And perhaps – I sometimes think so – it could have been otherwise. (It *was* otherwise, a number of people believe, or believed, right up to the outbreak of the fire that still rages before my eyes.) Perhaps there could have been a different ending. (There *was* a different ending, some people say; and there are others – oh, I know there will still be others out on their properties, beyond the reach of the fire – who will insist that there has not been an ending yet, that the ending is still to come.) But even those who believe that a certain kind of ending has taken place, even they cannot help asking themselves if it might have been different. Perhaps Oyster could have remained what he seemed to be in the beginning, and it was the cast of characters and the circumstances of Outer Maroo which turned him into what he became.

I don't know. I don't know.

I do know that in the beginning he arrived as rain arrives in the outback. He was our miracle, the one we had been waiting for. He changed the air. He put a spring in everyone's step, and everyone was drawn to him.

Almost everyone.

There were, *almost* from the start, a few resisters: my prickly self, though perhaps this does not count, since I am wary of everyone; and there was Charles Given; and there was Susannah Rover, though Susannah came late and left early. Oyster had already been in Outer Maroo for a year when Susannah arrived, and he set his cap at her, I remember. He was dazzled, he wanted her badly. To no avail. She was immune, as Charles Given was immune, though God knows, those two would seem to have had little enough in common, other than a pig-headed refusal to compromise their spiky and altogether inconvenient integrities, or to shut up and be sensibly silent in their own best interests. Still. For what their refusal to succumb said about everyone else, the town has not been disposed to forgive them.

This should hardly be surprising. Perhaps it was *their* fault, people began to tell themselves. They were troublemakers, those two. They were stirrers. This theory came to seem more and more plausible to people as time went on. They spread mistrust, those two, people murmured. They never gave Oyster a chance. They spread lies.

That is why things got out of hand.

That is what made Oyster change – and everyone agrees he did change. He twisted. He became twisted; but he was, some feel, bent by bad will.

That is why payment had to be exacted and meted out.

To be scrupulously accurate, it should be acknowledged that

Mercy Given was also among the first resisters: but Mercy was only twelve years old when Oyster came, and children have an unfair advantage. There is, after all, some fierce and atavistic chemistry which informs them, unerringly, of the difference between those they can trust and those from whom they should draw back. Older people lose the knack of it. They age into too much dissembling and too many masks of their own.

As for masks . . .

Oyster, it turned out, had a wardrobe full of them.

Outside Bernie's at 2.23 on that particular December afternoon just before Christmas, he was boyish and handsome and charming. He was one of those ageless young-old, old-young men with greying hair that hung in a shock of curls on his forehead. His eyes were a piercing blue, but not piercing in the usual way because the blue was a strange blue, pallid, washed out, a whitish mauve-ish blue, almost the colour of jacaranda blossoms just before they die, just before they finally succumb to the heat and scatter themselves on the lawns of Brisbane, and it was this curious, almost milky pallor that made the eyes so disturbing. When he looked at you, in his fixed attentive way, you knew you were being singled out in an extraordinary way. You had the sensation, a *physical* sensation, even as you scoffed at yourself, even as you were embarrassed by your own reaction, that a spring in your life was being wound more tightly and that your nerve ends were gearing up for significant change.

I remember reading somewhere that all that is required, in order to exert influence on, to attract, to seduce another human being, is to maintain fixed eye contact for several seconds longer than is socially acceptable; the recipient, in spite of himself (or herself), cannot resist the flattery. Perhaps Oyster's power was as simple as that; or perhaps it was the eeriness of those limpid blue opalescent eyes; or perhaps, on that hot December day, it was the fizzing aura of compressed energy he gave off even though he was on the point of fainting from heatstroke and pain.

At any rate everyone thought: here is a man in his fifties who is prematurely grey but remarkably vigorous, and who looks scarcely older than forty; though in fact it is possible, if more recent information is reliable (Nick's information), that he may have been sixty – not that any information with respect to Oyster can be considered more than provisionally reliable. Perhaps because there was nothing at all at the core of Oyster (that is one of my theories), he had the fluid capacity of fitting the shape of everyone's dreams and of being whatever age one needed him to be.

I think young Donny Becker was the first to speak, and he asked a simple enough question. 'What happened to you?' – because the stranger was limping, and there was that ghastly mess of blood clotted along one leg. His right foot seemed to have been caught in a mangle, or perhaps rolled over by a jeep. The dark stain, a thick, blackish red, almost plum-coloured, on his white trouser leg and white boot was quite shocking.

Oyster turned his pale eyes full on Donny for several seconds, and for some reason everyone looked at Donny too, as though the asking of the question, rather than the answer, had become the significant thing. Donny swallowed. He was just a sixteen-year-old kid at the time, and to be singled out in this way, to be the focus of everyone's eyes, paralysed him with embarrassment. A mottled rash suddenly reddened the left side of his neck and branched upward on to his face. He lifted his left hand to his cheek. When he dropped it again, I could see the white imprint of his fingers against the flushed skin.

'Who are you?' someone else demanded, but this intrusion energised Donny. It was as though, suddenly, he became unwilling to relinquish the intensity of Oyster's gaze, and he said in a rush: 'Did your jeep roll over you? Did you hit a 'roo? What happened? How did you get here?' – because no one could see any sign of an unknown vehicle in the street, no one had heard anything unfamiliar arriving, and outback people know the signature sound of everything on wheels the way city people recognise faces.

Oyster said something, but very softly, as though he were giving Donny a private answer. Maybe he did no more than move his lips. Whatever he said, or didn't say, no one heard it, and everyone leaned in closer. There was a shuffling, a kind of swarming together, a hum of *What? We didn't hear you. What did you say? What did he . . .? We couldn't hear . . .*

I was watching Donny and I saw his eyes widen, as though the answer, intended only for him, was not at all the kind of answer he had bargained on.

Then Bernie spoke. 'Who are you?' he demanded roughly, authoritatively, slightly irritably. 'Where are you from?'

Oyster shifted his gaze from Donny, and as he did so, Donny put both hands to his cheeks. Everyone registered this, and then everyone turned with Oyster to look at Bernie, and Bernie frowned. I'm more than used to Bernie's short fuse. Oyster looked at Bernie for so long that I knew something exceptional was happening by the mere fact that Bernie did not swear, or spit, or turn away. I was astonished. I was fascinated. I kept expecting Bernie's usual kind of deadpan over-the-top line: *What's the matter, mate? Haven't you ever seen a red-blooded transvestite before?* And when Bernie said nothing at all, when his eyes kept swimming in the watery blue-mauve of Oyster's eyes, I felt a slow burn of excitement, though excitement was something I'd trained myself not to feel for a good few years. Perhaps this stranger can hypnotise, I thought; perhaps he has hypnotised Bernie so that Bernie cannot lower his eyes and cannot turn away.

'What did you say?' Oyster asked. He spoke very courteously and very quietly, but everyone heard him.

And Bernie stammered: 'Who . . .?' – and cleared his throat and began again. 'I said . . .' And he cleared his throat again.

'Yes.' The stranger nodded, as though Bernie's difficulties were a tribute which he accepted, and as though he had heard the question in its unspoken form. 'Yes. Of course you are curious.' He nodded again. Then he beckoned to everyone with both hands and we all leaned closer. 'I am Oyster,' he said.

Ahh . . ., we murmured uncertainly.

A collective sigh slipped through the verandah railings and down to the street where the stranger still stood, drooping a little, and sometimes wincing from the pain in his leg. He was pale, and there were beads of sweat on his face, and no one would have been surprised if he had fainted before our eyes. Nevertheless it still amazes me in retrospect that no one asked 'Oyster who?' – though later, of course, later, in the brief period between the end of the honeymoon and the state of undeclared war with the Reef, this moment became the long-running serial gag of Outer Maroo, an endless game, with more versions and more re-runs than Dad-and-Dave jokes.

Knock, knock.
Who's there?
Oyster.
Oyster who?
Oystro-enteritis, otherwise known as pearl-up-the-arse.

Knock, knock.
Who's there?
Oyster.
Oyster who?
'Oist 'er up 'ere , mate, where me drilling rig fits in her opal shaft.

Knock, knock.
Who's there?
Oyster.

Oyster who?

'Oist 'im, *mate; 'oist 'im, not 'er; 'oist 'im on 'is own petard.*

And so on, and so on, for ever and ever amen in Bernie's pub, non-stop through the cold war period, right on up until the Disappearance, after which all jokes and all discussion abruptly stopped.

Of course I should not be remembering the jokes now, out of sequence, because the memory falsifies the mood of that first afternoon, a mood which swung from astonishment, to anxiety, to awe. There was no shred of jokiness in the air that day. On the day of Oyster's arrival, not one single person, in a pub chock full of habitual larrikins and knockers, not one of them so much as thought of the question *Oyster who?*

No one spoke at all. We just waited. We *gaped*, I suppose.

I wish someone had taken a photograph of us from where Oyster stood. These days, I find myself imagining us in a painting by Drysdale: the terracotta earth all around, the stark verandah rails, a gaunt vertical cluster of lost souls with staring eyes and open mouths, all of them looking as though they had seen a ghost.

We just stood there waiting.

For the mounting of the sermon, Susannah Rover laughed a year later. You were set up, she was to say often and sardonically. You were set up. For the mounting of the sermon and the B platitudes, she claimed, but she'd give Oyster an A for seduction.

Very funny, Susannah, Pete Burnett would say.

Can't you see that you were set up? she would ask. Just days before Christmas? Honestly.

Blessed are the graziers, she would mock, who live on vast cattle properties and who believe the government is out to get them, for they shall be protected from state and federal interference.

She had an uncanny way of mimicking Oyster's voice, the rise and fall of it, the passionate fortes and intimate lows.

Blessed are they who hunger and thirst for a taxless cash economy, she would say, for they shall be in on my opal spree. And blessed are ye, o little towns of the outback, when all men revile you and persecute you, blessed are ye, all ye cow cockies and yobbos with a persecution complex, for a white knight with a rifle on his back will arrive when the Christmas star is in the sky . . . but at about this point Pete Burnett would stop her mouth with a long wet kiss. You're a raving lunatic, love, he would say, but nervously, in case anyone else but himself and me had heard her. It was never a smart idea to make fun of gullibility in Outer Maroo. It was not a way to endear yourself to the town.

It takes two to demythologise, Pete, she would say. One to go over the top, and the other to undercut. Half the time, he never knew what the hell she was on about, but he loved watching her talk. He loved the perfume of danger on her. He got high on it. I'm the undercutter, she would say. And guess who is over the top?

She could not leave the topic alone. She kept hearing different accounts, all embroidered, and increasingly so, of Oyster's first manifestation – that was *her* term for it, ironical; but funnily enough it caught on and came to be used straight, without any self-consciousness, so that people would speak of *that hot afternoon, a Friday, wasn't it? the day of Oyster's first manifestation*, or they might say *There was something he said at the second manifestation that keeps . . .* and so on, and they would say these things much as they might say *That day Bernie's truck broke down, you remember?*

Susannah kept hearing stories and she could not resist setting to work, snip snip snip, with her scissoring mind.

With apologies to Dickens, she would say, in a puckering Pickwick kind of voice, they've got very good power of suction, Pete, oysters have. Oyster would ha' made an uncommon fine oyster himself if he'd been born in that station o' life.

With apologies to Swift, she would say, he was a bold, rash man, Pete, he who first swallowed an Oyster.

But I should stop myself from remembering this sort of thing out of sequence, because it skews things, I keep skewing things, I keep bringing to bear a knowingness and a scepticism that were simply not present that first afternoon (though I'm not averse to pretending there was something of Susannah in me right from the start, because of course I'm embarrassed, thinking back; perhaps I'll become more like Susannah as my chronicle proceeds. Of course I'd like to pretend to myself that if Susannah had been there that first day, she would have succumbed like everyone else, at least for a day or two. I wonder? But no, I suspect not; not Susannah). Anyway, I should try to be more rigorously honest. I should not muddle up pristine and retrospective attitudes, except for the fact that it does not seem to be possible to think about Oyster in only one way at a time.

And yet on that first day, of course, everyone did. There were no complex levels to our reactions. We were apprehensive as we always are with strangers, and then we were intensely curious, and then we were beguiled. We had no cynicism.

'I am Oyster,' he said, and we simply stood there, patiently waiting.

'I used to have another name,' he said. 'An ordinary name. But it belonged to another life.'

('That,' Nick was to tell me, 'is the understatement of the century. He had other *lives*.'

Ah well, I thought, who hasn't? In Outer Maroo, who hasn't?

'And not one of them edifying,' Nick said.)

Oyster smiled disarmingly and looked from person to person in a slow and deliberate way as though he were searching for someone he knew, letting his eyes rest on each face for whole seconds. You know what I mean about another name and another life, his eyes said; and of course we did. Most people in Outer Maroo knew exactly what he meant. When he looked at me, his smile deepened in a complicit, knowing way, and he nodded slightly, and for a few seconds I had the eerie and totally unnerving sensation that he could see the bar and the back alley in Roma where I had so hurriedly shed the skin of my past life. I had the sensation that he saw all my selves in multiple exposure (gypsy child, rural convent girl, city student, government surveyor, violent offender, and finally me, Old Silence, at home beyond the end of the railway line). It is mortifying for a strong-willed person like myself to admit to having experienced this sensation of transparency, this sensation of . . . of what . . .? of momentary fusion, of the illusion of momentary fusion. How did he do it? How did he sense so unerringly everyone's Achilles' heel? No, that is not the way to put it. How did he make everyone *believe* that he had access to secret shames? It is my own collusion in this, even though it was brief, that still disturbs me. I still cannot account for it. His eye contact was intense, and lingered longer than was comfortable, and when he nodded again and moved on to the next person, I found myself, like Donny, putting a hand to my flushed cheek.

When he had finished his survey of the little crowd on the verandah – I suppose there were fifteen of us, and he gave the impression that he had memorised each face – Oyster wiped his forehead with the back of one forearm and began to drag his injured right foot towards the steps. He grimaced and swayed again, and hands reached over to steady him. We could see where the foot left smears of blood in the dust. He had to pull himself up, step by step, both hands on the banister, though that is a ludicrously refined word for the rough-sawn chunk of wood that served the purpose. Predictably (maybe even intentionally?) there came a moment when he gave a sharp gasp of pain and lifted his hand as though scalded. We could all see the thick jag of splinter, big as a casuarina pine-needle, and the bead of blood like a jewel in the palm of his hand. He stared at his blood and turned pale, though it was hardly to be compared with the congealing mess of it at his ankle. He looked around in a bewildered way and then his eyes settled on me and he extended his hand like a child.

What I remember is a sudden intense flare of inner conflict, extreme, and entirely disproportionate to the moment, because I was still under the spell of his beauty, and his improbability, and his . . .well, *theatricality*, but I do not like to be given orders, implicit or otherwise. I don't like it now, I didn't then, I never have. I have an intense, highly allergic, gypsy railway-ganger's reaction to the slightest hint of coercion. Yet it would have been a pointless discourtesy not to respond. I remember actually thinking that. Oyster swayed slightly, and the swag and the rifle lurched away from him, and that settled it, I suppose, because I respond equally instinctively, equally haplessly, to vulnerability; though now that I think back to that moment and hold it up to the light and study it, I realise (with a giddy sense of relief and self-congratulation) that it is not completely true that there was no cynicism whatsoever in my earliest response. I remember now that I had a sense of being manipulated, and that I felt irritated, but that simultaneously I felt it was churlish and ridiculous of me to be annoyed with a man who was clearly exhausted and injured (his foot, I mean; not the splinter) and I felt ashamed of myself.

I stepped forward and cradled his hand in both of mine, and pulled the splinter out in one deft painless motion. There was a bubble of blood about the size of a ruby and I found that I had his hand in my mouth, sucking it, cauterising the puncture with my tongue. I had no recollection of deciding to do this; in fact, I rather think it was he who propelled his hand towards my lips (but perhaps that is retrospective dishonesty again). 'Thank you,' he said. And then he carried our joined hands to his own lips. He did not kiss my hand, though that is what the salute would have looked like to anyone else: a fleeting gesture of chivalry, a formality (though of a kind not commonly seen in outback pubs, as I imagine I have no need to point out). But no, he did not kiss my hand.

He slid my fingertips into his mouth and licked them, his eyes on mine. I know what you want, his tongue said, casually arrogant.

And yes, I felt a stirring of primitive sexual excitement, purely animal.

I do not forgive him.

I think even then (in fact I am sure of it; I am virtually certain; I am almost entirely sure), I think I resented him for it. His eyes offered some sort of dare; mine (I am sure of this) offered nothing.

Then he returned my hand to my side, accompanying it for the length of its trip in an exotically formal and gentlemanly way, his eyes now milkily expressionless though still fixed on mine.

You have a feverish imagination, his eyes said politely, with just a faint suggestion of hostility. (Was I aware of that then, or is it only now, in retrospect? Was the menace really there? Or am I adding it, now that I know what I know, what I think I know?)

If you think that anything unusual has happened, his eyes seemed to say, it is all in your mind.

He released my hand and pulled himself a little further along the verandah. He set the swag down, but kept the rifle slung across his back.

The rifle. We all keep a rifle in the car. Everyone in the outback does; everyone west of the coastal cities does; it's purely humane. Along with four-wheel drive, a spare tyre, spare parts, spare petrol tank, and a 'roo bar, it is a simple driving accessory, indispensable. None of us wants to leave a kangaroo or an emu or a prime example of Simmenthal heifer writhing in a pool of blood beside the road. No one (well, almost no one; there are, I'm afraid, sadistic hoodlums) wants to hit such creatures in the first place, the damage inflicted on both parties by collisions often being extraordinarily severe, but sudden encounters at high speeds are not infrequent, and a rifle behind the driver's seat is simply a compassionate act. We do not leave animals to die in slow pain. So. Oyster's rifle meant nothing; but the absence of a vehicle meant much. It disposed us, you see, to accept his coming as miraculous. It predisposed us to let him get away with talking in the way he did.

Oyster's rifle clattered against the verandah post, and he adjusted it, and eased his back against the railing, and everyone settled warily around.

'The blackest waters have passed over me,' he said solemnly, conversationally, as though he were saying: it's been a bugger of a drought, hasn't it? 'As they have passed over many of you,' he said.

There was a long silence while we pondered these words, while we wondered what it meant that someone would speak like this on the verandah of a pub, rather than saying, for example, *I've been up shit creek without a paddle, mates*, and we wondered about someone who could make such an earnest way of speaking seem ordinary.

It seemed to go with his arriving out of the blue.

Across the road, cars and utes were beginning to arrive at the Living Word for the afternoon prayer meeting. Here come the holy rollers, someone murmured, but Oyster frowned at that, and for some reason people wanted his approval, and so the usual round of jokey comments did not start up, though, in general, in small outback towns, the godly and the ungodly accommodate one another quite affectionately. They shear sheep at the same shearing time, they muster cattle the same way, that is what counts. They are as interdependent as night and day. They need each other. 'We are the seed ripe unto bloody harvest,' Ma's Bill is in the habit of saying, speaking on behalf of the ungodly. 'Who else would they have to bloody pray for? If we all up and got saved, the whole prayer-meeting kit and caboodle would come tumbling down.'

And then there is also this: both the godly and the ungodly in outback towns distrust equally the government, the coastal cities, the newspapers, the ABC, the Department of Education, the godless Other, the World, the Flesh, the Devil, all the people out there who are not in the little crucible of pastoral *us*. This binds the two camps into one family.

Across the road, the Given family was arriving in a battered Holden ute. Bernie raised his hand in greeting to Charles Given, and the pastor returned the salute. Brian and Mercy clambered out of the back of the truck. Mercy would have been twelve at the time, but she was small for her age and could have passed for nine or ten. She was one of those children whom people instantly take to, the way they do to kittens, to newborn puppies, to foals, to lambs, to day-old calves.

'Will you look at that little monkey?' Ma's Bill said fondly. 'Someone's gonna pick her up and put her in his pocket before she's eighteen, eh Donny?' – and Donny coloured up like beetroot water.

'Hello darlin'!' Ma's Bill called, and Mercy waved and blew kisses.

Oyster turned to look.

'Who is that beautiful child?' he asked, and I don't know why, but the way he asked it made me deeply uneasy.

'That's young Mercy Given, the pastor's kid,' Ma's Bill told him.

I watched Oyster closely. Who knows? Perhaps my motives were of the basest kind. Perhaps I was still in the confusing middle of that finger-licking buzz, perhaps I felt a stirring of the most primitive kind of sexual jealousy. I won't even try, from this distance, to sort that out. What I do know, intent as I was on his intent gaze, is this: it was not Mercy his eye rested on, but Brian.

People used to joke about the Givens. Given this, and given that, they would say, and given a bit of a mix-up at birth, Brian is too bloody girl-beautiful and Mercy has the brains of a boy.

They do not make jokes like that any more; certainly not on the subject of Brian.

Mercy saw Major Miner on the verandah and ran halfway across the road. 'Major Miner,' she called, 'can I come and see your boulder-opal mine again? Will you take me again? Please, please, *please*?'

'Well . . .' Major Miner said, teasing her. 'I don't know. I'll have to think about it.'

'Oh please,' she said. 'Jess, please make him take me.'

I might as well admit that Mercy Given has been able to wrap me around her little finger from Day One, and for reasons that I don't pretend to hide. She is a kind of weird reversal of myself, of my gypsy railway-ganger and my convent-girl years. She has the same kind of innocence (frightening), and limitless ignorance about the world, that those environments (both cloistered, in their totally different ways) gave me; and the same kind of unconventional knowingness. I want to hover around like her guardian angel. I don't want her to make my mistakes.

'Jess?' she cajoled. 'Tell Major Miner he has to take me,' though she knew very well, the young minx, that she was not going to get me to speak. Not in public.

'G'day, Mercy,' Donny Becker said, blushing.

'G'day, Donny. Hey, I found a great new place to catch lizards.'

'Mercy,' her father called sternly, and Mercy turned and ran towards the Living Word.

'Ah, Donny.' Charles Given said. 'We haven't seen you in prayer meeting for a while.' It was meant obliquely, I think, as parental warning, but Donny took it as invitation.

'I was just coming, Pastor Given.' And then he called out with such uncharacteristic bravado that I can only assume Oyster's gaze had transformed him. 'Hey, Mercy! Wait for me!'

Mercy turned.

Oyster watched her, and this time, yes, his eyes were on her, and I bridled, I felt a different kind of jealousy, I felt like a mother lion watching her cub.

Oyster watched her. Everyone watched her. She was quite as beautiful as her brother Brian, but of course her beauty sat on her more easily, more casually, than it did on him. It was not an advantage in an outback town, or in any Australian town for that matter, for a boy to look as Brian Given did. But there was also the matter of Mercy's fizzing little mind. She was a stirrer. She came out with startling ideas, as though some vinegary person, pickled, a hundred years old, were curled up inside her and were pushing words out through her mouth. Everyone was as wary of her as they were fond of her. People treated her as though she were some sort of exotic rainforest lorikeet inexplicably blown off course and over the Great Divide and on into Outer Maroo. She might suddenly bite as a cockatoo bites, but more likely she would simply fly away. We all watched Mercy and Donny Becker and Brian and Charles Given disappear into the shadows of the Living Word.

'Amen,' Ma's Bill said. 'Jess, how about more beers all around? This one's on me.'

'Amen,' Oyster said, and as I began to move back into the bar, he put his hand in his pocket and withdrew it and then held out his open palm. Three opals the size of walnuts, only roughly cut, and only partially polished, nestled there. The shimmer of the blues and reds, in particular, was extraordinary and of a brilliance only possible when the undernotes were dark; they were like the black opals of Lightning Ridge.

Opals are something we know about in Outer Maroo, even though only half a dozen loners, Major Miner among them, were working the old seams and the old fields and the open-cut boulder-opal cliffs in the breakaways at that time. Most of us have found floaters of some value out among the breakaways. As for Bugger Harvey and Scotty McTavish and Big Leather Jack and the rest, they were certifiably crazy, and we saw them once in a blue moon when they sidled into Bernie's back room and reached into their socks or their underwear and fished out their little bags of stones.

So. Opals we know about.

But Oyster had our instant awed attention with his stones, and everyone, myself included, forgot about the next round of beer.

'Holy shit!' Major Miner said with reverence.

'A pure child,' Oyster said, 'is like one of these. Those children who have just entered the House of the Lord are like these gemstones. Goodness absorbs the light and gives it back. *Verily, I say unto you, whosoever shall not receive the kingdom of God as a little child, he shall not enter therein.*'

Now this is the kind of thing that is no doubt comfortably said in places like the Living Word Gospel Hall, but it is not said on the verandahs of pubs. I do not know, even now, how Oyster got away with it, I simply do not know; but the opals, and the rifle, and the absence of any visible means of transport, and perhaps also his bloodied foot, and the heat of the day, and the hour of mirages, all that must have swung it, I suppose. All I can vouch for is that we were mesmerised.

'Holy shit,' Major Miner said again, staring at the opals. I almost thought he was going to cross himself. 'I want to touch them,' he breathed. 'I want to kiss them.' And when Oyster extended them towards him, he did. That is exactly what he did. Anyone who has been to Coober Pedy or Lightning Ridge or Yowah will have no trouble believing this. The devotees of opal will prostrate themselves before its colorific and prismatic silica flames. They will offer up house, mortgage, bank account, spouse, children, life itself, to opalescent fire. They smoulder with passion, they burn.

'Where did those come from?' Major Miner breathed.

'They were given to me,' Oyster said. 'Our Mother Earth gave them to me. My new name was given to me. A hand rose up out of the ocean of time and gave them to me. If you are drowning, and you know you are drowning, and someone throws you a lifeline, everything changes. Everything is different.'

Everyone shifted uneasily, watching him.

I saw him casting invisible lines, hooking people, winding them in. The opals won their respect; and beyond that perhaps it was his eyes; perhaps it was his voice; perhaps it was the sheer absence of self-consciousness. Oyster believed in himself.

'Consider the oyster,' he said. 'The oyster is a bivalve mollusc. It produces its own eggs and its own sperm. It fertilises itself. It is male and female, both. It is complete in itself. It is perfect.'

Dazed, we considered the perfection of oysters.

'Have you ever visited an oyster farm?' he asked. 'Well, out here . . . out here, I suppose not . . .' It was a little joke, and his eyes invited us to laugh.

'I've got fossilised oysters out on the Great Extended,' Major Miner said. 'That's my stake,' he explained. 'My claim. Boulder opal, though, not like those, nothing like that . . .' – and his awe at the stones was like a hot breath fogging them. 'I've found a couple of opalised ones too, oysters I mean, I mean the fossils have become opalised, and one opalised sea horse.'

Oyster seemed slightly disconcerted by this interruption. It was like an ill-mannered bit of flotsam sticking up suddenly in the path of the prepared floodwater of his speech. (Did I really think 'prepared' then, or was I swept along like everyone else? I would like to believe I was already wary by then; I think I was; but I also know how the devious memory picks over and re-edits the past; and I also know, I am also compelled to admit, that I was in any case spellbound, and I still can't really account for how he got away with it, except to concede, as even Susannah always did, that whatever else Oyster was, he was brilliant, he was a consummate choreographer, a master of ceremonies, an actor of the most exceptional kind.) In any case, after Major Miner spoke there was a pause, and then Oyster's words flowed on around the obstruction.

'On the oyster farms at Broome,' he said, 'and the ones off the Queensland coast, in the Gulf, and at Thursday Island . . . the *pearl* oysters, I mean . . . they are different, you know, not edible . . .'

Very few people in Outer Maroo have had close acquaintance with oysters of either genre, or not, so to speak, in the flesh. And most certainly not in the fresh. They did not know oysters, that is to say, in the biblical sense of knowing, in the carnal sensation of viscous sea-food on the tongue; though fossilised specimens and opalised shells lined our drawers and our windowsills. Nevertheless we were dazzled.

The range of topics for conversation in Bernie's has always been narrow, and such intricate knowledge of crustaceans was exotic to us. It was like a breeze, like a raincloud, like a monsoon tale from a thousand and one ocean nights. It sent a buzz of excitement along the verandah boards. I could feel it against the balls of my feet.

Oyster turned to look westward and shaded his eyes as though he could see Broome over there on the north-west coast of the continent, just a couple of thousand miles away, nothing but scrub in between. 'It's extraordinary,' he said dreamily, and everyone turned towards Broome, we all seemed to go under that blue sky like divers, the Indian Ocean lapping us; 'so *intense*,' Oyster said, 'that blueness, that equatorial blueness, you can't *imagine* . . .' He made some graceful motion with his hand as though drawing back a curtain, parting the air – the magus, I remember thinking; or if I didn't think it then, I can see it now, the way he held the magician's baton in his hand – and everyone swayed, we all leaned into his vision, we were stunned by the blue wave washing us, the tide coming in, shussing back over lost sands, picking up fossilised shells it had dropped on an ancient ebb. We saw Broome, we saw the Indian Ocean, we saw the curves of pale sand, the white shavings of surf, we turned languid in the lush coastal humidity of Oyster's words.

'They dive for the oysters as they always have,' he said. 'They bring up shells by the thousand. But this is no longer harvest, you know. It is not the end point. It is cropping. It is just the beginning.'

He turned from Broome and from the equatorial waters of the Gulf, he motioned Thursday Island off stage with a flick of his hand. There was a slow fade, the red dust drifted in. He addressed himself again to the little orchestra pit of Outer Maroo. It must have pleased him: fifteen of us hanging on his every word, the whole continent as endless stage on every side.

'What they do,' he said, 'after the divers bring up the shells . . . What they do . . . and it's a very delicate operation . . . They take each shell, they take the shells one by one, and they prise them apart very gently with a very sharp knife, forcing the adductor muscle, which holds the shell like this' – he clenched his fist – 'to release its grip. Inside, the oyster breathes like a baby. You can hear it snuffle and gurgle very very softly, a poignant sound. Then the pearler takes a silver instrument, a fine pair of tweezers, a jeweller's tool, and he reaches in . . . the two shell halves are propped slightly, just slightly ajar like this' – he held his thumb and forefinger a whisker apart to demonstrate – 'and he reaches in . . .

'Now the oyster is a bivalve mollusc, as I explained, and the pearler reaches in, he holds open the valve like this . . . It's like . . .' He was breathing raggedly. He had us all in the palm of his story, he was braiding narrative into the hot drugged air that filled our lungs. 'There is the soft muscle, the mucous membrane which he must part, and it's like easing apart . . . it's like separating and spreading . . . and then slipping it in . . . letting it swim up that warm, swim upwards. It is an incredibly moving, an incredibly beautiful thing, a virginal thing, the virginal aspect is the most . . . And what they do, the pearlers, what they do, in this opening they have made: they insert foreign matter, *grit*, a small seed pearl, a little nub of nacreous substance . . .'

We were dazed. Our breathing fogged the hot air. Something steamy, something akin to desire slipped into all crevices: gaping mouths, wide eyes, minds reeling open; and each person asked himself furtively, nervously, if such silences, such omissions, could possibly have been unspoken on the verandah of an outback pub.

'And what they do,' Oyster said, gesturing colourfully with his hands, orchestrating shock, conducting us, directing our fantasies, 'the pearlers, what they do: they insert this foreign matter, the small seed pearl . . .

'They just set it there . . .

'And then they let the valve close over it. They let those soft nether lips of the oyster kiss it. They close the shell. They attach the shell to a mesh rack, a rope mesh, a fishing net full of seeded molluscs. They attend to the oyster racks with such gentleness, such exquisite grace, the pearlers.'

Like the Holy Spirit hovering over a crop of Marys, full of grace and lustrous concretions, Susannah Rover said tartly, much later, *Blessed art thou among molluscs, and blessed is the pearl of thy womb.*

I should not let her interrupt, but she does that, she always did, she had a gift for irreverent interjection, though Oyster too was gifted with unwanted intrusion, coating it, pearling it, slicking it over with words.

'And they lower the racks of shells,' he said, 'into the blood-warm equatorial ocean of time. For seven years, my people' – and all of us, dumbfounded, breathless, absorbed, were willing for the moment to be his people, at least for as long as his story and his voice and his eyes had us swaying like seaweed on undersea racks – 'and seven is a very significant number in the codes of the Lord; seven, I say unto you, is the perfect number, that is what the compilers of the Bible believed, and the first disciples believed it, and all the mystics and martyrs, and the ancients knew it, for there were Seven Wonders of the Ancient World, and it is still true today, for there are seven days in the week, and seven states in Australia if we count, as we should, the Northern Territory, and leave out, as we should, Canberra and the ACT, that nest of vipers, and the Lord rested on the seventh day, and it is the seventh angel who will open the seventh seal, and it is for seven years that the racks of the seeded shells are lowered back into the ocean by the growers of pearls. They are suspended from a man-made reef of nautical rope and marker buoys and nets, and *at night they sway and wander/ in the waters far under/ and morning rolls them in the foam.*

'For seven years they are monitored by the pearling luggers, they are watched and tended and caressed. The racks are lifted from the sea every few weeks, and the shells are scraped and cleaned and keelhauled, in order that the tabernacle of the pearl may be pure, and that the oysters be left inviolate at their secret work, and then the racks are lowered again to the deeps. And then lo, after seven years, exactly as the disciples pulled in the nets on the Sea of Galilee, the pearling luggers tow their reefs to shore.

'And what has happened to that seed of irritation? That carnal moment, that *incarnation*, that hard little kernel of foreign matter and bodily pain taken into the sex of the oyster?

'Ah, my people, it has been layered over with the milk of divinity, with mother-of-pearl, with layer upon layer of an exquisite nacreous distillation. It has become the cultured pearl of great price. Men will die for it, they will kill to own it, they will give fortunes for it. It will fetch anything from $2,000 to $8,000 in the Japanese gem wholesalers' market.'

No one moved. No one made a sound. We stared at him, awed. There is a kind of excitement, you see, that gifted orators have, and there can never be a full accounting for it outside the atmosphere that they themselves create.

Oyster smiled at us, boyishly, disarmingly, as though he had just given a lighthearted set of instructions for making damper or for travelling beyond the Barcoo.

'That is what happened to me,' he said, shrugging. 'I was chosen.' He said this as someone else might say: my mother was Irish; that's why I have red hair. 'God touched my orifices,' he said. 'I was tested as Job was tested. Pain and evil entered into me, I was tormented, I suffered.' He bent over slightly, and pressed his fists into his stomach, and the memory of past torment was present and visceral in us all. We all winced, I think. We all bent forward a little, self-protectively. 'And within me,' he said, 'the suffering was transformed.' He lifted his fists from his stomach and held out his hand again, and the opals shimmered bluefire in the afternoon sun.

In opal country, you respect a man with stones like those, the way you would respect, at high noon in a western, the man who has already drawn his gun. Whatever private reservations you may have about the man, you accept that the game is his. He is calling the shots. If an inner whisper tells you the man may be a lunatic, you grant him – under the circumstances – even greater respect. You do not want to mess around with him. You fall back. You let him have his head.

That is how, from this distance, I account for why we let him go on. And he did go on. And on.

'As it is written,' he said, '*And when the seven thunders had uttered their voices, I, Oyster, being caught up in the Spirit, was about to write: and I heard a voice from heaven saying unto me, Seal up those things which the seven thunders uttered, and write them not.*

'But go to a place that I will shew thee, and to a people that I will shew thee. And I will shew to thee a reef where all the colours of mother-of-pearl clap their hands and where opal sings. And you will lead the people of that town to repentance, and when they are pure in my eyes, you will share with them the riches of my reef. And glory and honour and power shall be given unto them.

'And the seventh angel which I saw stand upon the sea and upon the earth lifted up his hand to heaven. And sware by him that liveth for ever and ever . . . that there should be time no longer.

'My people, these things were told to me by the seventh angel, after the black waters had passed over me.

'I was struck down by a white light, like Saul on the road to Damascus. And the angel showed me the shining mathematics of heaven, and I saw spinning discs of sevens, I saw sevens multiplied since the beginning of time, and the angel moved them among the mystical numbers and passed his hand over them, and they became the year 2000, and the angel said to me: when this year is come upon you, time shall be no more.'

Oyster paused and looked around him.

We were all, I suppose, more than a little bewildered by this time, a little stunned. I don't think any of us quite took in his words. They simply hung there like a mirage, and we were used to mirages. We were mesmerised by the lilt of his voice. He had a way of gesturing with his hands, his eyes flashed opals, he had everyone's absolute, awed, and undivided attention. But as for belief or disbelief . . .?

I suppose you could say that some sort of division set in from that very first day, because no one in Outer Maroo outside the congregation of the Living Word (whose members, both before and after Oyster, were perpetually expecting the Second Coming and the end of the world, and expecting them as imminent events), but apart from the Living Worders, not one of whom was on Bernie's verandah that afternoon, no one else in Outer Maroo ever really believed all that business about 2000 and the end of the world; whereas all the young foreigners did.

They began arriving within days, it seemed to us, all those young backpackers from Brisbane and Sydney and overseas. Certainly within a few weeks, after Oyster went to Brisbane and then came back, we had more strangers in town than we'd had in the previous ten years. They came in waves, and we were like recluses hauled into a crowd: we were blinking, bewildered, affronted, frightened, shocked. We did not know that people dressed like that, or spoke like that. They kept arriving. Oyster had recruiters, and they must have been on fire. They worked up and down the coast and in the big cities, and they found devotees ripe unto harvest: all those bright young seekers so desperately certain that their days were shunted hard up against the end point of time.

In Outer Maroo we were bewildered.

But just the same, people told one another in Bernie's, as long as they stay out there at the Reef . . .

As long as we're in on it . . .

No skin off our noses, if they want to sing and pray all night and mine opal all day . . .

If they all up and vanish in the year 2000, more opal for us . . .

They look strange, but they're harmless enough . . .

In the beginning, Oyster had Outer Maroo on his side; he had people in his pocket and under his thumb. He seduced them. They were in on the cut. They were cutters, and grinders, and polishers, and truck drivers, and mullock heap sifters, and they had opals forever dancing in their eyes.

Oyster's got a few ratbag ideas, but he's all right, they'd say in the pub. He knows opals. Got his head screwed on. Got his heart in the right place. And mind you, about the government, and the way the world is going to pot, and stuff like that, he's absolutely spot-on there.

For Oyster's sermon on the verandah was followed, in weeks to come, by many more. He did not stop at oysters. There were wars and rumours of wars everywhere, he would say, and who could disagree? There were fornications and perversions, there were men who were not men and women who were not women, and Australia should return to the way the world was meant to be. This was fertile ground. Governments were not trusted, he said, by the people they governed, and everyone passionately agreed. Politicians were as ravening wolves, he said, and our governments, state and federal, spied on us and stole from us and squandered our hard-earned cash.

In Bernie's, they lapped it up, they kept the rounds going, 'Another jug, Jess,' and 'It's on us, Oyster,' they would plead. 'Keep up the good work, mate.' But he would never join in; he did not touch alcohol; he would never enter the bar. He sat on the verandah, white and shining, and all he drank was awe. There were sure signs, he would say, warming up, winding up, there were signs that we were living in the latter days, and sure signs that on the first day of January in the year 2000 . . .

'Yeah, well, the bloody republic,' someone would shrug. 'Time's running out, all right.'

'The bloody ratbag politicians.'

'We know what they've got up their sleeves.'

'It's our land they're after, the buggers. World heritage, national parks, the bloody Abos, one damned excuse after another.'

There was a confluence of apocalyptical fears, and Bernie's regulars would swim in the currents of Oyster's dreams. 'At the Reef, I am rebuilding Eden,' he would say. 'We will be the end and the new beginning. I am what I am.'

Where the light touched him, he would burn like a sunflash opal himself. His lips were parted. I would imagine his oyster bivalves vibrating in climax, and I would remember again that first afternoon, and the way we all stood there, after his mad-eyed sermon, and the way Ma's Bill spoke for all of us.

'Jesus,' Ma's Bill said softly, and we could hear for a moment the hum of the end of time drawing close, and then out of the hum, at the same moment, came two four-wheel drives, both of them Toyota Land Cruisers. They arrived in a skirl of red dust and parked on opposite sides of the street: the little world of our local aristocracy, our squatters, our *squattocracy*, our robber barons, our princely landed graziers, behold, *tan-ta-ra*: the lords of Jimjimba and Dirran-Dirran. Our cow cockies, as is uncharitably said in the pub. Dukke Prophet got out of one Land Rover, his bible under his arm. He did not look at Bernie's, and the Living Word swallowed him whole. Andrew Godwin swung himself out of the other and tossed his Akubra on to the front seat. He raised his eyebrows at the crowded veranda.

'Heard on the CB that we got company,' he said. 'What's he after?'

Oyster turned to look at him.

'I was *sent*,' Oyster said.

'What?' Andrew Godwin, philandering sheep-and-cattle man, part swaggerer, part grazier thug, was about to take the verandah steps in one booted stride, but he paused and blinked.

'I was sent to you. You are the one. My reef is on your property.'

'What the hell is this fuckwit talking about?' Andrew Godwin wanted to know.

Oyster fixed his eyes on Andrew Godwin, and Andrew Godwin raised his brows sardonically and curled his lips in polite and amused disdain, but then his expression seemed to droop and float back towards neutral. It was a staring match. Andrew Godwin was a man who always took what he wanted, who always wanted what he took. In any sort of competition, he would certainly never be the first to lower his eyes.

'If you follow me,' Oyster said, 'he whom you have lost to violent death will be restored to you.'

It was as though he had hit Andrew Godwin with a stone between the eyes. I know Andrew Godwin intimately; more intimately than I would have liked, as a matter of fact, since, drunk or sober, but especially drunk, he is amorously inclined. I saw his eyes widen with shock. I saw a flash of anger, and simultaneously a sort of buckling. He was winded. He sank down right where he was, on the steps. His hands shook, though at the funeral for his son Ross, whose suicide is never mentioned in Outer Maroo, his hands were steady, and he did not weep.

'There was an opal floater found by your son,' Oyster said. 'You keep it hidden in your shearing shed.'

Andrew Godwin turned very pale. We could see the line of sweat above his lip.

'The opal came from my Reef,' Oyster said. 'There is enough opal to make all of us rich. It is on your land. I will make you a fisher of opal,' he said, 'if you follow me.'

A vibration moved through Andrew Godwin's body. There were people on the verandah who will swear they saw Andrew Godwin weep. I have heard them, drunk and solitary, telling their pint pots as though the astonishing fact must be set down. I have heard them talking in their sleep. Andrew's weeping, if that is what it was, was barely audible. It was like the soft gurgle of an oyster being seeded in its shell.

2. Dreams of Black Opal

Even before Oyster had lifted his hand and displayed those lozenges of opalescent fire on Bernie's verandah, Major Miner could tell by the racing of his heartbeat and the singing in his ears that some rare sound was in the air, something new and stunning, which was also disorienting – like the quarter-notes of African jazz, say – because it could not be attached to any known scale. He could feel the follicles in his inner ear go crazy.

The memory of that moment, of that excitement, is still strong with him four years later, even though darkness is closing in and the bushfire still rages, and even though, more and more often in dreams, he has found himself in the bamboo cage again, and the cage is being lowered deeper and deeper into a black pit, and there do not seem to be any spaces or slivers of light at all, nor even any niches where a stick of dynamite might be lodged.

He has had ghastly dreams, since the Reef disappeared, of licking a stick of gelignite, lubricating it, and sticking it up himself, the last refuge: he has sometimes felt that he is swimming towards Oyster's

2000, he has felt the final climacteric building in him, felt the incredible release as he floats with his final fragments into peace.

Major Miner sighs heavily and fearfully and reaches out in the dark. 'Jess,' he calls, out of a half-sleep, tossing. 'Jess, hold me.'

'It's all right,' I say. 'We'll be all right. I think the fire is beginning to slow down.'

'What?' he says startled, sitting up, and we stare at the glow over at the edge of the sky. 'I was dreaming again,' he says. 'Singapore dreams.'

His breath feels leaden to him; he has to strain to push it out, pull it in.

'We can begin again,' I say.

One can always begin again, with less visible baggage each time, but more of the invisible kind. There is always more sombre knowledge to drag along, and it can't be left in a cloakroom, it can't be abandoned, it can't be cut loose. But then again, the journey never ceases to surprise: thigh against thigh, the sweet close body smell, the soft interlocking. I explore with my fingers. I love, in particular, the silky hollow at the groin, and the kinked knotted veins at the back of his neck.

'The strange thing was,' he says in a low voice, 'that day Oyster arrived in town, when I listened to those stones in his hand, I knew I'd heard the same sound just a couple of weeks earlier. The same sort of sound, I mean. The same frequency. It was when Bugger Harvey dropped by the Great Extended.'

Opal rushes and gold rushes, Major Miner thinks, are like bush-fires: in the morning, not a flame is in sight; then suddenly you notice a lick of orange here, a crackle there, and another one over there, half a dozen separate little burns, a dozen, twenty . . . and then by early afternoon there are a hundred thousand acres of billowing firestorm.

Speaking of which . . . 'Fires,' he says, apprehensive, noting the way the glowing arc is now extending itself in a small sickle at its southern end. 'Fires always remind me of the Japanese raids . . . It's bloody incredible, more than fifty years later, the way panic attacks . . .'

'Hush,' I murmur, holding him. For all those years in Outer Maroo, I would never have known he lived with panic. But then, I suppose, he would never have known what my silence was designed to protect, though it would hardly be new to him, the wish to disappear from a former life. He himself, after the war, had wished to cease being Major Somebody Else. It was not as simple as he had hoped.

He can see Joe Blow waiting for him at the edge of the night. The prison camp is everywhere, Joe Blow says. The world is a prison, he says. The Tao, he reminds, is a way to be when the worst arrives.

Is it? the Major wonders.

We lie naked, not exactly entwined – it is far too hot for that – but close, slack, in post-coital lassitude. Through the shed window, we can see a curved brow of the breakaways and the glow of the bushfire and a few hundred million stars. It is January again, the season of hot/hot. There are two seasons in Outer Maroo: the season of burning days and of freezing desert-winter nights; and the other one, the longer one, of hot hot hot, of burning burning, when darkness brings not even a memory of cool.

The season of hell, the Major thinks; the season when Oyster arrived, and when he left; the season of Bugger Harvey's farewell.

He has never spoken to anyone before of the Bugger's last visit. In fact, he had more or less forgotten it, but lately it keeps coming back. He does not understand why he forgot it, because it was the Bugger who taught him how to dispense with gelignite.

It is not exactly accurate, he thinks, to say he had forgotten Bugger Harvey; it was the Bugger's *absence* he forgot. The Bugger has always been hanging around the diggings: around the Great Extended and the Reef. It is more that, since the war, the Major has known so many dead people that he has got into the way of dispensing with bodily presence as a condition for conversations and exchange. But he had definitely forgotten the specific occasion of the last supper with Bugger Harvey, and now he is puzzled as to why.

The Bugger was an RSL-er too, and this was a bond between them, though the Bugger's reclusiveness was extreme. Possibly things had been even worse in New Guinea; possibly the prison camps there had been worse, though 'worse' is a difficult concept to ponder when it comes to extremes, and especially when it comes to highly refined conditions of powerlessness. In any case, the Bugger's surliness and occasional outbursts of drunken ferocity meant that not even the Major could take him straight for long. And then there was that other thing, the way Bugger Harvey took to aligning himself with the Murris and to getting drunk with them in their camps along the riverbeds, which put him beyond the pale for Outer Maroo, which made things tricky and complicated, for the Bugger had gone over the line.

Major Miner tried to sort out what he felt about that, and there was no black-and-white answer, he thought, smiling grimly at the way language itself made bad jokes. How the Murris got along with the miners was a grey area, and the only word Major Miner could come up with was *foreign*. Not that the Murris seemed foreign to him, so much; well, they did, of course, but that didn't matter. It was that he himself felt profoundly foreign among them. He felt that they tolerated his presence and his opal fossicking, as long as he stayed clear of the bora rings; they did not like his blasting, he knew that; they were friendly enough, but he felt that they viewed him as alien, and that they did not like having him sit with them in their camps. And yet they accepted Bugger Harvey as one of themselves.

Major Miner did not understand the convolutions involved.

He understood even less the kind of animosity towards the Murris that came off Andrew Godwin and Dukke Prophet. It made no sense to him whatsoever. It was as though they believed that such difference threatened the sequence of night and day, as though it were the force that withheld the rain.

He knew the Murris couldn't care less what the graziers thought, or what he himself thought.

There was something else that bothered him greatly: it was the obliging way that some of the Murris used to sit out on the verandah at Bernie's, never venturing into the bar; the obliging way they moved off when they were ordered to; the obliging way they offered – in the beginning – their skills to Oyster. It was the way they held their bodies and their smiles. He recognised it. He had seen it in the camps when men decided to give up. Once you saw that slackness in the body, that benign smile, you knew that an inner deal had been made about not resisting, you knew a man had accepted death's terms.

There were other Murris who had not accepted the terms of decay: the young ones whose eyes gave back nothing; the ones who never drank at Bernie's, the ones who wore T-shirts silk-screened with the Aboriginal flag. He had seen them giving Oyster the finger behind his back. That he understood. He was not surprised to learn that they were the ones who led the insurrection at the Reef, the ones who organised the Vanishing, the ones who were now in Bourke.

Good on yer, mates, he wanted to say – not that they gave a damn about Major Miner's opinion on the matter.

As for Bugger Harvey: he had walked the line ever since New Guinea. Sometimes he took on the world; and sometimes he just curled up and drank himself legless and blind, and it was this ambivalence, this dual way of living, Major Miner had decided, that made the Bugger so at ease with the Murris, and the Murris so at ease with him.

Nevertheless, it was Bugger Harvey who had startled Major Miner one day, who had, in fact, inadvertently perhaps, pushed him deeper into the way of the Tao, coming up behind him unexpectedly at the very moment when an ironstone slope in the breakaways flew apart like a flock of cockatoos rising. It had been beautifully done. Against the sky, great slices of rock traced slow arcs as delicate as feathers on the glide, and there, on the rockface so exposed, Major Miner could see a vein of pipe opal like vivid blue-green lightning descending through whooshes of fire. Chuang-tzu and Joe Blow were watching, as always. You have done well, they said. Truly, a great cutter does not cut. The finest work is effortless.

The Tao does all by doing nothing, they said.

'Hack work,' growled Bugger Harvey from behind him. 'Completely unnecessary violence. Completely senseless.'

'God, don't *do* that, you crazy old bugger!' The Major clutched at his heart. 'You gave me one hell of a scare.'

'Not surprised,' the Bugger sniffed. 'You'd block out the end of the world with a butcher of a blast like that.'

Major Miner was offended. 'If you care to go and look closely, that entire run of pipe opal is unscratched.'

'That,' said Bugger Harvey mournfully, studying the cliff face as though he felt its ravages in his gut, 'is what I would call mutilation.'

'What?'

'Of a very beautiful mesa.'

'You're off your rocker again.'

'If that pipe opal is meant for you,' the Bugger said, 'there'll already be a way in. You could learn a thing or two from the Murris, you destructive clod.'

'I see they've taught you some very refined behaviour, Bugger.'

'That's right,' the Bugger said. 'They have. They've taught me that anything that can't be reached with a pointed stick doesn't belong to us, and I say they are bloody well right. You know what happened here in 1873?'

'Is this going to be a sermon?' the Major asked.

'All I'm saying is, the earth is our mother, like the Murris say, and you can't cut her up and get away with it,' Bugger Harvey said. 'And you don't *need* to tear her up, you stupid oaf, because she's generous. I'll show you.'

He walked towards the breakaway face, from which great slabs of rock were still flaking away like slow drifting soot. Though it seemed to the eye of Major Miner's appreciation of his skills that the slabs floated weightlessly as ash, he knew better than to walk into their black rain.

'You crazy old suicidal drunk!' he yelled.

But Bugger Harvey had taken off at a tangent, and he made for a particular point, beyond the range of the falling rock, where a line of wild native orange trees straggled up the slope. Major Miner followed. He saw the Bugger begin to climb, and then the Bugger disappeared. Exasperated, muttering colourful words beneath his breath, Major Miner climbed too. To his relief, he found the Bugger flattened against the underside of a gigantic rounded boulder at the base of a rubbled pyramid of rocks. A bush orange tree pushed its way out from between the rocks, and the Bugger was sucking at one of its hard and woody little fruits.

'There's water in here,' he said. 'Where there's bush orange, there's a fault line, and where there's a fault line, there's water, and where there's water, there's a waterway, and where there's a waterway, there's hydrated silica, and where there's etcetera, there's opal, right?'

'Right,' Major Miner said, disgusted. 'That's why I blasted, you barmy old galoot.'

'Uncalled for.' The Bugger squirmed into the narrow opening between two boulders.

'I'll call you whatever I bloody want.'

'The blasting was uncalled for.'

'You're gonna dislodge them, you fuckwit,' the Major yelled. 'You're gonna start a bloody landslide. You'll get us both crushed, you stupid fucking dehydrated raving –'

'Got enough room to swing two cats here,' the Bugger called. His voice came out manifold, resonant, as from echo chambers. 'Come and see.'

Major Miner had run out of breath and words. Warily, he crawled through the gap.

'How's that for pipe opal?' the Bugger asked.

'Holy shit.'

'The Murris know a damn sight more than we do,' Bugger Harvey said. 'They've been around longer.'

Oyster thought so too.

In the beginning, he sat in the riverbeds with them. We share our secrets, he told Major Miner. We are all God's children. At the End of Time, the First Ones will be there, as they were in the beginning . . .

In the beginning, a lot of Murris moved into the burrows and tunnels of Oyster's Reef. They gave their hearts to the Lord, they sang hymns, they listened to Oyster's Bible lessons, they showed Oyster where the opal ran. And then all those camp followers, all those young kids from Brisbane and Sydney and Melbourne, from New York and Timbuctoo, from God knows where, all those kids began to arrive. It seemed to be all one big happy family, black and white, white and black, at the Reef.

'I don't like this,' Bernie told Major Miner at the pub. 'If I were you, I'd leave a bit of gelignite around, accidentally on purpose, if you know what I mean. It's going to be us or them, I reckon.'

'Don't be daft,' Major Miner said. 'They're a bunch of kids.'

We don't like this, people told one another in Beresford's and at Bernie's. It's going to be us or them.

'Who's getting hurt, for God's sake?' Major Miner asked Bernie. 'Besides, you're doing pretty well out of all this.'

Bernie frowned. 'We'd be doing a whole lot better if we took over the mining ourselves.'

'You're getting a lot of free labour,' Major Miner pointed out.

'Oh sure,' Bernie growled. 'Trouble's free.'

It interested the Major that a ragtag camp of thirty Murris and another sixty or so backpacking kids could generate so much fear. Not one of either group was armed, so far as he knew, unless you counted boomerangs and Oyster's rifle. He found himself quoting Bugger Harvey. 'Maybe we could learn a thing or two from the Murris,' he told Bernie. 'They've been around longer than us.'

'Reckon you've shown your colours,' Bernie said.

'There are more of them than of us,' Ma's Bill pointed out. 'It stands to reason, Major M. We hafta do something.'

Major Miner did something; he stayed out in the breakaways with his boulder opal. He found that several boxes of explosives had gone missing. He began to hear old voices. The world is a prison, the echoes called. It doesn't matter how far into the outback you go, Joe Blow said. It's still part of the prison camp. Freedom is an inner condition.

'How could it have come to this?' the Major asks me in the dark. 'Just spaced-out kids and a Murri camp and ordinary people in an outback town. How could we have turned that into the fall of Singapore?'

'There's the Old Fuckatoo, don't forget. And the opal. And the drought. They had something to do with it.'

He is haunted by his own stolen explosives. In dreams, the gelignite lodges itself in every crevice: mouth, nose, ears, and private parts. A man of violence, Chuang-tzu whispers, will come to a violent end.

Major Miner puts his head in his hands. He should have got rid of that stuff, he should have listened to Bugger Harvey, and suddenly, unpredictably here is the Bugger again, large in memory, larger than life, arriving with the last supper wrapped up in a bit of newspaper and cloth. Here comes the Bugger, against all probability, bearing gifts: a bottle of whisky and a round of damper still doughy and hot from his blackened pan.

'I was even more surprised than I was suspicious, Jess. You can imagine . . . that cranky old bastard.

'"I've got meself a Christmas present, Major," he says to me. He was practically pissing himself with excitement. "I don't mind telling you because you're straight as a die," he says. "You've still got the army and all that bloody pommie-officer guff they drummed into us like a steel rod up through your arse. Besides, there's . . . you know . . ." He meant we'd both been fucked over in the camps, which isn't something you talk about, but it's always there. "Rather die than rat on someone, that sort of thing," he says. "I may be white meself," he says, "though I'm less and less sure about that, but you're the last white man I trust besides meself. I've come to see things from the Murris' point of view. You can't trust a white man as far as you can throw him. Just the same, I reckon I'm bursting to tell some other white man, in case that's what I am after all, so bully for you, Major, I picked on you."

'Of course, he didn't have to tell me anything. I knew. And I knew why he could only tell me. After the war . . . after the camp . . . after stuff like that . . . you can only talk to other ex-prisoners-of-war . . .'

Major Miner had tried for a while, after the war. He had tried to stay in the army, stay in the world, get married, have children, have a life, but the marriage was done for almost before it began, the children fathered on various army bases did not know him, did not want to know him, he seemed to treat everyone badly and then he seemed to treat everyone worse, he seemed to be mostly drunk, he seemed to be violent . . .

'I just wanted to blow everything up at first,' he tells me. 'That's the truth. I wanted to blow everything to kingdom come, once and for all.'

That was why he had had to head for the outback. He had needed to be where no one else was. That was why he had bought a jeep, a few cases of whisky, and six boxes of assorted explosives. He drove to nowhere. He drove aimlessly and bumped into Lightning Ridge and got blotto. In the pub someone had asked him: 'Are you a miner?'

'Nah,' he said, deadpan. 'I *look* young, but I'm old enough to drink, cross me heart.'

It went down well in the bar, it was a hit. They laughed all over Lightning Ridge and all the way to the White Cliffs field. They laughed all over their beer slops and they bought him another round of drinks. 'I used to be a Major in the army,' he allowed, and it turned out that sitting right there in the bar with him, surprise surprise, there were other RSL types, other ex-Changi, ex-Tobruk, ex-New Guinea flotsam, other bits of war wreckage, and they took him right into their hearts and into their mines. He offered his blasting expertise. Overnight, he stopped drinking and switched his addiction to opal. He took on a new life, a new name. He was hooked. He moved on, he worked all the fields in New South Wales and South Australia, but Queensland boulder opal lured him in the end because it was so intransigent, it was so bloody hard to get, it required such delicate blasting skills, it required the wisdom of Chuang-tzu and the patience of Prince Wen Hui's cook. It required the Tao.

Also: it was beyond the margins of maps.

Out on the opal fields, like calls to like, and Bugger Harvey and Major Miner boil a billy and eat damper together.

'That day . . .' he begins to tell me again.

He can see it: the old jeep chugging up in its private heat haze, the whisky, the hot flour-and-water bread. He shakes his head fondly. He has a soft spot for Bugger Harvey. He misses him. 'The minute he got out of his jeep, even before I smelt the damper, I could hear the opals like gamma rays squealing in a satellite dish. Hell, he *taught* me how to hear that stuff. Like angel sopranos, they were. They gave me a hard-on. They gave *him* a hard-on too. He was practically shaking with excitement. He looked as though he had the DTs.

'"G'day, Major," he says.

'"G'day, Bugger."

'"I'm heading down the Innamincka track," he says, "but that's a decoy. Three hours, and I'll cut across the back way to Thargomindah, and then to Bourke, where I reckon I'll have a party-and-a-half with a few of me old mates –"

'"The Murris," I say.

'"Right," he says. "Got something bloody incredible to show 'em. And then I head on down to Lightning Ridge."

'"Bloody awful track," I say. "The Innamincka track, and the back way to Thargomindah."

'"Yeah," he says. "But I gotta get to Lightning Ridge, and I sure as hell am not gonna go via Quilpie."

'"What's wrong with Quilpie?"

'"Spies," he says. "Sniffers. Bernie's eyes and ears, Bernie's little hirelings. Don't trust 'em as far as I could throw 'em. Lightning Ridge is where the serious deals are, and besides, they know black opal when they see it."

'I could hear those opals singing a Gloria. I stayed calm, though. I said: "No black opal in these parts, Bugger."

'"That's what you think," he says.

'"You got something worth selling, eh, Bugger?"

'"You bet your sweet arse," he says. "And no bloody way I'll let Bernie or Eromanga or Quilpie set eyes on these. We're not talking boulder opal, Major. We're not even talking good pipe opal here."

'"So what are we talking, Bugger?"

'"We're talking a pure crystal vein as long as Cooper's Creek," he says. "We're talking stones like Lightning Ridge gets, the black beauty, the real McCoy. I got three of 'em, three fiery black beauties, on me now."

'Oh, I could hear the real McCoys, Jess. I could hear them singing the Hallelujah Chorus in the little pouch he had shoved down his sock. I could see them burning a hole in his leg.'

He sighs regretfully. 'I never saw them,' he says. 'But I wasn't surprised that someone else picked up the signal too. I wasn't really surprised when Oyster showed up, and then all those kids with starflash in their eyes.'

Major Miner has a theory: that once the Bugger had found the way in, once he had brought some samples up for air, the seam began transmitting loud and clear. The real miracle, he thinks, was that half the world didn't hear it, just the groupies, just the ragbag army of Oyster's kids.

'I can still remember,' he says, 'when Oyster showed us those stones just two weeks later on Bernie's verandah. I felt my ticker turn a somersault. That's it, then, I thought. That's the same angel choir I heard on the Bugger. Oyster's picked up the signal and tapped into another doorway to the Bugger's seam.'

In spite of everything, in spite of what happened, Major Miner still finds it difficult to believe that someone tuned into opal so attentively . . . he does not understand how Oyster could be *entirely* . . . at least in the beginning, he thinks, before the darkening, before all that, in the beginning, then surely, surely, there must have been something inspired, something pure, some idealism that later went horribly astray.

A memory comes to him.

It is just before dusk, and before the Murris have cleared out, and the sun is great throbbing red disc behind the mulga clumps and that maze of bora rings. He is at the edge of Oyster's Reef, and he sees the large circle around the campfire. Oyster is there, and a few dozen of those spaced-out innocent-faced kids that keep showing up, and the Murris, and a didgeridoo is playing, and there is singing and swaying, gospel hymns and didgeridoos, weird, he thinks, but in spite of himself, Major Miner is moved. He can feel something warm and glowing spreading around his heart.

'Come and join us,' Oyster calls, seeing him.

And he is surrounded, it seems to him, by innocence and warmth. Oyster is telling Tully Wollaston and Percy Marks stories. Of course, Major Miner knows these stories, every digger on every opal field in Australia knows them, and Oyster knows them, and Major Miner is reassured by this, that Oyster must have worked all the fields, that he is a true opal addict, he knows the lore. Major Miner has no idea whether or not these stories are true, but every field he has worked on subscribes to them. For the patron saints of opal-seekers in Australia are Tully Wollaston and Percy Marks. It was *faith*, Oyster said, that had sustained those men. At the turn of the century, they had known pure beauty when they saw it, before there was a market for it. Tully Wollaston trekked through the desert and bought at the mineheads, and Percy Marks fashioned black-opal jewellery that dealers would give a king's ransom for today.

But they had no takers at first.

The only opal Europe knew was the pale and milky Hungarian opal, and no one knew what to make of the dark untried barbaric fire. Tully Wollaston and Percy Marks had to give it away. They gave away pieces of the sun, moon and stars in single stones; they gave away splendour. They gave black-opal fabulations to Queen Alexandra, to the Duke of Gloucester, to Sousa the American band-master on tour Down Under, to Dame Nellie Melba. They turned the dreams of the famous into fire, and the bushfire word spread, and the famous began to covet Australian dreaming . . .

And Tully Wollaston . . .

He'd always believed, he'd been a believer since he first peddled dream opal in London in 1890. He had to take raw stones over . . . there was no one in Sydney or Melbourne who knew how to cut and polish as he wished, as he imagined, as he dreamed. He had to match the cutters to his inner vision. He had to travel and search until he found. He found De Beers. He had to cajole the De Beers people, the diamond people, he had to hire them to cut and polish his stones . . .

So Tully Wollaston had the stones cut, and Percy Marks fashioned them into magic, and in 1908 they exhibited at the Franco-British International in London, and seduction took place, and Europe fell under the spell. Australian opal had them in thrall.

And De Beers panicked . . .

Or so everyone says on the opal fields of Australia.

So all the opal old-timers say.

It's a story that eddies through shafts and tunnels and open-cut blastings from Coober Pedy to Outer Maroo: how De Beers feared black opal, how they feared a drop of value in diamonds; how back then, at the dawn of the century they expended a fortune to discredit the Aussie gem, how they dug up the bad luck legend of opal and marketed it with the subterranean discretion that only millions of dollars can buy.

'There's no evidence it existed, this bad luck legend, before the turn of the century,' Major Miner tells me. 'It didn't exist before Tully Wollaston had De Beers cut his stones from Lightning Ridge. And then suddenly it cropped up all over the place. It grew retroactively. It trawled up bad luck from centuries past, though the bad luck connection wasn't noticed back then.

But what Oyster said to his wide-eyed kids was that it did not matter any more, for truth and beauty had won in the end, as they always and inevitably do. They were building a new Eden, he said, and they would live beyond time as opal did; for Australia's national treasure had been required to wait through a few millennia, discreet, modest, doing nothing except guarding its purity, and now its hour of triumph had come.

And it was true. There were Swiss buyers, Japanese buyers, American buyers falling all over themselves to fly in low and buy direct from every opal field in Australia: and Oyster's kids and the Murris laughed and sang, and Major Miner sang along with them.

Someone asked him to take a photograph, he remembers. He remembers it was an American girl with long blonde hair, shy and skittish as a rock wallaby. She had a Polaroid camera, and she asked him would he mind . . .? He wonders what happened to that photograph. He wonders how many layers deep in Ma's locked mailroom it lies.

'They were happy that night,' Major Miner says. 'I think, back then, before things went wrong, it *was* a sort of Eden out there.'

That is what he wants to believe; but Oyster did change, and the weather in Eden turned bad; yet even so, he cannot hold Oyster alone accountable, he cannot condemn him as the sole agent of harm. Major Miner knows better. He knows worse. He knows that someone stole a dozen boxes of explosives from his shack, his entire remaining supply. In dreams, Joe Blow and Chuang-tzu regard him sorrowfully. A man of violence, Chuang-tzu says, will come to a violent end. He sees that his own hands are covered with blood. He sees young bodies, innocent, falling out of the air. Chuang-tzu hands him a lubricated stick of gelignite. There's a price to be paid, he says.

'Jess,' Major Miner whispers in anguish. 'It was my fault, that ghastly, ghastly thing.'

'Rubbish,' I murmur. 'Nobody needed your explosives. There was enough stuff to blow up the country already at the Reef, and in Andrew Godwin's bunker, and at Dukke Prophet's, and in Bernie's shed, and who knows where else.'

'But it's my gelignite that went missing.'

He should have got rid of the stuff, he should have blown up his own hopelessly flawed life, he should have listened to Bugger Harvey . . . and then what puzzles him, suddenly, is why it was that the Bugger never came back.

'It's strange,' he says, 'it's so strange to walk out on a claim, on a seam like that one.'

The Bugger would have sold his black opals to Herman the Shark (*Come in and be ripped off!*), the broker with the bottomless pocket in Lightning Ridge, the broker whose buyers come right to the minehead in low-flying planes. He must have made a fortune from his pouchful of stones. He must have buggered off to Sydney and good luck to him too.

Nevertheless. To vacate such a claim . . .

It is not like an opal junkie.

It is not like Bugger Harvey, not at all.

'It's really very peculiar, Jess,' he says, 'that he never came back. It's not like him. I reckon I was too distracted by Oyster's arrival to give it much thought at the time.' He thinks about it now. 'One of these days,' he decides, 'he will come back. Actually, for all we know, the sly old Bugger *is* back.'

Major Miner can imagine him holed up underground somewhere on the outer breakaway edges of Andrew Godwin's property, living off goanna meat and smoking himself high on gidgee leaves. He can imagine the Bugger sneaking down the Innamincka track to throw them off the scent, then striking out east to Lightning Ridge: doing a Chuang-tzu. Major Miner smiles to himself. He can well imagine Bugger Harvey making his way through the gaps.

'He'll pop up through a chink in Bernie's verandah one day, Jess.'

But I am thinking of Bugger Harvey's last damper supper, and of Bugger Harvey's three stones, and of Oyster's three stones just two weeks later, and I am remembering Oyster's first night in town. I remember the way he slid into my room, limping, and stood against the window in the moonlight and looked at me. I sat on the bed and stared back. You might have knocked, my eye said, and Oyster smiled. He undid the buttons on his loose shirt-tunic and took it off. His body was golden. There was a nap of soft hair on his chest. He undid the cord on his trousers and let them fall.

I watched, impassive.

Oyster crossed the room and stood so that the silken hair of his crotch was at my lips and his yeasty smell in my nostrils. 'Blessed are ye who hunger and thirst after righteousness,' he murmured. He stroked my hair. 'For you shall be satisfied.' He put his right hand on the back of my head and pressed my face against his body. 'Come unto me,' he murmured, 'and I will come. Come, let us come together. Let us be joyful before the Lord.'

I did not move. I neither resisted nor yielded. I did think of biting him, but for reasons of past rashness, I held myself back.

Seconds passed.

Oyster released me and crossed to the window. He washed himself in moonlight. He preened under the Southern Cross.

'I never coerce,' he said easily, as he put on his clothes. 'But you will desire me. You will come to desire me.' In the moonlight, his milky eyes gleamed. He smiled, and I saw his teeth. His mouth was crowded with them, and they gleamed like white fangs. 'I promise you,' he said. His voice was as sleek and lustrous with menace as the pearled inner membrane of a shell. 'I will be like a hunger,' he promised. 'I will be a thirst that you cannot quench. You will never be able to stop thinking about me.'

But what I cannot stop thinking about is his foot.

There was nothing wrong with his foot.

He was soaked in someone else's blood.

'Bugger Harvey went down the Innamincka track,' I tell Major Miner, 'just as Oyster was coming up. From Coober Pedy, I'd say.'

Major Miner stares at me.

'The same three high notes of opal,' I remind him. 'He could have hidden the Bugger's truck in the breakaways and walked in from there. He knew a lot of local gossip when he came.'

'Holy shit,' Major Miner says softly.

'Oyster's leg,' I say. 'His foot. I saw it that night. There was nothing wrong with it. He was covered with someone else's blood.'

Major Miner's sleep is full of skyrockets and shooting stars. His own gelignite drenches him, he is rained on by Oyster's Reef, he is soaked to the skin with screams, with opalised legs and arms, with Singapore falling, with the Bugger falling out of the sky. He is covered in other people's blood.

'Jess!' he calls, tossing. 'Hold me.'

And I do.

3. The Seventh Angel

Freakish things happen in outback air, especially in winter when diurnal extremes are so . . . extreme. Roiling currents are set up between the burning days, the 50-degree-Celsius days, and nights that seem as cold as the stars, and at first light there is a rind of frost on the Mitchell grass. Campfire embers glisten with splinters of white, shearers wake with chilblains, stockmen with tiny icicles in their lashes and in their hair. Cattle stand bemused at a waterhole gone milky beneath a wafer of ice.

Freakish things happen high above, in the upper layers of air.

In Outer Maroo, the weather can turn dark; not dark with rainclouds, although it is not unknown for mirages of rainclouds to scud by and mock us in their dry, arch manner, telling of water falling in channel country, or north around the Gulf, or in various places that are hundreds of kilometres away. But a different kind of darkness, a twilight, a sort of doomsday murk, can settle in for several hours or several days. It speaks of exceptional instability in the upper air: there may be snowstorms, dust storms, hailstorms, or torrential rain, all happening a few kilometres straight above. The rain may be whipped towards the sun; it may fall up. Gusts of wind, full of red dust, can take the roof off a shed.

These are dangerous and unpredictable times.

In Outer Maroo, the weather was turning dark.

We have to do something, people said. There are more of them than of us, they murmured, frowning, and the murmuring ran to the Reef.

We should not rock any boats, others said. We should not look a gift oyster in the mouth.

From out of the breakaways, fierce winds, hot, blew saltbush tufts and jagged spears of gidgee root through the town. A window in Beresford's was broken, and a black tortured twist of gidgeewood came through. Dead birds were found on Bernie's verandah. The air was the colour of dark blood.

The Old Fuckatoo is roosting again, we said.

Cattle died, sheep rotted, the waterholes shrank and stank, the bore water gave off a sulphurous fog.

The weather turned freakish.

There was lightning, both day and night, high above, like the flash of great seraphic wings. There were dull thunderous booms.

In the first winter after Oyster arrived in town, a twilight fell on us like a thick russet cloak for three days, and out of the murk, out of the hot choppy wind, Oyster came.

He came out of the red dust, alone, in his loose white clothes, at the hour of the afternoon prayer meeting. He stood under the gidgee trees and raised his arms. From Beresford's and Bernie's, and from the Living Word Gospel Hall, people stared. It was fiercely hot and eerily dark, but the Old Fuckatoo had lifted just a little, had seemed to fan us with its wings so that there was a hint of fresh air and a brief false promise of change. Such days are cruel: nobody will say aloud that the sweeter cloudiness could mean hope because this would surely extinguish the possibility.

Everyone waits.

Under the twisted black trunks of the gidgee trees, Oyster waited, his arms lifted to the sky.

Major Miner was on the verandah at Bernie's. I was watching from behind the bar. One by one, from Beresford's, from Bernie's, people came outside to stare. Even those on their way to the Living Word stopped to gaze, and did not go inside. They stood in the street. They edged closer.

Oyster waited, his arms raised, his eyes fixed on the sky.

He's gone crazy, people whispered. He's in a trance, others said. The Murris have told him that rain is on the way, someone said, because everyone is aware that the Old People have mysterious ways of knowing such things.

At a certain point, when most of Outer Maroo had gathered in the street, as though he had been waiting for an audience of a certain acceptable size, Oyster lowered his eyes and looked around him. 'Follow me,' he said. He turned towards the steps of the Living Word, and we all crowded in behind. Major Miner had never been inside the Gospel Hall before; nor had Bernie; nor had I. Even for funerals, we non-believers always clustered outside. For many people in Outer Maroo it was the first time, and the spare puritan place, beautiful in its austere way, had its own power, it cast its own spell.

Oyster said something privately to Charles Given, who frowned, and appeared a little puzzled, a little distressed. Oyster, I noted, was looking at the floor, not at Charles Given, and was talking in a low intense voice. Charles Given reached out and put his hand on Oyster's arm, and Oyster raised his head then, and the two of them were eye to eye, for five seconds, eight, ten, it seemed interminable. A shuffling began, because most people could not see what was happening, and the crushing was considerable. There was standing room only; the heat and the dust and the twilight murk and the body fug were suffocating. Charles Given never dropped his eyes from Oyster's, he never wavered in focus, but he did seem to concede something. Compassion came too easily to him, I think, and not always at the right time.

'All right,' I heard him say, and I actually saw him squeeze Oyster's arm, a sort of brotherly gesture, the kind of thing that would probably translate roughly as: my friend, these states of agony pass; these dark nights of the soul roll away and then morning comes.

Oyster climbed into the pulpit and raised both arms, slanting them outwards, embracing us, and the wide white sleeves of his tunic hung like wings. The moving and shuffling ceased. For several seconds, he let the silence grow.

'The last days are coming,' he said. 'The last days are coming, and are even now upon us, for darkness shall be upon the face of the earth, and there will be a mighty rushing wind, and the Beast of the Apocalypse will stalk the land, and the seventh angel will speak. The last days are upon us, and very soon time shall be no more, but the earth is offering us refuge and wealth. She will shelter us in the last days, but she will shelter only those who are pure in heart and are without a spirit of dissension.'

There was movement again, a slight thing, like small choppy waves before a storm, and there was a low murmur, because we knew that the reference to dissension was meant for us, and we did not like it.

'A spirit of dissension,' Oyster said, 'will divide us, but a spirit of trust will unite.' He reached into the pockets of his tunic, and then pushed his pocketed arms toward us in a strange way, so that he appeared to offer us hooded hands. 'He who is for us, saith the Lord, to him will be given the riches of the Kingdom.' He flicked his wrists free of the pockets and held out his fists towards us and opened them.

His hands were full of opal.

Major Miner held his breath. He could hear the high singing in his ears.

'Follow me,' Oyster said, 'and I will continue to share the abundance of my Reef, and I will lead you safely beyond the end of time. But he that is not for me is against me and will be cut down.'

Can you picture this?

People do not laugh at madmen, they give them a certain kind of respect. They are hushed. There is something about hubris, about genuine hubris, that does inspire genuine awe. It is a true mystery; its pedigree is long and full of terror; it has a history that no one treats lightly, a history that tolls names as a death bell tolls: Attila, Robespierre, Hitler, Stalin, Idi Amin, Saddam Hussein, Jim Jones . . .

Something else about hubris: those afflicted with it are, at one and the same time, clowns, carnival barkers, dress-up artists, madmen, magicians, monsters; yet always clowns. They are ridiculous; they are alarming. They wave their batons; they lift a curtain; they have the power to divide into two. There will be those who stand back, chilled, silent, with due respect for dark power, to watch the tumbrils roll across the stage; and there will be others who pass through the curtain, who leap up on stage, who enter the play.

On stage, on the other side of that curtain, the laws of nature change. Logic changes. People see with the madman's eyes. For true madness has this gift, and this potency, that it makes its own complete world. It has its own space. Others can enter it.

'We are the last of God's free people in the wilderness,' Oyster said. 'We are His chosen ones. The people of Outer Maroo are chosen. They are custodians of the wealth of the Lord God of Hosts.'

And he came down from the pulpit and walked among us and distributed opals. And many, perhaps most, with who knows what mixed emotions, held out their hands, cupped, as for a sacrament, their eyes flashing, their lips slightly parted, their breathing fast. Some kept their hands deep and defiantly and contemptuously in their pockets, but most held them out, and here was the deviant brilliance of Oyster, that connoisseur of purity of heart, because an unseemly shuffling began. There were ripples of anxiety from those who had decided to partake, but who feared they might miss out on a stone. There were sideways glances, there were comparisons of size and cut and play of colour. Little serpents of greed, of rivalry, of discontentment hissed about. There was a competitive desire for the special touch of Oyster's watery eyes and gemmy hands.

Then Oyster returned to the pulpit and raised his arms and closed his eyes.

'It is not I who speaks to you,' he said. 'I am merely the instrument, the channel. He who speaks through me has words to say. He that hath ears to hear, let him hear.'

Major Miner remembers rubbing a hand across his eyes, dazed. He remembers looking about him. For a frightening moment, he thought he saw Singapore mud, shaved heads, hollow eyes, and the prison camp commandant out in front. He shuddered. He felt as though he were swaying in a sleep.

'For I call upon my righteous servant, Dukke vanKerk,' Oyster said, 'a man upright in the sight of God, I call upon him to be my right-hand man, to be my Prophet, yea, he will be my Prophet in the midst of my people, to keep my people faithful unto death, that they may acknowledge me in all their ways. And I shall direct their paths; and my Prophet shall develop those veins of my treasure which are on and under his land . . .

'And I call upon my servant Andrew Godwin to look to those veins of my treasure which are on and under his land, and to guide my people thereto, and to look to the defence of my people . . . for he shall be my Warrior and my right-hand man . . .

'But I must warn you, my people, that envy shall arise round about us. And evil powers shall arise, godless powers, the powers of government and of tax inspectors, the powers of the godless who shall gnash their teeth and shall seek to take from you that which is rightfully mine and rightfully yours . . .

'And you must arm yourselves, my people . . . you must protect yourself from those without . . . For in those days which are coming upon us, this town will be your shield and buckler. And you must separate yourselves from the world, for the world is evil. Yea, those of you who have your children in school in Quilpie or Toowoomba or Brisbane must bring them home as sheep to the fold, where the teachers of the godless shall not corrupt them. And you shall have your own school and your own teachings, as I will direct you, and you shall cause to be brought hither your own teacher who shall teach the precepts of the Lord in your school. The world will be against you, my people, but they that shall endure to the end will be saved, for the great and terrible Day of the Lord is coming, my people, the great and terrible battle is coming, the final battle of Good and Evil, a battle when You, my people, shall be against Them, the forces of darkness. For this is that battle which has been foretold in the Book of Revelation, my people, the last great battle of Armageddon, the last –'

'*Stop!*'

There was a shocked and terrifying silence, and for the space of two whole seconds, no one moved. Every living soul heard the thump of heartblood against the wall of the chest.

'This is demagoguery,' Pastor Given said angrily. 'God is not a showman.' He stood and surveyed them. He walked to the pulpit. 'Excuse me,' he said politely to Oyster. 'The Spirit of the Lord,' he said, addressing the congregation in the quieter voice of someone mildly embarrassed by a spasm of outrage, 'is gentle.'

He stood in the pulpit and opened the Bible and read quietly, tried to read quietly, tried to read, from the Old Testament, and from the Book of Kings:

> '*And, behold, the Lord passed by, and a great and strong wind rent the mountains, and brake in pieces the rocks before the Lord; but the Lord was not in the wind: and after the wind an earthquake; but the Lord was not in the earthquake:*

And after the earthquake a fire; but the Lord was not in the fire: and after the fire a still small voice . . .'

But there were interruptions, there were shouts, it was very difficult to hear, and so Charles Given closed the Bible and raised his head and spoke in such a low voice that the congregation fell silent again and had to lean forward like Mitchell grass in the path of a wind to hear.

'God is not a showman,' Charles Given said. 'God speaks in a still small voice. He speaks in a whisper. No one, no other living soul, can hear what God says to you.' And there was a shuffling of feet, and a murmuring, and 'Let us not forget what the Gospel of Matthew warns . . .' the pastor said, but the shuffling was shoving by then, '*for there shall arise false Christs, and false prophets, and shall shew great signs and wonders*,' and then Mr Prophet rose to his feet, '. . . *deceive the very elect*,' Charles Given said, and then, and then, '*wherefore if they shall say unto you*,' he said, and a great tumult arose, '*behold, he is in the desert . . . believe it not*, for the spirit of the Lord is gentle. It is not full of pomp and circumstance and the lust for personal power and greed. It is not –'

'It is not puffed up,' Mr Dukke vanKerk shouted, striding forward, jabbing his finger at Pastor Given. 'It is not full of the vain pride of human learning and of books.'

'Amen,' Oyster said, his eyes lifted to the rafters. 'My Prophet has spoken. Hear, o my people, my Prophet.'

'My people,' Pastor Given said, 'the Spirit of the Lord is full of love. The Spirit of the Lord does not bribe with offers of wealth. Remember, I beg you, that the Bible warns of false prophets who shall come promising –'

Sit down, people shouted, and there were hands that grabbed Pastor Given, there was shuffling and growling and calls of *Oyster, Oyster*, and *opals*, and *we want to hear, we want to know, let Oyster speak . . .*

'*And the sixth angel*,' Oyster roared, reading from the book that was in the pulpit, '*the sixth angel poured out his vial upon the great river Euphrates, and the water thereof was dried up, that the way of the kings of the east might be prepared . . .*

'God speaks to us here of the drought,' Oyster said. 'And after the great drought shall come tribulation and earth tremors and hail . . . And evil spirits shall arise to do battle with the Lord's Anointed, and the forces of the Lord and the forces of Evil shall do battle . . .

'Hear the words of the Lord in the Book of Revelation:

And he gathered them together into a place called in the Hebrew tongue Armageddon. And the seventh angel poured out his vial into the air; and there came a great voice out of the temple of heaven, from the throne, saying, It is done. And there were voices, and thunders, and lightnings, and there was a great earthquake . . .'

Oyster held up his right arm as Moses once did above the waters.

From the Reef, came the distant rumble of blasting. The Living Word shook.

'Hark,' Oyster called, 'to the voice of the seventh angel.'

And the great wind roared from the north, and the windows rattled and were dark with red dust.

'*And there fell upon men a great hail out of heaven,*' Oyster read; '*every stone about the weight of a talent: and men blasphemed God because of the plague of the hail; for the plague thereof was exceeding great.*'

'Hark!' Oyster said.

And we all listened, nervous and amazed, as hailstones the size of tennis balls pelted against the iron roof. Children cried, and mothers held them. We thought the world was falling apart around our ears. Major Miner felt panic twist like a dervish in his mind, and felt bombs falling. The clatter went on and on. A window broke. There were flying shards of glass. There was cut flesh, screams, blood.

And then there was a terrible quiet.

'The seventh angel hath spoken,' Oyster said, and he beckoned the congregation with both hands, and there were people who entered the space that Oyster and the hail had made. Dukke Prophet leapt to the pulpit and fire flew from him, incendiary words, and then events piled up so fast after that, so fast, it was scarcely even possible to know what was happening . . . the rushing, the shouting, the ransacking of the Pastor's study, the bonfire, the book burning, the sudden violence, the brawls . . .

A mob is a mob is a mob, Major Miner thought then.

'I still feel sick,' he tells me, 'when I think of that insane day . . . I feel sick that I didn't do anything to stop that . . . that madness . . . I can't understand it. I can't forgive myself. I couldn't seem to realise what was happening, but I don't forgive myself for letting it happen. I don't forgive myself for not doing anything.'

'You did do something,' I tell him. 'You reached into the fire, grabbing books like an idiot. You were beaten unconscious.'

He stares at me. 'I did?' Some very faint echo of this, the shadow of a shadow, comes back to him like the edge of a dream.

'You did,' I say.

'Thank God.'

He is so grateful, so overwhelmed, that he turns from me and walks away, fast, jerkily, and loses himself in a fold in the breakaways. He goes into one of the fissures, I know that. He communes with his boulder opal. He remains out of sight for an hour and then comes back.

'Every time I try to think about Oyster,' he says, 'I feel sicker, and I feel more confused.'

But there is Oyster in the pulpit, again and always, offering everyone his private dreams. Ah, but some of those dreams . . . It is a murky thing, Major Miner thinks, to let loose some people's dreams.

4. Letters Never Sent

To St Paul, Minnesota, USA:
Dear Luce,

Remember how we used to lie on the grass outside the library and make those vows that wherever we ended up after college, no matter what country, no matter if we stayed together or not, we'd still check in with each other every year? At least once every year, we said. We'd send the letters to our parents' address if we lost track of where the other was. We didn't believe we ever would lose track, at least I didn't then, and I don't think you did either.

We both said we'd travel, but we were going to do it together after graduation. Well, I know it was me who messed things up. She left me before we even got out of London, you'll be pleased to know. Went off with someone she met in a pub. Not that you'll care, probably. You're probably married or something by now. The thing is, Luce, I can't stop thinking about you lately, and I'm kind of hoping there's just a chance you'll come and join me. You always said you wanted to live in some sort of community, a commune in the country somewhere, you wanted to live off the land. Well, I've found the perfect one. I hope this isn't going to sound too corny, but I've found God too.

We live out in the desert like shamans used to do, in tunnels and caves and tents. It's an opal mining community and we're self-sufficient. It's incredibly beautiful out here, and we're like a family, all one in the mystical Body of Christ. There's no racism either. I mean all the things we believed in in college, they're here. We live together, black and white, the Australian Aborigines and us (they call themselves Murris), and we work extremely hard, and meditate, and every night there are meetings and singing and discussions and the teachings of Oyster – he's the leader. Well, you get the picture.

I'm sending this to your mother's address. If you're interested in coming out, get yourself to Brisbane, then you have to take a train or a bus to Quilpie, then hitch a ride on to Oyster's Reef. Anyway, Luce, I keep thinking about you. Please write.

Lots of love,

Simon Peter (formerly Rob)

To Melbourne:

Dear Jimbo,

Well, you may have been right, after all, but you were so high and mighty about it in Brisbane, and I hate to give you the pleasure of saying *I told you so*, so you can guess how desperate I am to be writing to you, mate. You can be a real pain in the arse sometimes, but you turned out to be right about that guy Gideon, he's got a ramrod up his whatsit and he's holier than God Almighty himself, though believe me, he's nothing compared to the fat cat who's Lord High Mucky-Muck out here. Yeah, yeah, I remember the jokes you made in Brisbane, anyone who swallows an oyster sucks. Very funny, even though you turned out to be right. Actually, it was all pretty good at first, it really was, and lots of very nifty sheilas around, but they make us live like bloody monks, except for Oyster, who's a real poker, he likes to keep them all for himself, but just the same, I really had a pretty good time for a while, and I liked the hard work, and I've learned plenty about opals. In fact, you and me should head for Coober Pedy after this, mate. Trouble is, here, we don't keep a brass razoo for ourselves, it all goes to Oyster and Gideon and the commune and crap like that, we're slave labour, that's what it is, and the prayer stuff is getting to be just a bit too much. As a matter of fact, it's getting a bit crazy around here, and much bloody harder to get out than I realised when I came. So what I'm asking (and yeah, yeah, I'll eat shit, I'll kiss your arse), is could you send some dosh, a postal order for a few hundred'll do. Don't send a cheque, there's no bank. Send it to me care of Beresford's, Outer Maroo, west of Quilpie. And don't tell Dad, or I'll crush your nuts when I get back. Once I'm in Melbourne, I'm gonna sleep for a week, we only get about three hours a night, we get preached at till the morning star is in the sky, I'm scribbling this at the rate of knots, hope you can read, it's not allowed, which'll give you some idea, and then I'll cart you off to Coober Pedy, mate, and make us both rich.

Your dumb brother,

Matt

(a.k.a. around here as Habbakuk, I kid you not. No jokes, please.)

To Sydney:

Dear Mum and Dad,

It is easier for a camel to go through the eye of a needle, than for a rich man to enter the kingdom of God. That is hard for you to understand. Here, we keep nothing for ourselves, we give ourselves totally, and so we find ourselves. I am bathed in the peace that passeth understanding, and I think of you with sorrow and with pity, so full of the poison of ambition and rush, getting and spending, laying waste your powers. I pray for you. I am filled with a radiant white light, and when I meditate, when Oyster directs our radiance out into the world, I clothe you with it. The world is rapidly returning to the chaos out of which it was once called forth by God, but I will draw you into the light that will take us beyond time and into the unchanging present of eternity. I pray that you will be saved in spite of yourselves by the force of the love of God. I clothe you in white light.

Love,

your daughter in Christ,
Balm of Gilead (formerly Ginnie)

To Boston:

Dear Sarah,

I have come home. It's one of those feelings deep down in the bone. I believe now that everything is ordained, every seemingly chance encounter is meant to be. I know Dad has gone. It's OK. I saw him in a dream. He was standing on the dock, down by the lake, and I walked down, and in the dream he kept watching me the whole way until I reached the dock, and then he turned away and dived into the water and never came up.

It's OK.

Out here there's so much sky, and so many stars at night, and the rocks are so ancient, and I have this feeling that nothing ever passes away. It's all here. It's all with us. That is what Oyster says. It's all ours. Last night there was a dingo outside my tent. They are very beautiful, very *Other*, somehow, not dangerous at all. We just looked at each other, the dingo and me, and I suddenly realised that he had Dad's eyes. I felt the most incredible peace.

I can feel you with me too, Sarah.

I have never known such peace and happiness. I will confess a secret: I'm in love. All the women are in love with Oyster, and he is kind to everyone, he loves everyone, but I am his Special One. It is an honour and a joy that overwhelms me. I keep it secret, because he wants me to, so that none of the others will be jealous.

I have a new name, by the way. Oyster gives each of us his own special name. We have a ceremony and we are baptised with our new name. We are born again. Mine's Rose of Sharon, which I find very beautiful.

I'll write when I can, though we don't get much time, and we're not supposed to write letters, but I do feel I owe you this one, Sarah, and if Oyster knew our past history, he would permit it. We work terribly hard, and we meditate, and study Oyster's teachings, and we're all very happy together. When I meditate, you are with me, Sarah. All things were meant to be.

Love,

Rose of Sharon (formerly Amy)

Dear Sarah,

When we meditate, we see a white light, brighter than anything you can imagine or have ever seen. We visualise it in the heart of an oyster shell. Oyster talks to us very softly, and teaches us, and the light grows and grows and swallows everything. I cannot describe how incredibly beautiful this is, but what I want you to know, Sarah, is that I reach out with the light and cover you with it in my mind.

Love,

Rose of Sharon

Dear Sarah,

It's hard getting used to the heat sometimes. A lot of the girls faint in the middle of the day, and one died from heatstroke. It was awful. So Oyster is changing the rules. He says we have to come into alignment with the rules of the universe. Even the animals obey very strict rules, the males live one way, the females another.

So the girls cook, and they sew clothes. The guys are learning to hunt the way the Aborigines do, and we are learning to cook in the same ancient way. We're not allowed to go into town on the trucks so much now, but nobody wants to anyway, because we can see the people in town don't like us. If we go, we have to go in threes, for safety. I really believe in the way we're living here, but I'm very tired, and not very well. I might come and see you for a holiday, but then I'd come back.

Love,
Rose of Sharon

Dear Sarah,

Winter's harder than summer, because it's so cold at night, below freezing, but just as hot in the day. There's been some very strange weather. We've had dust storms and freak hailstorms. I never knew hailstones could be so huge.

Oyster says the town is against us, and he's tightening the rules. There's impurity at the Reef itself, he says, and he's right, because we are supposed to keep ourselves pure, but a number of the girls are pregnant. There are a number of babies and toddlers now, and they are looked after by a specially chosen group. Oyster adores the children. We all have to wear scarves tied around our head now, the girls, I mean, to show that we are modest and our thoughts are pure.

I'm not feeling very well lately. I'll write when I can. It's hard to get a chance to go in and mail our letters these days.

Love,
Rose of Sharon

Dear Sarah,

I'm making you come out of the white light so I can talk to you. I'm very upset. We're not supposed to talk to each other any more while we're working, or ever really. We meditate all the time, we're contemplatives, Oyster says. It's a way to make the world pure. But I was working over a campfire with Jillian, we were roasting roots in the hot coals the way the Murris showed us, and suddenly Jillian just began crying and she couldn't stop. I asked her what was the matter and she said she didn't know what they'd done with her baby. It was Oyster's baby, she said. I don't know whether to believe her or not. Oyster says a lot of the other women have fantasies about him, and some of the men are not keeping themselves sexually pure. I think sometimes, even in perfect communes, things can go wrong. I'm thinking of leaving for a while, just to think things out.

Love,

Rose of Sharon

Dear Sarah,

Some of the opal tunnels that are worked out have been widened out into rooms. The men do it with small drilling machines, though the noise is giving me terrible headaches lately. So anyhow, now most of us live underground instead of in tents or sheds. In some ways, it's much better. It's so much cooler underground by day, and it stays exactly the same at night. The temperature is constant down here, so this will be much better when next winter comes, though I don't think I'm going to stay until then. There's a special team to look after the babies and toddlers, but some of the babies have died. The toddlers seem terribly quiet and still to me, not at all the way little children usually are. They hardly ever even cry. It worries me, but Oyster says it is because they were born into an aura of peace. There are always girls pregnant, and there are births, but the mothers have to give their babies to the special team. One of them was so upset she tried to kill herself, but at camp meeting (which we have every night), she testified that she accepted the will of God and she confessed her sin of rebellion and she said she was filled with joy and white light, except the next day, when we were doing laundry duty together, she started crying and couldn't stop. There are a lot of things I find hard to understand, and I'm not feeling very well, but I do believe in Oyster. I do love him. When I meditate, I feel at perfect peace, and I try to let the white light fill my mind for the whole day.

Love,
Rose of Sharon

Dear Sarah,

I haven't written for a long time, and I haven't told you about many things that happen here, because I couldn't. I couldn't even think about them. I blamed myself. I blamed my impure thoughts. But something's happened, I know it's not just me now, I know something's gone wrong. Someone came here and then managed to get away, and it's changed things for me. I've suddenly remembered there is another reality out there, outside the Reef. Remember ages ago, I told you about Gideon (his real name's Angelo), the one who first told me about the Reef? Well, he's seen it too, and it's incredible to have someone to talk to, though we hardly ever get a chance. I'm going to leave here. I'll see you soon, Sarah, and I promise I won't run away again.

Love,
Amy (formerly Rose of Sharon)

Dear Sarah,

Almost impossible to leave Reef at all now, even to get into town in threes, but am determined. *Must* mail this so you'll know what happened if I never. Forgive scrawl, hard to find time and place, almost impossible, dangerous. Amazing diff. now Angelo and I can talk, *really* talk, tho vry diff to talk at all, talking not allowed anymore except wk, prayers, always 3s.

Angelo and I can't understand ourselves now, why it took us so long, how we lived with, why we put up . . . Hope you cn read. Not much time. It was like a madness, it was sick, hard to explain. Weren't ourselves. Always too tired to *think*, work too hard, and then all night practically, sermon and singing, and too much meditating, fried our brains, I think; like being on drugs, being tranquillised for years.

Oyster quite mad now, we think, and getting worse. Dangerous. Angelo told me Oyster has big plan for next week. Big ceremony, everyone underground, candles, middle of night. *Service of Final Purification and Deliverance*, we don't like sound. All the vestal virgins waiting, Oyster says, *for the Bridegroom Cometh*. Angelo knows his moods, doesn't like this at all. Going to take us all across the Great Divide, Oyster says, and into the Promised Land. Going to take us beyond time. Like the babies, Angelo says, and the other ones, the chosen ones, who keep disappearing, tho we're all too exhausted most of the time to know who's missing or not. Angelo asked about the children dying and the missing. Offering to God, Oyster said. Caught up in the Rapture, Final Purity, Deliverance, changed in the twinkling of an eye, gone to be with God.

Don't like sound at all. Must mail. Angelo and I made up minds to get away, make a break. Coming home, I promise.

Pray for me, Sarah. I'm scared.

Love, Amy

5. Shafted

The rabbit-hole went straight on like a tunnel for some way, Miss Rover read, *and then dipped suddenly down, so suddenly that Alice had not a moment to think about stopping before she found herself falling down what seemed to be a very deep mine shaft.*

Mercy, falling through nightmares and yesterdays and past lateral tunnels and the roar of drilling rigs and winches and the sucking sound of Cretaceous dirt being vacuumed in below her, and blown back out above ground as mullock heaps, tried to ascertain which chapter and verse she was in, which prophecy, which mine: Oyster's Reef, or Aladdin's Rush, or Potch Point, or Major Miner's Great Extended, or simply one of the drill-and-abandon sites. It was hard to tell from the main shaft.

It was hard to see anything but dread through the skeins of white dust. *Miss Rover come over*, she prayed, and the words turned over and over with each slow sickening cartwheel of her fall. They rolled around Mercy like gemstones clattering down a well. She clutched at them and kept them tight in her fist, and Miss Rover's name was warm against her palm, a fire opal sending out sparks. When she rubbed it, her own fearless genie broke loose from her body. 'Where am I?' she called. 'I can't see . . .' Her lungs filled with mullock dust and she was seized by a coughing fit. *Miss Rover*, she coughed, and Miss Rover will-o'-the-wisped forth from from a lateral tunnel, chalk-dusted.

'I've been looking for you,' Mercy said, joyful. She could not stop coughing. 'It's the mullock dust,' she gasped. 'It's killing me. But it doesn't matter now. I'm so glad I found you. They said you'd been transferred.'

'Translated,' Miss Rover said, 'to a higher sphere. They promoted me.'

She was hitting the blackboard duster with a ruler, and small white clouds rose like balloons. 'The dust is a problem,' she acknowledged, 'though it could be just the poor-quality classroom chalk.' Nevertheless, she entered *mullock dust* and *mullock heaps* on a fresh page. She was keeping a journal of gaps in the curriculum. 'You may be right,' she said. 'It may be mullock dust in the lungs that is killing people off. A lot of people do seem to be dying around here. But the thing is, in the long scheme of things, Mercy, in the sweep of history, this little end-of-the-world sideshow doesn't count for very much, although of course it does not seem that way to those of us caught up in it. Everyone is ridiculously arrogant in that way, you know. We all place ourselves front and centre in world history, but the world has already ended once for Outer Maroo, and who remembers?'

'I remember,' Mercy said. 'In 1873. You taught us.'

'Very good,' Miss Rover said. She swept her duster across the classroom board, erasing dates. 'For various peoples and places, there've been other Armageddons, and I regret to say there'll be more.' She blew a cloud of chalk dust out the window. 'One person's end-of-the-world cataclysm is another person's footnote, Mercy. Take the Armageddon that began in 1788. We are only just beginning to know chapter and verse on that.'

She sat down at the teacher's table and put her head in her hands. 'What haunts me,' she said, 'is how little I achieved. I will be honest with you, Mercy. Even in my new posting, it gives me no peace.'

She shuffled a pack of report cards, and the cards rose and fell like white birds. 'I achieved nothing,' she said. She was still overwhelmed by how inadequately a Queensland education prepared one for Queensland. She was overwhelmed by unfinished work. She could not release herself. 'I am still in Outer Maroo,' she said.

Something about the way she said this frightened Mercy, who felt a need to shield herself from dreams, and especially from unwanted revelations. 'I know you have sent me letters,' she told Miss Rover. 'I know they can't be delivered because of Ma. It's so cold here.'

'It's the wind off the Reef,' Miss Rover said. 'It's the wind off Inner Maroo. It's called the chill factor. Just ignore it. I'll go on reading because I'm still here.'

Miss Rover is still reading *Alice in Wonderland*. There are thirteen children in the one-teacher school and their ages range from six to eighteen. Mercy sits in the back row. 'Children's stories,' Miss Rover explains, 'are rarely *just* children's stories. And this one in particular,' she says, 'seems pertinent, since suspensions of normal logic hold sway.'

'How do you know what *normal* is?' Brian asks.

'Exactly,' Miss Rover says. 'People arrive and then they vanish. It's normal in Outer Maroo.'

'They don't vanish,' Brian says. 'They withdraw from the world, which is altogether a different thing. They seek to purify themselves.'

'And death,' Miss Rover says. 'Death is normal here too.'

'Death is always normal in the outback,' Brian says.

Mercy has to agree. It's true. The drought, the dead cattle, the dead sheep. And people too. In cattle country, sheep country, the cancer statistics are high. Cattle dips, insecticides, crop and forage spraying, it can't be helped. And there is a rule in Outer Maroo that upsets Miss Rover: the rule that a man with cancer does not burden his family with slow death. He disposes of himself, discreetly, somewhere on the outer boundaries, where one of his stockmen will find him, muzzle in mouth.

Pete has explained it to her, Mercy has heard him. 'That's what separates the men from the city boys, love,' he has told her. 'As for forage-dusting and shooting 'roos and mining on the so-called sacred sites, she's a real bugger, the land. If you don't slap her round a bit, the land gives too much damn cheek.'

'I see,' Miss Rover says.

'No, you don't,' Pete says. 'You *don't*. Because the land always wins, see, in the end. We *know* that. Shit. There's a whole townful of skeletons and rotting foundations just the other side of the break-aways. This town's already come and gone once. I mean, gone. Absolutely. All that's left of Inner Maroo is nothing.' Pete snaps his fingers, then kisses their tips and blows the kiss away. 'That could happen to us, Susannah. We could all go under to the drought, every last one of us. I mean, all these carcasses . . . you must have noticed. The smell of death hangs over us. Or we could all be washed away in flash floods. She's a tough old bitch, is the land. We respect her, and that's why we give her no quarter. We're talking about passion here,' he says.

'Really?' Miss Rover raises her eyebrows. 'Passion?' she says.

Pete is angry. 'You don't understand our way of loving.'

'No,' Miss Rover agrees, unwinding his arm from her shoulder, and they seem to be sitting on Bernie's verandah, and Mercy is sitting on the steps. 'Sounds more like rape to me,' Miss Rover says.

'Now don't get difficult,' Pete cajoles. He takes one of her hands and traces the up and down of her fingers with his own. 'Tell you what. After you've survived a few droughts and a few flash floods and a bushfire or two, we'll give you a gold-plated soapbox, no questions asked. And we'll all listen like Sunday School kids.'

But Miss Rover has a terrible taste for making trouble. 'Foot-in-mouth disease,' Pete sighs, 'and a terminal case.' And here is Andrew

Godwin choosing the very moment to swing himself out of his truck and up Bernie's steps. He empties a small sack of severed emu heads on the floorboards. 'How about that?' he asks proudly. 'That'll teach the buggers to swipe forage from my cows in a drought.'

Miss Rover, fully mounted on soapbox, rising, pushing both deckchair and Pete aside, asks coldly: 'Aren't emus protected?'

Andrew Godwin blinks.

He has to pause and replay the question to himself.

Then he laughs. 'Only by their feathers, love,' he says.

'God, she's something!' he tells Pete, and the merriment is so general, so infectious, that everyone is inclined to forgive Susannah and to buy her a drink. Isn't she something? they say. These Brisbane sheilas, aren't they something these days? Strike me blue.

'If you'll forgive me,' Miss Rover says, trembling, smoothing her skirt. 'I've got lessons to prepare and thirteen children waiting. Come on, Mercy. Let's go.'

And they are walking away up the street, hand in hand and heads high.

'Like two jabirus,' Pete tells them later.

Mercy watches the way he watches Miss Rover. She knows that Miss Rover seems to him as graceful and flighty and wild as the long-legged birds of the waterholes. Dangerous, too. The men watch the way her cotton skirt whispers around her legs. Mercy knows that Miss Rover is angry. Pete knows it too.

'Don't make trouble, Susannah,' he begs, low-voiced. He slides his hand along her arm. 'The living's rough out here. You have to make allowances, that's all.'

'Believe me, Pete,' she says. 'I've been making allowances.'

She is keeping a private record of allowances made.

She is compiling a textbook, unorthodox, unasked for, 'because,' she tells Mercy, 'we need proper local reference points for Outer Maroo.' Mercy studies the flow of her fountain pen, the thickness of the downstrokes, the elegance of the loops. The secrets are hidden in my writing, Miss Rover says.

'*Mullock heaps*,' Mercy reads.

Mullock heaps are small mountains of coarse white chalk dust at the head of every shaft. They are deposited by the winches attached to the drilling rigs. They often contain fractured pieces of precious opal and also much opal potch. Various tourists (usually young backpackers) and also Aboriginal tribespeople (the displaced fringe-dwellers of the mining areas; the Wangkumara in the vicinity of Outer Maroo) have picked up fortunes by noodling through mullock heaps at many opal fields throughout Australia.

Noodling

'Noodling' means sifting through the chalk dust for pieces of opal, although most of what is found is potch.

Potch

About 95 per cent of all opal is potch, that is to say, opal without a play of colour. Although frequently very beautiful, potch has little or no commercial value. It may be milky and pearlised, or black, or clear, or honey-coloured. It is used in the production of 'doublets' – that is, as backing for thin veneers of precious and colorific opal found as thin surfaces, which could otherwise not be displayed. While doublets have a mere fraction of the value of solid opal, the difference in appearance is not detectable to the untrained eye. The origin of the word *potch* is obscure, but it is probably a miner's corruption of *pot-shard*. The children in Outer Maroo love to go noodling for potch, though the practice is very bad for the lungs and causes serious coughing fits.

'Everyone already knows this,' Mercy tells her.

'In Outer Maroo they know it,' Miss Rover says. 'But this textbook is for my next school.'

Mercy is still falling and coughing. She keeps passing Miss Rover and losing her again. She seems to be spinning in slow circles as she falls, like an astronaut in space, a phenomenon she has witnessed on Miss Rover's television set. She falls into the schoolroom then out again. In several lateral tunnels, as she passes, she sees Pete with Miss Rover. She sees the way blue sparks leap between them, anger or passion, it is hard to tell which. Mercy wonders how Miss Rover can distinguish.

She cannot stop coughing.

She is noodling with Brian near Oyster's Reef and Brian is coughing until threads of blood make stars in the chalk-white dirt. A fine white dust covers all the noodlers like a shroud. When they move, jam jars of water in hand to clean the stones and to keep them from crazing, knees bent, heads lowered, the noodlers look like dancers in a ghost corroboree.

Mercy sees ghosts. She sees Brian consumed by intensity. She sees Amy with all her unsent letters in flames. Bodies are advancing rank upon rank, like sheep, into conflagration. There is Oyster, crisped and candescent in martyrdom as he'd always wanted to be, going out in style, in good company, thronged around by the votive candles of his power.

It's all done with smoke and faggots, he laughs, and his laughter turns into flakes of fire and scorches Mercy as she falls.

Miss Rover Miss Rover come over, she whispers frantically.

She tells Miss Rover's name like beads that pass between her fingers. Like opals. Like pearls.

I'm back in Oyster's Reef, she thinks with despair.

'How clever you are, my little pearl,' Oyster croons. 'You're in my own private grief, my private Reef,' and his voice bounces around the mine shaft like an echo gone berserk, my reefreefREEFREEFreefreefreefreef.

'Welcome, Alice, to my little inferno,' he says. 'Welcome, welcome, welcome.'

Wel*come-come-come*, the echoes call.

'I'm not Alice,' Mercy says.

'Down here,' Oyster tells her, 'your name is whatever I tell you it is.'

Either the mine shaft was very deep, Miss Rover reads, *or Mercy fell very slowly, for she had plenty of time as she went down to look about her, and to wonder what was going to happen next . . .*

'I'm not Mercy,' Alice says, frantic. 'At least, I don't think so. Not any more. Am I? Am I?'

'You'll have to decide,' Miss Rover says. 'It's up to you. Whatever your name is, you still have to think for yourself. You have to look yourself in the eye. You have to decide what you are willing to live with, Mercy, and what you will die for.'

'I don't want to die for anything,' Mercy weeps.

'Nobody does,' Miss Rover says. 'But sometimes it happens that we have to make a choice. There are lines we won't cross, but we draw the lines ourselves. Nobody makes us do it.'

'I don't know where my line is,' Mercy says. 'I don't even know if I'm falling up or falling down.'

Down, down, down, Miss Rover reads. *Would the fall* never *come to an end? 'I wonder how many miles I've fallen by this time?' Alice said aloud. 'I must be getting somewhere near the centre of the earth. Let me see: that would be four thousand miles down, I think . . .*

'That's silly,' Mercy says. She feels exasperated. 'Opal shafts are not very deep. I must be falling slowly, that's all.'

'In nightmares,' Miss Rover says, 'the sleeper falls slowly because the unconscious is free to choose its own playback speed and to map its own routes.'

Mercy is relieved. 'This is a nightmare,' she says. 'I knew it was. I knew I'd wake up, and you would still be here, and Brian would still be here, and Oyster would *not* be here, he would *never* have been here, and it's just a nightmare.'

'Outer Maroo is a nightmare,' Miss Rover says, 'but a serious one. Not everyone manages to wake out of it. As for depth statistics,' she says, 'you are right. Speaking comparatively, among the planet's geological nips and tucks, it is true that opal shafts are mere pinpricks in the epidermal layer of the terrestrial crust, though they are deep enough to violate the earth under Aboriginal law. As the Old People say: you cannot mutilate your mother without repercussions.'

'I think I've stopped falling,' Mercy says.

Although the light is poor, she can see along several lateral tunnels to other mines. In one tunnel, she is catching lizards with Donny Becker. In another, she can see Oyster arriving in town.

'A significant question to ponder,' Miss Rover says, 'is which came first: opal or Oyster?'

> It is rumoured, *she writes in her journal*, that Oyster, before the secret of world salvation was vouchsafed to him, had come from an earlier life as something else in Coober Pedy, and as something else before that on the pearling luggers at Broome. It would be wise, I am sure, not to enquire too closely into what that something else was. But once he saw the calibre of the opal floaters here, he put a word in the ears of Bernie, and of Andrew Godwin, and of Mr Dukke Prophet. These pillars of the community – may their names be blessed, may their names be recorded in the Book of My Unspendable Salary – crossed the South Australian border and bought a drilling rig and winches and trucked them up the Birdsville Track.
>
> Could anything other than opal and the recurring fantasy of the end of the world, *Miss Rover writes*, have wedded Bernie and Andrew Godwin and and Dukke Prophet and Oyster?

Behold the prophecy of a schoolteacher whose sense
of adventure ran away with her: here, if ever, is a
marriage made in hell.

Here is a *ménage-à-quatre* made for violent divorce.'

Mercy has definitely stopped falling, but feels giddy. The tunnels are spinning. Will you join the dance? Miss Rover asks.

Will you, won't you, will you, won't you, *won't* you join the dance? the twelve other children sing.

They hold out their hands and pull Mercy into the ring, shrieking with laughter. They form a conga line around the one-teacher schoolroom and they dance through the tunnels and up and down the ladders in the shafts. *The Walrus and the Carpenter*, they sing, leaping and kicking up their legs.

The Walrus and the Carpenter
Were walking close at hand:
They wept like anything to see
Such barren salt-panned land:
'If this were only opal mined,'
They said, 'it would be grand!'

The Walrus and the Carpenter
Walked on a mile or so,
And then they rested on a rock
Conveniently low:
And all the little Oysters stood
And waited in a row.

'The time has come,' the Walrus said,
'To talk of many things:
Of 6-6-6 and sealing wax –
Of mullock heaps and kings –

'This isn't funny,' Brian says.

'This is blasphemy,' Mr Prophet roars, 'and the fire of the Lord shall descend and shall burn the singers to a crisp,' and Mercy can see the end of the song approaching, the Walrus weeping as he eats, the Carpenter shedding crocodile tears, and all the passive little oysters disappearing one by one.

I wonder if I shall fall right through *the earth!* Miss Rover reads. *How funny it'll seem to come out among the people that walk with their heads downwards! The Antipathies, I think – but I shall have to ask them what the name of the country is, you know. Please, Ma'am, is this New Zealand? Or Australia?'*

'Of course, Mercy,' Miss Rover says, 'you understand that a book always reveals things about an author that the author himself is not aware of. Attitudes. Assumptions. Cultural blind spots. Down here in the Antipathies, as a consequence, we have an advantage or two. We know how *Here* looks from *Over There*, because they keep telling us what they see and we've always had to listen. But we also know how *Over There* looks from *Here*, and they don't, which gives us a tactical edge.'

'Do you mean for the republic?' Mercy asks. 'By the year 2000, the way the Prime Minister says? Or do you mean the end of the world, like Oyster says?'

'I mean,' Miss Rover says, 'that whenever there's a top dog and an underdog, the underdog *knows* more.'

'Knows more about what?' Mercy asks.

'Well, for one example,' Miss Rover says, 'the Murris know how the miners and the cattle cockies think, don't they? But not vice versa. Everyone thinks the Murris have disappeared for good, shot through to Bourke and Innamincka, but I do not believe that will be the end of the story.

'Or take Ethel,' she says. 'Ethel knows how Mrs Godwin thinks, doesn't she? But Mrs Godwin doesn't have a clue about Ethel.

'And for another example . . .' Miss Rover laughs quietly to herself and turns the pages of the book she is reading. She does not seem to see the page she is looking at. Mercy has learned that laughter may have many translations, and when Miss Rover laughs she can hear a wild undernote, the kind of sound you hear a kangaroo making in its throat when a pack of cattle dogs has bailed it up. The kangaroo will stay on its hind legs to the end; it will bat at the dogs with its forepaws, disdainfully, full of contempt, as they tear it apart; it will die making that eerie laughing noise in its throat.

'For another example,' Miss Rover says, 'what does the private school board of Outer Maroo know about me?' She tips her chair back and turns her face up to the ceiling and seems to shake with merriment at some internal joke, but her laughter this time is quite silent.

'We have to ask ourselves, Mercy, why certain people can find Outer Maroo without difficulty, in spite of its absence from maps. These people never come from the direction of Brisbane or Quilpie, but always from the north or north-west, have you noticed? I'm talking about the small planes that fly in low . . . perhaps you've heard them . . .? they fly in low and fly out again, and nobody ever mentions them. If I mention them, nobody knows where they come from or where they go.'

'They come down from Darwin and the Gulf,' Mercy says.

'Yes, they must. How did you know?'

'Everyone knows,' Mercy says.

'I see,' Miss Rover says.

'They buy opals.'

'I'd like to know where the opals end up.'

'Singapore,' Mercy says. 'That's where they sell them, Ma Beresford says, the best stones. She says the stuff she takes down to Brisbane isn't worth much. She says you can sell any kind of opal junk to tourists, they'll even buy potch.'

'Oyster is potch,' Miss Rover says. 'But he's dangerous potch.'

Composition of Opal, she writes in her textbook.

The water content of opal may be as high as one-fifth of total mass, but the most precious stones contain about 10 per cent water.

The microspheres of silica are packed densely together and arranged in regular patterns. The more uniform the size of the particles, and the more regular the arrangement, the more brilliant the colour and the greater the variegation and flash, though it is, in fact, the minute void spaces between the silica particles that cause the light to be diffracted.

In potch, the microspheres of silica have no pattern, no system. They are lumped together like a wet load of clothes on washday. They have no void space.

In precious opal, the void, being an orderly three-dimensional design between stratified silica cells – a strict system of absence – splits incoming light into its full spectrum of colours . . . thus proving that something comes of nothing, that a ray of light falling into nowhere is splintered but not lost.

But Mercy keeps falling and falling into nowhere, and Brian is lost among the pure.

'The secrecy at the Reef . . .' Miss Rover says. 'I have a very bad feeling about it, Mercy. The way the kids are always in threes when they come into town. The way some go out there, and then we never see them again.'

'We never see Brian now,' Mercy says, and she is falling, spinning, and Brian has been gone two months without a word, and Mercy's mother keeps crying, and it isn't like Brian, it isn't like Brian at all. But then Brian hasn't been like Brian for some time, Mercy thinks. Not since Oyster stood in the pulpit and the seventh angel spoke.

'We have to let air in,' Miss Rover says, breathing strangely. 'We have to get out, Mercy. We have to get out.'

'Will you go back to Brisbane?' Mercy asks anxiously. 'If you get out?'

'Now that,' Miss Rover says, pressing her hands against her chest to help the air in and out, 'is an interesting question. That is a very interesting question. Will I ever get back to Brisbane? I wonder what long-range planning the private school board of Outer Maroo has in mind. I must be quite a worry to them, I would think. I was not what they bargained for.'

Mercy keeps falling.

She falls back into a certain day in Beresford's . . . Oyster is there. He is moving between hardware and rows of canned beans. She knows it is Oyster, though her face is pressed against boxes on the highest shelves. She is on the stepladder, reaching for something, stretching. Shoebox labels, too close to her eyes, are distorted. There is someone at the foot of the ladder. She knows it is Oyster. She presses her legs together, pushing her soft cotton skirt between her legs, and holding it there, bunched. She knows it is Oyster. Perhaps, from the top of the ladder, she saw him at the edge of her eye in the street without realising it. Or perhaps there was something about the sound of the door as it opened, the way it was pushed, or the sound of his footsteps in the shop. Perhaps it was a faint and particular body smell that caused Mercy to stiffen. In any case, she knows it is Oyster. And she knows now how a tortoise feels pulling into its shell. She can feel a layer of air – it is actually something she does with her mind and with her nerve ends – she can feel a layer of air against her skin turn hard, like a carapace.

'Come on down,' Oyster says, his voice milky. 'I won't bite you.'

She does not want to climb down, but she does not want to stay up there above him either, her skirt bunched between her legs. She does not know what to do. She does nothing.

'Brian asked me to give you a message,' Oyster says.

Mercy can feel a small jolt, like electric currents, through her body. She climbs down slowly. When she reaches a certain level, she feels

Oyster's hands on her ankles. Her calves slide through Oyster's fingers, her thighs slide into his hands. She can feel his thumbs slip under the elastic in her knickers.

Her body goes hard, like a shell.

'You like that, my little pearl, don't you?' he whispers, his lips in her hair.

She is completely wrapped, like a tortoise, inside the bone of her will. 'What did Brian say?' she asks.

'He wants me to bring you to the Reef,' Oyster says. 'He wants to tell you something himself.'

'All right.'

'I have my car outside,' Oyster says.

'All right.'

At the Reef, she does not see Brian. She sees gunyahs of corrugated iron leaning against gidgee trees. Cockatoos rise in soft fleecy clouds, but she can scarcely hear their screeching for the great burr of noise: the drills, winches, the graders, the generators. Smoke and dust and fumes fill the air. The mullock heaps, pale and chalky, glisten like mounds of talcum powder against the red earth. People in lines come and go. Mercy feels dizzy from the heat and the dust and the noise and the patterns of movement, the movement itself shimmering like a mirage so that she has the impression of some great, tentacled, cogwheeled machine, fuzzy at its edges, with people as sprockets who circle and file and defile, bearing buckets of powdered rock. When they pass close to Mercy, she sees the white hollows of their eyes ringed with red. They are shrouded in mullock dust: ghosts, revenants, the living dead. Their sandalled feet are rust-coloured. Sometimes one or another of them drops soundlessly in the heat, folding neatly into itself like a silk scarf. When this happens, there is always a young woman from a small team reserved for the purpose – they all have kerchiefs tied around their heads, these young women; they all look like nuns; they are all pregnant, the women in the water-bearing team; their swollen bellies move ahead of them like announcements – and the young woman will bring a flask of water tipped with a rubber nipple, like a baby's bottle, and she will press it between the lips of the fallen one. The water-bearing team also seems to be looking after a cluster of toddlers. The children sit in the dust very quietly and play with coloured stones. They look at Mercy with listless eyes.

This could be a dream, Mercy thinks. Or it could be a moon colony; or it could be hell.

'I don't see Brian,' she says.

'Brian is one of the elite,' Oyster tells her. 'Those whom I have chosen to be close to me work underground, where it is cool. Follow me.'

She sees the shafts and the iron ladders bolted into rock. On the rungs, her shoes ring, and each footstep sings a lower and more plaintive note. The uprights hum against her fingers like tuning forks. Down, down – the temperature dropping with each step. At the foot of the ladder, tunnels unfurl themselves into coolness. Some of the tunnels have been widened into cavernous rooms and the rooms are crowded with sleeping bags. Somewhere above, in the heat, a generator throbs, and Mercy can feel its heartbeat. She can feel her own heart thumping, but not keeping time; it jumps about unevenly, like a cockatoo with frantic damaged wings.

There is light. Lanterns dangle from a thick black cord that snakes overhead, and the lanterns sway and dip so that the light shifts itself about in great golden discs. The walls are the colour of whipped cream. They are washed down in honeyed fog. Here and there vents are visible – long cylinders of nothing, with circles of blue sky at their tips.

Ant colony, Mercy thinks, because young people, a constant stream of them, like dark kernels within the clouds of ferrous dust and golden light, move along the tunnels with hand-held electric drills. They jab at the walls, jarring themselves and vibrating, and scoring the curved rock with long wounds. Someone follows each driller, tapping with a mallet. Someone follows the hammerers with a bucket.

It is impossible to talk, but Oyster moves on, often touching people as he passes. He and Mercy leave the drillers behind. They enter a large chamber where women, kerchiefs on their heads, peel vegetables at trestle tables. Others bend over steaming cauldrons on the electric plates of great stoves. These stoves must have been brought down the shafts in pieces, Mercy thinks, and then reassembled. The faces of the women gleam with sweat. They do not talk. They look at Mercy briefly and guardedly then lower their eyes.

Oyster moves on until the kitchen noises and the roar of the drills are background surf. It is as though they have reached a new country: the Tunnel of Quietness. Here, suddenly, their voices have an unnatural clarity and richness.

'Well,' Oyster whispers, close to her ear, and each word is like a small silver bell. 'Here we are, my little bird. You are at nest in my gilded cage.' And his voice comes back from the curved walls as a carillion, as a bell-ringers' chorus, rich and mellow.

'Where is Brian?' Mercy asks.

'In fact, you must begin to think differently now,' Oyster tells her. 'There is no Brian here. Here, we shed the Old Self the way a snake sheds its skin. We die in Christ. We descend into the womb of the earth, and then we are born again. We rise in newness of life and we take on new names.'

'What is Brian's new name?' she asks.

'If you become pure,' Oyster says, 'he will tell you himself, but I will give you a clue. It means *God is with us*. He does not wish to speak to you until you purify yourself. Until you have been baptised. Are you ready for baptism?'

'All right,' she says, because whatever she has to do to see Brian, she will do.

'Gideon will bring you when I am ready,' Oyster says. 'This is where you wait.'

There is a small bulge, like the inside of a gourd, like a monk's cell, in the wall of the tunnel. There is a mat on the floor and a cushion.

'You must kneel there and pray,' Oyster says. 'You must not move. If you do not continue to kneel and pray until I am ready, you will be punished. Gideon will come for you when I want you.'

Mercy kneels on the cushion. There is a lantern hanging in the tunnel just outside the cell, and it throws shadows and tongues of light around her. The light braids her into the cell and plaits thick coils of shadows all around. It is like being inside an eggshell, Mercy thinks. It is very peaceful, very quiet, very beautiful. She closes her eyes and bows her head. She prays. She prays for Brian and for Miss Rover and for her parents. Her mind wanders to Jess. Her mind wanders to Donny Becker, to the lizards, to the time in prayer meeting when he put his hand on her leg, to the time just a few days ago when he came into Ma Beresford's store.

'G'day, Mercy,' he said. He looked around and then he dropped his voice. 'You heard from Brian?'

'No,' she said sadly. 'Not since he left.'

Donny looked around again, furtively. 'Is anyone here?' he whispered.

'Only me.'

'Good,' he said. Nevertheless he continued to whisper. 'I drive the truck out there now, did you know? At the Reef, I mean. I bring the stones in to Bernie.'

'I didn't know. Did you see Brian?' she asked eagerly.

'No. But I . . . but I heard something. I got some news. From one of the kids out there. The ones who load the trucks.'

'What? What news?'

'They didn't call him Brian, it was some other name, I forget what it is. They've all got Bible names. But I knew they meant him.'

'What did they say?'

'Well,' he said awkwardly, blushing. 'I heard he's . . . uh . . .' – he began playing with one of the elastic bands in a little tray beside the cash register; he began twisting it round his fingers – 'I heard he's one of Oyster's favourites.'

'I know,' Mercy said. 'We know that. From the first day. That's why Brian went. Mum says –'

'No, I mean . . . I don't mean like that. I mean . . .'

'What?' she asked, impatient. '*What*?'

'I mean . . . Oyster . . . Oyster, you know . . . he likes girls *and* boys.'

'I know,' Mercy said. 'I know that.'

'No, you don't,' Donny said. 'You don't know what I mean. I don't mean like that.'

Mercy was puzzled. 'Well what do you mean then?'

Donny looked at her, desperate, then looked away. 'I can't tell you,' he said. 'But I reckon I had to tell you what that kid said, that's all. He said it meant Brian wouldn't last long.'

A rash was spreading up from Donny's neck, across his cheeks. Mercy stared at him across the counter, her lips slightly parted. She could feel Donny's nervousness seeping into her. It made her feel as though she were catching a cold. 'What do you mean, not last long? You mean he'll come home again?'

'No,' Donny said. 'No, I . . . I don't think anyone's allowed to leave. I reckon you'd better pray for him, Mercy.'

'We do,' she said. She had something caught in her throat, a bone-splinter of anxiety. 'We do. We pray for him every night.'

'Yes,' he said. 'Well, yes . . . but I mean . . . you should *pray* . . .' He suddenly leaned across the counter and kissed her full on the lips. 'I don't know what you should do. I just had to tell you, that's all.' He was breathless. Mercy could feel a burning on her lips. They stared at each other.

Then he bolted.

Mercy, kneeling on her cushion in Oyster's Reef, prays for Donny Becker and for Brian.

Her knees are beginning to hurt. It seems a long time since Oyster left her. She is probably imagining it, but the lantern in the tunnel seems dimmer now, and the shadows longer. She prays for Brian who is one of Oyster's favourites and whom she will see again soon if she does as she is told.

I will see Brian soon, she whispers, and her voice comes bouncing back as thick and shussy as opals that the hand scrunches and plays with in a sack, a sibilant crescendo rising softly from susurration to full crashing surf. She experiments, whispering: soon I will see Brian, I will soon see, will I see him soon? Brian soon I will see, will I see? and the soons come sooning back, the Brians boomerang, the sees seesaw like a hissing sea of swooning lightheadedness.

She feels giddy. She puts out a hand to steady herself.

We will see, she says to herself, and starts to giggle.

The light in the tunnel goes out. It is pitch dark.

She says to herself: The light in the tunnel has gone out. It is pitch dark.

. . . and *piiiitch*, the echoes bell and caw, they call and beck, and *darkdarkdark* they say, and *hark* how the bevelled angles sing, the Ps popping plosively against the wall like soap bubbles and the Ks kick-kickkicking and hopping and pocking off the walls like kangaroos.

Pitch dark, she thinks. Pitch. High and low. She hums two notes and listens to them skirmishing. Pitch is also the thick black paste that is used for mending rust holes in rainwater tanks, though too many drought years have come and gone for anyone to notice whether or not the tanks have holes. She imagines the bottom of a full tank is like this, sludge, muck, or the bottom of the ocean perhaps: the sheer weight of darkness pressing down, the sheer weight of terror. The darkness touches everywhere like water.

Mercy can feel her panic rising. It is rising like steam. It is rising like the steam in her mother's pressure cooker, it is going to blow.

'Halloo!' she calls, her heart thumping. She gropes for the opening. 'Halloo!' she calls down the tunnel, and her voice comes back like a rattle of hailstones in a well. Pieces of word bounce and ricochet and multiply themselves, then gradually sink back into the thick silence.

The darkness is like something crawling on her skin.

Her breath is choppy now and full of needles. *Miss Rover come over*, she whispers, and the whisper overandunders her and underovers and rovers the tunnel with ropy breath. She makes herself breathe slowly.

She tells herself: I will feel my way back along the tunnel to the kitchen.

And then.

And then there is a hand on the back of her neck.

Mercy screams.

'The scream is the cry of the soul in sin,' Oyster whispers in her ear. 'I'm afraid you must be punished. I told you not to move. I told you to wait until Gideon came to get you.'

Mercy has seen a kangaroo shot in the arc of its leap. That is how she feels. She is tailspinning down, she is in the bottomless pit of the Book of Revelation. She has nothing to lose. Something flashes itself across the black funnel of her freefall: an image of Miss Rover on the day she was transferred, an image of the menace on Bernie's verandah and of Miss Rover's clear and steady voice.

Mercy twists away from the hand on her neck. 'I don't like you,' she says to Oyster, and her voice comes out steady. 'I don't like the way you do things. I don't like the way you quote the Bible either. It makes me want to be sick.'

She can feel him close, like something feral, in the dark. Her back is against the tunnel wall and she is conscious of the imprint of the long grooves and welts left by the drills. The blackness could be molasses.

There is a small scurrying sound, a rat perhaps, or a snake.

A shiver passes across the surface of Mercy's skin, and she can feel goosebumps careening across the landscape of her body, up its hills and down its valleys and into its shafts.

She can hear Oyster's breath. She can feel the light mist of it on her cheek.

'It is Brian who asked me to put you to the test,' Oyster says.

'I don't believe you.'

'You are free to go,' he says sweetly, and Mercy thinks that she finds his voice more sinister when it smiles. 'If you don't wish to see your brother. It's up to you.'

Mercy imagines Oyster's gaze in the dark. She imagines that even if there were light, and they were still standing there eye to eye, nothing at all would be reflected in the milky blue.

'I want to see Brian now,' Mercy says. 'Right now.'

Oyster puts his hand on her arm and then slides it up to her shoulder, and then to the back of her neck. He propels her ahead of himself in the darkness, deeper into the tunnels and into the womb of the earth. Perhaps he can see in the dark, Mercy thinks. Like a bat. Like a devil. Like someone not yet born. Not human.

Something soft touches her face: a curtain, heavy, made of satin brocade, she thinks.

Oyster lifts it aside and pushes her through. 'Wait,' he says. She can hear him moving about. She hears the soft sound of cloth, then of a match being struck.

There is a candle. There is a hurricane lamp.

By its light, she sees that Oyster is on some sort of throne of scarlet cushions. He has wrapped himself in a scarlet robe.

'Approach,' he says.

Mercy does not move.

'If you want to see your brother,' Oyster says, 'you must kneel, and move forward on your knees.'

Mercy kneels. The rock floor presses and cuts.

When she has reached the cushions, Oyster opens his robe, and she sees his white naked flesh. His sex stands up like a pulpit.

'Kiss the sceptre of power,' he says, and then he pushes her head down, he pushes the sceptre into her mouth, he grabs her hair by the handful and he pushes and pulls, he pushes and pulls, she is gasping, she is sobbing, she is gagging, and Oyster is laughing and moving and shouting something, 'the Tree of Knowledge,' she hears, 'except ye eat of the fruit of the Tree of Knowledge,' and he is pushing and pulling and she cannot breathe, 'and ye shall be as gods,' she hears, 'and ye shall know all things, and all your desires shall be given unto you,' and everything is purple and black and red and smells of fish, smells of frozen fish melting in Ma's storage room, smells of oysters, smells of mouldy bread gone ripe, gone to fermentation, gone to yeast, and Mercy's ears are ringing and bursting and 'your brother,' she hears, 'whatever you want to know and if you eat of the fruit . . . and if you eat of the fruit . . . and when the fruit of the Tree of Knowledge . . . and when the seed . . . and it will ripen in your belly, little oysterling, and you will bear fruit, you will bring forth a pearl and will be as a goddess and everything you ever wanted to know, it shall all be revealed, and time shall end,' and now time has ended and she is being rolled over and over to eternity and a drill is jabbing and ramming and she can see something like sunflash opal, like a meteor, like a pulsing star, like something exploding, and then there is black.

Black.

Silence.

A moving light, possibly a candle.

A voice.

'I'm sorry,' it says. 'Drink this.' There is an undernote to its accent; it is Australian, but with something else underneath. It hands her a tin mug and when she puts it to her lips she is filled with something warm and sweet that turns the air into waves. She sways in them. 'It'll help,' the voice says.

She can see a face, not Oyster's.

'I'm Gideon,' he says. 'I have to take you up to the meeting now.'

'Where are you from?' she asks.

'It's the Campfire Meeting,' he says. 'We have one every night, and everyone has to go. It's above ground. Can you walk?'

The question surprises Mercy. Of course she can walk. She stands and the air tips itself crazily in all directions at once. There is a terrible pain between her legs. She feels as though a boulder has been tied there and the weight of it is dragging at her. She reaches down, puzzled, and her hand comes away warm and wet. She blinks at her fingers in the candlelight. They are smeared with blood.

She holds her hand out to Gideon, as question or offering or confusing evidence, she is not sure which.

Gideon bites his lip. 'Yes,' he says. 'I know. It's . . . I know it must . . . I'm sorry. But you've been on cattle stations, right? On Jimjimba and Dirran-Dirran? You've seen brumbies?' He rushes into his words now, like a wild horse on the gallop. 'You've seen the brumbies broken? It's good for 'em, right?' His phrases lift themselves in odd places, like the tails of brumbies in the breakaways. 'Gotta be done. I mean, we don't always understand, but His ways are not our ways. Gotta trust Him, you know. Gotta accept.'

She stares at him. She lifts her hand slowly, as though she is asleep, and rests it against his cheek and strokes it. She stares at the lines of blood on his face.

Gideon swallows and wipes his cheek nervously with the back of his arm. He is wearing a loose white tunic and the violent smear of red on the sleeve agitates him. '*The sacrifices of God are a broken spirit*,' he says, as though he is being given rapid-fire questions in a test. 'As it is written: *a broken and a contrite heart, O God, thou wilt not despise*.'

Mercy feels extremely calm now because she is in a dream. She knows this because she can feel the darkness all around her like warm water and she is swimming in it, floating, coasting, treading water languidly. She knows this kind of thing only happens in dreams. 'Where are you from?' she asks Gideon.

He frowns. 'Whaddya mean?'

'Your accent.'

He looks annoyed. 'Me dad's Greek. Used to talk Greek at home. I was born in Melbourne.' He seems to feel he has failed something under interrogation. 'But that's an old life,' he says irritably. 'I'm done with that. I've been born again and my country is Oyster. As it is written: *There is neither Jew nor Greek, there is neither bond nor free, there is neither male nor female: for we are all one in Christ, and we are all one in Oyster's Reef.*'

'St Paul's Epistle to the Galatians, chapter 3, verse 28,' Mercy says. She can see her words floating in front of her. She is sliding on the skin of something like sleep. 'I can say all the books of the Bible off by heart, can you?' She begins: 'Genesis, Exodus, Leviticus, Numbers, Deuteronomy, Josh . . .' The waves of air are getting higher and deeper again, they are lifting her up on their crests and then sliding her down into their troughs, she is feeling giddy, she is feeling all at sea. 'Joshua, Judges, Ruth,' she says, but then First and Second Samuel slam into her like wrecked ships and she is going under, she is drowning, she curls into herself like a shellfish so that she will float and sees with sleepy interest that a great deal of blood is running down her legs.

'I'll carry you,' Gideon says. 'We have to go to the meeting. We'll be late. Oh, shit,' he says, frightened. '*Shit!*' because the blood is very messy and is covering his white tunic and white trousers and Mercy supposes that he is a tidy person who likes to keep his clothes clean and uncrushed. It is very strange, she thinks, to go up a ladder this way, with her head hanging down. This is how a sack of potatoes feels, she realises. She thinks about the wild horses being broken, which is good for them, it must be done. She wonders if the brumbies think so too. A girl is above her, reaching down towards the ladder, taking her hand, and Mercy says to her, 'Some brumbies can't be broken, they break loose again,' and the girl stares at her with wide eyes.

And now the meeting is all around them, everyone sitting cross-legged on the red dust and Oyster is up there on a box or something, with the moon behind him like a plate against his head, like the paintings of saints in Miss Rover's book, and he is preaching and preaching and reading the Bible and explaining and everyone is saying *Amen, amen* and sometimes lifting their arms and waving them and then everyone is singing and swaying and some are laughing and some are rolling over on the ground, it is just like prayer meeting in the Living Word, except that it is outside under the moon and it seems to go on and on and on and Mercy realises that everyone is very tired, that everyone is exhausted, that the skin on everyone's face is stretched very tight and shines as though a bulb was switched on under the bone, and they all just want to sleep to sleep to sleep as Mercy does and the blackness is coming up to get her again and then Gideon is carrying her back down the ladder and the meeting seems to be over and she has to eat of the fruit of the Tree of Knowledge again and there is more blackness and then there is Gideon's face again and he is taking her up the ladder again and it is twilight, early morning twilight, and Gideon is saying something, 'Your brother is not here any more,' he is saying, 'I shouldn't be telling you,' and then she thinks she sees Donny Becker and she is being put under the front seat of his truck and there is a blanket and 'Just *go*, go, go!' Gideon is saying urgently, and they are bumping and driving and she can hardly breathe for dust and the blackness comes again.

She is climbing slowly up the ladder out of blackness and above her, swimming in the waving air, is her mother's face, her father's face.

'Brian isn't there any more,' she tells them. 'He's not at the Reef.'

'Thanks be to God,' her mother says. And she is laughing or sobbing, Mercy cannot tell which. 'Wherever he is,' she says, 'he'll be all right now. God will protect him.'

It is difficult, sometimes, Mercy thinks, to tell good news from bad, and it is difficult to get her bearings while her mother weeplaughs and Miss Rover is reading aloud, which brings us, Alice, Miss Rover says, to what you must ask the Cheshire Cat.

'I'm not Alice,' Mercy says. 'Alice Godwin is Alice, but she's not me.'

'As Mercy said to the Cheshire Cat,' Miss Rover reads, '"*Would you tell me please, which way I ought to go from here?*"

'"*That depends a good deal on where you want to get to,*" *said the Cat.*

"*I don't much care where –*" *said Mercy.*

"*Then it doesn't matter which way you go,*" *said the Cat.*"

'But it does,' Mercy said. 'It does! This isn't right, it's crazy.'

"*Oh, you can't help that,*" *said the Cat:* "*we're all mad here. I'm mad. You're mad.*"

"*How do you know I'm mad?*" *said Mercy.*

"*You must be,*" *said the Cat,* "*or you wouldn't have come here.*"

"*Let the jury consider their verdict,*" *the King said . . .*

"*No, no!*" *said Mr Prophet.* "*Sentence first – verdict afterwards!*"

"*Stuff and nonsense!*" *said Mercy loudly.* "*The idea of having the sentence first!*"

"*Hold your tongue!*" *said Mr Prophet, turning purple.*

"*I won't*" *said Mercy.*

"*Off with her head!*" *Mr Prophet shouted at the top of his voice,*' and Mercy opened her eyes and saw the roots of the gidgee trees and the red earth and the rabbit holes. She shielded her eyes from the sun and turned, and there, suspended over her, was the grin of the

Cheshire Cat. A face began to appear around the teeth and she saw that it belonged to Mr Prophet.

'Daddy says you can come home with us,' Beverley tells her.

But there's jostling, there are others, she sees Ethel, she sees Major Miner, and then Jess is there, Jess is scooping her up, she is in Jess's arms.

6. Sunday, Bloody Sunday Again

In the prison camps, Major Miner remembers, the worst things, the things that even nightmares shied away from, occurred in the last days before Liberation. Some special madness, more refined than all the madnesses that had gone before, seemed to swamp the captors. There were moments when one could almost have felt sorry for them, because the prisoners, too, knew that the tide had turned; knew it, in fact, from that very excess of arbitrary power by which the captors sought to disguise the waning of their ascendancy and their certain knowledge of doom. The prisoners could feel the seesaw tipping, they could feel their strength coming back in great gouts from the air they breathed, they could feel their spirits lofting them into a future – a *future*! – on trembling wings; and so they could almost commiserate with the guards who now went to bed each night with absence-of-future, a frigid lover; they could almost feel a detached pity for the thugs floundering in their wave of vengeful frenzy, so obviously out of control, so lost to rage. To the prisoners, the bloodlust was proof – proof absolute – of imminent change, so that the final random horrors were, in a curious and inverse way, energising . . . that is, for those who were left, for those who escaped the final triage, for those who made the last cut.

This is what Major Miner is thinking as he drives in from the breakaways toward the Given household on Sunday morning. He knows he will be able to talk to Charles Given, as he had known he would be able to talk to Jess. He will explain that he has Nick and Sarah safely hidden in his shack for the moment, but that a sixth sense tells him it will not be safe for long. They must leave as soon as possible, though he has not yet shown them the Reef. He dreads showing them. He keeps putting it off. There is just one good thing, one hopeful thing, he will say. Unexpectedly, Andrew Godwin's Troopie has come into their possession, with its reserve tanks full, and he has hidden it deep in the breakaways. Jess and I think, he will say, that you two and Mercy should go with them. We think you must leave tonight.

He blinks at a cloud of dust approaching at great speed. At the core of the red fog are three four-wheel drives, Godwin vehicles. He catches a glimpse of Godwin stockmen and miners as they skirl past him, and sees that each truck is packed with men, and that the men are armed with weapons ominously bigger than roo-hunting guns. They halloo Major Miner and brandish their weapons in the air. They are drunk. They are high on the thrill of aggression.

Major Miner accelerates, an old sickness of the heart swamping him.

There is a glow on the horizon, a great soft bloom of coral against the sky. It is arced like the curve of a fire opal, shot through with light. He knows that sort of shimmer. His heartbeat skids about in jazz riffs. He waits for a terrible sound. He waits for the quick silent pain in the ears, and the strange cottonwool feeling that follows. His hands are shaking, he puts his head down on the wheel, he finds he is sobbing, he cannot see, but he keeps pushing towards the glow.

He can see the seed pod, now, of that carmine bloom.

He is in time to see the Given house begin to collapse in on itself like a silk scarf falling to the floor. He drives right up to the roaring verandah, but the heat beats him back and he is afraid his petrol tank will go. He reverses, leaps out of his truck, throws the car blanket over his head, and gets as far as the french doors, which still stand. A post crashes behind him. The bullnose verandah-awning lists crazily, and the glowing galvanised metal scorches where it touches his arm. The floorboards give way, and he is battling through smoke and flame and blackened timber. He drags himself out.

He lies on the ground and sobs and thumps the earth with his fists. 'No!' he screams at the sun. 'No! No! No!'

The beast is truly on the loose now, he knows, and there will be more horror, because it always goes that way. There will be the same kind of hysteria that ballooned out of nowhere the day Susannah Rover . . . The beast will gorge itself until it drops from surfeit, he knows that. His intuition is so potent that he can *see* mutilation, see tomorrow, see the arsenals itching to display themselves, see fire, feral pigs, the disposal of evidence. He gags and drags himself into his truck and drives into Outer Maroo. He drives like a maniac. He can feel the claws of the Old Fuckatoo on his neck.

It's happening, he thinks. Outside the Living Word, he sees a crowd. He sees Jess, he sees Dorothy Godwin, he sees Ethel, he sees Dukke Prophet, he sees Mercy lying on the ground . . .

It's happening, he thinks.

He sees Jess scoop up Mercy in her arms, and all his own limbs go weirdly soft, he feels as though he is walking in a dream, walking through treacle, walking underwater, but something apparently is working, he must be functioning on automatic pilot because here he is in the kitchen at Bernie's again, and Jess is here, and Ethel, and Jess is saying to him, 'Get some ice, and get some Scotch. She's passed out again.'

He looks around bewildered, slow, but Ethel comes to his rescue. 'Here,' she says, putting a tray of ice cubes in his hands. 'Make yourself useful, Major M, and don't blow anything up.'

He takes the ice tray dumbly and obediently and offers it to Jess. 'I have something to tell you,' he says in a low urgent voice.

'She's feverish,' Jess says. 'She's dehydrated. There's Lucozade in the cupboard next to the fridge.'

Ethel says: 'I'll get it. I'll smoke her, Jess. I'll smoke her with gidgee leaves. She'll be right then, mate.'

'Jess,' Major Miner says again. 'I have to tell you something.'

'Tell,' she says, impatient.

'I can't tell you in front of Mercy.'

'She's passed out. She can't hear you.'

'Just the same,' he says.

'You go, Jess,' Ethel says. 'I'll do this.' She takes the bowl of water and the cloth, and spreads coolness over Mercy's burning skin.

'Well,' Jess says, abrupt with him, looking away. She leans against the door frame and studies the sky. 'What?'

But when he tells her, she turns pale and stifles a cry with her fist. 'Did you –?'

'I tried. I tried. It was too late.'

She can feel darkness swooping at her, she can feel the Old Fuckatoo diving, rapacious, a bird of prey. She covers her eyes.

'I know,' he says. 'I know. It was horrible.'

'We mustn't let Mercy know, not till later. If she knows, she won't leave. We have to get her – we have to get the three of them out. And the others?'

'In my shack, but we have to move them fast. Andrew Godwin is roaring around playing war games.'

Jess grimaces. 'I heard. Outside forces are moving in, that's the word going around on CB. They reckon Charles Given phoned Brisbane. Someone intercepted police radio in Quilpie, and they reckon police detachments are on the way.'

'There's some very serious craziness about, Jess.'

'Yeah. Armageddon,' she says with derision, but the joke is bitter. 'And Andrew's Troopie . . .?'

'It's hidden in the breakaways, I'll get it. But first I'll have to take Nick and Sarah to the one place no one will go.'

She stares at him. 'Yes. The Reef. They're entitled anyway. I'll meet you there with Mercy as soon as I can.'

'Bring Ethel too. She won't be safe.'

'I know. I will.'

'Jess,' Mercy calls, and Jess is there, she has Mercy in her arms, she gives her Lucozade.

'There,' she says, 'you'll be right as rain in a minute, as soon as you get some fluid. And we *need* you right as rain, because you have to drive Nick and Sarah to Brisbane. We need someone who can drive the Troopie on open ground.'

'The photograph,' Mercy says. 'I have to get the photograph.'

'What photograph?'

'The one Amy gave me. I've kept it safe, it's hidden in Beresford's, I have to get it. Gideon gave it to Amy to give to his dad. It's Nick, isn't it? He's Gideon's dad.'

'Yes, it's Nick.'

'We have to get it.'

'We'll get it,' Jess says soothingly. 'Don't worry. We'll get it before we go.'

And Major Miner leaves then.

The Reef, he thinks, driving towards the breakaways. He knew it would all come back to the Reef, back to Inner Maroo, back to the bora rings, back to the beginning again.

And then he sees that the coral bloom flowering above the Given house has put out tendrils. So much tinder, he thinks. There is no water, there is nothing that can be done. He hopes the wind stays low. He hopes the paddocks around the Given place have been cropped bare enough by famished sheep. He hopes there will be no fodder to feed the fire.

7. Armageddon

When Major Miner sees again the desolate place, the great charred skeletons of the winches, the scorched trees, the black bowl of rock, it seems to him that the distance between the war and the present is no longer than the blink of an eye. He presses his forehead against the steering wheel. He can never prepare himself.

'Oh my God,' Sarah says in a faint voice. 'Oh my God.'

Nick stares and then wrenches open the door and leaps out. He walks very fast, very jerkily, to the edge of the awful tar pit. He pauses there, but only momentarily, and begins to trace its circumference, clockwise, in the same fast jerky motion, a marionette on someone else's strings. He begins to run, hugging the rim of the burned circle, as though the pressure of horror and grief and rage are pushing against his body like a gun.

'Oh God,' Sarah says. 'Was this –?'

'The Reef. I'm sorry.'

A bubble of something catches in Sarah's throat. 'How –?' she tries to say.

But Major Miner cannot answer her. His own stolen sticks of gelignite rise spectral before him, like the yardarms of winches, like gibbets, like judges, like the blackened hosts of bodies on fire. On the far side of the great saucer of ashes, Nick is a small stick figure running furiously. A desert wind scuds out of the breakaways and the ash lifts into wraiths. The wraiths twirl on their pointed toes like dervishes. One of them twists towards the car and spins, poised, in front of the windshield.

Sarah turns pale and puts a hand over her mouth.

The wraith doubles itself over then scatters and vanishes.

Nick is between three and six on the ghastly dial of the Reef; he passes six and keeps on running, a second loop. He has to run interference: there are pieces of charred metal and bits of machinery that roll and buck in the wind. Sometimes he has to swerve, sometimes jump. Once he trips and throws out a hand to break his fall. His hand is covered in coalblack. The heat in the rock startles him, though it should not, since the fierce midday sun falls on his head and shoulders like axe blows. Before his eyes are spinning orange discs. He keeps running.

Major Miner is still slumped at the wheel, head buried in his arms. Sarah touches him. 'Everyone?' she asks in a low voice. 'Did everyone . . .?'

'Yes.'

'Is there any chance . . .? Is there any faint hope that *some* . . .?'

'I don't think so.' He gestures at the desert. 'Where would they go?' He sighs heavily. 'Actually, having said that, I must tell you that there are more and more people in Outer Maroo who claim . . . who believe . . . who have convinced themselves . . . that no one died. Not for good reasons, I fear.' First the claim, he thinks; then the belief.

'So . . . the bodies? There aren't any bodies?'

'Oh,' he sighs. 'The bodies. There are all sorts of stories. About the way the bodies . . .' He tries to shut out the memory of the ghastly night when young Donny Becker, drunk as a bandicoot, came careering out to the Great Extended in his jeep and raved on and on and on.

They were all lying flat on their faces with their arms stretched out, their hands praying . . . like Oyster ordered them not to move or something . . . I couldn't stop vomiting . . .

Mr Prophet made me . . . it was like he was furious with those bodies . . . like he was disgusted . . . you'da thought we were loading hay . . .

He made me and Tim Doolan carry all those ones up, the ones close to the ladder . . . He used the grader . . . we dumped them all in this big pit in the breakaways . . . I couldn't stop vomiting . . .

'In the deeper tunnels . . .' the Major says. 'Who knows? It's . . . you can feel it . . . it's powerfully haunted. No one comes here.'

'So no bodies . . .? So there's no proof,' she asks, her voice trembling, her voice wanting to believe in some outside edge of hope.

He cannot bring himself to tell her about what Donny Becker said; nor of the boom, of the great end-of-the-world fireball in the sky with its pendant rockets and shooting stars, the very sign and symbol – so Mr Prophet later roared from the pulpit – of Armageddon, that armed struggle described in the Book of Revelation, the last great battle in the war between darkness and light. He cannot bring himself to mention the dread aroma of barbecue, of some gargantuan cookout for barbaric gods, the terrible succulent smell of roasting flesh that lasted for days . . .

'When?' Sarah asks. 'When did it happen?'

'Middle of the night. They used to have a prayer mee—'

'No,' she says, upset. 'I mean, how long ago?'

'Uh . . . a year. Just over. A year and one month.'

She thinks of her hope as a frail and guttering candle. She has kept it alive. It goes out. 'So if anyone had got away . . . they would have . . . by now, they would have reached . . .'

'Yes,' he says. 'Or died out there somewhere in the desert.'

Nick goes careering past six again, and keeps running. He is staggering now. He is like a drunk man. Soon he will pass out from heatstroke and dehydration, but Major Miner does not feel he has the right to meddle with grief. He keeps his eye on the drunken runner, watching for the moment when he will take the bottle of water and essential salts . . .

'It happened in the middle of the night,' he says. 'They used to have a sort of religious meeting after dark, up here, until about two in the morning, sometimes later. Bible studies. Oyster used to preach for hours, apparently. Then they all slept underground, well, almost everyone, because it's cooler, you know. So whoever . . . it seemed to have been carefully timed . . . The explosion happened about three in the morning.'

'Who did it?'

'No one knows. Of course, it could have been an accident. There are always explosives . . . around mines, I mean.' There are enough explosives in Outer Maroo, he thinks, to blow up Queensland. His own missing sticks of gelignite rise up again, accusatory. He feels a terrible weariness.

'But you don't think it was an accident,' she says quietly.

'Oyster got more and more paranoid toward the end . . .' He makes an oscillating gesture with his right hand. 'No one ever quite figured him out. But things went to his head, that's certain. He seemed to believe he was God, he felt embattled, he thought almost everyone else was Satan in the end. Maybe he thought he was taking his chosen few to the Promised Land. I don't know. I honestly don't know. Nobody knows.'

'Could it have been anyone else . . .?'

'Who knows?' he sighs. 'Who knows what to think?'

The weariness is so great that his words seem to have to climb up infinitely long and infinitely steep ladders to connect with his voice. 'You see,' he says, 'almost everyone wanted them gone. Not right at the beginning, but they came to want them gone.' He makes a vague gesture with his hand, a gesture of helpless irritation. 'I mean, there were more of them than of us, at least up until the Murris left. Counting the Murris, there were more out here on the Reef than in Outer Maroo. Most people didn't like that. They wanted them gone. Not like *that*, of course; but they did want them gone. That creates a certain climate, you know, and Oyster was a weatherman of sorts. He was a dealer in signs and portents.'

Oyster, he thinks, was like one of those bacterial forces that blindly and ruthlessly seek out the culture that will nourish them. In Outer Maroo, he found it. Outer Maroo was his petri dish, ideal.

'And then, you know, the opal dealing complicated things. All that money.' Invisible cash economies are volatile things, he thinks. They can blow up.

'Ah, look!' Sarah cries.

Nick is at four on the dial but his arms are flailing in slow circles like a top winding down. Major Miner grabs the water and salts. 'Gimme a hand,' he says. Nick is racked with sobs when they reach him; the sobs sound like whooping cough, and each one seems to punch him violently.

'Drink,' Major Miner orders, pushing the bottle between his lips.

Nick splutters and dribbles, but in seconds the fluid and salts begin to calm him.

'I have to leave you,' Major Miner says. 'You'll have to go down the main shaft. The ladder's still bolted there. I'm . . . sorry, but it's the only safe place to hide at the moment . . . There's some serious craziness about.'

He and Jess will come back, he tells them, with Andrew Godwin's Troopie which he has hidden in a ravine in the breakaways. They should have enough petrol to get to Quilpie, and then they will be OK, they will be back on the map, they will be able to get petrol merely by paying for it, they can head on down the Warrego Highway to Brisbane.

And Mercy. Jess will bring her, he tells them, as soon as Jess manages to get away. They should take Mercy with them to Brisbane.

Another world, he thinks. He can dimly remember it.

But they will have to swing south of Outer Maroo; they will have to make a big arc over open ground, they will have to steer by instinct, more or less, which Mercy can certainly do. And they will also have to avoid Eromanga, where too many of Bernie's cousins . . . If they swing south towards Thargomindah and then north again towards Quilpie . . .

'But until we get back, you will have to stay underground. There's a torch here,' he says. 'And water and food. Good luck.'

If they make it to Brisbane, he thinks, it will mean simply that the seesaw can always be tipped the other way. That is all one can ask, he thinks: to move between the spaces like Prince Wen Hui's cook.

8. Notes From Underground

It is as though, Sarah thinks, something has been cosmically arranged. It is as though something has required that she should live the nightmares of relatives she never knew, nightmares that all her life she has tried to flee, nightmares that her sister and her sister's children have fiercely embraced. Is there, after all, a Prime Trickster, the he-she mischief-maker of those belief systems tied most closely to earth and sun and stars and natural forces?

Sarah is in an oven.

She is actually sitting cross-legged on the floor of an oven, in the belly of a joke so black she feels faint. Blackout, she thinks. I am going to black out. What she cannot bear, what she cannot bear, is that Amy should have been trapped in the same web. How could that be, that doom should be passed on not only to the third and fourth generation, but across bloodlines to a step-generation, across faith boundaries, across traditions? Is harm as deadly in the breath as in the blood?

'There's no safe place,' she says. She has not meant to say it aloud.

'No,' Nick agrees, sighing, but when she looks at him, she sees this has nothing to do with her words. He is somewhere else altogether. He is buffeted by inner conversations of his own.

We are like a Rembrandt painting, Sarah thinks: two faces, luminous, within a little fog of softer light, and everywhere else, thick blackness. The torch – it is a sort of emergency lantern, a miner's lamp perhaps – is on the rock floor between them and throws up a cone of light. Within the cone, Sarah can see dimples and fist-sized cavities and scored grooves in the rock. The grooves (Sarah supposes they are the teeth marks of drills) are the length of her forearm, each one straight as a ramrod, and they all face the same way, as though a blizzard of dashes had been forced into the tunnel from some machine. Everything is coal black, but if she touches the wall or the floor, the surface comes away like a blister and below it she sees the pale buttery colour of the rock itself. The tunnel smells like an ashtray. It smells as though the Old Fuckatoo has a nest deep inside.

'Both my mother's parents,' Sarah says, 'my grandparents, died in the camps. I have cousins whose parents died there. I have a great-aunt who survived.'

'Yes,' Nick says from some other place. 'I know.'

Sarah puts the back of her hand against her mouth and bites it. She is appalled to find her thoughts slopping about in public like this. It is the black tunnel, she thinks, that is inducing such helplessness. There is something so fearful about the smell of ash. It is like being in an interrogation cell. There is something about the smell that makes her babble. I am going to black out, she thinks again. I have to keep talking to stop myself blacking out.

'My father wanted to escape history, he wanted to bleach the past out of us. That was the gift of America, he believed, a chance to escape the European past. He was passionately secular. Religiously non-observant, you could say.'

Nick looks at her and frowns but says nothing.

'But it drove my sister into orthodoxy. She is ultra-orthodox, she accused me of being part of the Final Solution for marrying a non-Jew. She said I was doing the work for them. She wouldn't speak to me for years, she broke my heart.'

Nick watches her lips, as though she speaks in a language he does not know. 'Yes?' he says vaguely.

'I just wanted to find a little happiness,' Sarah says. 'I just wanted to be somewhere safe.'

'It doesn't help,' Nick says, frowning, apparently concentrating, as though here and there, fleetingly, one of her words holds meaning. But no, she thinks, studying him; more likely there has been a random intersection of two thought paths.

'Extremism is everywhere,' she says. 'There's no safe place. My sister's daughter Rachel, my niece, has joined the Lubavitchers in New York. She has terrible arguments with her parents. They aren't orthodox enough, she says; they aren't pure. She breaks her orthodox mother's heart. My nephew Jeremy, my sister's son, is in the Israeli army. He worships Ygal Amir. My father won't watch the news any more. He says he doesn't know which he's more afraid of seeing: an Islamic terrorist bomb in the street where his daughter lives; or his grandson laughing like Ygal Amir in the dock.'

Sarah wonders why she, why her father, should be surprised that being secular offers no protection from the true believers, or from the irrational, or from extremes. All the celibates in the world, she thinks, have not by one whit reduced the sexual voltage of humankind. Sex goes on degrading and exalting the way it has since history began. The religious impulse, she thinks, is the same. It is simply there, biding its time, manifesting itself in forms both horrific and sublime, regardless of where an individual places himself on its scale.

'The thing about Angelo,' Nick says, 'is he always managed to tie me in knots. Always. I can't . . . I can't . . .' He can't decide. Was it Angelo who always relied on Nick to straighten out the messes? Or was that something Nick imposed upon himself? Was he a failure as a parent? Or was he too protective, too ready to bail Angelo out of every scrape? 'He was always in trouble as a kid. Stealing apples from gardens, that sort of thing, harmless at first. But you couldn't . . . no one could . . . because he was also generous and reckless and loving, kind to old ladies, you know, that kind of . . . everyone loved him. You could never stay angry with him.'

Sarah is listening. She is watching him. For some of us, she thinks, life consists of figuring out other people's lives.

'He had no fear of anything,' Nick sighs.

When he moves like that, precipitously, flakes of black drift from the wall. Eventually, Sarah supposes, all the black will crumble away, and there will be a line of ash along the floor of a wide cream-coloured pipe. Or perhaps not. Perhaps an agent of movement is required. She looks down the tunnel into blackness, and shivers. Amy's bones may be down there somewhere. She wants to do something religious for them, she does not know what. Some ritual of passage seems called for, but she does not know any.

She has a sudden queasy memory of the Boston subway, the Red Line train careering down the black tunnel to Harvard Square. The subway car is packed, it is peak hour, and she and Amy are standing, hanging on to one of the chrome columns, swaying violently with the movement of the train. It is not possible to fall, the press of travellers being so great. Amy gives herself to the safe turbulence with a kind of ecstasy as the train hurls itself around a bend. She laughs aloud in a high breathless way. Sarah is startled. It is a rare show of uncensored emotion.

Perhaps life consists of a series of templates and treadmills, she thinks. Perhaps we unconsciously seek them out, or respond to them, simply because they are familiar. Perhaps Amy loved this tunnel.

'Angelo was risk addicted,' Nick says. 'My little boy.' He laughs, a tired unhappy sound. 'He was taller than me. That never stopped me from feeling I had to keep him under my wing, I don't know why. Well, partly because his mother left us when he was very young, abandoned us . . . left me, I should say. She never wanted to leave her son, but I – ' He puts his head in his hands. 'She left me for another man. She wasn't Greek, his mother. In my parents' culture, you know . . . it was not something I . . . I was devastated.' The shame of it. The humiliation. He had not thought he would find the will to go on living, but he tapped into it via anger and pride. 'I fought for sole custody rights. It wasn't hard. Adultery . . . unfit mother. I destroyed her, and I was glad. I took my son back to Greece.'

He twists sideways and bangs his forehead against the wall of the tunnel, a slow, rhythmic, self-punitive act. When he turns again, his face is streaked in black.

Sackcloth and ashes, Sarah thinks.

'His mother was killed in a car crash,' Nick says. 'No other car involved. She was driving alone at night up the Pacific Highway. She drove over the cliff.' He rakes his fingers through his hair. 'Revenge never solves anything,' he sighs. 'Greek history should have taught me that. And after that, you know, I felt I had to keep Angelo in my pocket, keep him safe. But he felt the same, I think. Well, maybe not . . . Maybe he resented it. I'm not sure about anything. But it became a habit. He contacted me when things went wrong.'

'Yes.' Sarah nods. 'But with Amy . . . I always knew I was partly looking after myself. Trying, somehow, to make sure the ending came out right.'

'Then his scrapes began to get a bit more serious,' Nick says. 'Or maybe it was a way of . . . I think, looking back, I was pretty strict. The more worried I got, the more I laid down the law. Maybe I drove him to it, anyway he dropped out of high school, got into drugs, things like that. He'd call from Broken Hill or somewhere, back-packing. He'd been arrested in some scam he got mixed up in. Swore he didn't know it was illegal, which was probably true.' He had a fatal capacity for trusting the wrong people, Nick thinks. 'He was a sort of perpetual Unholy Innocent.'

He has begun to peel the black off the floor as he talks. Sarah watches how neat he is, scratching at small recalcitrant smudges with his thumbnail. Incongruously, she thinks of the obsessive way some people pick at peeling skin after sunburn. The buttery colour of the rock spreads. Nick moves and begins on another patch.

'About six years ago he got into some kind of trouble in Brisbane,' he says. 'So I went up. I was still living in Melbourne then, but Angelo took off to Sydney a couple of days after I got him out on bail. That's where the action was, he said.'

He bends low and blows at the blistering skin of the floor. He peels off a piece as large as a man's handkerchief and sets it delicately to one side.

'I felt pretty desolate when he left. I felt all I'd done was blame him. I felt I'd driven him away. So I drove up the north coast. I didn't know where I was going, really. I just stopped at some point and went and sat on the beach and stared at the ocean. It was Noosa. Noosa Heads. I was going to stay for a week, then I made it two. I sat on the beach every day. Then I added a third week. It reminded me of the Aegean, you know. I fell in love with the place and never left. I wasn't expecting it. It took me by surprise.'

He is chipping away at the blackness faster and faster. He keeps moving slightly, further into the tunnel, cleaning as he goes. He casts about for some sort of tool, then takes his sandal off and uses it as a scraper. Sarah feels obliged to pick up the torch and move it towards him. He needs light. She begins to scrape her side of the floor.

'Sunrise and sunset every day,' he says, 'I always sit on the sand and watch the ocean. Every single day. I watch the sun coming out of it, and dropping back in.' He pauses in his peeling and looks at her. 'You can't pollute the ocean,' he says. 'It just throws everything back out on the shore eventually, even oil slicks. That comforts me. That there's something, you know, that goes on resisting.'

Sarah pushes the torch a little further down the tunnel. 'But we should concentrate on one area,' she says. 'Walls and ceiling, I mean.'

'Yes. You're right.' He picks up the torch and crawls back to their starting point. He begins on the wall. 'The trouble is,' he says, 'the ocean threw up Oyster. They were like two magnets, Angelo and Oyster. The minute I met him I had a horrible premonition that the chemistry would be fatal.'

'You met Oyster?'

'With Angelo,' Nick says, '. . . there were always as many good impulses as bad ones . . . But Oyster, he was a different kettle of fish altogether.'

He turns around again from the wine racks, he is always just turning around from the wine racks, and Angelo is always arriving with the companion in the white linen tunic and pants. Angelo hugs Nick, 'I'm not me, actually, Dad,' he says in Greek. 'I'm not the person you know. I've completely changed. I've been born again. I'm Gideon now. This is Oyster. And this is going to be a sort of baptismal dinner and a celebration.'

There is a manic edge to Angelo's voice which Nick notes uneasily.

'Gideon,' he says, weighing it. 'Why Gideon?'

Angelo says solemnly: 'After a Gideon bible in a motel room.'

'That is how God spoke,' Oyster says.

'Dad,' Angelo says earnestly. 'I can't explain it to you.' He presses his hand against his heart. 'It's something inside,' he says. 'It's like a fire. I've never felt this way before, Dad. There was a hole, there's always been this *hole* inside me. And now God is there.'

'That's good,' Nick says, embarrassed. 'So what next?'

'Opal mining,' Angelo says. 'Oyster's staked a claim out west, west of Quilpie.' Oyster knows the gem market, Angelo explains, because he used to be a pearler at Broome, and then he worked opal at Coober Pedy after that. 'We're going to be self-sufficient. We're going to live in a new way.' It was going to be a pure community, a commune, a born-again world.

Another racket, Nick thinks. 'And who was Oyster,' he asks casually, 'before he was born again?'

He sees the light change in Oyster's milky eyes and feels a chill. He knows that what would attract Angelo is this dangerous buzz of intensity. Oyster smiles with the basilisk charm of a cat. His eye contact is so intense that Nick expects his wine to turn sour. He sips it warily, to experiment. It tastes like vinegar. He imagines that dining with Rasputin would have been like this. He is exasperated when he catches himself thinking this way. It is the way his grandmother thought, and he knows he has a few hundred years of Greek-village superstition in his veins. He tries to discount it. He sips his wine again, but it does not taste as it should.

Oyster says lightly: 'I was a bad boy, Big Daddy. But God spoke to me.' He moves his voice into a performing register, low and intense: '*And he fell to the earth, and heard a voice saying unto him, Saul, Saul, why persecutest thou me*? Do you recognise it?'

'Uh . . . no,' Nick says.

'The miraculous conversion, on the road to Damascus, of bad boy Saul, persecutor of Christians. He became St Paul. That was the chapter I was reading in the Gideon bible. It hit me like a laser and transformed me.'

'And what was the former bad boy's name before he was Oyster?' Nick persists. 'Just for interest's sake.'

'But it is of no interest and no relevance whatsoever,' Oyster says. 'The old is dead. I have put on the new man in Christ. I will build a new heaven and new earth.'

'And where exactly will the new heaven be?' Nick asks.

'The kind of community we will have,' Oyster says, 'can't be put on conventional maps.'

'I did some research after they left,' Nick tells Sarah. 'I had just two clues: Coober Pedy and Broome. And I had an instinct. I found out why he'd want to put on the new man in Christ, all right.' Police records, mug shots, it took him months. 'He'd discarded as many names as the rest of us have thrown out old shoes.' He would tell Sarah some day, if a day came when they could bear to talk about the Reef. 'Oyster was nothing if not brilliant,' he says.

'If only they'd known,' Sarah says. 'If only Amy had known.'

'I don't know,' Nick sighs. 'I don't know if it would have helped. Angelo showed up again one day,' he says. 'Out of the blue, as usual. Recruiting along the north coast, he said, where the young tourists are. So I told him what I'd found out. It shook him, I think. But then he said that was *before*. Oyster was born again now. He was someone else.

'I didn't believe him,' Nick tells Sarah. 'But I wanted to believe him.'

'Here,' Sarah says. 'This'll make the work easier.' She has found two knives in the food basket. She gives one to Nick.

'This is great,' he says.

They scrape from the ceiling down towards the floor. Nick has to stoop slightly when he stands; Sarah does not.

'I was too strict, too demanding,' Nick says. 'Too proud. Too stupid. I just wanted one more chance, one moment . . . I just . . .'

'Yes,' Sarah sighs. It seems to her a miracle that there are any moments of safety or moments of happiness at all. They work steadily, scraping and blowing carbon dust from the wall.

'I should have come looking sooner,' Nick says wretchedly. 'I left it too late.'

'Yes,' Sarah says. The lateness, the terrible permanence of it, suddenly pushes her like a blast of dead air. She stops scraping, paralysed. She can feel an unstoppable flash flood of sobbing, a tidal wave, coming at her from the depths of the tunnel, rising and rising and rising . . .

'No, listen,' Nick says. He drops his knife. She can hear it clatter and ring against the rock. 'Listen,' he says helplessly. He puts his arm around her and she buries her face against his shoulder. Her sobbing is violent but noiseless. He holds her. 'Listen,' he says. 'The ocean . . . Think of the ocean."

Her sobbing is noisy now. It bounces off the rock walls and reverberates and echoes back from deeper down. An ocean of mourning fills the tunnel. They sit in the small cleaned sand-coloured space and listen to the dirge of it. The light from the torch washes them. He strokes her hair. He kisses her. They huddle like frightened children, holding each other, and stare into the dark.

Epilogue

Everything is going up in smoke, the years crackle like kindling, the feathers of the Old Fuckatoo smell black and singed. From here in the breakaways, we can now see two separate fires, but we cannot be sure that both are real. Where there's smoke, there's fire, but not always simultaneously; where there are mirages, the truth is bent. One blaze could be a twisted message from a crooked time, or perhaps both are ghost fires. Perhaps both are burning somewhere else, somewhere much further off.

Smoke and heat haze hang like draperies in the air, they sway and twist, the years get in my eyes, they drift, I am giddy with time.

'Did you know that it took the Great Fire of London in 1666 to wipe out the plague?' I ask Major Miner, but he is somewhere else, and where he is, Singapore still burns. Ethel leans into past millennia, blowing on the flames of her little fire, fanning herself with gidgee smoke. At least the fire will burn the carcasses off, I think. The Old Fuckatoo will flap its slow wings and bugger off, at least for a while, just as the Great Plague was cauterised by flame. *London's burning,*

London's burning, we chanted it at the convent, it was a game, it was a history lesson: 1666. Dukke Prophet would make something of that, it suddenly strikes me: one millennium plus 666, footprint of the beast, or act of God?

Major Miner cries out, as though from sleep, though he has not been asleep, he has been sitting staring into the haze. 'Jess!' he calls, like a child in the night. 'Jess!' But when I go to him, he blinks vaguely. 'Where am I?' he says.

'With me.'

'It's hungry, the beast,' he says, 'once it tastes blood. It'll gorge till it drops.'

'It'll be all right now,' I say, calming him. 'There've been no explosions for hours.'

'But we did it anyway. We moved through the gaps. In spite of the beast, we got them out.'

'Yes,' I say, but I'm watching him, I'm keeping my eye on him, because the shivers keep taking him, the bushfire, Singapore, the thought of the three of them in that truck with the fire at their heels. It would have been touch and go. 'The explosions have stopped,' I say again. 'All the cars and the tanks must have gone up by now. It should run out of fuel.'

'Depending on the wind.'

'Yes.'

'There were two separate fires,' he says. 'They joined up. It wasn't just the spread from the Givens' house. It was that shooting spree in town. They must have fired into Beresford's tanks by accident.'

'Yes.' That would have been the first huge explosion, the one that had thrown Ethel and Mercy and me into a great skidding arc on the edge of town. We had almost rolled. We felt the explosion in our ears and against our skin like a punch on the side of the head. The wind was in our favour then, though the great fireball bounced at our tail. We were lucky. The wind favoured us.

But since then? For the others?

'Drive south, drive south as far as you can,' I shouted at Mercy. 'Curve around it on the south side, give it as wide a berth as you can.'

'I have to go back for Mum and Dad,' she said, aghast at the blaze. She was frantic.

'You can't,' I said. 'You can't. It's too late. You'll have to drive for your lives.' And then I lied through my teeth; it was the last gift I had. 'We'll go back for them,' I promised. 'Don't worry, we'll keep them safe.' Later, later, I would tell the black truth, but not until they were safely on their way. 'I promise,' I shouted, and she gunned the truck and they took off.

But the whole place is nothing but tinder for hundreds of miles, and everything hangs on the wind.

Ethel sits a little away from the bora rings now, in the spindly shade of acacias. 'This is my tree, Jess,' she says. 'I was born under this tree.'

'You going to push off to Bourke when the fire dies down, Ethel? Or what?'

'Staying here, Jess,' she says. 'This is my country here, my tree. My mob'll come home now, any day now, you'll see. They'll hear on the bush telegraph, they'll all start showing up from Bourke.'

'What about you, Jess?' Major Miner asks.

'I don't know,' I say. 'What about you? You heading back on to the map?'

'Nah,' he says. 'Not me. I've paid me dues to the world. I prefer rocks to people, present company excepted. I'll just keep pottering on at the Great Extended till the end of the next world, the one after this. Me and the opal and me nightmares and that bloody great sky.'

Me too, I think. The railway-ganger's life is my style. We don't need much. We've got what we need. We travel light.

'You could move in for keeps,' he says.

'Shack up together, you mean?'

'Yeah. Why not?'

'We're rotten bad luck, us railway-ganger brats.'

'I'll take my chances,' he says. 'Why not?'

Why not? I think. I play with my jacks, I hold my fossilised mussel in my hand, I toss Major Miner's opalised oyster in the air. I imagine Andrew Godwin's Troopie heading east.

'They'll be back on the map by now, I reckon. East of Quilpie.'

'Yeah,' he says, 'as long as, you know . . .'

We both know it depends on where they were when the second and third explosions . . . and how the wind . . . but we will not say it. We will not. We insist that they outstripped the fire.

I can see the three of them now, up high in the cabin, Mercy driving, because she knows outback terrain so well . . .

The waiting seems interminable. Mercy imagines that a chrysalis must feel like this, locked inside the cocoon, blind, the wings damp and pressed shut and useless. Waiting. Waiting. The minutes feel like constrictions on her breathing, like swaddling bands. The three of them sit high and close in the Troopie's cabin. Mercy drives. They feel the explosion like a blow to the side of the truck. It rocks them, they tip, they are poised like a ballerina *à point*, on two tyres. A funnel of freak winds twists them, they teeter, they can feel the sickening arc of the beginning of the roll, they hesitate, they drop back on all fours.

'Holy shit,' Nick breathes, and the pyramid of bottles in his grandmother's cellar comes lurching at him, and he crosses himself.

The fire reaches out like an octopus, like a many-pointed star. The fire is like vast red batwings on three sides.

Mercy drives for the gap. She keeps her mind on it, that opening between the flames. Beyond it lies the edge of the map.

Cards riffle through my mind like a waterfall of light: beginnings, arrivals, departures, Susannah and the elders, Oyster in the pulpit, Mercy's card.

The dealer calls.

The dealer calls, and I insist on dealing the cards the way I want.

Especially the last card.

I see the three of them moving east like a charmed arrow, the sun gilding them, the fire like wings at their heels. I see them passing Thargomindah, I see them somewhere east of Quilpie by now.

'Gonna be rain,' Ethel says suddenly, jumping up and raising her arms to the sky. 'Rain on the way. I know these things. It's coming down from the Gulf. Three days, maybe four, you'll see.'

And I believe her, I believe her, I believe the weather is going to change. I believe the Old Fuckatoo has fucked off.

I can see the Troopie flying down the Warrego Highway, and I can see Mercy reaching inside her shirt and taking the photograph out.

'We got Mercy's photograph,' I tell Major Miner. 'That one you took at the Reef. She hid it in the one place she knew Ma would never look. She hid it in the Gideon bible that Ma kept stuck in a cupboard at the back.'

'They were happy that night,' Major Miner says wistfully. 'They were laughing and singing when I took that shot. I think it was still a kind of Eden out there then. It seemed to be.'

I see Mercy hand it to them, I listen to her explain, I see her conjuring up the day that Amy came into the shop. I watch Nick and Sarah as they stare at the Polaroid past, they stare at Oyster who is in the middle, and at Angelo who is on his right, and at Amy on his left. They consider the meaning of the smiles.

Nick turns the photograph over.

Dear Dad,

Thought you'd like to see how happy we are.

I miss you.

Love, Angelo

'It was Gideon,' Mercy says, 'I mean Angelo, who got me away from the Reef. It was Gideon who saved my life.'

Nick cannot speak.

He winds the window down and leans out. He leans far out.

'My son,' he shouts into the hot wind and the red dust and the great blue dome of the sky. 'Oh my son, my son Angelo!' He begins to sob noisily like a child and cannot stop.

Sarah holds him as though he were her own lost waif.

Mercy drives always for the gap where Brisbane lies, Brisbane the beautiful, the city of dreams, the fabulous city of anecdotes, of her mother's thousand and one embroidered tales, and she will bring her parents, she will go back for them, because I remember, Mercy, her mother says, how we used to drive down the range from Toowoomba when I was a girl, and I would imagine the city long before I could see it, and the sun would be on all the tall buildings, and on the glass windows, and it would be shining like the New Jerusalem, you know, in the Book of Revelation: *and the city was pure gold, like unto clear glass.*

And Mercy imagines Brisbane, the golden city. She imagines the great river with water in it. She thinks of grass, ferns, trees, ocean, sand. She imagines herself running into the ocean as into the world. She will let the world crest and froth about her.

She is driving back on to the map. She imagines that some qualitative change will occur. Perhaps the light will be different. Perhaps the pull of gravity will shift.

The Warrego Highway stretches ahead, and in the distance, always floating, beckoning, shifting, sometimes upside down, sometimes not, the golden city shimmers in the heat.